Divided Loyalties

Copyright © 2006 Richard E. Witten
All rights reserved.
ISBN: 1-4196-4387-8

To order additional copies, please contact us.
BookSurge, LLC
www.booksurge.com
1-866-308-6235
orders@booksurge.com

RICHARD E. WITTEN

DIVIDED LOYALTIES

2006

Divided Loyalties

Few Are Guilty, But All Are Responsible.
Abraham J. Heschel

Dedication and Acknowledgements

This book is dedicated to my father, Carl Witten, whose love, warmth and relentless support carries me to this day, and my father-in-law, Harry R. Hayes II, whose heroic experiences in the Second World War inspired this story and moved me to embark on a second career.

There is no doubt that Divided Loyalties would not have seen the light of day without the encouragement and collaboration of my wonderful family. I am grateful for the wise counsel and loving support of my wife, Lisa, enabling me to stay on a (somewhat) straight and narrow course towards completion of this novel. Annie Witten, my eldest child, provided invaluable editorial and critical advice, and my two sons, Alex and Jeffrey, suffered my idiosyncratic behavior with restraint and understanding.

Special thanks are due to Herb Bass, whose extensive advice during the early stages of this novel was invaluable, and to Jeffrey Kellogg, editor par excellence.

CHAPTER 1

Sam Hart hoisted the knapsack across his broad back and braced himself for the impact of over 40 pounds of equipment, ammunition and food. The pack came to rest with a dull thud that day as it had every day for the past 11 months. He adjusted the straps, donned his helmet, grabbed his automatic rifle and headed down the muddy road that led to the briefing tent of the 14th Infantry Regiment.

0500 hours. Sam was getting used to catching sleep here and there, even standing. While some of the guys bitched about moving out so early, Sam didn't care. He'd rather get up early and have something to do than sit around.

After six months of basic training at Fort Bragg, seven weeks of advanced training at Fort Benning and another month hanging around Le Havre, waiting for fuel, the Company had finally been moved by box car to Laon, France, and from there trucked to Bitche, just west of the old Maginot Line.

Once limber, Sam now felt tight and thick and plodding. He worried that the long periods of inaction had dulled his senses and instincts, a scary thought when the inevitable occurred and his unit was forced into battle.

At the briefing, Lieutenant Miller welcomed Company B to the Regiment. "It's not the Riviera, and we're a long way from Paris, but sooner or later the rain will stop and you'll get a chance to enjoy the countryside. Maybe even clean up the mess the Krauts have left us."

Miller paused to let the GIs appreciate his humor. Sam tapped his foot, waiting for the day's assignment. "Let's go, let's go," he said under his breath.

"All right, then." The Lieutenant turned to a large map standing on an elevated easel to his left. "Our assignment is to clear the area in the triangle, here, between the Mosel and Rhine Rivers. We've got about 80 kilometers to cover, and there have been reports of enemy troops retreating through the area, particularly around Saarbrucken. Company B and C, you're going northwest toward Koblenz. A and D, you are to head due west on a line straight to the Rhine's banks. We meet up at Weisbaden, in three days. Be careful, and use your heads."

The knot in Sam's stomach was just like the one that had almost crippled him aboard the *Serpentine*, Company B's rickety transport for the two-week journey from Georgia to France. Ten days into the sail, and literally bored to tears, Sam had snuck up on two officers sharing a private story on deck late that evening. One of them, a tall and blond Texan, said, in between drags of his unfiltered cigarette, "We're heading right into a firefight: German counter-offensive. They're throwing all their weight into stopping us. No chance they'll give up."

The other officer, a lieutenant named Anderson, nodded in agreement. "I was talking to one of the first officers, who spoke to his brother when we left port. That guy is in the 7Th Armored Division near Antwerp. They stopped the Krauts' counteroffensive on the Meuse River. He told me things were looking really pretty good, pushing those bastards back left and right—GIs fighting mad. Word got out that the Nazis executed 100 POWs who were captured when their unit got separated from the main army. The guys surrendered when surrounded. The fuckin' Germans shot 'em in the road. A couple of Joes escaped, and got back to HQ. They told the story, and word got around."

"Shit," said the Texan. "Don't spread that. These guys are already losing their cookies and they've got a few more days of puking ahead of them."

The dread extended deep into Sam's bowel. Until now, he'd done what he was told, followed the script, and went along. He complained about the food, the officers, and their lack of activity. But he was safe.

No longer. He thought about surrendering American soldiers being gunned down by panicked Germans. The same terrified Germans he was likely to encounter on today's mission. The knot pulled tighter.

***

"Whoosh"
"Wham"
"Thud"

The tall, lanky GI slammed into the ground face first, blood spurting from the side of his neck. Sam was frozen in place for an eternal second as he put the facts together.

"Sniper" he yelled, diving headlong behind a tree. His heart was pounding as he watched his infantry mates hit the deck.

"Shit," he muttered, turning back to see the result of the second "wham" he had heard. Feeney, the kid from South Boston who always had a smart-ass answer for everything, lay face-up with a bloody hole in his forehead.

"Whoosh"
"Shit, shit, shit."
"Whoosh"
"Ten o'clock! Ten o'clock--in the trees. Stay down."

"Whoosh"

"There's two of 'em. Stay down."

A moment later, Sam's world erupted with noise and smoke and panic and chaos. Automatic rifle fire from a dozen prostate American infantrymen shredded the air. Dirt and debris flew from the area where the snipers' attack had presumably begun. Sam held his fire. The only sound of the enemy's bullets was the rushing of the air around them as they hurtled toward their targets, suggesting to Sam they were out of range for their infantryman's weapons. He sensed a trap.

He saw the movement to his left—shaking bushes, a few man-shaped forms sliding slowly toward them—several hundred meters away. Sam bellied over to a twosome of GIs squatting behind a cluster of boulders. He pointed out the advancing enemy, and yelled at them to tell the others.

Sam waited for their acknowledgement, and then dove behind another group of infantrymen. As he somersaulted into position behind a large maple tree, something grazed his foot. Only after delivering his message did he see that the entire heel of his left boot had been shot off.

As news of the would-be ambushing spread, the random shooting diminished enough for the Sergeant to issue new orders. Using hand signs, he instructed Sam, Dalton and Hoffman to advance toward the snipers and keep up the barrage. The others, on the Sarge's signal, were to attack the circling enemy with everything they had.

Hoffman took the lead, yelling "Cover me" as he tightened his long form into a small target, bolted out from behind the rocks and zigzagged in the direction of a cluster of thick bushes 25 yards ahead to the southeast. He drew sniper fire almost immediately, which gave Sam and Dalton a general area at which to aim their covering salvos.

DIVIDED LOYALTIES

Sam could see Hoffman dive to a safe spot before he and Dalton were chased to the ground by the enemy's bullets. Dalton thumped his rifle across his chest, and after receiving Sam's acknowledgement, darted southwest behind a large oak tree. Sam stood again to cover him, but a bullet whistling past his ear forced him down.

"Stupid," he said aloud. The enemy knew his position. Sam could picture the German sharpshooter sitting in a tree, high-powered rifle trained on the spot where Sam's head would emerge from behind the rocks. He was petrified.

Hoffman's screams jarred Sam back. "Dalton's hit. Hart, get there! I'll draw their fire."

Sam waited for the automatic fire to begin from Hoffman's location to move from his sanctuary toward his fallen comrade. Sam counted the steps as he sprinted, trying to think of nothing else. It wasn't until he reached the wounded soldier, and bent over him, that he realized that bullets were whizzing around him.

Sam fired several shots while trying to pull Dalton forward, into the trees.

"Leave me," moaned Dalton.

"Wha'?" said Sam, sure he had misheard him. "Can you move?"

Hoffman was darting in an out of the field, firing furiously at the trees and distracting the snipers with some success.

"Get the fuck out of here. Let them think I'm dead. Go over to Hoffman, and I'll go behind 'em."

Sam paused for a moment to make sure he got it, then dropped Dalton's arms and ran toward the large oak. He yelled out, "Hoffman, he's dead."

"Shit. Stay there. We need to spread out."

Sam fired repeatedly as he moved, tree by tree, away from Dalton.

When Sam had progressed a fair distance away, he snuck a look back. Dalton was no longer where he had fallen, and Sam thought he could make him out crawling on his belly on a circumnavigational course.

Hoffman had resumed moving and shooting. Between the two of them, Sam reckoned, they could give Dalton a chance.

Sam spent the next 15 minutes running and firing, dodging and diving, pausing and listening, trying not to think about how all this might end. Finally, a burst of gunfire and the sound of a man falling provided a clue.

Hoffman stood out from behind a rotted elm and fired at the remaining sniper's position. Sam joined in, and could see that fire was also coming from the ground just below the trees. Within a minute, the second sharpshooter lay dead on the ground.

"Now!" yelled the Sergeant.

The men of Company B surprised their ambushers. Four Germans were killed immediately, four surrendered and two ran into the deepest part of the woods. Sam and Hoffman, rushing back to join their colleagues, gave chase and quickly closed the gap.

Hoffman yelled "Stop!" but the Germans ignored him. He stopped running, knelt on one knee and calmly brought one of the enemy soldiers down with a shot to the shoulder.

The second German turned back to face Sam with his handgun drawn and fired wildly. Sam became infuriated, and pounced on the man like a blitzing middle linebacker in pursuit of a quarterback. The German fell flat on the ground, and Sam tumbled over him on his back.

DIVIDED LOYALTIES

The hard contact dazed them both. As Sam sat up and got his wind back, he saw the German crawling on his knees, appearing to look for his weapon. Sam reached into his holster, drew his sidearm, and fired into the side of the German soldier's face.

***

Five weeks later, spring had turned into summer. Company B had been slogging west into the heat and humidity of the new season, and everything—the pack, the rifle, and especially the boots—dragged them down.

When the soldiers had moved out this morning—a late start at 0830—the cloyingly sweet odor of wet hay and burning manure almost choked them. Now, hours later and miles behind them, they could breathe again.

It had been quiet the past few days, and the weather was improving as the day wore on. Company B had been re-supplied with food, dry clothing and letters from home just two days ago, and the soldiers were generally at ease, and in good humor. As they approached within 10 kilometers of the small town of Gunskirchen, which purportedly housed a munitions factory, Sam lifted his nose to the sky and sniffed.

Something acidic, like smoke, scratched the back of his throat. As they neared the village, the smell thickened and deepened until several of the soldiers were gagging and others tried to clear their mouths by drinking from their canteens. Soon the stench enveloped them.

Several GIs vomited violently and when the soldier marching in front of him, Billy Adams from St. Louis, threw up, Sam lost control as well.

"What the hell *is* that?" stammered the Missourian, wiping his lips and taking a swig from his canteen. "It smells like shit!"

Sam groaned and held his midsection. He lit a cigarette, but that only compounded the sensory assault and made him more nauseous. Dry heaves followed.

Sergeant Yancy put a kerchief to his mouth and the rest of the men followed suit. They advanced until they reached a street paved with loose gravel. The forest ended, and the road led into a huge clearing. Yancy signaled his men to stop, pulled a map out of his backpack and motioned for his radioman to join him.

About a kilometer ahead a series of 12 coarse, wood buildings formed a rectangle, surrounded by 10-foot-high stockade fences and barbed wire. Guard towers acted as the right angles of the box.

Nothing moved. No smoke, no people. Even the breeze had died. The sun was bright above Sam's head, but by the time the light penetrated the infected atmosphere, the air seemed filled with choking smog. Bright blue and white above, gray and black below. *What kind of factory was this?*

Sam shifted his gaze to the area outside the fences. Bodies lay on the ground a small distance from the gate. At first he only saw a few, then, as he looked closer, he saw more of them—hundreds, perhaps.

Finally, Yancy handed the field phone back to the radioman. He split the Company into four groups, each approaching the camp from a different direction. The intelligence report Yancy had just received said that the German guards had vacated the "plant" a day or so earlier. Nonetheless, Yancy cautioned his men to anticipate trouble. As Sam and his team approached the main gate, dread roiled his stomach

He passed several dozen bodies, twisted in death, sprawled on the ground. The figures were barely clothed, in coarse, off-white pajamas with vertical gray stripes. Most of those grim uniforms bore a faded yellow star, sewn above the heart, with the word "Jude" at its center.

It was almost impossible to make out the ages of the victims. All were bald and emaciated, and most lay in pools of their own waste. A few had bullet holes and bloodstains on their backs. The Americans moved past, single file; all had been rendered mute by the atrocity.

Ahead, Sam looked through the huge, open gate and into the courtyard. Both sides of the road were littered with bodies, in similar condition to those they had first come across. As Company B entered, the numbers of bodies increased logarithmically. There were rough piles of corpses outside the doors of many of the wooden structures, presumably barracks. Clearly, they had been thrown there in haste, like old furniture being discarded from a basement. Other bodies were strewn across the compound in horizontal patterns, on their backs, suggesting to Sam that the inmates had been lined up and executed by automatic weapon fire.

Sam felt empty to his core. His pack was a burden, his legs as thick and heavy as tree trunks. He even stopped blinking.

He wasn't sure how long he remained motionless. The cries of "Hey, this one's alive!" and "Medic! Medic! Get over here," slowly pierced the haze and spurred Sam to refocus. His colleagues were searching through the piles for any sign of life.

Sam joined them, desperately hoping to feel a twitch, a breath. A reed-thin figure, lying on its back, moaned softly.

His jaw and pronounced Adam's apple marked him as a man—probably in his mid-20s, Sam thought—and the yellow star on his shirt pronounced his faith. The man lifted his hand to his mouth, forming a "V" with his fore and index fingers. "Yes, we're here," Sam said. "Wir sind Amerikaner. Sie sind jetzt sicher."

The inmate shook his head slightly and slowly moved his fingers up to his face. It wasn't until the man touched his lips that Sam understood the message.

He pulled a crumbled pack of Lucky Strikes from his shirt pocket and lit a cigarette with a Zippo lighter from his ammo belt. The man was too weak to hold the cigarette so Sam cradled his head in one hand and held the Lucky to his mouth with the other. The prisoner eagerly drew the smoke into his own lungs. After a few tugs, the man smiled at Sam, turned his head to the side, and exhaled for the last time.

CHAPTER 2

For half a century, Sam had steadfastly refused to talk about his experiences during the War except in the most general terms and only in response to a specific question. He declined invitations to Company reunions, despite the warmth and respect he bore for the men he had marched and battled with, and when the dark memories came calling, he too often found solace in drink.

Fifty years later Sam still abhorred cigarettes. The acrid smoke dragged him back to the invasive air of Gunskirchen, poisoned with the smells of death and decay, human excrement, and cheap German tobacco, and the horrifying image of the man who had spent his last breaths in Sam's arms, puffing a Lucky Strike.

Five decades of reasonably successful avoidance, Sam sighed as he stepped out of the shower with a towel wrapped around his thickening, but still respectable waist. He hoped that the morning routine would take his mind off of the chores awaiting him that day. For a time—shaving, drying his hair, and dressing— seemed to work, at least until his wife stepped into the dressing room.

"You're up early," she said, garbed in a white terry-cloth bathrobe two sizes too large.

Despite the hour—it was just barely six in the morning—Sam wasn't surprised to see Gloria up and about. She'd always been a light sleeper, but lately her malady had worsened and her sleeping times were now best characterized as purely random events.

Gloria Hart was a petite, meticulously groomed 67-year old, one of those women whose obvious beauty had been worn down by time and an unfortunate gene pool. Once a highly regarded school principal and administrator, she had entered retirement reluctantly, channeling her substantial energies and intellect into volunteer work. All that seemed to come to a crashing halt about four months ago when Gloria began behaving erratically. It seemed to Sam that he hadn't had a stress free day since then.

Gloria patted Sam on the rear end playfully. "Putting on a few pounds, big boy?"

Sam shot a barbed look at his wife. "Thanks for the compliment."

"Don't get grumpy with me, young man!"

Sam suppressed an angry retort, not wanting to provoke an "episode." Unfortunately, the trance had been broken and his thoughts turned to his schedule for that day: eight o'clock Executive Committee breakfast meeting; 9:30 visit with Mr. Kobayashi of Sumitomo Bank; 11 o'clock conference call with his senior managers regarding the bonus pool. Then, rush back to leafy Westchester to pick up his wife and bring her to the neurologist at Columbia Medical Center.

Gloria, who had been standing next to him the whole time, moved close and touched him on arm. "Dear, you just got so pale. Are you all right?"

Sam was surprised by the urgency of her tone. He caught a glimpse of himself in the wardrobe mirror. He looked like an old man, gray-faced and stooped. He brushed it off. "I'm fine. Just need my coffee."

***

"I don't think I can keep them with $1 million. It's got to be at least 2," pleaded the corpulent vice president. "Credit

Bank announced bonus increases of 35 percent across the board."

Sam rolled his eyes, letting everyone in the cramped conference room know just what he thought about Brenner's pleas. Sam hated this part of his job—divvying up the bonus pool. The irony of it all was that the more money that was available to be distributed, the more contentious the process of apportionment became.

"Spare me. I warned you that this wasn't a one-way street. I offered them plenty last year, and then begged upstairs to get them more when they whined and threatened to defect. This year, they were barely mediocre. They deserve less, and that's what they'll get." Sam turned the page in his flip book, ready to move on to the next adjudication.

Brenner kept himself on center stage by thumping his forefinger on the table to get Sam's attention. Sam slowly looked up at the manager of his high-yield bond desk and stared at him through watery brown eyes. He was thinking, *One more word out of you and I'll fire your smarmy ass,* and hoped he hadn't said it.

Perspiration stains darkened Brenner's underarms. "I'm not saying I like these guys, Sam. I wouldn't let any of them date my daughter or invite them over for dinner. They're mercenaries, absolutely. But unless I can pay Johnson and Carver more, they'll go across the street. If they leave, I'll probably lose Steiner and Marvin too. Forget about loyalty and culture. Without the money, there's nothing I can do."

Sam knew he had a decision to make: throw a platitude at Brenner ("You're exaggerating, Tom. Let's talk later,") and get on to the next desk, or excoriate the pain-in-the-ass in front of his peers. He chose the latter.

"Tom, you're making an important point here. Thanks. By the way, what did I pay you last year?"

"Wha—?"

"A million, four-hundred-thousand. That's what you got paid."

"I'm a partner," whispered Brenner. "Profit share."

"I set your share last year. And I'll set it again this year. Sounds to me like you haven't done much to create loyalty and team spirit on your desk if they're ready to leave us for a couple of bucks. So, tell me what I'm getting for the one-point-four million dollars?"

Before Brenner could mount his defense, Sam plowed ahead. "You've just answered my question." Sam pulled a yellow pad from the stack on the table and began writing "So here's what we'll do: give Johnson and Carver each another hundred-fifty-thousand. Steiner, umm, say, 50. Same for Marvin. That's 400K. Let's spread another hundred-thousand around the trading and sales desks, for a total of five-hundred-thousand. We'll fund that from your points, OK, Tom?"

Sam intended to cut him back another couple of hundred thousand if he said another word. Brenner obviously sensed that, because he sank back in his seat, half a million dollars poorer for his efforts.

Sam tried not to appear too pleased with himself, although he was happy to have set an example so early in the process. The rest of the session would go much smoother.

"OK," he said. "Who's next?"

***

Two hours later, exhausted from the intensity of the bonus-setting process and sore from the arthritis that was attacking his lower back, Sam hunched over the steering wheel of his black Mercedes and cursed the midday traffic. He thought he had dodged a bullet when, knowing that his meeting would run longer than scheduled, he had arranged for Gloria's sister to pick her up at the house and bring her to the medical center. That would save him at least an hour-and-a-half.

But of course, he was still late. He had 20 minutes to get uptown and the West Side Highway wasn't moving. He hoped Eileen could handle Gloria, who, under the best of circumstances, was neurotically punctual. Now, in her "altered state," and apprehensive about seeing a new doctor...Sam shuddered to think of the shit she was capable of dishing out.

He caught a break after the Holland Tunnel where the traffic eased. Sam calculated that he just might make it there in time, pushed down on the accelerator, gradually at first, and had no idea he was doing 80 when he saw the flashing lights behind him.

The state trooper was all business. Sam tried to explain that he was rushing to get to his wife in the hospital, but the cop had heard it all before. As he impatiently waited for his summons, Sam downed two Rheumatrix pills with the warm remnants of a Diet Coke. What he really wished for was a cold martini.

By the time he parked the car and hustled to the hospital lobby, Sam was almost 30 minutes late. He spotted Eileen and Gloria on an upholstered bench near the gift shop, sitting a full arm's-length apart. Sam knew that didn't bode well.

"Hi, dear. Hi, Eileen. Sorry, the traffic was just awful. I was stuck on the highway for a full half-hour without moving. There was an accident on the bridge."

The look Gloria gave him strongly suggested she knew he was lying. Eileen's face, on the other hand, shone of relief.

Eileen rose and kissed her brother-in-law on the cheek. She said, softly, in Sam's ear, "I tried to take her up to the doctor's office, but she wouldn't go without you. She hasn't said a word since."

Sam hugged her gently and reached out his hand to Gloria. "Come, dear. Let's go up to the doctor now."

After a few minutes of cajoling, Gloria stood to take Sam's hand. Eileen said "I'll come by the house tonight and bring dinner."

Gloria looked at her sister as if she hadn't understood a word of what she was saying. Sam headed-off the predictable uncomfortable confrontation by putting his arm around Gloria's shoulders and gently but firmly moving her down the hallway and away from Eileen. "This way, dear. We've got to go to the fifth floor."

Sam glanced over his shoulder and saw Eileen wipe tears from her eyes with her fingers. He breathed in deeply to keep his identical feelings in check, and led his wife into an opening elevator. Gloria muttered something under her breath, and Sam asked her to repeat it.

"She's a bitch," Gloria said, so loud that the three other people in the elevator turned their heads. "She always gets what she wants. Mama gives her everything."

Sam tried to pull her close, but she resisted with a lowered shoulder. "Don't do that. You're always standing up for her. Are you *sleeping* with her?"

Having spent the past months learning the hard way, Sam knew it was best not to respond directly when Gloria got like this. He'd have to try to change the subject, quickly, because the elevator was moving excruciatingly slowly, stopping at every floor.

DIVIDED LOYALTIES

The fifth floor lobby was, for all intents and purposes, a large waiting room servicing the dozens of doctors in the neurology and oncology departments. Sam found a seat for Gloria near a huge and colorful fish tank, positioned so he could keep his eye on her—and more importantly, where she could see him—as he joined the queue in front of a sign entitled "Patient Registration."

The line moved slowly, Sam's arthritis medication wasn't working, and the strains of the day were wearing through his resolve. Under his breath at first, at then audibly, he drew upon a large database of profanities to inveigh against the stupidity of a place which put one through so many bureaucratic hoops to get to see a goddamn doctor.

Finally, Sam got to the front of the line and checked in. He was advised by an officious young woman with short, greasy hair to "Take a seat. We'll call you when the doctor is ready."

Turning back to rejoin Gloria, Sam looked around the room and the dozens of others who had taken a seat, and almost snapped. The crowded, overheated waiting room was teaming with tension. He sat down next to his wife and tried to make conversation, but Gloria was clearly nervous and uncooperative. After 15 minutes of waiting in silence, he began to feel light-headed, and didn't know how much more of this he could take.

Sam was within seconds of grabbing his wife and leaving for home when a tall, black woman wearing a white lab coat entered the waiting room from a hallway behind the registration desk. She was holding a manila folder, which she looked at for a second before calling out "Karetske? Anton Karetske?"

Sam recognized the name from a newspaper article he had clipped just a few days before and read several times since. He instinctively sat up straight and extended his neck to get a better view of the room. Within seconds, a short, red-haired woman in a brown overcoat, pushing a man in a wheelchair, responded to the call.

They stood in front of the hallway, talking quietly with the nurse. Sam strained to eavesdrop, but they were too far away. He considered getting up to get a glimpse of Karetske when another white-coated woman entered the room and barked "Hart? Gloria Hart?"

***

Although Dr. Nelson's waiting area was much less crowded and thankfully cool, Sam couldn't get comfortable. A nurse had asked him to wait there for "just a few minutes" while Gloria got undressed, but wasn't at all clear what would happen next.

A "few minutes" became a half-hour, and again Sam got progressively agitated. He could feel his heart rate increase, and he was sweating through his shirt into his suit jacket. Sam tossed the out-of-date copy of *People* magazine he had been flipping through on a coffee table and opened his briefcase. Several minutes of aggressive searching ended with Sam locating what he was looking for.

> White Plains Resident, Holocaust Survivor, Brings Message of Tolerance to High School.
> At an assembly of 375 high school students on Monday, Holocaust survivor and White Plains resident Anton Karetske spoke of the importance of tolerance and understanding in a world where tensions are increasing between peoples of differing ethnic and religious backgrounds. In Hungarian-accented

English, Karetske, who has lived in Westchester County since 1963, told the 15- to 18-year-old audiences that "the lessons of the Holocaust are clear. We cannot allow anyone, any person, religion, or country, to claim they possess the only truths. There is no perfect truth. There is no single way to think, or live. God created all of us, and made us all different. We must love those differences, learn from them and embrace them."

The assembly was the second in a series of events held at the Arthur Scales High School to promote tolerance of religious and racial differences. Last year, several racially-motivated incidents occurred at the high school, causing school administrators to cancel the senior prom and sports rallies.

Karetske was taken from his home in Budapest in his late teens and separated from his parents, whom he has never seen since. He was liberated two days before the end of the war in Europe from a concentration camp in Gunskirchen, Germany by the American Infantry. He spent time in Holland and Israel after the war, and eventually moved to New York City with his daughter after his wife died during childbirth. He founded a jewelry fabrication business in Manhattan in 1963, which he continues to operate, and moved to Westchester County in 1963.

Karetske has been active in working with youth groups, particularly in inner city situations. "I lost much of my childhood because the Nazis stole it from me. Racism and bigotry stole it from me. In the end, I survived because the Americans found us. In that sense, I was lucky. A few more days and I would have been dead. I feel I need to return the favor, to maybe find a child who needs some help, and be his luck."

Sam walked to the cooler and drank two cups of water, crumbled the cup and chucked it into a waste basket. He walked slowly to the assistant's desk in the corner of the waiting room, and was about to engage her when her phone rang. She held up a finger, answered the phone, said "OK, I'll send him right in," and smiled at Sam.
"She's ready. Please follow me."
Sam's impatience turned to anxiety. He had hoped for a private meeting with Doctor Nelson, the geriatric neurologist who had been recommended by Gloria's internist. He knew that nothing good could possibly come from describing his wife's recent aberrant and aggressive behavior in her presence.
He followed the assistant through a doorway into a large, airy office. A lab-coated woman with white hair rose behind a bulky English desk to her full six foot height and extended her hand to Sam. "I'm Dr. Nelson. Your wife in is the examination room getting dressed. I'd like to ask you a few questions before she comes back in. Please sit down."
Sam did as he was told, taken a bit aback by the no-nonsense appearance and approach of the neurologist. "How is she?" he said in a loud whisper, looking toward a slightly ajar door at the other end of the doctor's office.
The doctor didn't change her expression. "Something's going on, but it's not readily apparent to me what it is. I went through some standard cognition tests with her, and there does appear to be some impairment compared to the norm for a woman her age. Has she fallen, or had any head injury that you are aware of?"

Sam shook his head.

"Tell me about her. What's normal, and how has she been acting lately?'

Sam's eyes watered thinking about his wife of 45 years. "Gloria has always been a sweet, kind woman. She never had a bad thing to say about anyone. Over the past month or so she's used words I didn't think were in her vocabulary. She's lashed out at her sister, her friends, me. She accuses people of stealing, and me of cheating on her.

"And the crying. We'll be at a movie, or having dinner, and she'll get morose and start crying. I'll ask her what's wrong and she says she doesn't know. It can go on for hours, and usually ends by her falling asleep.

"But then at other times, she's totally fine. She'll go to her committee meetings, take care of her garden, and it's like it always is. I've tried to find correlations and causations between her dark periods and other events, but I can't put it together."

Dr. Nelson scribbled a few notes on a yellow pad and pulled a multi-page letter from a manila folder on her desk. "This is from your wife's internist. Her blood pressure was extremely high--220 over 95--at her last checkup at the beginning of the year. It was almost that high when I took it a few minutes ago. He prescribed Tenormin. Has she been taking it?"

Sam flopped back in his chair. He hadn't known Gloria had high blood pressure, much less that she was supposed to be taking medication. "I had no idea."

"Well, that could be one of our problems. Unchecked hypertension can cause TIAs or mini-strokes. It's often the cause of dementia in people her age. I don't think its Alzheimer's, but we can't rule that out yet.

"I've ordered a series of tests for today: a CT scan and an MRI. My guess is that your wife will lose patience quickly unless we can give her something to lighten her mood. Nothing too dramatic—I'm thinking a low dose of Celexa would work. I need your permission to do that."

"Yes, of course. Should I stay with her?"

The doctor turned as Gloria entered the room, scowling as she tried to button her sleeve. "That would be a good idea. You will need to go across the street to the Minor Pavilion for the radiological tests."

Dr. Nelson got up and escorted Gloria to the chair next to Sam's. She got down on one knee to be eye-to-eye with her patient, held her hand and said firmly, "Mrs. Hart, I'm going to give you a pill which you need to take for the tests we've got scheduled for you. When you get home, you must take your blood pressure pill. That's a doctor's order. OK? You have to take it every day, or you'll have a stroke. Every day."

Gloria shot a cold look at Sam and snapped, "I don't have high blood pressure."

Dr. Nelson commandeered Gloria's attention back to her. "Yes, you do. You have dangerously high pressure. I'm the doctor, and I've just given you an order. I'll call you every day if I have to."

Gloria looked sullen in defeat. She accepted the small white pill from Dr. Nelson and a cup of water, and took her anti-depressant without complaint.

***

The cafeteria was like every other place of its type Sam had ever had the misfortune of visiting. The fluorescent lighting added to the austerity and gloom of the undersized, windowless room in the basement of the Minor Pavilion. Sam had called his office twice, inquiring about the fate of a very large currency risk position one of his divisions was running, and about which he was taking a lot of flak from his Management Committee colleagues. To his enormous frustration and growing sense of irrelevance, Sam was told the head trader couldn't speak to him because, as Sam's secretary put it, "The markets are going bananas."

Sam looked at his watch. He had at least another 45 minutes before he had to report to Radiology to pick up Gloria, which was not enough time to get to his office but way too much time to spend in that gloomy cafeteria. Donning his khaki raincoat, Sam took the elevator up to the ground floor, walked through the lobby and out onto the street.

The drizzle turned into a steady rain by the time Sam had only three blocks' worth of a stroll under his belt. With no umbrella, and no alternative destination, Sam hastened back toward the main hospital where he and Gloria had first started their day, remembering that there was a newsstand in the lobby. Possibly, mercifully, he would be able to find some distraction there for the remaining–Sam looked at his watch again—half-hour he need spend in limbo.

Sam stepped out of the rain into the hospital, and almost immediately spotted the redhead who responded to the "Karetske" name in the Admitting Department. She was sitting on the end of an upholstered bench, facing a man seated in a low armchair. Sam circled the lobby to get a closer look.

The man's gray hair was just longer than stubble, suggesting new growth. He was broad-shouldered, of uncertain height, but the dark sports jacket he was wearing seemed too big for his frame. As Sam got closer, he noticed that the man's blue eyes appeared almost luminescent, framed as they were in his drawn and bony face.

Sam got within a few yards of the Karetskes when the woman got up and started buttoning her coat. She said, "Papa, I'll get the car and bring it right up to the door, so wait here.

I had to park in the lot on Maple Street, so maybe I'll be 10 minutes."

Anton shrugged, smiled and watched his daughter head to the door. He hadn't noticed that Sam had taken her spot on the bench until he spoke.

"Mr. Karetske?"

Anton turned his eyes to Sam. "Yes."

"I'm Sam Hart. You don't know me, and I'm sorry to intrude. Can I ask you a question?'

"Of course."

"I read an article in the local paper recently about someone with the same name who talks to kids about World War II. Are you that person?"

The response was immediate and vigorous. "I don't talk to them *about* the War. I try to discuss prejudice and discrimination as someone who survived these things *in* the War."

Sam regretted the inexactitude of his wording, but nonetheless went right to the point. "The article said you were at Gunskirchen at the end of the War."

Anton searched Sam's face for a few long seconds. "You were there, too."

Sam held out his hand and gave in to the firmness of Anton's clasp. "One day. May 4, 1945."

Gratitude radiated from Anton's face. "I'm Karetske. I was there for many days. It's an honor to meet you."

***

Anton's daughter, Helene, was back in exactly 10 minutes. This gave Sam only enough time to learn that Anton ran a jewelry business in Manhattan and lived nearby in Rye, New York. He had just finished an experimental chemotherapy protocol for prostate cancer with encouraging results. The disease had gone into remission, and the side effects—loss of hair and appetite, occasional joint and back pain—were "trivial" in Anton's opinion. He pronounced himself ready to go back to work full-time, starting the following week.

Anton popped out of his chair with an ease that surprised Sam as Helene moved through the lobby toward him. "Come, Papa. I can't leave the car there."

Anton grabbed his daughter's arm and pulled her toward him. "This is Mr. Hart, a friend from a long time ago. Sam, this is my wonderful daughter Helene."

Sam and Helene exchanged hellos, but it was clear the conversation would go no further. "I'm sorry," she said, "but I promised the guard I'd be right out."

Sam fished a business card out of his wallet and a pen from the inside of his jacket. He wrote his home number on the back of the card and handed it to Anton. He asked "Could we talk again?"

Anton looked over the card carefully. "Of course. Sorry I don't have a card with me, and I never remember my own number. I'll call you, or you can look me up in the yellow pages—Tikkun Jewelers. 'T-I-K-K-U-N'—on 46th Street."

Sam wrote this down on a scrap of paper, extended his hand to Anton and turned to face his daughter. "It was a pleasure meeting you, Helene. Sorry to keep you."

Sam watched Anton and Helene leave the hospital, feeling postive and energized. It was as if he had received some really good news as a result of this chance meeting, although Sam couldn't quantify or identify what that might be.

It only lasted a fleeting minute, however. Sam caught a glimpse of a large digital clock on the wall above the elevators and realized it was time to cross the street to collect his wife. He re-buttoned his raincoat, cinched the belt tightly around his waist and lifted the collar to cover his ears, and with a deep sigh ventured back into the rain.

***

Mercifully, Sam thought, Gloria slept most of the ride home. The silence gave him a chance to think about Dr. Nelson's initial diagnosis, and that she had said any damage that may have occurred would be irreversible. Sam tried to inventory the dozens of questions—some obvious, some not—that were surfacing for the next time he spoke with the doctor.

Although Dr. Nelson hadn't talked at all about treatment in their short, private dialogue, Sam got the clear impression—either from the tone of her voice or the softness in her eyes—that taking care of his wife would be a profound responsibility. He tried to remain disciplined and clinical in his approach, but try as he might to stay on track, he couldn't help but give in to self-pity.

He was only 68 years old! He wasn't ready to pack it in and move to Florida. Retirement had been an option he and Gloria had been discussing for a few years now, but they were in agreement that it wouldn't be good for either of them. Sam never anticipated that something like this might force his hand, and it was upsetting him, and scaring him.

Sam headed toward the longest line at the toll booths at the Larchmont exit on Interstate 95, not liking the way he was feeling and hoping that the change in tempo would clear his head. He turned to the small woman resting comfortably next to him and reminded himself that she'd been there, at his side, for more than four decades. They'd had ups and downs in their lives, but never in their marriage. Sam readily admitted to himself that Gloria had put up with a lot more "sh-tuff"—as she put it—in dealing with Sam than the other way around.

The tightness in Sam's head was easing, and he was taking on a more positive mental attitude. With Gloria's blood pressure under control, there'd be no more TIAs. Drugs could moderate, if not eliminate, the mood swings. They'd get more domestic help in the house. Sam would travel less and put fewer demands on Gloria for business entertaining.

A blaring horn snapped Sam back to the highway. Several cars had moved up in the toll line, leaving a large gap in front of Sam. As he took his foot off the brake and the car moved forward, Sam heard Gloria shift her position and try to unbuckle her seat belt.

"Almost home, dear," Sam said, reassuringly.

"Where are you taking me? I want to know, where are we going?" Gloria sounded petrified.

"Home. We're going home."

"I don't live here. This isn't New York."

Sam could see from the bright lights at the toll plaza that Gloria was moving her hands across the inside of the car, her back turned to Sam. He pushed the door lock control on his side, hoping it would buy some time as he powered down his window and paid the toll.

Sam accelerated, and reached out to take Gloria's hand. She shrank from his touch, and began pulling on the door handle. "Let me out, damn you. Let me out."

Sam pulled over to the side of the road, put the car in park and checked to make sure the doors were still locked. "Take it easy, Gloria. You just woke up. You're acting crazy."

The muscles around Gloria's eyes tightened and she glared at her husband. "Crazy! You're the miserable, cheating, crazy son-of-a-bitch. I've had it with you. I'm leaving, now."

She pulled on the handle again, and again, and began

banging on the side windows with her fists. When that provided no result, she turned to Sam and began swinging at him.

Sam grabbed her hands and held them tight. "Gloria. Look at me," Sam implored. "Please, look at me."

When her eyes met his, another transformation took place. Gloria's face softened and her eyes filled with tears. When Sam let go of her hands, she buried her face in them and sobbed quietly.

Sam let her cry for a little while, not knowing what else to do. Eventually, as she seemed to be winding down, Sam offered her his handkerchief, which she accepted without looking at him.

"It's OK. You were sleeping and woke up suddenly. You probably had a nightmare."

Gloria shook her head, still looking at her hands which were now folded in her lap. "No, you had it right. I'm crazy. I get these ideas and I know they must be wrong but they seem so right. I can't stop them. They take over."

Sam's mind worked frantically for a response, but nothing came. All he could do was to reach out and touch Gloria's shoulder.

They sat there in silence, in the breakdown lane, for a few minutes, until Gloria blew her nose into Sam's handkerchief and turned her tear-stained face toward him. Her voice was clear but fragile. "Sam, what's happening to me?"

It was all Sam could do to keep from breaking down, right then and there. His head was pounding and his heart racing. "It's nothing serious, Gloria. It's nothing we can't handle. Let's get home and we can talk about it."

***

Sam stayed close to Gloria for the next two days, Saturday and Sunday. He took it upon himself to cancel all social activities that involved other people, and they spent time alone together taking walks, watching television, going to the movies and eating at local restaurants.

Gloria was relaxed and calm and charming, again. She didn't bring up the emotional outbursts of the past few days, and Sam left well enough alone. It was as if her episodic difficulties were a virus that had run its course and were gone for good. And even though he knew deep down that the other shoe would most likely drop soon, he clung to the hope that maybe, just maybe, they'd be lucky.

Sam was very reluctant to leave Gloria alone at home on Monday, but she assured him she was fine. His mind was so active during the drive down to Wall Street—filled with emotion-laden images of his wife—that when he got to his parking garage he had no recollection of how he got there.

Sam poured himself a cup of coffee from the dispenser outside his office and picked up a large stack of pink phone slips from the previous Friday. Although several of the messages suggested he wouldn't have an easy day ahead, Sam was grateful for having things to distract him. He sat down at his desk, sorted the messages according to urgency, and began making his first round of calls to Europe.

By 8:30, Sam was finishing up his third cup of coffee and a four-way conference call, and he desperately needed a bathroom break. He rushed out of his office to the men's room at the opposite end of the full floor trading room, used the facilities, and took his time coming back, meandering from cubicle to cubicle, chatting and gossiping as he went. Almost a half-hour had elapsed since Sam left his office, and he wasn't surprised to see two more message slips on his desk, one of which was from his boss, Stanley Masters, Chairman and CEO of GSC, saying, "Leaving for Asia within the hour. Call ASAP."

The second message was from Anton Karetske. The slip left his number and a simple "please call" notation.

Sam reread the new messages, and looked at his watch, doing the math. He felt his heart racing—probably from the coffee, he thought—sat down, and punched some digits into his phone.

A male voice, with a slight Eastern European accent answered politely "Tikkun Jewelers." Sam could have sworn he had dialed the other number.

In their brief conversation, Sam and Anton agreed to meet for lunch the following day in midtown, near Anton's store in the diamond district. Sam suggested the Harvard Club, but Anton countered with Magyar on 47th Street, winning the battle conclusively when he told Sam he refused to put on a jacket and tie just to have lunch.

Over goose liver pâté, veal cutlets and Tokay wine, Anton was generous in sharing the details of his post-war life. The German guards had abandoned Gunskirchen the evening before Infantry B arrived. Anton, then only 17, was one of the few inmates who had the physical strength and the courage to venture outside the gates in search of food and assistance. Feeling his way through the dense forest surrounding the camp in the pre-dawn fog, Anton literally bumped into two advance Army scouts, and followed them back to Company B for the first real meal he'd had in two years.

Anton led the American soldiers into Gunskirchen a few hours later. He was rewarded for his efforts with a direct trip to a field hospital, where he remained for three weeks fighting off a nasty infection and dehydration. After a year in a displaced persons camp outside Salzburg, Anton left to find his sister and a distant cousin on his mother's side, in Amsterdam.

In Holland, Anton learned the jewelry trade. He had married Sarah when he was 22, and they moved to Israel after four years. Helene was born 11 months later.

Sarah died giving birth to their son, Jacob—named after Anton's father, who died in the war—three years thereafter, but Jacob had a defective heart valve and lived for only a few months. Anton and Helene came to New York almost immediately after Jacob was buried in Tel Aviv.

Anton reported proudly that Helene was a wonderful daughter. Not because she had turned down a merit scholarship from Stanford to study statistics and computer science because she didn't want to leave her father all alone, but rather because she was self-confident, centered and held herself, and other, to high standards.

Anton almost remarried several years earlier, with his daughter's earnest blessing. He confessed to Sam that he backed out at the last minute, causing the woman—"a kind, lovely lady from Great Neck"—no small amount of pain and embarrassment. He enjoyed living alone and his business in New York City (manufacturing gold settings for precious stone jewelry) was thriving.

Sam was not nearly as forthcoming. He told Anton that he had practiced law for a while, hated it, and got lucky when he was recruited to join an investment bank 30 years ago. He now ran its trading division and traveled a lot.

Anton pressed for more details, which Sam only grudgingly gave him. Visibly exasperated, Anton apparently tried a different tack. "You have children?"

"One. Jeffrey. He's....40, no 41, I think, and lives in

Washington." Sam looked down at his hands, hoping Anton wouldn't ask for more details.

"Are there grandchildren?"

Sam paused for a moment, savoring a quick flash of his darling granddaughter. "Yes. Rebecca. She's in her early twenties. She also lives in Washington. A real delight and we just can't get enough of her."

"She's an adult already. That must be wonderful. Mine are still tots. I hope I get to see them grow, so we can have real conversations."

Sam sensed a slight bit of melancholy in Anton's voice, and thought it best not to pursue it. The men were silent for a few minutes, the first awkward moment in their brief time together.

***

Several days later, after a long and tension-filled risk management meeting, Sam came back to his office seeking refuge. He closed the door, turned down the lights, kicked off his shoes and collapsed onto the leather couch, hoping the quiet would calm him down. He hadn't yet begun to relax when he heard a soft but forceful knock on the door, which opened a crack to reveal the face of his secretary.

"Sorry to bother you, Sam. But Dr. Nelson is on 7355. You said you wanted to be interrupted if she called. Also…"

Sam grabbed for his phone, not letting his secretary finish.

"Hi, Dr. Nelson. Sam Hart. Did you get the tests back?"

The results were inconclusive, the doctor explained, as they usually were in this type of situation. There were some darkened areas in the scan that may indicate small lesions in the brain, which could have been caused by TIAs, but, maybe not. The MRI was similarly inconclusive.

Dr. Nelson suggested that the appropriate course of action

here was to employ one or more of a new type of anti-depressant to take the edge off of Gloria's mood, and watch to see if that alone improved the paranoid and anti-social behavior. "It's a lot more art than science," she explained.

Sam pressed her for more specifics. "Is this something that will get worse as she gets older, or can the drugs stop the progress? What are the side effects of the anti-depressants?"

"I'm just a neurologist, Mr. Hart. I only deal with cells and synapses that we can see. This other realm belongs to the psychiatrists, and I think your wife should definitely see one. I can recommend a team here at Columbia that specializes in geriatrics, which is important because they've most likely seen many cases like your wife's."

Sam took down the names and number of the geriatric psycho-pharmacologists, thanked Dr. Nelson, and hung up. He had been anxiously looking forward to her call, hoping to arrive at some clarity, but all he was left with was more uncertainty and many more questions.

There was another knock on the door, and his secretary again appeared. "Mr. Karetske is here. He said he had an appointment."

Sam sat silently on his couch, not having processed this new information. He continued reviewing what Dr. Nelson had told him when he watched Anton enter his office.

"We need to leave now to make it to the school by 3," he said. "You'll be back by 5."

"What school? What are you doing here?"

Anton grabbed Sam's wrist and gently pulled him up off of the couch. "Martin Luther King School, in Hunts Point. I've got a car downstairs."

"I can't go now. I've got to make a call. I've got meetings," stammered Sam, offering only a token bit of physical resistance to Anton's tugs.

"We," Anton said, smiling warmly at Sam's secretary and accepting her nod graciously "have taken care of your afternoon. Come, let's go. I'll fill you in on the way."

Anton was electric as he described the High School Tolerance program he'd been involved in for the past few months. "Every day, these kids see on the TV what they don't have, and believe that they can't have it. By the time they get to high school, they're victims without hope. They don't believe anyone cares about them because they're poor, black or Hispanic. They get bitter and hateful. It's very frightening.

"What we do is show them that they aren't alone. Old men, like us, understand what they are going through because we experienced similar things. We try to get them to stop feeling like victims and regain their hope and aspirations."

Sam listened, trying to figure out his place in all of this. He shuddered when he thought he put some of the pieces together. "Do you talk about Gunskirchen?"

Anton moved his head slightly side to side. "I don't talk about the camp. I try not to think about the camp. There is no future in dwelling on the past. *That's* what I talk about. I say that I was picked on only because I was Jewish, just like some of the families of the students in the room were picked on because of the color of their skin or the language they spoke at home. But things are different now—maybe still very hard, but better. Rather than focus your energy on hating the people that beat you down, I tell them, try to use that energy to lift yourself up."

"So, I'm a prop?" Sam asked, beginning to feel annoyed.

Anton responded firmly. "Only if you want to be. I was

rather hoping that you'd tell these kids that you left the warm, secure comfort of your middle-class home to risk your life for people like me, half-way around the world, and that you'd do it again for people like them. Maybe you'd mention that you're a lawyer, and that there are lots of lawyers out there fighting to enforce the rules against discrimination and prejudice. Maybe you'd urge them to push, to keep going, because it's not easy and may take years but in the end it's worth it.

"Or, you could just sit there and listen. Or, you can take the car back after it drops me off."

***

Sam felt uncomfortable and out of place in the cavernous, run-down high school auditorium in one of the poorest Bronx neighborhoods. He sat on the side of the elevated stage—a compromise he had worked out with Anton during their trip to the school—while Anton, two other volunteer speakers and a handful of teachers and administrators, addressed the issue of discrimination. Sam peered through the spotlights into the crowd of high school kids who occupied almost every seat. To him, the audience seemed genuinely disinterested and mostly disrespectful, slouched in their seats, baseball caps worn backwards, whispering to each other during the speakers' presentations.

When the assembly was over, the principal thanked the guests for their time and instructed the students to go to their next class. Sam positioned himself next to Anton, who was chatting with a high school teacher, wondering whether he should congratulate him or to brave the more sincere question, "Do you really think this helps?" As he got close, Sam noticed that a thin, light brown-skinned young man was standing nearby, clearly waiting for a chance to talk to Anton. Sam hung back, and moved a bit closer only when the teacher left and the young man approached.

Sam heard the young man say "Can I see your number?"

Anton looked at him carefully for a few moments, and then rolled up the sleeve of his left arm to the elbow. He held out his forearm to show the 11 digit tattoo that had been burned there in 1944.

The teen nodded. "I got one, too," he said. He turned around, his back toward Anton, gathered a handful of dreadlocks and pulled them up to the ceiling. On the nape of his neck was inscribed, in raised and rough script, "L69."

Sam heard Anton's gasp at the same time as he heard his own.

"They cut my ear off, too," said the young man, displaying that fact by pulling up more hair.

"Why? Who did this?" Anton asked.

"Los Diablos. I wouldn't pay them, so they used me as an example."

"Wouldn't pay them for what?"

"Protection, man. All the Haitian kids have to pay, or they get beat up. I wouldn't, so they cut me."

Anton reached out, put his arms on the young man's shoulders and lowered his neck so that their foreheads touched gently. They stayed like that for several quiet minutes.

Sam stood there, experiencing the combination of sorrow and anger that explained why Anton was right.

CHAPTER 3

Sam looked at the young man in the gray pajamas for a long while, cradling his head in his lap, willing him to open his eyes. The grateful look on his face when Sam held the cigarette to his lips was one of the most gratifying moments in Sam's life. The peaceful expression he had on his face when he exhaled the smoke and turned his head, to rest, encouraged Sam momentarily. But there had been no movement since.

Sam moved the man's head gently, left and right, up and down. He moved his free hand in front of the man's mouth, hoping to feel some breath. Around him, American soldiers were searching the heaps of bodies for survivors. In the corner of his eye, Sam saw a helmet bearing a white circle and the Red Cross, and shouted for help.

"He was just talking to me," he told the medic. "Help him."

The medic felt for a pulse on the man's neck and wrist. He put his ear over the man's heart. The soldier straightened up from a kneeling position, and shook his head slowly.

"He's gone. Sorry. It's probably for the best. Look at him. He wouldn't have made it much longer anyway."

The medic tried to help Sam get to his feet, but Sam wouldn't move. All he could think about was that he had failed. If he had summoned the medic sooner, maybe he could have saved this poor man.

Before he walked away in response to a distant cry for help, the medic whispered, "They're all like this. Starved and beaten. Or shot. It's hard to imagine anyone surviving this hellhole. C'mon, Joe, leave him there. The guys behind us will make sure he's decently buried."

Sam got up slowly, wiped the sweat from his face with his sleeve, and pulled a cigarette from his pocket and lit it. His mind was numb, his brain on hold. He inhaled, and the vile taste of the smoke and the cloying smell of death accosted him. He doubled over and vomited in the dirt until there was nothing left to throw up. He flicked away the cigarette in disgust. It was the last cigarette he would ever touch. He washed his mouth out with a sip of water from his canteen and walked on.

Here death was inescapable. Death in piles of bodies, face down in shit and muck, in wheel barrels and open trenches and in front of bullet-pocked wooden fences. Through the haze and stench, Sam noted that each death was marked with a little yellow star.

Sergeant Yancy didn't appear to be holding it together better than Sam or any of the men of Company B as they moved out of Gunskirchen and headed east. The men were horrified and more, they were furious. The soldier beside Sam said, "I hope we find the fuckers responsible for this!"

Yancy's whistle stopped the Company in its tracks.

"Dyrszka, Bradley, Pixner, Hoffman, LaBianca, Hart—over here, on the double!"

Yancy took the men off the road, away from the rest of the Company. "Intel spotted four or five German soldiers moving northwest of our position, away from the camp. They're probably the last of the guards to leave, and we want them for interrogation. Find 'em, and bring 'em back."

Yancy looked at the angry faces of his men. "A couple of them, anyway."

Sam was surprised at how quickly they located the German SS guards. After a two-hour walk, in the direction of Speyr, they heard two gunshots and placed the sounds near an old, ramshackle barn a hundred yards off the dirt road. The sun hadn't yet set, and a fresh breeze picked up from the southwest. After the death stench of Gunskirchen, the air felt cleansing.

Dyrszka and Sam headed toward the barn, using boulders and shadows for cover, giving them a direct look into the open door. Bradley and Pixner broke off and circled around the back of the building. Hoffman and LaBianca moved forward at a more deliberate pace, providing cover for the other pairs of men.

The Americans froze when four Germans, in the dark blue uniforms of the SS, staggered out of the barn. A tall, thin and balding soldier held a pistol in one hand and a tinted wine bottle in the other. His compatriots appeared to be without weapons, and they were skunk drunk.

Dyrszka had a clear shot at the Germans, and indicated his intention to take out the armed soldier while the others moved in. Bradley held up his hand to wait, signaling that he wanted to make sure there were no others in the barn. Dyrszka nodded, steadied himself against a tree and took aim. He'd killed Germans before, several times, but always in the heat of battle. With that said, he showed no hesitation in aiming his weapon between the ears of the enemy soldier.

Minutes later, Bradley emerged from behind the barn and reassumed his position just off center of the Germans, who were playfully fighting over the bottle. Pixner had stayed behind, ready to move into the barn through a back door as the attack unfolded. Dyrszka was ready when Bradley flashed a thumb's up, and his shot struck the gun toting German in the forehead.

The Americans fired at the feet of the standing guards, who raised their arms in surrender even before Sam had finished yelling, in perfect textbook German, "Hands on your head. Hands on your head or we shoot you."

Sam heard a shot fired inside the barn, and then Pixner's voice. "There's another one in here—an officer. I'm bringing him out."

***

Hoffman bound the ankles of the last SS guard and rolled him on his stomach. He stood up and said, to no one in particular, "Do we march them back to Unit now? It's almost dark. It'll take us hours before we catch up."

Bradley lit a cigarette and picked a strand of tobacco out of his teeth. "We're not due to rendezvous back until 1300 tomorrow—there's no rush. We've got food, shelter and ammo." The slender Kentuckian strode over to one of the bound Germans and booted him in the ribs. He kicked him again. "We've even got some entertainment."

Hoffman spat, and stomped his size twelve's down on the back of the knee of the soldier he had just tied up. "Scumbag," he said. "We should take you back to that camp. They'd tear your skin off with their bare hands. They'd pry your eyes out with a stick. You don't deserve to be a POW. You don't deserve another second."

He had picked up his rifle, and was about to use it to bludgeon the soldier when the German officer, sitting against a tree under Sam's watchful eye, intervened. "Halt! Nein!! Geneva Convention."

Hoffman stopped his assault in mid-air, flipped the rifle and positioned it firmly against his shoulder. He aimed it at the officer, hate in his eyes. "Geneva Convention? Are you out of your fucking mind? Where was the Geneva Convention for the people you starved to death? I saw children with bullet holes in their heads, in a pile outside of the fences. You did that, you fucking sick fuck. You did that!!!"

Hoffman paused just long enough for his fellow GIs to appreciate the truth of what he had just said. Sam knew that no one would fault Hoffman for shooting the German. But as mad as he was, as insanely mad as he must have been, Hoffman paused.

The German officer, sensing a reprieve, made a terrible mistake when he said "Wir waren nur machend, was wir erzählt wurden, zu machen. Wir sind Soldaten, gleich wie Sie."

Sam's face turned a number of colors—black, blue, red and purple—as he silently decoded the officer's statement. His heart began beating violently and his face flushed with anger. Sam unsheathed his bayonet and moved in the direction of the German, who curled up in a protective position.

In one motion, Sam cut the rope that held the officers legs and yelled, "Stehen Sie jetzt Bewegung auf!"

The officer struggled to his feet and Sam pushed him toward the barn. "Gehen Sie. Schnell."

Bradley had moved his hand down to his holster, and he turned to follow Sam and the prisoner. "What'd that fucker say, Hart? What was that jabber?"

There was just enough light left to see the panic in the officer's face as Sam pushed him against the barn wall. Hoffman and Bradley had followed them in. Sam said, "Cover me," as he handed his rifle to Bradley, turned the prisoner and cut his arms free.

Sam retrieved his rifle and placed its barrel just above the bridge of the German's nose, and lightly fingered the trigger. He said very slowly, "Nien, sind Sie nicht gerade wie ich." Then he pulled the trigger.

Sam looked at Hoffman, and walked out of the barn. Bradley emptied his rifle into the dead prisoner, as did Hoffman.

***

Sam felt the tugging on his arm before he heard and recognized Anton's voice.

"Sam, Sam. We're back."

Sam looked out the passenger side window of the town car and took in the familiar picture of his office building on Wall Street. The problem was that he didn't know why he was there.

"You had a nice snooze there," said Anton. "A bit noisy, too. I got you back here by 5, almost. We're a few minutes late."

Sam rubbed his eyes as the pieces fell into place. "I fell asleep on you. I'm so sorry."

"Not to worry. We had a nice talk before we hit traffic."

Sam sat up, combed back what remained of his hair with his fingertips, and straightened his tie. "Thanks for dragging me along. I'd like to go with you again."

"But this time, you get a speaking part. Right?"

Sam nodded, opened the car door and stepped out into the noise and commotion of rush-hour Wall Street. He pushed forward against the tide of the clerical staff leaving for the day and entered the elevator of the GSC headquarters.

Sam, still a bit groggy from his accidental nap, walked right past his secretary en route to his office. Before the door closed behind him, she yelled out, "Stanley's called several times for you, Sam. He doesn't sound happy."

He raised his right hand to indicate he'd heard the message, waited a moment to be sure he couldn't be heard, and mumbled "Fuck 'em." As tired and drained as he was, he knew his day was far from over.

***

Gloria was waiting at the front door for Sam when he got home that evening, even though it was well after eight o'clock. Sam could see she'd been crying, and although she tried to make chitchat with him while he took off his tie and poured himself a drink, he knew she had a lot on her mind and was desperate to talk.

Sam grabbed his martini and a stack of mail from the kitchen table, and motioned for Gloria to join him in the living room. "What's going on? You seem very upset."

"I spoke with Dr. Nelson this afternoon." Gloria tugged nervously at her fingers and her voice trembled. "She wants me to see a psychiatrist."

"Is that what you're upset about? It's no big deal, Gloria. It's actually good news. There's nothing wrong with your brain. You'll just get some medication to help with your mood. Did you take your pills today?"

Gloria shook her head and lightly banged her hand on the couch. "The doctor told me I probably didn't have a stroke, but that there was nothing she could do for me. That's why I need to see a shrink—because I'm crazy!"

Sam took a deep breath, reluctantly resigned to the fact that he would not be relaxing any time soon, slowly got up and moved to sit next to his wife. Knowing better, he didn't try to physically comfort her, but softened the timbre of his voice to try and calm her down.

"You are *not* crazy—not even close. Being depressed isn't being crazy. It's like high blood pressure, Gloria. You take the medicine and you're back to normal, that's it. But you have to take the pills—especially the blood pressure pills. If you don't, you *will* have a stroke."

Gloria sat without responding for a few moments, but Sam could tell from the reddening of her face that her silence wasn't a positive sign.

She exploded from her seat and walked hurriedly toward the kitchen door. "No. My mother, my grandmother. It's happening to me. You'll send me away. I'll die there. No, no, no."

Sam moved quickly, placing himself in front of her and the exit. "Your mother and grandmother were alone when they got sick. You're not. They didn't know they had hypertension and depression. We do know, and there are drugs that work.

"Please, Gloria. Trust me. Let's go upstairs and take your pills. Come."

An hour later, Sam headed to the den that adjoined his bedroom, having coaxed Gloria to take her medications and lie down with the TV on. His empty stomach growled, but he was just too tired to move to the kitchen and scrounge something to eat. He made himself another martini from the bar, kicked off his shoes and sat at his desk, hoping to relax.

He tried not to think about the complexities of Gloria's situation—not because he wanted to avoid the issues, but because he was just too exhausted to be able to deal with them thoughtfully. He tried to focus on his time with Anton, but that too was a strain. His eyes searched the desk, hoping for a simple distraction.

Sam found what he was looking for in a sterling silver frame—the college graduation photograph of his now 23-year-old granddaughter, Rebecca. He smiled freely thinking of her.

Rebecca got more beautiful as she aged, he thought. The crescent-shaped scar that partially encircled her left eye and cheek, and which had dominated her appearance after the accident, had almost completely faded, and with the help of makeup was indistinguishable. She was short of stature, but very long on energy. Sam envied her proclivity to take risks and rely on her instincts to get through unexpected situations. He loved her all the more for her ability to put a tragic situation behind her and, as she had once crudely put it, take things on "by the balls."

Rebecca's childhood had been a mess—a haphazard, emotionally exasperating muddle. The fact that her parents divorced when she was seven didn't change to any material degree the circumstances of her upbringing—before and after the separation Rebecca was primarily reared by hired help. The divorce did provide her mother, Margaret, with a fine apartment on Park Avenue and handsome alimony and child support payments, which she parlayed into an elaborate society life. That left virtually no time for her only child, and Rebecca became increasingly aware as she matured that she was little more than an afterthought.

Rebecca lived with her mother and hated her. Margaret spent hours at the spa to stay slim and coiffed. She shopped the Madison Avenue boutiques obsessively, and never with her daughter. Rebecca's disdain for her mother blossomed the day she overheard Margaret tell a friend—a nauseatingly skinny, affected Upper Eastsider straight out of *Bonfire of the Vanities*—that her settlement with her ex was so good she'd never have any interest in remarrying.

On the other hand, Rebecca didn't know her father well enough to hate him. She had few personal memories of him from the pre-divorce period other than standing by at a birthday party or the occasional appearance at a weekend breakfast table. Jeffrey Hart had been a prominent banker, Rebecca remembered being told by one of her nannies, a famous and rich man of whom she should be proud.

Rebecca wanted to be proud of him, especially as her revulsion of Margaret grew. On the few occasions when Jeffrey would arrange to visit her, or take her to lunch, she would desperately hope for some personal contact with her father, some connection or sign of affection. But Jeffrey was always awkward and formal with her. By the time Rebecca was 13, their time together dwindled to one or two meetings a year, which caused Rebecca to fall into a deep and profound funk for days thereafter. The extravagant gifts Jeffrey would send to her after these get-togethers made matters even worse.

When Rebecca started 8th grade, she "graduated" to the Hallows Academy, an elite prep school populated by the children of Manhattan's rich and famous. Adopting a slogan of "fuck it," she collected a group of friends with comparably disaffected backgrounds and demeanors. These kids were angry and resentful. They had few limiting influences on their behavior, and lots of available cash. The combination was a potent one, leading to aggressive anti-establishment behavior, drug and alcohol use and promiscuity. Eventually, by the time she entered her junior year in high school, Rebecca's acting out impacted her grades materially, followed by formal warnings from the school.

Margaret flipped out, suddenly taking interest in her daughter. She screamed at Rebecca daily. She threatened to cut off her access to discretionary funds, and to send her "upstate" to boarding school. Most of the time Rebecca just stood silently as her mother, waving a glass of Chardonnay in one hand and a cigarette in the other, babbled on about responsibility and social standing and *blah-blah-blah.* There was a sort of comic theatre about all of this, Rebecca thought, and sometimes she rather enjoyed it.

Rebecca hoped to hear from her father. She wanted to tell him about Margaret's ranting and raving. She wanted Jeffrey to tell her he understood what she was going through, that he would take her away from her mother and make things better for her. She would have listened to him. She would have moved away with him.

Jeffrey didn't call. He had recently been given some hotshot diplomatic position and was traveling all the time. At least that's what his executive assistant said the one instance that Rebecca got up the courage to call him.

Margaret's drinking binge continued unabated, and she became more and more abusive. One night, in a drunken rage, she accused Rebecca of acting to sabotage her social standing.

"You have everything, but it's not enough, is it? You have to punish me. That's what you want. Well, damn it, you're doing it. People are talking about you and your friends. They're talking about me. I won't have it. I won't have you deliberately trying to hurt everything I've built for myself."

Rebecca felt the blood rush to her face, and thought seriously about picking up the heavy glass ashtray on the nearby table and smashing her mother's head with it. Instead, she looked down at her feet and mumbled, "Fuck it."

"What did you say to me?" Margaret demanded, getting close enough that Rebecca could smell the alcohol on her breath.

Rebecca walked around her mother to the door. It was the last time she would be talk to her mother, face-to-face. "Nothing. I said nothing."

Rebecca stopped going to school. Just before the Christmas break, a letter was sent home summoning Rebecca and her parents to the headmaster's office. Rebecca refused to respond to the notes Margaret slipped under her door or the messages left on her personal answering machine. She wanted to be left alone. She didn't care about school, and it was clear her parents didn't care about her. And anyway, she had met this guy, Gary Roberts, at a bar in the Village and he was fun and had his own room at NYU where they slept together.

They had only known each other for a few months before the accident, and although Gary wasn't her first lover, he was her first love. He was cute and slender, with dark eyes and a mop of curly brown hair. His laugh was genuine and copious, making Rebecca feel light and fine. She liked his friends, too. They were smarter and happier and more fun than her petulant high school crowd. When she was with them, she didn't think about her mother or father or care about school.

There had been a moment or two when Rebecca considered showing up for her "hearing" at Hallows. But that idea vanished before it was expressed when Gary asked her to go with him, her best friend Stephie and her boyfriend Marley to his uncle's ski house in Vermont. Rebecca rationalized her decision as providentially dictated, and snuck into and out of her mother's apartment the day before they were to leave to collect winter clothing and ski equipment.

Rebecca and Gary stayed up almost the entire night, making love enthusiastically in anticipation of a few days together in a private room with a large bed and burning fireplace. They were tired and bleary when they got up just after noon, and by the time they headed out of the city, the sky was darkening and a cold, wet chill moved in from the north.

Rebecca sat in the back of the old Audi Fox, generously offering the front passenger seat to the king-sized Marley. They rode up the FDR Drive on the east coast of Manhattan Island, and Rebecca felt a lightness of expectancy she hadn't experienced since her parents put her on a bus for summer camp. As they passed through Connecticut and crossed the Massachusetts border heading north, Marley pulled a pint of Jack Daniel's from his jacket pocket and took a big swig.

Rebecca heard the sleet on the windshield before she actually saw it. The sun was almost completely down, and there was much more traffic ahead of them than earlier. Gary put on his windshield wipers and moved into the right-hand lane.

"This weather sucks."

Marley drank a second time from the bottle, and said while swallowing, "Hey, maybe it's snow in Vermont. That would be cool. Here, Gary. You want some?."

Marley placed the open bottle in Gary's outstretched hand. He held it for a few moments watching two large trucks, one right behind the other, accelerate onto the highway from an entrance ramp. Gary looked in his side mirror, and moved into the middle lane. He took a small sip of bourbon and reached back to give it to Rebecca.

Rebecca was staring out of the side window, oblivious to the gesture. The dark and dreary weather was making Rebecca blue. So too was the fact that, for some reason, she couldn't help thinking about her father. After a few seconds, Gary turned his head 90 degrees and said, "Hey, Becca. Do you want some, or not?"

Rebecca turned to Gary's voice, and as she did so she saw the wheels of the silver tractor-trailer move left, sending the truck directly in their path. She yelled, "Watch out!" but knew that Gary had been looking at her, not the road. He braked as the cab of the truck banged into the left side of the Audi, crushing the front fender and snapping Marley violently back into his seat. Rebecca could hear shattering glass and Stephie's screams. The impact shoved their car into the passing lane and only the seat belt kept Rebecca from flying into her girlfriend. She felt sharp pain on her cheek, and had just enough time to see Gary's head smash into the driver's side windows before the force of the oncoming car caused her unconsciousness.

The evening the accident happened, Sam was dining in a private room at GSC with the rest of the Management Committee. Just as the dessert course was being served, an attendant came in and handed Sam a folded-up note. Sam looked at his watch, wondering who was trying to get hold of him at 10 p.m., as he opened the note. It said simply, "Margaret Hart needs to speak with you, urgently."

All the blood drained from Sam's face. He stood up, excused himself, and walked briskly into the butler's pantry, where he knew there was a phone. He tried not to let his mind speculate on why his daughter-in-law would be calling him at the office, but deep down Sam knew something was terribly wrong.

Margaret was hyperventilating. She could hardly get the words out, and Sam had to use his firm, "control" voice to get her to focus. Rebecca had been in a serious car accident. The car, driven by her boyfriend, had overturned on the New England Thruway, and the four teenaged passengers had been rushed to a hospital near Springfield, Massachusetts. The boyfriend was dead on arrival. Rebecca and the others were in critical condition.

Margaret was afraid to go alone and Jeffrey was nowhere to be found. She pleaded with Sam to pick her up and take her to see her daughter.

Sam was the first person to see Rebecca when she awoke the next day, immobilized and drowsy. He fought through the tears and smiled gently at his granddaughter, stroking her hand and whispering her name. For the next several hours, Rebecca slipped in and out of awareness, but Sam refused to move, insisting that he be by her side each time she opened her eyes.

He was there when she asked what had happened, and when she asked for her friends. Sam held her, as best he could, given the casts, splints and bandages that covered her body, when she began crying hysterically at the news that Gary and Stephie and Marley had died. He stayed when the police came to question her, guiding her answers to their cold and leading questions. Sam stood by her when Margaret came, protecting Rebecca from her mother's recriminations and counterfeit concern.

Two days later, Rebecca was well enough to be transferred to a hospital in New York. And although most of the next eight days of convalescence was a thick blur, Rebecca did have vivid memories of the time when her father, Jeffrey, finally came to visit.

Sam had been with her in the morning, to talk to the doctors. Rebecca was drowsy from the pain medication, floating in and out of sleep, and was surprised when the nurse shook her gently to say that her father was outside. Rebecca looked around for Sam, who uncharacteristically wasn't at her bedside when she needed him.

Rebecca told herself to get it together as the nurse sat her up in the bed. She knew she must look awful, her face still bandaged and hair cut raggedly short. She just hoped she wouldn't cry.

Jeffrey tiptoed into the room, holding a bouquet of roses against his stiffly-tailored grey suit. He held his distance, and an uncertain expression, until Rebecca reached up to him with her one free arm and sobbed, "Daddy."

He rushed to her side, whispering, "I'm so sorry" over and over while she wept. Jeffrey touched his daughter's face and hair for the first time in such a long time, slowly caressing the bandages that hid her scars.

Rebecca wanted Jeffrey to ask her what happened. She was desperate for an outlet for all the horrific things that had ensued and the terrible things she had done. More importantly, Rebecca hoped Jeffrey would show some interest in her, so that she could explain it all—how Margaret baited and hated her; how she needed to get away and be with him; and how she was responsible for Gary's death. Rebecca lay back on her pillow and desperately needed her father to do more than stroke her hand and gaze distractedly out the window.

They sat there for a while saying nothing. Eventually, Rebecca's hopes were kindled when Jeffrey shifted his position in the chair, and cleared his throat as if to speak. She turned to face him, her heart pumping with expectation. Jeffrey returned the look, his dark brown eyes now more focused and intense. He tightened the grip on her hand, and said, "Rebecca, I know I haven't been there for you. But..."

Jeffrey raised his eyes to the window and stopped speaking in mid-sentence. His face paled and his hand felt cold. Rebecca turned to the window, and then back to the doorway. Sam stood there, nervously looking at the two of them.

He began backing out the door. "I'm sorry. I didn't mean to barge in. I'll come back later."

Jeffrey dropped Rebecca's hand and stood up stiffly. Her heart sank when he said, "Hello, father. It's OK; I've got to be going anyway."

He cleared his throat again. "I'll try and come back tomorrow, Rebecca. You're doing great." He bent down and kissed her gently on the cheek, and whispered in her ear, "I love you."

Jeffrey gathered his briefcase and overcoat and moved out of the room. Rebecca watched through the tears as Jeffrey and Sam stood by the doorway, at arm's length. Neither man said a word. Jeffrey turned back to Rebecca, said "bye" and walked past his father into the hallway.

Sam paused for a moment, and followed Jeffrey out.

"Jeffrey. Wait a minute." Sam's voice had urgency.

"Yes, father," Jeffrey responded, sounding like the ill-tempered teenager he never seemed to outgrow.

"We need to talk about Rebecca. I don't think she should go back to the apartment with Margaret."

Jeffrey shook his head slowly and pursed his lips while looking over his father's shoulder. "She's got custody. Not much I can do about it."

Sam reached out and grabbed Jeffrey's arm, squeezing until Jeffrey looked at him. "Goddamn it. This is your daughter we're speaking about. Margaret's a dysfunctional alcoholic and completely incapable of dealing with Rebecca under the best of circumstances. I'd be really worried about what might happen if she goes back to her mother. If you were around more often, you'd know how close to the edge Rebecca is."

Jeffrey struggled to free himself from Sam's grasp. "Let go. I'm not 16, I don't work for you and I'm no longer your whipping boy."

Sam relaxed his hand and saw the hatred in his son's eyes. He looked from the hallway into Rebecca's room, where his eyes met hers in the reflection of a glass framed picture handing on the wall opposite her bed. It was obvious to Sam that Rebecca had seen, and heard, the entire exchange.

"Sorry," Sam muttered unconvincingly.

Jeffrey brushed the wrinkles from his suit jacket and took a step away from Sam. "I'll call my lawyer and see if he can get through to Margaret—she certainly won't talk directly to me. I'm the bad guy, you see. I'm to blame for her dependencies, for Rebecca's delinquencies, for the fact that she's not on the 'A' list with Brooke Astor."

He shifted his briefcase from one hand to the next, took one step down the hall and stopped. Jeffrey turned back to Sam and said, "I'll try. But I think hell would first freeze over before Margaret would give me anything I asked for."

Sam nodded awkwardly, attempting to acknowledge Jeffrey's grand gesture. Inside, however, Sam had already decided what needed to be done. No sooner had his son rounded the corner toward the elevators than Sam commandeered a phone at the nurses' station. He called his private attorney--a rottweiler of a man named Bleustein-- and told him to prepare for an off-the-run custody case. If Jeffrey didn't have the ways or means to protect Rebecca, he would.

CHAPTER 4

The outhouse walls had been made of sheets of corrugated tin, nailed to a plywood roof coated with tar. The floor was also plywood, covered by stitched scraps of linoleum, which the villagers were fortunate to have found in the huge waste bins from the refinery. One got to the outhouses from the riverbank, where wooden planks on progressively taller stilts led to a platform, about 10 feet offshore. There were no lights marking the way, making a trip to the bathroom on a moonless or stormy night an unwelcome adventure.

Midway back to shore after a visit to the outhouse on a hot and steamy morning, about a week after she first arrived at Bahia de Caraquez, Ecuador, Rebecca watched several shirtless men, in makeshift skiffs only a few feet away from the platform where she stood, hauling in nets filled with crabs and small, boney fish. For the rest of her stay in Bahia, she declined to dine on the local catch.

The quality of her living accommodations was completely consistent with that of the bathroom facilities. She and three other Peace Corps members occupied a tiny, two-room house about a quarter-mile from the riverbank. The four Americans had designated the room with a light bulb as the "family room," and it contained a metal desk and desk chair, a beat-up easy chair, and a small dining table with two stools. The other room was for sleeping, such as it was in the equatorial humidity of the village. Thankfully, the mattresses were relatively new and only moderately stained and each of them had a bed frame that elevated the mattresses above the dirt floor.

Rebecca's house was situated in a compound of 15 similarly-sized structures owned by Mama Baja, the acknowledged matriarch of the community. Mama had been born in the village some 60 years earlier, the only daughter of eight children. Her father prospered there, parlaying cash flow from fishing into real estate. He built the compound of small houses the year after his wife died, and used the income from renting those houses to develop a large general store on the grounds. His timing was superb, coinciding as it did with the expansion of the AZTEC Oil pumping station and refinery across from Bahia de Caraquez on the Chone River.

Mama Baja managed the store, and the family's finances. She attracted the attention of an engineer from AZTEC Oil, who was on temporary assignment at the refinery, and at age 16 she married him and moved to Quito. Widowed 18 years later, she went back to Bahia with two of her three children to take care of her aging father and reassume control of the family business.

While the AZTEC Oil Company enlarged its facilities, employing more of the men and women in the village and bringing in more outsiders with valuable foreign exchange, Mama Baja's enterprise prospered. Then, in 1992, the Shining Light Revolutionary Army seized on the danger of all foreign, capitalist influences in South America, and chose the AZTEC facilities to highlight the seriousness of its message. Six months of kidnappings, car bombings and various other attacks on the refinery resulted in the temporary closing of the facility. But it also brought the national army into the region, supported by American "advisors" (who wore fatigues, carried rifles and piloted Ranger attack helicopters). Within days of their arrival,

DIVIDED LOYALTIES

Bahia de Caraquez became a bloody battleground as heavily armed government forces attacked and tracked down Shining Light commandos who had taken up positions in the village and surrounding marsh lands.

Much of the village was destroyed in the violence. Mama Baja's store was looted and gutted by the fleeing revolutionaries. Half the compound was raked by machine gun fire, which literally tore the little houses into tiny pieces. To make matters worse, her father died during the height of the fighting, when the ferocity of the gunfire confined all the villagers to quarters. It was three days before the family could leave the compound to bury the 90-year-old man.

Bahia de Caraquez was thrown into a downward spiral. The shuttered refinery neither employed villagers nor bought food or products from local farmers, fishermen or retailers. Wealthy American and European executives from the parent company no longer bought Chilean wine or Colombian flowers. Electricity, provided by generators owned and operated by the refinery, stopped flowing, and work on connecting sanitary facilities to an underground septic system ceased entirely.

Mama Baja told her friends that she was seriously considering returning to Quito to live with her eldest son, Ernesto, who had risen to mid-level prominence in the country's legislative bureaucracy. But in the end, she refused to abandon what was left of her heritage in the small, riverside community. With a fierce determination and uncommon directness, and the complete support of the village's elders, Mama Baja mounted a campaign to secure governmental aid to rebuild Bahia de Caraquez and convince the Euro-American conglomerate to re-open the refinery.

With respect to the former, Mama Baja had no effect. Her village was one of hundreds in the country in desperate need of infrastructural investment and government assistance. Quito denied the request, stating that if they helped one, they would have to help them all. The perverse logic of the statement wasn't lost on Mama Baja, but there was no official venue available for her to argue the point.

Finally, however, some luck seemed to be coming Bahia de Caraquez's way. Higher oil prices, global economic growth and the consolidation in the worldwide oil market made investment in the nation's petroleum industry more attractive for foreign interests. The government suspended all environmental restrictions on oil drilling and refining, and lowered the official tax rate on the profit from these activities from 50 percent to 15. (Of course, there continued to be an "unofficial" revenue tax of 25 percent, in cash, payable to the offshore accounts of two dozen well-placed government officials). The Chone River refinery had remained relatively unharmed by the violence, thanks to protective measures by the American-assisted national army, and the refinery re-opened only one year after it had been shuttered.

The villagers were overwhelmed with the good news, giving Mama Baja credit for the victory. At first, the refinery's reactivation brought a rush of money and good will into the village. Bahians again filled menial jobs at the plant as they manned the cafeteria, mowed lawns and watered plants, cleaned the offices and hauled the garbage. Local farmers and fisherman again had markets for their labors, and Mama Baja was able to rebuild her store and a few of the lost units in her compound.

Over time, the rush of euphoria ebbed, and bad things started happening in the village. The ancestral burial grounds, on the northernmost banks of the Chone, were a foot or two under water at least half the time. Other riverside areas showed evidence of incremental flooding as well. Fishermen complained of smaller catches, skimpier fish and a greater incidence of deformed crustaceans. The flow of electricity from the generators maintained by the refinery was cut back to three hours a day, and it was more likely than not that even this meager allotment was curtailed because of malfunctions in the equipment.

Some village leaders, especially Mama Baja, grew frustrated in their discussions with the "liaison officials" designated by the refinery. Not only was the company resisting re-commencing the septic project, but they also seemed to be reneging on promises made to provide funding for a local health clinic and to help build a new school house.

And yet, money seemed to be plentiful across the river. The refinery plant expanded endlessly. The men and women who worked there returned to the village with vivid descriptions of the sumptuous offices and living quarters being built for foreign employees there, replete with air conditioning, tennis courts and salad bars. There was even a school being built for the children of the expatriate employees, filled with colorful walls, bright lighting and new desks and chalkboards.

Bahia's elected officials turned the other way when some residents complained of the disparity of conditions on the two shores and the unwillingness of the company to consider the village's complaints. Clearly, the refinery had taken care of *their* interests. Just look at the new clothes, pickup trucks and private generators.

Each evening, more and more of the conversation among the villagers revolved around the changes in their community and the difference in the standard of living on each side of the narrow river. Depictions of the opulent lifestyles at the plant mixed with anecdotes of the continual degradation of the environment around the village, and people got angrier and angrier.

"Mama, I tell you it's like paradise. The air is cool and soft, like just after an evening rain. There is electricity all the time. The toilets don't smell, and there's hot water in the bathrooms. If they can have that across the river, why can't we have it here?" said Xanatu, whose leathered face belied her relatively young age.

That caused a buzz of agreement among the 12 women who had congregated on the wooden benches in front of Mama Baja's store one late afternoon. A bottle of spring water was passed around as Marta spread her palms and cleared her throat before speaking:

"That paradise is not for us. They bring America with them, even in our jungle. At least they give us work. Don't forget what our life was like after the fighting, when the plant was closed."

Mama Baja clapped her enormous hands together once, making a loud "POP" that got everyone's attention. "Marta, stop! It could always be worse, of course. And the fact is it is getting worse. Xanatu is saying things should be better, but they are not. Our river is dirty, even dirtier than before, because the refinery is putting its garbage in there. And our land is flooding, because of all the work they are doing over there. My parents' graves are now under water. Our leaders buy new houses and trucks with the money the refinery gives them, but our medical building has not been built and our roads are still dirt."

Marta sank into the bench as the other women nodded approvingly at Mama's statement. She was about to launch into the second stage of her invective when she was interrupted by the laughter of two eight-year-old boys, resting atop the broad shoulders of the Peace Corps worker heading Mama's way. Charley, who was bearded, huge and cheerful, had ingratiated himself to the village children through regular bribes of candy and soda purchased for hard currency at Mama's store. He had also apparently worked his magic on the cute American woman volunteer who was his constant companion and roommate, according to the local gossip.

Charley bent down on one knee to unload his passengers and asked Mama for cokes and gum for the boys and cigarettes for himself. Rebecca entered the store a few moments later, holding the hand of a beautiful little girl. She said hello to Mama, nodded at the group of women sitting outside her store and inquired, "What's the talk of the town today?"

The woman first looked at Charley before glancing back at Rebecca. "It's the same—always the same. The people work at the refinery and come back upset. They want to know why the Americans have electricity and clean water, and we don't. They see the houses for the families there, with cold air and indoor plumbing, and we have outhouses that empty into our river. Our girls sell themselves to the visitors for money, and then get sick and we have no doctors or hospitals to help them."

This was not the first time that Rebecca had heard the villagers complain of the tension with the refinery, but her previous encounters with the issue had been indirect—a conversation overheard or a sidebar with one of her fellow Peace Corps-niks. Obviously, the issue had become so prominent that the villagers were willing to discuss it directly with anyone they came in contact with. "Mama," she said, "Have you talked to the mayor? Aren't there others in the local government who can help?"

Charley snickered at Rebecca's naïve response. She responded with a swift kick to his shin, which brought him down a full foot and a half. Rebecca took full advantage of this unusual opportunity to look him in the eye, at least on a vertical basis, as she muttered in English, "Asshole."

Mama smiled warmly at these two, who she often referred to as her "puppies." She paused before responding to Rebecca. "The mayor is a happy man. He doesn't see the filth or the flooding. He only sees the money in his pocket and his new girlfriends. My son lives in Quito, and works for the government. He has tried to help us, but there is no one to listen. There is no one there who cares. No, this is our problem."

Charley had taken a seat on a plastic milk crate near the front door of the store to nurse his wounds. As he rubbed his sore leg, he looked up at Mama Baja and said, "You're right. No one in the government will do anything. You need to make the Americans look bad—make them feel guilty. They've got the money, and they obviously use it to make peace. That's why the mayor gets rich."

Rebecca walked over to Charley and put her arm on his huge shoulders. "He's right. We've got to show them that they have to make us happy too."

Rebecca's transition from "tu" to "nosotros" wasn't lost on Mama Baja, who opened her large hands and said, "And how do *we* do that, little one?"

The inflection in Mama's voice stimulated endorphins in Rebecca's brain, setting off a highly pleasurable buzz.

Rebecca's first year in the Corps had been a mixed bag of new experiences and frustrating daily routines. She ached for significance and found little personal reward in the painfully slow process of teaching preschool children and building daycare facilities. This was her chance to *do* something.

Rebecca turned quickly toward Charley, who was still stroking his shin. He looked dubious, but not completely negative. Rebecca knew he was putty in her hands. She then walked over to Mama Baja and melodramatically grabbed, and squeezed, her hands. *"We'll* show them who really runs this place, Mama. It's hard to refine oil if no one's there to turn on the lights."

***

A week into the process, Rebecca was beginning to admit that Mama Baja had been right about the village men. They just weren't buying into the urgency of the problem. She had placed posters all around the village, announcing a meeting to discuss "the welfare of Bahia de Caraquez." Of the 30 villagers who came, only a half-dozen or so were men and not one of them seemed interested or even bothered to ask questions. Assuming that her gender might have something to do with it, Rebecca pushed Charley to specifically invite the men to come to a second rally at the village docks. Even with a promise of refreshments, the turn-out was disappointingly small and the reception tepid, at best.

"What are we missing?" Rebecca said into her beer after the second meeting petered out only a half-hour after it began.

Mama shot a hard glance at Rebecca. "I told you that the men wouldn't be interested. They see no chance for winning, so they see no reason to argue. "

Rebecca was surprised at the bite in Mama's retort. "But we showed them how unfair it is, how they are exploited and don't get fair pay. We talked about the broken promises to build a clinic and a new school and the power generator and the sewage system. Don't they care? Don't they get angry? What do we have to do to get them involved?"

Mama stood and smoothed out the wrinkles from her colorful skirt. She narrowed the distance between her and Rebecca to a few feet, and put her hands on her hips, waiting.

Rebecca stood in response.

"You keep saying *we* talked, or *we* showed. But it's been *you*. Not *me* or *we*. I told you that Bahian men won't accept losing face, so they won't take on a risky situation. It's that simple. Only the women will take chances here. And they have more at stake. It's their children who are getting sick from the dirty water. It's their daughters who have no choice but to sell themselves to the foreigners. I told you this, but you didn't listen."

Rebecca flushed with embarrassment, recognizing the truth of Mama Baja's words. Typically, she took it personally, questioning her own competence and self-worth. Rebecca had been arrogant when she dismissed Mama's earlier tactical suggestions. Valuable time was wasted, and Rebecca's credibility was damaged.

"I'm sorry." Rebecca sat back down on the rotting wooden bench near the gangway to the dock, and sighed audibly. "If we—sorry, if *you*—can't get the men to join in, how do we—er—*you* put pressure on the refinery? The women don't have many jobs over there, and they aren't the ones that can slow the place down. The men drive the trucks and pilot the boats. The women clean the place and work in the kitchen."

Mama smiled, exposing her perfect white teeth to the one streetlight at the end of the dock. "*We*—the village women—stop *our* men from going to work. Simple."

***

Charley lay on his back in the cot while Rebecca rested on her side, curled up on Charley's bare chest, wearing a grey

Georgetown t-shirt in the equatorial heat. Neither of them was sleepy, several beers and athletic lovemaking notwithstanding.

"Its nuts," Charley said. "No way this works. There's no plan here—it's an arbitrary event. You should stop it before someone gets hurt."

Rebecca snuggled closer to his massive body. "No one's going to get hurt. And it's worth a try."

Charley played with a few strands of Rebecca's hair while he smoked a local, nasty cigarette. "Maybe you can shut the plant down for a day or two. But that's all. It won't mean anything to AZTEC. They're a gazillion-dollar company. I think we've got to keep plugging away at an old fashioned, organized worker's strike that has some staying power and some impact on the company's bank account. That's the only place they'll feel it. We need a plan."

Rebecca shook her head, signifying her disagreement with Charley and that his fondling was getting annoying. "We tried getting the men to bite, but nothing happened. Organizing a strike will take a long time, if it could ever happen. So we'll try this. What's the downside?"

"Well, let's see. The women can get roughed up—or busted. That's one. You and I could get thrown out of the Peace Corps. That's two. Or *we* could get roughed up or busted. I'm up to three already. Ouch...shit!"

Rebecca pulled away and sat on the edge of the bed, taking a handful of Charley's chest hair with her. "Sarcastic asshole," she muttered.

Charley propped himself up on one elbow while he massaged the red spot in between his nipples with his free hand. "Damn, Rebecca. That hurt. You've got to get over this thing you have about criticism. It's really not healthy."

Rebecca stood up, and with her back to Charley, gave him the finger over her shoulder. She slipped on her blue jeans and flip-flops and headed to the door.

"Don't go. C'mon. We're just having a grown-up conversation here."

Rebecca paused. She liked Charley, actually quite a bit. He was strong and funny, and one of the very few men she'd met whom she respected intellectually. But she wouldn't let him hold her back.

Rebecca walked out the door, ignoring Charley's pleas for her to come back and her own surprising desire to do so.

***

Almost two weeks later, Rebecca paced the "living room," nervous and uncertain and unable to sit still. She recalled Charley's warning that notwithstanding the endless contingency planning she and he had engaged in, there were still a large number of variables that they couldn't control. Rebecca recognized that they would have to be very, very lucky for this to work, and she wondered whether the risks were just too great to proceed.

Adding to her concern was the letter she received from her father just a few days earlier. Rebecca had proudly written to Jeffrey with a brief description of her efforts in organizing the village to remind AZTEC Oil of its promises to the community. She was surprised when she received his response—by DHL courier—just a week after her letter was posted, and utterly disappointed with the substance of his note. Rather than a "way to go, girl" message, Jeffrey admonished her to take seriously her contractual promises to the Peace Corps. He warned that Latin cultures wouldn't necessarily recognize "passive resistance as protected activity" and ominously added that, "The company probably has government officials in its sphere of influence, making police or military intervention much more likely."

Rebecca considered that Jeffrey's concerns were purely of the fatherly, protective kind. She would be pleased if that were so, but she had her doubts given their improving, but still somewhat distant, relationship. Most likely, she reasoned, Jeffrey was worried that Rebecca's activism might jeopardize his own position as the head of a huge supranational organization. Taking a deep, cleansing breath, Rebecca unsuccessfully tried to dismiss this concern with a nostalgic "fuck it."

At 6:00 a.m. the following morning, the first of 12 boatloads of ladies left the village dock. When they landed at the refinery, Mama Baja was there to greet them and go over the plans and logistics for food, rest and bathroom facilities.

Charley had succumbed to Mama's requests that he pilot the launch even though he wasn't feeling particularly lucky that day. By 7:30, he had ferried 146 Bahian women and food and water from the village to the plant.

Rebecca stood among them, next to Mama Baja, as they massed in front of the main door of the refinery. The sun rose over the town, and Rebecca felt small, but warm and secure, in the crowd of women who were holding hands and humming rhythmically. .

At 8:00, the day shift workers began to arrive in buses and ferries from numerous surrounding communities. Most stopped in their tracks when they saw their entrance to the plant impeded, unsure what to make of the grouped women. As that crowd grew, a few workers moved close to the Bahians, asking for an explanation. The women responded with silence.

Eventually, a tall, dark man arrived wearing a blue blazer sporting the AZTEC Oil corporate logo on his breast pocket. He held a walkie-talkie and moved it repeatedly from his ear to his mouth, while he eyed the protestors. After several minutes of what appeared to Rebecca to be pantomime, the man lowered the device and moved to the front of the crowd.

"Hello?" he said three times. "Who is here to talk to?"

Mama Baja looked quizzically at Rebecca. Rebecca shook her head ever so slightly, and lifted her palm so that only Mama could see. She knew Mama was anxious and wanted to start the process of negotiation, but this was neither the right time to start talking nor the right guy with whom to begin.

"Come on now, ladies. This is not a game. You are stopping people from going to their work, and getting paid. You have to go." The man surveyed the crowd from his tiptoes. When the women began to quietly chant again, the man turned away, walkie-talkie at his lips.

Rebecca grabbed Mama's hand, and whispered to her, "He was just a guard. We need to talk to a corporate guy, probably an American, to show them we're serious."

Mama nodded, and looked side-to-side and behind her, catching the eyes of many of the villagers. As she did, the chanting gained strength.

By this time, a large group of workers had assembled in front of the refinery and on the dock. They were clearly confused about where to go, or what to do. A number of men began yelling at the protestors: "Crazy ladies, go back to your children"; "Maybe you don't need to work, but my family needs the money. Go away!" But the Bahians stayed together, hands together, voices together.

The tall company man came back, followed by five other men, in security guard uniforms.

Holding a megaphone, the man said, "You are trespassing. You do not work here, and are stopping other people from going to their jobs. If you don't leave immediately, we will be forced to make you leave. If you get hurt, that's your own fault."

Some of the women stopped humming and exchanged glances, and searched out Mama Baja with their eyes. She tightened her grip on Rebecca's hand and chanted more loudly.

The guards looked nervously at each other, and the man giving orders. He raised the megaphone again. "This is your last chance."

A few seconds later, he turned to the security guards and motioned them to move toward the women. They hesitated, and finally one—the largest one—advanced, followed by the others. A few steps before the guards reached the crowd, Mama dropped Rebecca's hand and began unbuttoning her blouse. The others responded in similar fashion to Mama's signal.

The guards stopped in their tracks as blouses came off and breasts exposed. One hundred forty-six topless women— old and young—re-clasped hands and began to sing. The guards moved back, away from the Bahian women. They muttered and stammered and swore. The corporate official's jaw remained wide open until the squawk of his walkie-talkie got his attention.

The delayed workers gasped in unison. A moment later, Rebecca could hear cruel epithets from some of the men, and cheers of encouragement from some of the women. But it worked. Mama was right. Their collective nakedness would protect and empower them.

Within an hour a blond, well-dressed man emerged from a chauffeured car that had been driven within a hundred feet of the assembled Bahian women. He introduced himself as John Collins, the American resident manager of the refinery, and asked to talk with a spokesperson. He seemed to be trying to look the women in the eye, and nowhere else.

Rebecca nudged Mama Baja forward—gently but firmly—and stayed physically close behind. Mama began a conversation with Collins, describing AZTEC's broken promises to the village. Rebecca could hear Collins offering to meet with Mama, right then and there, if only she would disband the protest.

Mama looked back at Rebecca, and raised her eyebrows. Rebecca nodded, signaling that they should stick with the response they had scripted in preparing for just this likelihood. Mama faced Collins, and told him she would like to meet with him, and that she did have time now, but that her friends would stay in their places until their meeting was concluded.

Collins was obviously displeased with Mama's answer, and shifted his gaze several times from Mama to Rebecca while, presumably, he was considering his options. Rebecca guessed from the looks that he shot her way (this time, however, he let his gaze wander) that he had figured out she wasn't Ecuadorian.

After a few moments, Collins agreed. "Fine. Now please put your clothes back on before we go in. And would you ask the women to put their shirts on? The men are very upset."

She said, "Will you promise not to have your guards threaten my sisters?"

Collins nodded.

Mama smiled broadly, untied the blouse from her waist and put it on.

Collins called over a security officer and instructed him to stand down until further notice. Mama turned to the Bahian women, and told them to dress but to stay in place.

Collins pointed to the front door, blocked by the protesters. Mama headed in that direction as the crowd parted, and looked back just before entering. Rebecca was dying to join them and help negotiate a settlement. She felt the bridesmaid for a successful outcome she had inspired and engineered, and for an instant considered catching up with Mama and Collins as they entered the building. That feeling was squelched quickly, however, when she realized that Collins was staring at her again. This time, there was anger in his eyes.

Mama emerged an hour later, her lips turned up slightly in a restrained smile. She huddled with Rebecca and a few of the women leaders and delivered her report. She had agreed to set up a group of people from the village to meet with AZTEC officials to create a detailed list of what AZTEC would do. She demanded, however, a sign of good faith before giving up the protest—even temporarily. Collins promised that he would send engineers that day to fix the on-again, off-again electrical generator that serviced the village and agreed to deliver at least a month's worth of fuel for the generator.

Rebecca couldn't restrain herself. "Did you get him to sign the letter?"

Mama wrinkled her nose. "No, it did not seem right to insist. He agreed to everything we asked. It would have been rude."

Rebecca sighed deeply, but left the matter there. She respected Mama for believing in Collins' integrity, but knew it was likely to be naïve. She had prepared the agreement that Mama was to insist the AZTEC people sign. She had spent a lot of time on the language, trying to get it just right.

***

Rebecca was on the last boat back to the village. She stood next to Charley, exhausted, and put her head against his shoulder. It was the first time she had touched him in weeks.

"Seems to me you won. How come you're down?'

"Tired."

"It's more than that. I've seen you tired."

Rebecca pulled back and faced Charley, and at the same time articulated her own concerns. "I think they're going to jerk us around. Promise us this and that. Set up committees. Put us off."

"You knew that was a possibility. Did they sign the letter?"

Rebecca shook her head, sadly.

Charley reached out and patted Rebecca's arm. "Sorry. That's a problem. Guess we'll just have to rely on the pictures."

Pictures! Rebecca had almost forgotten. "You got some?'

Charley expanded his chest and pointed to the huge camera and telephoto lens at his feet. "Yeah, I got a lot of pictures—with and without shirts on. I'll keep the ones of you topless for my personal collection."

The AZTEC mechanics did fix the generator, but it took several days to complete. The fuel never showed up. Similarly, while Mama fulfilled her part of the bargain and organized a citizens' committee—including the mayor of the village whom she detested—a meeting with Collins was not arranged because, according to his assistant, he would be "traveling for the rest of the month."

As days turned into weeks, even Mama began to lose patience. She found Rebecca one morning, on break from teaching her reading class, and began venting her frustrations energetically.

Rebecca listened patiently, the irony of role reversal not lost on her. When Mama was finished, Rebecca pulled some papers from her back pocket.

"We may be in for a change of luck, Mama. I got this in my mail yesterday. Remember that reporter who was here last week? She wrote the story and it got into the papers. Here's the article. It's in English—I'll tell you what it says. But take a look at the picture."

The picture had been taken from behind the Bahian women, whose naked backs were clearly visible. Mama Baja stood facing the crowd, and the camera, next to John Collins. She was buttoning her shirt.

"Perfect picture, don't you think?" Rebecca was smiling broadly. "The caption says, 'Ecuadorian women protest AZTEC Oil's broken promises.' It quotes the president of the Company as saying that he will personally make sure they take care of their environmental and community responsibilities in Bahia. This is good, Mama. They will have trouble running away from this."

One month later, construction had commenced on the new Health Clinic facility and the village septic system. The citizens' committee had regularly scheduled meetings with John Collins and his staff, and AZTEC Oil was using Bahia as a poster child for its social conscience.

Rebecca and Charley were no longer in Bahia. They were also no longer in the Peace Corps. Both were unceremoniously given their walking papers at just about the same time that AZTEC began cooperating in earnest with Mama Baja. John Collins lit the fast-burning fuse that eventually caught up with Rebecca and Charley.

***

Rebecca was more upset by the censure she anticipated from her father than she was by actually being fired. On the trip back to Washington from Quito, she tried to construct a scenario—admittedly fanciful—which would have her father realize the true greatness of what she had done and praise her for coming so far from the depths of her high school improprieties. He would invite her back into his house and seek her counsel on the techniques she brought to bear to successfully combine multi-national corporate interests with the cultural and environmental sensitivities of the local population. They could be a team, working together and being together and recapturing a relationship they barely had together.

The sweetness of this dream lasted only as long as Rebecca was in the construction phase, however. Once she got back to reality, and for most of that long flight, she knew she was in for either a whole lot of criticism or a whole lot of silent treatments.

The reality was, unfortunately, much worse. Somehow, a Washington gossip columnist picked up the details of the events in Bahia, and that the provocateur was one Rebecca Hart, the daughter of Jeffrey Hart, President of the Inter-American Development Bank, and the granddaughter of Sam Hart, a member of the Management Committee of GSC. Both men were caught unaware when asked to comment.

Jeffrey was the primary press target. He was the head of an organization already under fire for its lending policies in Latin America, and was subjected to ad hominem attacks in the normal course. He had been burned in effigy on the streets of La Paz, castigated as a "puppet of the American imperialist regime" by populist leaders in Buenos Aires, and rebuked in the U.S. Congress for bailing out corrupt and dictatorial administrations throughout South America. In each such case, Jeffrey's Teflon-coated response was right out of the text book—he never angered, broke a sweat or acted in the least bit hesitantly.

He didn't appear to react nearly as well to the suggestion that his own daughter was undermining American interests in the region and abusing her position in the Peace Corps. In a single press release, he publicly disassociated himself, and the IADB, from Rebecca's actions, and was quoted as doubting her maturity and judgment. He refused all other requests to comment on the matter, even off-the-record. When asked about his relationship with his daughter at a press conference called to announce a major new lending initiative in Colombia, he angrily barked at the reporter and told him to "mind his own goddamned business."

Jeffrey didn't return her phone calls, even after he issued the press release the day after she got back to Washington. Rebecca tried to visit him at his office, but was told he was traveling. She fell into a deep funk, and spent the better part of the next several days curled up in a sleeping bag on the floor of a friend's apartment.

Charley tried to use his considerable charms to distract Rebecca, but met with little success. She refused to come to the table for his famous, and her favorite, chicken penne with sun dried tomatoes, even though he made the dish in the apartment, used a ton of garlic, and serenaded her in Italian.

Charley called in some favors and got tickets to the Indigo Girls—whom he knew she loved and he could barely stomach—at the Ballroom in Georgetown, but was forced to give them away when Rebecca dismissed his offer out-of-hand.

Charley finally tried a more direct approach. He got down on the floor next to her, face to face, and tried to kiss her lips. Rebecca pulled her head back, told him to leave her alone, and rolled over with her face toward the wall.

"Shit, Rebecca. That won't help."

He found her pocketbook on a nearby chair and noisily rummaged through it. Eventually, he located what he had been looking for—her Filofax—and headed to the phone in the kitchen.

Rebecca didn't move, but listened intently as Charley dialed a number. *Who is he calling?*

"Hello, may I speak to Mr. Hart, please?"

Rebecca shifted her head around to look at Charley, and pulled herself to a sitting position on the floor. She screamed, "Who the hell do you think you are? Hang up right now, damn it!"

Charley looked her straight in the eye and continued his introduction. "It's Charles Robertson. I'm a friend of his *grand*daughter's."

Rebecca stopped yelling and turned her back on Charley. She felt weak and embarrassed, not just because she guessed wrong on Charley's call, but because she needed him to make the call in the first place. For all that she'd been through since her car accident, it didn't seem that much had changed. She found trouble, and dragged people she cared for into her messes. She had no relationship with her parents. And she had to rely on Sam, again, for support.

"Rebecca. I've got your grandfather on the phone. He wants to talk to you."

Rebecca laid there, a mass of confused thoughts and self-recriminations. She heard Charley, but ignored him until the third time he called her name. She inhaled deeply and slithered out of the sleeping bag. She pulled down the t-shirt she had been wearing for the past 48 hours to a decent length, walked over and, giving Charley a blank stare, grabbed the phone from him.

"Hello, Grandpa. Yes, I'm okay. I just keep screwing up."

Rebecca wouldn't let Charley comfort her through the

tears and sobs. She motioned him away, wanting to get rid of any witnesses to her emotional breakdown. She heard Charley leave the apartment with one ear as Sam tried to console her through the other.

CHAPTER 5

The wave of noise escapes, like a cloud of gas, when the glass doors leading onto the trading floor are opened. Hundreds of traders, salespeople, clerks and assistants, all attractive and fit and in their twenties, swarm the cavernous space oblivious to the cacophony. The noise is really a hundred different noises: people talking on the phone to clients and competitors and yelling across the rows of desks to each other. Not infrequently, there's even a component of the din that comes from people talking to themselves. A trading floor will do that to you.

"Two bid at seven. That's 62 at 67. Changing!! Now 65 at 70. Quickly!!"

"Nothing there. Sorry, Mike. He's looking for a better offer. What do you think? Will we be able to buy some at 60 the figure?"

"Jesus. Everyone is looking to buy dollars at the figure. That's why we can't get there. Tell your client—it's Billy at PIMCO, right? Tell Billy to let me work half his amount at 65 and we'll try to get the rest lower."

Mike Tillingham, known by everyone on "the Street" as Mike T, turned away from the tall, strawberry blond saleswoman and barked into his headset, "Done at 71? What? Goddamn it. That was my offer you just blew through. For 20 million! That's the last time for you guys. You're in the box for a month. Have Gill call me after the close."

The earphones and microphone went flying across the desk, toward the tray of hardening Krispy Kremes that the rookie analyst had brought in for the 6:00 a.m. conference call. Mike's look of disgust went from furrowed brow to bared teeth. "I really can't stand those sons of bitches at Layton's. They're all in MetroBank's pocket. Luis, when Gill calls, tell him I want him here tomorrow at noon, and tell him to bring a check and a new yen broker. I never want to speak to that moron again."

Betsy thought a bit of good news would cheer Mike up, so she walked over to the head trader's desk to deliver the message in person, instead of yelling it "over the top." "Billy said OK. You've got 50 million dollars to buy at 65, and another 50 at 61. He said there's more to go at lower levels, and he's only going to work with us for the day provided he likes our execution. I guess dinner Tuesday night paid off! Maybe it was the hundred-year-old port? Did you see how much that was?"

"Nah, I didn't notice. That's your job—you're the salesman. I'm just the lowly trader who gets dragged along to these fancy restaurants as the entertainment."

Betsy's response was automatic. "You're breaking my heart. I'll trade my bonus for yours on the spot."

The fact that Mike stopped yelling, and even produced a wan smile, made Betsy's day. It was already 10 a.m., four hours since she'd gotten to the office and made her first calls around the globe, and she'd booked almost a half-billion dollars of currency business for her firm. She loved the tension and the energy of her life in the middle of the worldwide currency business. She loved getting lost in the noise and being able to think and act clearly through the chaos of her environment.

When her parents sent her to Wellesley, they assumed Betsy would either go into teaching or get a law degree. They could never have imagined that their blond and blue-eyed beauty, with all the best training and all the advantages Greenwich could offer, would be magnetically attracted to the raw energy of a trading room. But Betsy was clearly and completely addicted, an adrenaline junkie personified. She got up at 4:30 each morning, and was in the gym in the basement of her building in Soho 15 minutes later. That gave her just enough time to do her cardio, down a cup of black coffee with a cereal bar, take a shower, scan the papers and get to her desk for the morning call.

The business was filled with people like Betsy, who got off on the intensity of the market and extracted energy from it. The noise level in the cavernous trading room ebbed and flowed during the day, with a breath-like cadence: sometimes asynchronous, often rhythmic, and always alive. Ten years ago, the ambience of "the floor" was enhanced by the clouds of smoke spewing from the dozens of cigarettes lit at any given point in time. The haze generated by these poisonous emissions, coupled with the heat from the hundreds of computer screens and sweating traders, and the bland, white light of overhead fluorescent bulbs, added to the bizarre and uncomfortable feel of a Wall Street trading floor. Although smoking on the floor was now banned, and the temperature moderated as a result of flat screen computer technology and better air conditioning (which ran 12 months a year, even when outside temperatures were frigid), the trading floor still projected an intense, edgy feeling.

Surrounding the floor were a number of offices and conference rooms, which did their best to shut out the controlled chaos of the trading arena. Many of these spaces were designed with windows that opened out to spectacular views of the East or Hudson Rivers and were furnished with expensive furniture made of the finest cherry and mahogany woods, and decorated with plastic-looking trees and an occasional flower arrangement. Office location was the surest indication of seniority on a trading floor, and Sam's was right on the edge of the proprietary trading desk, commensurate with his role as the global head of the company's trading businesses.

One wall of the office was made up entirely of glass panels, facing the trading room, enabling its occupant to have an unobstructed view of the risk and reward of his enterprise. Sam worked at a late 18th century George II partner's desk, deemed "important" by the antiques dealer in London where it was purchased, because of its unusually large dimensions and abundant cabinet space. A pair of large computer screens sat atop the tooled leather, one for his email and web browsing needs, and the other devoted solely to displaying market news and prices for currencies, bonds and stocks. Two winged back chairs were placed in front of Sam's desk, purposefully uncomfortable to discourage lingering visitors. When hospitality was absolutely necessary, guests were offered a leather loveseat along a full wall to the left of his desk because it lay across from the glass showcase and provided an impressive view of the trading floor.

Sam sat with his back to the door, looking out of his floor to ceiling windows at the sparkling waters of the lower Hudson River. He was on the phone with Anton, with whom Sam was supposed to meet later that day at a high school on the Lower East Side of Manhattan for the third of their discussion sessions. Anton had told Sam he wasn't going to be able to go—"There's something I have to take care of"—and hoped that Sam would run the event by himself.

Sam was immediately suspicious. They had spoken just a few days before, and Anton seemed to be looking forward to the session. Today, Anton seemed preoccupied and tentative.

"We should cancel, then. It doesn't make sense for me to do the program alone," said Sam, hoping that his friend would volunteer a reason for his absence.

"It would be good for you. You connect with the kids, and they're more interested in hearing from a soldier anyway."

Sam waited for more, and when nothing else was forthcoming, went straight to his concern. "Is everything alright? Is Helene OK?"

With each passing second of the long silence, Sam became more anxious. "Anton, what's going on?'

His sigh was deep and long. "I need to go back to the hospital. Hopefully just for one night."

"Why?"

Anton took another full, nasal breath. "I'll be fine. I'm bleeding. It's probably from the Coumadin."

Sam waved off his secretary, Pam, who had just stuck her head in his office to let him know that his London-based partner was on the phone. He shifted his position to alleviate the pressure on his sciatic nerve, and hoped he would be able to disguise the concern in his voice. "I'll take you. When?"

"I'm actually on my way out the door. Helene is here. I'll call you tonight to find out how the program went. Please go. I hate to disappoint the kids."

"Anton…"

"For me, Sam. I'll be fine. I've got to go now. I'll call you tonight."

Sam hung up the phone and stared out his windows, surprisingly thoughtless. The tips of his fingers were numbing, and he rotated his wrists to increase the circulation in his hands. When Pam entered the office again, Sam was appreciative of something concrete to focus on.

"Jon's back on the phone. He says he must speak with you."

"Yeah, yeah. I'll pick him up in a second. Did you get a hold of my wife?"

Pam turned her eyes downward, as if wanting to avert her boss's look. "Not yet. I've tried calling the house every 10 minutes or so, but no answer. And I don't think her cell phone is turned on, because it doesn't ring and I go right to her voicemail."

Sam tried to make a mental inventory of where Gloria might have been. He got the distinct impression that she was planning on staying home to garden, but maybe she had an appointment or meeting or something else he had forgotten about. He checked his watch, and decided not to let himself worry for another hour.

Sam picked up the phone and steadied himself against his partner's onslaught.

From an over-furnished office in London, also abutting a trading floor but with a depressing view of an airshaft, Jon Lavendar said, "What is this crap about not coming to Vienna. All of our major clients will be there, and our party is the social event of the whole goddamned conference. It's not an option."

Sam reached into the top drawer of his desk and withdrew a single sheet of paper: an invitation on plain white stock addressed to "The Veterans of Company B," in basic black and white. In commemoration of the 50th anniversary of the end of the war, Major General Wyman had organized a reunion of the company, retracing the soldiers' movements through Germany into what was now Austria. The concluding event was a gala dinner in the wine-growing section of Austria—the Grunzinger—just outside Vienna.

Sam had received and passed on similar invitations over the years, having no desire to revisit his painful past more than the daydreams and nightmares forced him to in the normal course. This one, however, was more interesting, scheduled to coincide perfectly with the IMF meetings in the same city.

Sam fingered the invitation for a moment thoughtfully and then came to his senses. "You'll manage without me. It's good practice. I'll be out of here soon, anyway."

"Is Stanley still busting your chops?"

Sam chuckled at Jon's gross understatement. "They're all busting my chops. Like vultures circling a wounded animal. I can actually see the saliva dripping down their lips when we do the business reviews. They're wearing me down, and between that and the other crap going on in my life, I'm just about ready to call it a day."

Jon's nasal whining snapped him back. "Please, Sam. Don't give up. This is a crucial time for me...I mean, *us*. Come to the IMF meetings. It'll clear your head. Fly over Monday night. That gets you to London on Tuesday morning. We can set up some meetings that afternoon. On Wednesday, I was hoping to get you to Budapest for lunch with Imre, George and maybe even the big guy. You like them. We need to be in Vienna for dinner Wednesday night, and we have meetings with the Austrian Post Office and, after that, the investment folks from the World Bank on Thursday. Don't forget the party is at Schonbrunn Palace Thursday night. You could probably catch an early flight from Vienna to London on Friday morning, and hook up to the first Concorde flight back to New York. You'd be in the office by 10 a.m., no sweat."

"Jesus! Is that all? Here I am telling you I'm not coming and your response is a kamikaze itinerary. Forget it. I'm not 40 years old anymore." Sam feigned annoyance, but in reality felt proud of the intensity of this man whom he had hired, nurtured and mentored for over 20 years. "I'll think about coming over for the prom. But don't make any appointments without clearing it with me first."

Sam hit the black "release" button on his phone terminal. He let out a long sigh and thought about how the constant and mercurial urgency of business crowded out the really important matters. Sam had hoped that diving back into work, after Gloria's diagnosis, would help regulate his physical and mental rhythms and make him feel normal again. But that hadn't happened. To the contrary, Sam felt more overwhelmed, confused and "lost in space" than before. And now, with Anton's sudden health reversal, Sam worried that he was near his personal limits.

He pivoted his chair toward the glass wall, in exasperation, just in time to see Betsy steaming toward him with a stack of papers clutched in her hands.

"Got a minute?" It was more statement than question, as Betsy took a seat on one of the wing chairs. "How is Gloria?"

It never ceased to amaze Sam that there were no secrets, personal or professional, on the trading floor. He had certainly not discussed Gloria's issues with Betsy, or any other subordinates in the firm, but there she was, asking after his wife as if her mental illness was the subject of a front-page article in the *Wall Street Journal*. Sam was in no mood to recite, again, the rehearsed answer to this question. So he merely nodded, murmured "Fine" and hoped that he successfully telegraphed his impatience and desire that Betsy get to the point, promptly.

"Good. We were worried about you both." She pulled a memo from the pile she had plopped on Sam's desk and handed it to him. "Here's the list of our people we should send to the

IMF meetings. They've all got clients there, and it's important that they show their faces."

Sam looked at the list, which was twice as long as it should have been. *Everything's a negotiation*, he thought to himself.

Sam pretended to study the names for a respectable period of time. He handed the memo back to Betsy, mumbled "Fine," and searched her face for the shock he knew would be there.

"Huh?"

Sam tried to suppress a smile. "It's OK with me. Is there anything else?"

"Thanks. Oh, can I get some of your time at the meetings? I can think of a half-dozen people you should meet with when you're there."

Sam really wanted to get off this topic, and said dismissively "I'm not sure what my schedule will be. Send me a note, and I'll see what works."

Betsy seemed to get the message, and stood to leave. Over her shoulder she said, "We'd better make travel and dinner arrangements soon. It's going to be a zoo there this year with all the globalization protests."

A cold sense of dread came over Sam. *Damn*, he thought. He hadn't focused on the likelihood that the anti-trade, anti-globalization, anti-whatever groups would be in Vienna. But of course they would. It would be perfect—world leaders, big corporations, global press coverage, and a congested and ancient city. Chaos personified.

That settles it... No way am I going.

He didn't have time to dwell on the satisfaction this resolve provided, however, because his concentration was diverted to an enormous roar from one of the trading desks in his direct line of sight. Traders were on their feet, some beckoning to salespeople across the aisle, others hunched over, cupping headsets to ears to hear over the clamor. Individual voices could be heard through the din:

"I need a price on Dollar-Yen for Fidelity!" screamed Arty Robbins, a seasoned salesman who covered the world's largest money managers and who had a reputation, to some notorious, for putting his clients' interests ahead of his employer's.

"Mike!" yelled Betsy. "I'm hearing from Tokyo that Miyazuma's resigned. Japanese city banks are dumping their dollars. Bonds are down at least a point!"

Mike turned to Betsy: "Tell Billy I've filled his order. And we're much lower now." And then, turning to Arty, he yelled, "What are those sons-of-bitches at Fidelity looking to do? No way am I making a two-way price with news on the table. They probably know more than we do. Do your job, bloke, and get an order."

Sam moved out to the floor, mindful of appearing calm and measured in approaching the trading desk. Any sign of concern in his face or gait would be disheartening to the troops, who knew quite well that the Firm had a lot of exposure to a falling dollar. First he paused to look at a screen, taking in the extent of the market reaction to the rumored resignation of the Japanese prime minister. Then he did the mental calculation of the day's losses: a two-percent decline on a billion dollars creates a $20 million loss. Not counting the options book, that wiped out the month.

Damn it. I knew I should have bought those puts. Now I've got to call Stanley.

Stanley Masters, the President of GSC, was a politically astute but market-wary chief executive. For most of the month, Sam had been on the defensive with the firm's Management Committee, justifying the size of the trading unit's positions and risk profile. Many of the executives on the Committee were openly disdainful of Sam's aggressive posture in the markets, which he racked up to pure jealousy. With that said, Sam recognized, the amount of risk they were carrying didn't leave a lot of margin for error, or global economic turmoil.

As Mike T's eyes met Sam's, it seemed as if everyone on the floor was watching, and for a few seconds, the decibel level receded to the normal buzz. Mike knew the routine, having lived through moments like these all too many times in his 10 years of currency trading experience. A spreadsheet always open on his desk, and constantly refreshing, tracked the Firm's global currency positions on a real time basis. This allowed Mike the ability to calculate the risk of those positions in statistical terms, using the most current data and algorithms developed by "rocket scientists" in the Firm's research group. So, he had the numbers at his disposal.

The facts and figures were the easy part of the job. Sam now had to deal with the hazy, subjective stuff. His trading staff and all of the sales force were in the process of obtaining information from clients and brokers about whether this market move was a panic, or correction, or a true change in sentiment. He had awakened the Firm's senior economist in Japan to advise her of the news, and was awaiting her analysis. This information, while lacking in statistical substance, was invaluable in gauging whether a two-percent change in the value of the dollar was real, or a "fake out." Too many times market players reacted to rumors that turned out to be false or to legitimate facts in an exaggerated or ill-advised way. Sam's experience told him to take his time, think things through, and obtain as much information as possible from as many good sources as possible, before making a decision in the face of this kind of volatility. With that said, each second that went by without action was a very expensive second. The dollar continued its decline, down another half a percent.

Mike put down his headset and walked over to his boss, about 10 feet from the main trading desk. Sam's question was the expected "What do you think?"

"I could use a cigarette right now, is what I think." Mike's deep voice, gravelly after years of smoking, reflected the tension in the room. "What pisses me off is that I spoke with Hiro last night, and he assured me that there was no way Miyazuma would quit. The Prime Minister's only been in office six months, and had the support of the big banks and exporters. I feel like we've been sandbagged."

"Yeah, whatever the reason, you know the drill. Should we stay in here? If the answer to that is 'yes,' should it be our full amount? And what levels should we set for stop losses? I've got to call Stanley in a few minutes, and you know he's going to ask me exactly those questions. So let's decide who to lynch later, and figure out now what we're going to do."

Sam's approach was straight from the manual, and he knew Mike was just letting off some steam with him because he couldn't do it in front of the more junior staff. "Let's get on the phone with London, Tokyo and Hong Kong and get down to it." Sam walked to his office and said to Pam, "Round 'em up for me—Jon, Hiro, Mara. Now, please. Also, tell the desk to put Rumiko through when she calls Mike, which should be any minute now. And find out where Stanley will be in the next hour, but don't tell his secretary why I'm asking."

Mike scooped up a number of sheets from the printer containing the position reports and risk analysis and joined Sam in his office. Pam assembled the senior foreign exchange staff and put them through to the conference phone on Sam's desk. As Mike went over the risk report, Sam tried not to let his mind wander back to the telephonic exchange with Anton earlier that morning.

It took a full 45 minutes, but a consensus was formed among the team. Mike T would begin to lighten the risk, and they would reconvene at the end of the trading day to reassess the position. For the overnight hours, at least one of the four senior executives would need to be reachable at all times. Risk reports would be run and circulated hourly, and any deviations from the limits agreed upon had to be noted immediately.

Sam had been here before, many times. By definition, there was always a crisis in the currency markets. That was the good news, as it meant there was always something to trade, always actors doing things in a panic as opposed to reacting to logic. Sometimes the craziness worked in your favor, sometimes it just made you crazy.

When everyone had left his office, Sam swiveled his chair toward the harbor, put his feet up on the window sill and leaned back, waiting for his muscles to relax. He was hoping for a few minutes respite to unwind and think deeply about whether the course of action they were embarking upon was really the right one. It all sounded good a few minutes ago, but Sam knew that he would gain more perspective as time allowed deeper absorption to occur.

He never got close. He heard Pam clear her throat behind him, and he turned his chair around to face her. She didn't have to say a word.

"Shit," he said violently. "Nothing?'

Pam shook her head timidly.

Sam's mind was racing to find a plausible reason why Gloria might have been *incommunicado* for—he looked at his watch and did the calculation—five hours now. All of them were bad answers, he knew. She had fallen in the shower and was lying unconscious or unable to move. She'd overdosed on her antidepressants. She'd had a car accident. She'd had an "episode" and run away.

He looked at Pam for some direction, and she asked, "Do you want me to call a friend?"

This concrete suggestion helped Sam to focus. "I'll do it. Look in my Rolodex for "Abrams", our next door neighbor.

Pam scurried out of this office and Sam tried calling his house. When the answering machine picked up, he punched in his code to retrieve the messages. In addition to the one from Pam from earlier in the day and several hang-ups, there were messages from two of Gloria's friends wondering if she was alright, having missed the book club meeting that morning.

Sam's stomach was roiling as he took his neighbor's number from Pam's shaking hand and dialed. The housekeeper answered, telling Sam that Mrs. Abrams wasn't home. Sam had to beg to get a cell phone number.

Thank God, was Sam's reaction when he heard Sheila Abrams' voice on the other end of a grainy line.

He tried to disguise his anxiety when he explained to Sheila that he hadn't heard from Gloria all day. While he was sure everything was alright, would she be a dear and check on the house?

"Of course," said Sheila. "I'm across town, so it may take me a few minutes. I'll call you when I get there."

Sam tried to force his thoughts away from a parade of horribles to what he might do should the house be empty--he'd call the police and head home.

Sam considered the dozens of loose ends he'd leave hanging by exiting now—all of them important, all of them pressing. He had to talk to Stanley. He couldn't just leave without reviewing the trading position.

And there was Anton! And the high school program that had to be cancelled. How could he leave now?

These contradictory thoughts were making Sam nauseous. He closed his eyes and tried breathing deeply, counting backwards from 25.

***

Sam and his three buddies were caught in a crossfire. Mortar shells exploded to the south, most likely friendly fire. The Rhine River was due east, cold and wide and lacking cover. To the north, the remnants of a German light infantry unit were dug in, spraying automatic fire directly in Sam's direction.

Sam, Reggie Tillingham, GilRo and Eddie Adams split off from the battalion a few hours back to find the river, follow it north, locate the German division and radio back its coordinates. Then, get the hell out of there before the ordnance came through.

The boys had done their job to perfection—that is, until some sharp-eyed Kraut sweeping the terrain with high powered binoculars spotted their antenna. GilRo, the radioman, was able to get the call through, at least most of it, before the equipment died on him. Clearly, though, not all of the coordinate information was relayed, because the mortar fire was off by double digit degrees and blocked the Americans' escape route.

Sam was back to back with Reggie in a deep squat behind a clump of short, thick bushes. Sam's arms were shaking and he was having trouble steadying his rifle against his shoulder. His voice cracked as he tried to speak in between artillery bursts and machine gun fire. "We're cooked. What do we do?"

Sam could feel Reggie's body behind him, strong and solid. "We have two choices. Wait here, and hope the good guys figure out where to aim the mortars. Problem is that if they don't, either we get hit by our own artillery or the Germans come get us and kill us. Tillingham votes against that option. The river is the only other alternative."

Sam wasn't encouraged by Reggie's analysis, but knew it was the correct conclusion. The two pair of GIs would have to leapfrog each other, one providing cover while the other advanced the 150 yards to the banks of the Rhine. The really dangerous part would be the last third, where the trees and bushes thinned out considerably by the shore of the river, to say nothing about the complete lack of cover while in the water.

Sam tried to suck it up.

"Can you see the other guys? Good. Let's go for that swim."

Reggie motioned for GilRo and Adams to move ahead. As they bellied forward, Reggie and Sam stood in a half-crouch, ready to open fire. Suddenly, a series of loud explosions took place just over their position, creating a wall of dirt and debris between the American soldiers and their enemy. Reggie stood straight up, screamed, "Move it. Run," and took off toward the river. He paused to yank GilRo and Adams off their bellies, and to check over his shoulder that Sam wasn't far behind.

They dove to a stop behind a small rise in the terrain, a hundred feet or so from the shore. Reggie slowly lifted his head and pulled a pair of field glasses from his jacket. After a minute surveying, he flipped over onto his back and slid down the hill to report back to the others. "Can't see much. It would be awfully useful if our colleagues in artillery would oblige with another salvo, wouldn't it? Wouldn't have to be a direct hit—not a time to be greedy—just enough to lower the curtain for the getaway."

Who is this guy? wondered Sam, fighting the cramps in his gut. He pulled himself up to one knee, grabbed Reggie's binoculars and poked his head up for a peek. A barrage of machine gun fire followed a few seconds later, exploding in the dirt in front of him and sending Sam reeling backwards.

"Shit, they've got us," growled Adams. He curled himself up into a sprinter's starting position as the bullets whizzed over their heads. "We've got to go for it, now."

Reggie reached down, grabbed Adam's coat with his huge hands, and pulled him closer to the others. "That would be suicide. A better idea is to wait for the next barrage. Even if it's off target, it will provide some distraction. One or two of us might make it."

"Unless we're the target," muttered Adams. "I'm leaving. GilRo, Hart, you with me?"

Sam tried to concentrate, but found it impossible to focus with all the noise and tension in the air. Instinctively, he knew he'd be better off staying with Reggie. He looked at Adams and shook his head.

"Suit yourself. Cover us, at least. Let's go."

Adams slid out from behind the hill, fired several rounds at the Germans while on the full run, and got about half way to the shore when he was hit. Several bullets clipped him on his right shoulder, spinning him around 180 degrees. Adams held his palm up to GilRo, which Sam took as a signal to stay in place, before a cascade of machine gun fire virtually sliced him in half.

"Oh my god, oh my god," moaned Sam. He saw himself in Adams' place, face contorted with pain, body shredded by hot shards of metal. Sam looked around in a panic, wanting to make sure he wasn't yet alone.

GilRo had heeded Adams' gesture and dove back to momentary safety. He had curled up in a defensive ball, his face buried in the dirt. Reggie remained in his squatted position, looking up to the sky. He was breathing steadily and deeply, his forehead wrinkled in a contemplative pose.

Sam saw Reggie's eyebrows lift, as if he'd heard something above the small arms fire. Reggie looked at Sam and said "Get ready. Get him up."

A few seconds later, the barrage scored a direct hit on the German position. Reggie screamed, "Go, go, go!" and pushed Sam toward the river. Sam grabbed a handful of GilRo and ran full tilt to the Rhine. He looked back only once, to see Reggie Tillingham haul what was left of Adams over his shoulder before heading for safety.

In the days that followed, Reggie had become Sam's best friend in the battalion, in spite of, or perhaps because, he was so completely different than anyone Sam had ever known before. He was Main Line to Sam's Upstate. Reggie was comfortable and casual in the most intense situations and regularly referred to himself in the third person: "Tillingham did this" or "Tillingham thought that."

In a quiet moment the day after their Rhine scouting mission, Sam and Reggie were talking before dinner, resting their backs against the trunk of a scarred oak. Sam was a bundle of nerves, tapping his thumb against his thigh and unable to relax. Reggie, on the other hand, inhaled cigarette smoke deeply into his lungs and silently exhaled through his nose, seemingly without a care in the world.

"I'm completely confused," Sam said. "We come this close to being butchered, and you're cool as a cucumber. We're heading out tomorrow after a brigade three times our size, and you're sitting here like it's the fucking opera. The only thing I can think of is that you're not human. You don't sweat. You don't seem to eat. You do breathe, but usually through a cigarette. So tell me the truth. You're from Mars, right?"

Reggie snickered and drew his left knee up to his chest. "Worse. Tillingham here is from Haverford. It's like Mars, only colder."

"And another thing,' Sam said, turning to face his friend. 'I never know what you're talking about. You're from Philadelphia. It's not cold there. And I know cold, brother."

"Point taken. Perhaps a better word would have been 'bloodless.'"

"There you go again. What the fuck does that mean?'

Reggie straightened his left leg and flexed his right. He lit another cigarette and stared straight ahead. "In Haverford, a Tillingham is taught to take things as they are. No mess, no fuss. Something about God's will. Crying and bleeding and emoting are of little consequence. Things just are. And that's how one copes."

Sam let the concept sink in for a few minutes. His world, at least the one before the war, was filled with noise and perspiration and hugs and threats. As the youngest of seven children, Sam wouldn't have considered subtlety and refinement key descriptors of his familial orientation.

Yet he wished he could have more control over himself in intense situations. He hated being so scared he couldn't move. He was humiliated by the debilitating impact fear had on his gut and sweat glands.

"So how do you do it? I mean, how do you keep from crying and bleeding? And don't tell me it's in the Haverford water."

Reggie lifted one eyebrow, paused for a second, and moved his head closer to Sam's. "So you want the secret, passed down through generations of Tillingham's, dating back from Plymouth Rock? It's a powerful notion. Can you be trusted?"

"Don't mess with me, Reggie."

"Father called it 'respiration.'"

"I'm warning you, don't make fun of me. I goddamned well know what that means, even though I'm not a Pilgrim. Breathing—that's the secret?"

"Simply put, yes. Deep, full breathing. In, so the lungs expand and fill the blood vessels with oxygen, the ultimate nutrient; out, to expel the spent fuel and relax the muscles and the mind. Breathe deeply enough, in and out, and the brain numbs. That's the Tillingham advantage."

Sam shook his head. This guy was a piece of work. "So that's the secret. I thought it was about money."

Reggie winked. "Oh, there's no Tillingham money—Grandfather saw to that. All that's left to pass on to the next generation is the breathing, and irresistible charm. Speaking of which, this Tillingham is off to town to find some female companionship. Care to join him?"

CHAPTER 6

Pam's light touch brought Sam back to the extreme present. "Sorry, Sam, but Mrs. Abrams is on the line."

Sam took a moment to place himself and loosened his tie with his right hand while grabbing for the phone with his left. "Hi. Any sign of her?"

"She's here. I found her sitting on the stoop by the back door. She was really upset."

"How long had she been there?"

"It's hard to say. She obviously didn't want to talk about it. I let her in, and she went right to her bedroom. I'm not sure what to do now."

Sam didn't either. "I really appreciate your help, Sheila. I hate to impose on you, but would you mind staying around for just a few more minutes while I try to talk to her?"

"Sure. Let me go upstairs and tell her you're on the phone."

After hearing no response to her first few knocks, Sheila let herself in to the master bedroom, and found Gloria standing with her back to the door, shoulders raised and tense, looking out a picture window over the backyard. "Sam's on the phone. He'd like to speak with you."

Gloria didn't respond at first, and only after Sheila repeated herself did Gloria move from the window. She wiped some tears from her eyes with a handkerchief she'd been holding, and smiled weakly at Sheila. "Thank you. I'm alright now," she said as she walked over to the edge of the bed, sat down and picked up the phone.

By this time, Sam was pacing as much of his office as the phone cord would allow. In response to Gloria's weak "Hello," Sam found himself barking at his wife.

"Where have you been all day?"

"Driving around."

"What? I've been worried sick about you. You missed your book club. You didn't answer your cell phone. What happened to you? Did you forget to take your medicine this morning? You know you have to take it, every day."

"Don't yell at me, Sam. I had a difficult day and don't need this."

"Sorry." In fact, Sam was terribly sorry for yelling at her, and knew that being angry was precisely the wrong way to feel and the wrong tactic to take with his wife. "I'll leave now and be home in an hour. Do you want Sheila to stay until I get there?'

"No, Sam. I'm alright now, really. Don't rush home on my account."

"I'm on my way."

As he gathered a stack of papers and shoved them into his briefcase, he yelled for Pam to come into his office. "I'm leaving now. I'll call you from the car when I get on the road, and you can find Stanley and patch me through. There are a couple of things you need to do for me while I'm talking to him. Call the Tolerance Project and tell them I have a business emergency and can't make the program today. Then, tell Mike T I had to run, but he should try me on my cell phone if he needs me for the next hour or so. We're supposed to have an end of day conference call—tell Mike to make the arrangements and just let me know when. I'll do it from home. And he should send me the reports by fax. And call the garage and tell them to have my car ready."

Sam was rattling off these instructions frenetically, his head scattered in a million different directions. He paused before leaving his office, knowing there was something important he was forgetting but not being able to calm down enough to go through a mental checklist. With a shrug, Sam grabbed his coat, slung his briefcase over his shoulder, and steamed toward the elevators.

Ten minutes later, Sam was steering his car onto the FDR Drive in the light, midday traffic. He wondered which Gloria he'd find when he got home. She sounded sad, but coherent, when they spoke on the phone. But Sheila said that Gloria was extremely upset when she found her. *Where had she been all day?*

Sam worried that Gloria could no longer be left alone. If that were true, clearly his life would be dramatically impacted as well. Would he have to quit his job to take care of her?

Sam mentally strained to find scenarios and rationalizations to avoid that conclusion. He wasn't qualified to care for her—she'd need professional help, of course. And he wasn't ready to quit, although he'd threatened it numerous times over the past few years. So much of himself was tied directly into his job that he couldn't imagine what he would be without it.

He bit the inside of his lip, punishment for thinking selfish thoughts. There was no avoiding the fact that Gloria was facing a serious, life-altering situation, which meant that he would, as well. *Respiration,* Sam muttered to himself, and inhaled deeply through his nostrils.

Loud and rhythmic honking on his right attracted his attention. When his eyes caught up to his ears, he noticed that a yellow taxi had pulled alongside. The cabbie, a thin, olive-skinned man with a thick black beard, was leaning on his horn with his right hand, while the middle finger of the other hand was defiantly extended out the window.

Sam looked at his speedometer, which registered almost 70 mph. He established that he was about to pass his exit, the path to which was blocked by this hostile combatant. Checking his rear view mirror almost as an afterthought, Sam hit the brakes hard and banked the car sharply to the right. He just missed the taxi's rear bumper as he swerved onto the ramp, narrowly escaping a collision with a dilapidated van also exiting the highway. Sam sped up again to create some distance between him and yet another honking vehicle. He realized that he had driven almost 15 miles since leaving the office, obviously at breakneck speed, with no recollection of any part of it. And, he had forgotten to call his boss.

Sam punched in his office number on the car phone and asked Pam to connect him with Stanley. He regretted it almost immediately. Stanley yelled at Sam for the first five minutes of the call. The firm depended on the earnings from the currency group, Sam was told. This was not the time to take big risks. "Get your act together."

Sam made a slow circle with his neck, trying to restrain his anger and hold back his frustration, and held the phone close to his mouth. "The risks are only big when we lose money, Stanley. But when we're in the black, I don't hear anybody complaining. The unit is well within its limits, and we've got it all under control. I'm not guaranteeing we won't lose some dough, but it's more likely that we'll come out of this relatively unscathed.

"The currency group has been consistently profitable for the past 10 years, and there's no reason why that won't continue. So why am I hearing that you're calling for a headcount reduction? I know other parts of the firm aren't keeping up, and maybe cutting overheard makes sense for them. But it's crazy for my group."

Stanley's icy voice snapped Sam back in his seat. "Every single business unit in the firm has to tighten its belt in this kind of environment. And every group has a credible excuse why it should be the one unit to get a pass. The currency group has done well over the recent past. So have mergers, and equity derivatives, and Japanese arbitrage. But each of them is cutting headcount, and not busting my chops about it. You've been at this a long time, Sam. You know the drill. I know it's hard, and I'm sure you're tired of it. But if you're going to stay here, you've got to stay with the program and get in line. I need a bunch of names, and don't give me first-year associates. Look at this as a chance to clear out some dead wood. Get rid of some of the older, expensive types to make room for the next generation--Mike T, for example. Hasn't his name been on the possible 'upgrade' list for the past couple of years? Think of the opportunities that open up for some of our young stars if he is retired. And think of the money we'd save from his seven-figure bonus."

It seemed as if Sam's body temperature was increasing by two degrees for each second Stanley was talking. His face felt as if it were melting, and his brain was screaming, *Who the hell do you think you are, telling* me *about my business, about* my *fading and up-and-coming stars, you goddamn bureaucrat.* Establishing some modicum of self-control, Sam sputtered into the mobile phone, "Let's not talk about firing Mike. He's not a guy we want to let go of now, at a time of huge volatility and risk. It's just not right, given all that he's done for our business.

"I understand your point about everyone needing to 'give at the office.' Hey, that's a line I've used myself when we've had to trim the business and my regional heads bust my chops about it--but 12 people? That's almost 10 percent of a growing business. How do I staff Singapore, or grow revenues?"

Stanley growled, "You're not making things easy, Sam. It's not a question of what's right, or what's wrong. There are no moral imperatives here—it's simply business. I've told Mark Todd that I need the names by tomorrow night. He'll come to see you in a few minutes to go over what you've got and help you with the rest. Be cooperative. It's the right thing, trust me."

Sam almost came back with what he was thinking: *Trust you, right! What you really want is for me to quit so you can divvy up my business.* Instead, he pushed the off button on the phone and pulled his car over to the side of the road. He sat there, trying to breathe deeply and establish some self-control. After a few moments, he called Pam back, who reconnected him to Stanley's office.

"Sorry. The call dropped. I missed the last part of what you were saying, Stanley."

"Sure." The sarcasm was unmistakable. "Did you hear the part about Mark Todd being on his way to your office to finalize the list of people you're going to fire?"

"Sorry, but I had to leave the office—family obligation. Not sure if I'll be in tomorrow either."

By now, Stanley was literally hissing. "Nice try. It's up to you. I thought you might want some say, but at this point I don't give a hoot. Call Mark Todd if you want, or don't. I'm heading off to Beijing tonight, and when I get back by the end of the week, 10 percent of your headcount will be cut, with you or without."

Sam had no rejoinder. He waited for Stanley to hang up and then flung the phone against the windshield. He opened the window half way, hoping the brisk air would help him move on to the other crisis at home.

***

Sam was surprised to hear opera, and smell the sweetness of cooking garlic, emanating from the back of the house. He dumped his coat and briefcase on the loveseat in the front hall and moved gingerly through the dining room. Peeking into the kitchen, he saw Gloria in an apron, leaning over a saucepan and humming along with an aria from *Rigoletto*. Nothing in her demeanor or composure suggested anything other than a typical day.

Sam thought the best thing to do was to play it dumb. He snuck up behind his wife, gently grabbed her slim waist, and put his lips to right ear. "Whatcha' cookin', good lookin'?"

Sam could feel Gloria tense slightly before leaning back into Sam's embrace. "You're home early. That's a nice surprise. I thought I'd make that Bolognese sauce you like so much."

Sam strained to detect any duress or falseness in Gloria's voice, but she seemed to be genuinely in a light-hearted mood. She was typically well-dressed, in a dark blue skirt and light grey sweater, not a hair was out of place and her makeup was applied perfectly. Sam wondered if, perhaps, he had overreacted.

"I love everything that you cook, especially when it's from the old country. I never knew your family had Italian roots."

"Hah. That's a good one. Father would have cut you off at the knees at the mere suggestion our blood wasn't pure Anglican blue."

Sam gave Gloria a soft kiss on the neck and backed away. He fingered the mail on the kitchen table and asked, "So, how was your day?" as casually as he could.

Gloria stopped stirring momentarily, and Sam thought he detected a slight twitch in her neck. "Fine," she said in a formal, stiff sort of way, "uneventful, actually. Did you tell me why you're home so early?"

"Well, ah, I was supposed to meet Anton at the Harlem High School of Science, you know, for one of our Tolerance programs. I was on my way when I got a call that it was canceled, so I just kept heading north. And here I am."

Gloria turned to look at Sam with a disbelieving look. "Things must be quiet at the office for you to take an afternoon off."

Sam decided to beat a hasty retreat. "Not really. As a matter of fact, all hell was breaking loose when I left, and I expect to be on the phone now for most of the rest of the day and night. Do you mind if I go make some calls from my den?"

"Of course not. I'll call you when dinner is ready."

Sam guessed that Gloria was as relieved as he was when he left the kitchen and headed upstairs. Her situation made no sense to him, he admitted. She could go from utter despair to nonchalance in a matter of hours, and that volatility had the potential to drive Sam berserk.

Sam changed out of his suit into more comfortable clothes and went into his study, a large, paneled room next to the master bedroom. He turned on his computer and market data terminal, and while waiting for them to boot, he grabbed a blank yellow pad and scribbled a "to-do" list for the rest of his day. He paused when he had finished, knowing that there was something important he had neglected to register, and hoping he would remember before starting his calls. Nothing came to him, however, and he sighed and called Pam.

"I'm at home. Who's looking for me?"

Pam hesitated for a second as she pulled the messages from her pad. "How is she?"

"Huh? Oh, Gloria. I guess she's fine. I haven't gotten the whole story yet, but she seems okay. Did Mike T call?"

"No. But Mark Todd was looking for you. He came by and seemed annoyed when I told him you weren't in the office and that you wouldn't be back for the rest of the day. He insisted I call your cell phone, which I pretended to do and told him I'd left a message. I didn't think you wanted to be interrupted—he's a really difficult man, isn't he?"

Sam had to laugh. He treasured how Pam protected him, even if it meant staring down, or lying to, a corporate executive. Most of Sam's senior-level colleagues thought his assistant overreached her role and was too casual in her dealing with management—so much so, that the topic often came up in peer reviews of Sam. But Sam defended her at each and every juncture, and he knew the feeling was mutual.

"The grim reaper, that's Todd. He's been doing Stanley's dirty work for years, and he's gotten damn good at it. Not worth much more than his melt value, but there's plenty of crap that needs to be done in a place this size, so he's a busy man. I guess I should call him before I sign off, but I'll leave him for last. Otherwise, it will sour all my other conversations--anything else?"

Pam rattled off the names of several other callers with non-essential issues, including a Mrs. Bobroff, whom Sam did not recognize and from whom there was no message, just a phone number. "Would you mind calling her back for me and find out what she wants? In the meantime, connect me with Mike T."

Sam still had that nagging feeling of something important forgotten when Mike picked up the phone. "We've stopped hemorrhaging, at least. I was able to reduce the risk by 15 percent without the competition smelling our blood in the water, so we may have caught a break. How did the boss take it?"

"I've had better," Sam said, and then bit his bottom lip firmly to ensure that he didn't supply any more information about that call than was necessary. "How does it feel for overnight in Asia?"

"'Don't know, but I'll watch the market tonight. I won't sleep anyway, between the phone calls and my own nerves, so I might as well be here." Mike coughed roughly, twirled the end of his pepper-red moustache, and rasped, "To tell the truth, I'd be more inclined to add to the position on a dip versus booking more losses, but you'd never let me do that, would you?"

"It's exactly the right play in almost every other situation except this one. No one else in the firm is making any money right now, and we've got to take that into account—unfortunately. So, we play it the way we discussed earlier: take us down as close to half the risk as you can without paying away too much. And stop smoking, for crying out loud. You're no good to me dead."

"From your lips to God's ears," wheezed Mike. "It's a genetic defect."

Sam smiled at the reference to Mike's father, and realized how much he missed Reggie. "I repeat, you're no good to me, or anyone else, dead. I'll check in with you later, or call me at home."

Mike fingered the near-empty pack of cigarettes in his shirt pocket and put the receiver closer to his lips. "How's Gloria?"

"She's fine. There's nothing to worry about. I'll call you later. Transfer me back to Pam, please."

Damn, Sam thought. *Does everyone know everything about me?*

Pam answered Sam's phone, and told him she had figured out who Mrs. Bobroff was. "Helene Bobroff. Anton Karetske's daughter."

"Shit," said Sam aloud, finally remembering what he had forgotten earlier. "Did you speak to her? Did she say anything about Anton?"

"They're hoping to get him into a private room this evening, so he doesn't have a phone yet. She'll call you when he has one."

"Did she say anything about how he's doing?" said Sam, obviously annoyed that Pam hadn't answered his question.

"No. I guess she assumed you knew."

I should know, he thought. *I should be with him right now.*

Sam, all of a sudden, felt exhausted. He had an overwhelming urge to lie down. He asked Pam to get as much detail about Anton as she could from the hospital, and call him back in 20 minutes.

"What about Mark Todd? He called again while you were on the phone with Mike."

Sam knew he'd be no match for Todd in his weakened state. "I'll deal with him later. Tell him I'm still on a conference call and I'll get back to him as soon as I can. Don't forget to call me back."

Sam hung up, kicked off his loafers under the desk and padded across the study to a couch designed for just this sort of situation. He rested his head on a heavily upholstered arm and stretched out, relaxing into the cool, supportive touch of the weathered leather. He closed his eyes, listening to the sound of opera coming from downstairs, and was asleep in less than a minute.

***

After the War, Sam visited Reggie as frequently as his class and vacation schedule allowed during his friend's nine-month recuperation at the Wilmington, Delaware VA Center. At first,

Sam would spend some time with Reggie's wife, Mona. But as Mona's complaining became chronic, and her sexual advances overt and aggressive, Sam scaled back his visits.

By the time Reggie was released from the hospital in late 1947, Sam was busy completing his degree requirements at NYU and working two jobs in Manhattan. Sam tried to stay close, but his free time was becoming increasingly limited, particularly when his relationship with Gloria became serious.

When Sam met Reggie at the train station in New York in December of 1948, it was the first time they had seen each other in almost a year, and Sam almost didn't recognize him. He looked fragile and his trademark carrot-colored hair had grayed and settled into a wreath around his head. When they hugged hello, all Sam could feel of his once hearty friend was bone and sinew. And even though Sam had insisted on carrying his suitcase, Reggie labored as he walked through Grand Central Station.

"What happened to Mona?" Sam asked, stopping at the top of the ramp which led to the subway, to give Reggie time to take a breath, and light another cigarette.

Reggie just shrugged.

Sam visited Reggie at least twice a year for the next 10 years, a period in which Sam's fortunes brightened and Reggie's declined with comparable rates of change. Reggie never fully recovered from the bullet that pierced his chest and lung, keeping him physically weak and sapping his focus and intellectual acuity. Sam, on the other hand, got stronger and bolder, moving seamlessly from college to law school to Wall Street.

In the summer of 1957, Mikey was born. Sadly, later that year Reggie was diagnosed with emphysema, a malady severely compounded by the fact that his lungs had never healed correctly from the War injury. By the time Christmas rolled around, Mona abandoned Reggie and their infant son for a used car salesman in Baltimore.

Reggie tried to continue to teach, but his failing health forced him into retirement soon thereafter. He insisted to Sam that he and Mikey could get by on his GI disability and pension benefits, supplemented by cash earned from after-school tutoring, but Sam knew he was lying. "At least let me give you money for Mikey—to take him to a game, buy him a new mitt, that kind of stuff," he pleaded over the phone. "You can say 'no' for yourself, but not for the kid."

Sam could hear a muffled sob on the other end of the line. And then he changed the topic.

Mikey—now "Mike"—had been a naturally gifted student, excelling in math and statistics in high school. With his father's encouragement, he applied to the Wharton School at the University of Pennsylvania, and with Sam's calling in some favors, Mike was admitted with a full financial scholarship. For the first year that Mike was in Philadelphia, Reggie successfully hid his deteriorating condition from his son. But at the beginning of Mike's sophomore year, Reggie was confined to his bed and clearly dying.

A week after Sam was promoted to a partner's position at GSC, in October 1974, he took the train to Wilmington to share his new good fortune with his old friend. In Reggie's living room, which had been, by necessity, converted to a hospice, Sam strained to hear Reggie's voice through the respirator mask. When Sam asked him to repeat what he had said, Reggie flung the device off his face and struggled to prop himself up on his elbows.

"Please look out for Mikey," Reggie said, gasping for

breath after every other word. "He's strong and smart, but he's too sensitive. He's still a boy."

"I'll do that, not to worry," replied Sam, trying hard to keep his voice steady.

Reggie lowered himself back on the pillows. "He's got to finish college. You've got to promise that. He wanted to take a leave of absence to stay here, but there's no sense in keeping vigil."

Reggie reached out his arm and motioned for Sam to come closer. Struggling for breath, he panted, "It's the last favor this Tillingham will ask of you, Sammy. Watch out for him, please."

***

"Dear?"

Sam thought it strange to hear Gloria's voice in Reggie's living room. He jumped up off the couch and blinked his eyes ferociously, trying to distinguish dream from reality.

"Pam's on the phone. She told me to get you."

"I must have fallen asleep," croaked Sam through an impossibly dry mouth. "Would you tell Pam I'll call her right back? I've got to wash up."

Gloria's annoyed look registered on Sam as he staggered to the bathroom. He soaked a wash cloth in cold water, squeezed it mostly dry, and threw the compress on his face. He let it stay there for a full minute, the cold towel shocking his synapses back to life.

Sam took a long drink of water, and straightened his shoulders while looking in the mirror. He brushed his thinning, gray hair and readied himself for the challenging conversation ahead.

Pam picked up on the first ring. "I just faxed to your home machine about a dozen pages that Todd insisted I get to you."

"Hold on, let me check." Sam put the receiver on his desk and walked across the room to his fax machine. In the paper tray was a series of spreadsheets listing the professional employees in the currency group, along with their years of service, compensation history for the past three years, and GPA, or grade point average, which was an overall rating system taken from performance reviews for the past two years. These spreadsheets were sorted alphabetically, by location, by compensation, by GPA, and by longevity. *Todd has done his homework.*

Sam knew that being completely unprepared was sometimes better than being partially prepared for these sorts of negotiating sessions, and didn't bother looking more closely at the paperwork.

"It's all here. Connect me to that SOB, please."

Sam could hear Pam snicker in the background before placing him on hold, and a moment later, he heard a man's voice take over.

"Todd."

"Sam Hart here. Sorry I missed you earlier."

"Right. I assume that you've reviewed the analysis I had sent to you."

Mark Todd's title was Chief Administrative Officer, a euphemism for his true calling, Chief Hatchet Man. Although impeccably tailored, and extremely fit, Sam always thought of Mark dressed in a long, flowing black robe, his face hidden by a hooded cowl. For the past decade, and of course behind his back, Sam whimsically referred to Mark as "the grim reaper" to those unfortunate colleagues who were forced to "downsize" their businesses under Mark's watchful eye. Until now, Sam had been spared that misfortune.

Todd continued: "We need to solve for 12. You've got my list. It's based on reviews, the strategic plan we went over last month, and a demographic analysis. We've only got a few minutes at this point to get these names in to Stanley, so let's focus on my list as a starting point."

They're going right for the jugular, thought Sam, spotting Mike T's name at the very top of the upgrade list.

"I've already told Stanley what I think about this, Mark. I'm not about to cut this deeply in the only profitable division of the firm," Sam said sternly, purposely attempting to pull rank.

"My instructions are to work with you to come up with 12 names, Sam. I've not been given a lot of discretion."

Sam knew Mark was right, and had little authority to deviate from Stanley's directives. But Sam also knew that he needed to present his position in order to get through to Stanley. Sam's entire negotiating strategy revolved around salvaging Mike T from the downsizing effort. He honestly felt that his headcount shouldn't be reduced, but just as honestly knew that the extent of the reductions he was asked for wouldn't have a material impact on the business. He could easily find a way to improve efficiency with the remaining troops, and knew from past exercises that he could replace any key positions lost in a short period of time.

However, Sam realized that if he complied generally with the downsizing, he would lose the specific fight over Mike. Stanley had made that clear in their earlier discussion. The only way to save Mike was to make his continued employment part of the *quid pro quo* for the downsizing. Sam articulated to himself the message Stanley needed to hear: *If you want Mike's head, you'll have to take it, but you'll get no more. If you want a 10 percent reduction in staffing, Mike stays.*

Sam knew this made him extremely vulnerable. And it wasn't lost on him that maybe, just maybe, this was Stanley's ultimate ploy. Push Sam to issue an ultimatum, and then call his bluff. Sam played this out as he extended the pause before he picked up the conversation with Todd: Stanley would order Sam to fire Mike T. That, in turn, could provoke a "constitutional' crisis that could easily end in Sam's resignation, assuming Stanley played his cards right with the GSC Board. The odds of that happening were swirling through Sam's head , mixing his own personal interests with those of doing the right thing by Mike and the Firm.

Sam ended the haggling session with Mark Todd exactly 20 minutes after it started--a time limit he had imposed upon himself at the outset. Although his head was pounding, Sam was satisfied that he had accomplished the limited objective he had laid out before the call. Stanley would know that Sam wasn't caving in, and that expensive political capital would be required to get his way. The question Sam didn't have the answer to was how badly Stanley wanted him out of the company.

Sam moved his chair toward the market data terminal and punched in the keystrokes to update the currency prices on the screen. As he waited for the numbers to refresh, he looked around his desk. His eyes rested on a 4" x 6" photo, now faded, of him and Reggie Tillingham in front of a bombed-out municipal building near Munich. The two young men pointed their rifles upwards, at complementary angles, forming an "X" above their heads. A cigarette dangled from Reggie's half-smiling lips. "I got his back," whispered Sam to the image of his dead friend. "Not to worry."

CHAPTER 7

Sam looked at the multi-faced clock on the desk in his study that was a present from the firm on the 25th anniversary of his employment at GSC. It read 5:30 p.m. in New York, 11:30 p.m. in London and 8:30 a.m. in Tokyo, a period known in the currency markets as "The Twilight Zone" because it was one of the few times when one of the three key trading markets wasn't in full, frenetic throttle. The numbers on his screen rarely changed, indicating the lack of activity. Sam welcomed the break, and leaned back in his chair.

He answered his assistant's call a few seconds later.

"I've got Mrs. Bobroff on the other line. Do you want to talk to her?"

Sam sat up straight. "Good. Patch her through."

Sam heard the "click" of being put on hold, the "buzz" of two lines being hooked together, and Pam's voice "Go ahead, Mrs. Bobroff. I've connected you to Mr. Hart."

"Hi, Helene. Are you at the hospital?'

"Yes. We finally got him into a room."

"Is he alright?" Sam's feelings of guilt were re-emerging. With a well placed phone call or two, he could have made the process for Anton much easier. *Damn it.*

"He hasn't been complaining, so I guess the pain is being managed. That's a huge improvement over last night." Sam could hear the remnants of distress in Helene's voice, and it hurt.

"Can I come over now?"

"I'm sure he'd love to see you. But take your time. He just fell asleep. I'll be here for a while."

Sam took down the room and phone number, found his shoes and put them on. He grabbed a sport jacket from his closet and descended the back staircase into the kitchen. Gloria was sitting at their small, glass topped kitchen table, looking out of the picture window over the sink into her late summer garden. The opera had stopped playing. The pungent odors of garlic and spices had faded. Sam could feel the sadness in the room.

He walked softly toward the counter and picked up his car keys. Gloria didn't move, even when he cleared his throat. "Honey," he said.

Gloria raised her eyebrows and turned her head only slightly. She seemed to be looking several yards to Sam's right.

"Anton's back in the hospital. I thought I'd run over to see him now. Do you want to come?"

Gloria shook her head demonstrably. "No, thanks--no hospitals for me."

Sam didn't like the way she said that—a challenge of sorts. He put his keys down and pulled a chair across from his wife. Sam took her hands and placed them on his, resting on Gloria's knees. He gently squeezed them until she made eye contact.

"Are you OK?"

Sam could tell Gloria was trying to hold it in by the tightening of her jaw and the hardening of the muscles around her eyes. He squeezed her hands again.

Gloria dissolved in a rush of tears and threw herself at Sam, burying her head in his chest. Sam held her firmly, trying not to think about where this was heading. When she finally stopped sobbing, he asked, "Have you taken your pills today?" and immediately regretted it.

Gloria pushed herself away with a forearm to Sam's solar plexus. She jumped up from her chair, moved several feet away and wiped the tears from her face with her sleeve. Then she yelled at her husband. "Goddamn it! All you seem to care about is whether I'm sedated. I don't want to walk around in a fog all the time, too stoned to feel bad, or good, for that matter. If that's the best I can do, I want out."

Sam never in a million years thought he'd hear his wife talk that way. Gloria was always the one to buck up his spirits when the strains of his job pushed him to an edge. She was the encouraging voice, whose mantra, "an inch is a cinch, a yard is hard," reminded Sam to put it all in perspective. The notion that Gloria would even suggest, albeit under duress, that suicide was an option sent Sam literally reeling.

He tried to stand, a bit dizzy, and reached out to grab the kitchen table for support. Sam leaned heavily on the edge, and it tipped toward him, smashing into his leg before hitting the stone floor. Sam arrested his own fall by holding onto his chair, but could do nothing to stop the glass top from exploding into thousands of pieces throughout the room.

He was stunned, and stared at a concentrated pool of glass bits reflecting multicolored shards of light right back at him. His eyes eventually found Gloria, who had begun to move toward him when he seemed ready to fall, and then was repelled back by the force of the explosion. There were several red spots on her shins and ankles where her nylons had been cut by the glass shrapnel. She was expressionless and pale.

Sam snapped back and rushed to her, checking her hands and face for additional injury. He led her to the nearby powder room, put the toilet seat cover down and gently pushed her to sit. "Let's take off those stockings and clean those cuts. It doesn't seem too serious."

As Gloria complied, she began shaking her head slowly and making a soft, guttural noise, looking past Sam into the mess in the kitchen. At first, Sam couldn't make out what she was saying, but after the third or fourth time, he was able to find words within the mumbles. "Breaking apart...It's all breaking apart."

***

Sam cleaned up the damage in the kitchen, warmed up the dinner that Gloria had prepared and abandoned, and they ate together in the dining room. A couple of glasses of wine with her pasta calmed Gloria down, and by 7:30 Sam considered trying, again, to visit Anton.

Gloria was sitting on the couch in the living room, paying scant attention to the sitcom on the television while she leafed through the pages of a *New Yorker* magazine. Drying his hands—which had been hard at work cleaning dishes— Sam plopped himself next to his wife and tried to assess her status.

"Are you OK?"

Gloria looked up, shrugged her shoulders and produced a half smile. "Sure, why not?"

Sam was looking for positive signs, knew he was stretching to interpret this that way, but succumbed to the strong urge he felt to get out of the house. "Mind if I go visit Anton? I'll be back in an hour and a half."

Gloria shrugged again.

"I'll have my cell phone with me. Call me if you need me...for anything, OK?"

She nodded without looking up from the magazine.

Sam surprised himself by getting up, grabbing his coat and car keys and heading out the door. Only when he had backed his car out of the garage and headed down the block did he allow himself to feel bad—guilty, stupid, at risk—about leaving his wife. He thought more than once about turning around, but proceeded to the Bronx nonetheless.

Sam called home on his mobile phone after parking his car but before entering the hospital. After four rings, the answering machine picked up. Instead of leaving a message, Sam called again, and again.

Finally, on the third try, Gloria answered. She was clearly annoyed. "I was in the bathroom."

"Sorry. Just wanted to make sure you were alright."

"Don't worry. I'll call you before I run away again."

Sam couldn't tell if Gloria was being sarcastic or humorous, but was grateful for either kind of response. He could relax for the moment, although he recognized that his wife's mercurial mood swings wouldn't necessarily give him much time.

Sam checked in at the front desk, got a visitors pass and headed for the 8th floor of the Milstein Pavilion. After waiting several minutes outside while a nurse finished her ministrations, Sam took a deep breath and entered Anton's hospital room.

He tried not to let his shock at Anton's appearance affect his demeanor, but Sam knew right away that might not be possible. A thick, black bruise traveled horizontally over the bridge of his nose, exaggerating the jaundiced color of Anton's skin and the dark rings around his eye sockets. He was propped up at a 45 degree angle, his shoulders pointy and hunched, making his once broad chest appear shallow and concave. Anton's thin, pocked arms hung listlessly by his side, decorated by a series of grey wires and tubes.

"Oh," groaned Sam, although he had hoped to contain it as a thought.

"That bad?" murmured Anton, who lifted his head just enough to establish eye contact with Sam.

"Sorry. No, you look fine. I just get this way in hospitals."

Anton tried to smile, but coughed instead. "Sure. The good news is that I look worse than I feel. Come, sit and talk to me."

Sam did as he was told, relocating an armchair next to Anton's bed. He tried to think of some upbeat topic to open their conversation, but Anton didn't give him a chance. "How did the session go?'

"Uh, well, uh…."

"I had a feeling you weren't going without me, Sam. It would have been good practice."

"Sorry. Things got crazy with Gloria, I mean…at work."

Anton's dark eyes softened as he caught Sam's eye. "I know you've got your hands full, Sammy. How bad is it?"

Sam cursed himself for his carelessness. The last thing he wanted was for Anton to have to worry about him, especially in this circumstance. "Nothing serious. We're still working on getting the medications right. But she'll be fine. What about you? Do you need anything? Can I help with the business or anything else until you get out?'

Anton tried another smile. "Helene's got it under control for now. She's a very strong girl. After I'm gone, though, she might need some help. Maybe you could check in with her."

Sam's involuntarily shivering reminded him of the death bed conversation with Reggie, decades ago. "Don't talk like that. You'll be out of here soon. I'll make sure of it."

Anton shook his head slowly. "Maybe, maybe not. The cancer has spread to my brain and my lungs, and that's that. I thank God I was able to finish my interview. I'm ready now."

Sam pulled himself closer to Anton's bed. "What interview?"

Anton reached a shaky arm for a cup on the stand next to his bed, which Sam retrieved and held while he sipped water from a straw. Anton cleared his throat with difficulty, and wiped his lips with his hand. "I told you about the Shoah people, didn't I?"

"I don't think so."

" I meant to. You know Steven Spielberg--the movie director? His mother is a survivor. He is taking the testimony of anyone still alive connected with the Shoah—the Holocaust—on video. To prove that it happened. To teach what happened. To make sure it never happens again. I was interviewed three weeks ago."

"Really?" Sam was floored.

"I got the tapes in the mail today. Helene brought them over, there..." Anton motioned his hand toward the bureau next to his bed, where Sam spotted two black tape cassette cases.

Sam reached over to grab the tape and asked, "Did you watch?" The white label said simply "Anton Karetske: Mauthausen and Gunskirchen" and gave the month and date of the interview.

Anton made a slight clicking sound with his tongue. "No, the tape players are locked up until the morning—that's what the nurse says."

Sam fingered the cassettes thoughtfully. "Was it hard, remembering everything?"

"I haven't stopped remembering, not for one day." Anton paused while a tremble waved through his body and clenched the bed sheets around him as if needing the physical support to go on. "The hard part was talking about it. I practiced to myself, trying to use words to describe my memories. But I never got very far...my thoughts kept racing ahead. I'd be talking about my family in Budapest and my mind would be at Gunskirchen." Anton coughed again, and Sam wondered whether the moisture forming in his dark eyes was due to the pain of the cough or uttering the name of the camp.

"Remarkable," said Sam, allowing his head to hang while he stared at a dark spot on the linoleum floor. "I do everything I can to not think about the war. I fight like hell when the memories try to rise to the surface. They scare the daylights out of me."

"I could tell. When you talk with the kids, you never speak about yourself—you know that?"

Sam nodded, without lifting his head or shifting his gaze.

Anton wiped some phlegm from his lips with his sleeve and cleared his throat. "You should talk to them. You should tell your story. You can't hide the pain in your face and your voice. Fifty years is too long to keep secrets inside."

Sam stiffened at the word "secrets," wondering how Anton knew. "I've got nothing different to tell them than a thousand other GIs. I'd just as soon stay as far away as I can from that time and place."

Anton's eyes drooped, and he responded by trying to shift his position. "The drugs are making me tired, but I have something important to tell you. Help me sit up."

Sam pushed the electronic controls on the hospital bed and adjusted Anton's pillows to help him get comfortable. After taking another sip of water, Anton fixed his eyes on his friend and breathed deeply. With renewed strength, he began speaking.

"When I was a boy in Hungary, my grandfather would tell me the story of man's fall from grace. God created the world by forming containers to hold His Divine Spirit in the form of light. As God prepared the containers they shattered, tumbling down to Earth. Our world became filled with the splinters holding sparks of the Divine Light. Only by collecting theses shattered pieces and recreating the whole can our broken world be fixed and our divine nature restored. That process is called 'Tikkun Olam', which means 'fix the world.'

"It was some time after our liberation from the camp that I understood the parable. Those shards are the components of human experience, some good, many awful. Each one of them, though, is precious. To repair our world each person must find goodness and piety to counteract the evil around them. The terrible memories of our scarred generation are just as important as our loving ones if we are to make peace with ourselves and sense of our lives. Otherwise, we risk falling into a black hole of ambivalence, which allows evil to spread. Telling my story on that tape is my final attempt to repair my life. You should think about it, too."

Anton closed his eyes and Sam sat and said nothing, absorbing the message by osmosis. Several minutes later, the night duty nurse arrived with a cup full of pills. She checked the IV lines before gently touching Anton's shoulder and waking him, and lowered the bed to its earlier position.

Anton looked at Sam and smiled through glassy eyes. "I'll rest now," he said.

"Of course." Sam stood, still holding the cassette, and was about to put it back on the bureau when he said "Do you mind if I take this home? I'll get it back to you tomorrow morning."

Anton smiled. "Take your time. I'm not going anywhere."

***

Sam was relieved to find Gloria sound asleep on the couch, the blaring television notwithstanding. An empty bottle of

Chardonnay stood next to an equally drained wine glass on the coffee table. For a moment, Sam worried that Gloria had also decided to take her antidepressants, but a quick inspection of the pill boxes lined up on the kitchen window sill confirmed that she had stuck to her resolve.

He looked at the clock—9:30—weighed the pros and cons of watching Anton's tape before or after putting Gloria to bed, and decided on the former course of action. The safest thing was to let his sleeping wife lie.

Covering Gloria with a light throw, Sam turned down the TV, poured himself some gin and quietly climbed the stairs to his study. After kicking off his shoes, he loaded the cassette into a VCR and turned it and the TV on. He made a point of switching off the screens to his computer and market data terminals when he sat down behind his desk.

Anton certainly looked, and sounded, much better on the screen than he did at the hospital. Sam was deeply saddened realizing just how much his friend had deteriorated in the past three weeks.

Anton was tentative at first, answering the off-camera interviewer's warm-up questions about his early years with his family in Budapest. As his story moved into the war period, Anton became more animated and concise, needing fewer questions to stimulate his narrative.

Anton's father, Jakab, was the general manager of the Magyar Esta Bank, a mid-sized financial firm in the Pest side of the city and an energetic civic volunteer in the lay and Jewish communities. Anton was 15 when his mother died in 1938 and he and his younger sister, Kata, were looked after by their housekeeper, who eventually moved in with the family and married their father two years later.

Although aware of numerous anti-Semitic laws passed

in Hungary at that time, Anton noted that the impact was mostly in the outer regions of the country. Urban Jews were more-or-less insulated until 1941, when Hitler's pressure on the country's leader, Nicholas Horthy, intensified. As a result, Anton's application to the University was returned without consideration on "ethnic grounds." His father was demoted from his position at the bank on the basis of new laws restricting Jews from leadership roles in financial institutions.

Nonetheless, the day-to-day impact of the new rules on Anton and his family was limited, and there was growing optimism that things were likely to get better in Hungary. Anton and his friends would exchange stories they picked up in their jobs or at the coffee houses about property confiscation and pogroms against Jews in Slovakia, and the actions of Hungarian border officials to allow many of those victimized to take refuge. Similarly, there was much discussion that, with the war not going well for the Germans, Horthy had refused Hitler's demands for the branding, confinement and deportation of Hungarian Jews.

It was against this false sense of security that the German occupation of Hungary, in March 1944, occurred. German soldiers, including large battalions of SS troopers, seemed to appear overnight in Budapest. Horthy announced a new, pro-German government, and within months all Jews were required to re-register with a newly formed Jewish Council, manned by urban Jews but overseen by German soldiers.

Jakab was a member of the Jewish Council. Adolph Eichmann appeared in Budapest in June, taking personal command of the registration process and interacting regularly with Anton's father. Jews were required to wear yellow stars and were subject to evening curfews. The deportations of suburban

Jews began within a month, and horrible rumors circulated that they were being sent to Poland for execution.

One day in early September, coming home from his job at the printing company where he had been able to find work, Anton found Jakab in a chair in the dining room, head in hand, weeping silently. He had never seen his father in any form of emotional distress, and stood quietly by.

Eventually his father noticed him, dried his eyes with a handkerchief, and motioned for Anton to come sit next to him.

"I'm sorry, son. I've made some terrible mistakes."

"No, father, I'm sure that's not so."

Jakab smiled for a brief moment. "We should have left months ago, when we had the chance. And then it became impossible. I thought we'd be safe, here in the city, but..."

He reached up and stroked his son's face. "Tomorrow, early, take your sister and go to the Swedish Embassy on Minerva Street. You are to see Mr. Wallenberg about a job."

Anton cocked his head in confusion.

"...with the embassy. The Germans won't bother you if you are working for the Swedes. You will have to live there, so take a suitcase with you."

Anton's heart sank. "Live there? What about you, father? I won't leave you."

Jakab moved his hand down to Anton's shoulder, which he grasped firmly. "Anton, you will go if you want to live. All the Jews in this city will be sent to Auschwitz before the end of the year—I have seen the document. I tried to hide some names, confuse the records, but they suspect me now. You must do this tomorrow, and I cannot go with you."

Anton and his sister did as they were told, and met with Raoul Wallenberg at the Swedish Embassy. Wallenberg was, technically, an official of the Swedish Red Cross, but he made it clear to the Karetske children that his mandate from his government was to save Hungarian Jews from persecution. They would assist him in production of documents, called "Schutz-Passes," intended to convince German and Hungarian authorities that the bearer was under the protection of Sweden, an officially neutral country.

Anton's first question was whether such a pass might be available for his father.

Wallenberg stroked the front of his balding forehead with the back of his hand. In fluent Hungarian, he said, "I offered one to him, but he declined. He was afraid it would diminish the value to others. He is a courageous man."

His position as an employee of the embassy allowed Anton to dispense with the yellow star on his clothing, and freed him from travel restrictions and curfews within the city. He was able to visit his father nightly for the next month, providing Jakab some relief from his terrifying awareness of the worsening plight of Hungarian Jews. The deportations had gathered momentum, and people were panicking. Civil order was breaking down and violent acts of anti-Semitism were commonplace.

In mid-October, Anton and numerous other "employees" gathered in the Swedish ambassador's office to listen to a radio address by President Horthy. The Hungarian leader declared that his government would seek peace with the Soviets. The cheer that resulted was short-lived, however. Thirty minutes later, a different announcer on the same radio station advised that President Horthy had "resigned" in favor of Ferenc Szalasi, the leader of the Arrow Cross, the Hungarian Nazi Party.

To Anton, the message was clear. The Nazis had taken control of the government, and the dangers to all Jews increased dramatically. Not even pausing to grab his coat to face the cold night, Anton rushed out the door toward his father's house.

As he neared the ghetto, the number of Hungarian and German soldiers on the street increased substantially. He watched as soldiers and civilians alike methodically smashed the windows of an entire block of stores, looting as they went. He heard the sounds of gunfire and women's screams coming from the very center of the Jewish section.

Anton stuck to the back streets he had known all his life, rushing through intersections and waiting in the darkness of doorways and alleys when people approached. A block from his family's street, he hid while a small troop of Hungarian soldiers—four or five—marched down the street. He could see that an older man, wearing a coat over what appeared to be a night shirt, was being dragged along. To his horror, Anton recognized him as Istvan Tors, a respected leader of the Jewish community whose father was once mayor of Pest.

Without thinking, Anton emerged from the shadows and followed the procession, heading directly for his home. He watched while two solders climbed the stairs, first banged, and then kicked the front door until it yielded. He could hear someone yelling "Jakab Karetske? Get your coat and your papers and come with us, now!"

Anton's heart was pounding. He took a step forward, and then stopped. He reached into his pants pocket for his wallet, and *his* papers, but felt nothing. He had left everything at the embassy in his haste to get here, and as such any chance of being useful to his father was also left behind.

A minute or two later, he saw his father emerge from the townhouse. At the top of the stairs, Jakab looked down the street and made eye contact with his son. He shook his head slightly, but clearly, in a sign of admonition, telling Anton not to intervene. At the bottom of the steps, Jakab paused to repeat the subtle warning. In response, one of the soldiers grabbed the yarmulke off Jakab's head and pushed him, almost causing him to lose his balance. "Move," he said.

Jakab straightened himself, brushed back his hair, and moved forward. Anton watched until his father turned the corner, fearing it might be the last time he would ever see him. He then sprinted back to the Embassy the way he came.

Over the next 24 hours, Wallenberg himself tried to intervene, complaining formally to numerous Hungarian ministries and offering cash "rewards" to individual policemen and government diplomatic personnel, but no useful information arose. Anton and Kata visited prisons, police stations and army garrisons through the city, protected with diplomatic passes, and came back empty-handed.

The following evening, Anton was smoking outside in the Embassy's back courtyard, too depressed to eat or sleep, blaming himself for not being able to save his father. His shame was interrupted by one of his colleagues, who announced that there was a woman in the lobby who wanted to speak with him.

Anton stubbed out his cigarette and went inside. He reached out his hand to a well-dressed, blond woman who appeared to be in her late forties. "Is there somewhere we can talk?" she asked, never looking up to establish eye-contact.

They went into a small meeting room a short way down the hall, one of the few remaining spaces in the embassy not devoted to housing protected Hungarian Jews. The woman introduced herself as Marta Evigny, who had worked for Anton's father for almost 20 years at the Bank. She greatly respected him, and thought his son should know what had happened.

Marta told Anton how the soldiers had been planning to

take Jakab and Istvan Tors to the Petr Street prison, but were confronted along the way by an angry mob of Arrow Cross elements. They demanded the soldiers give up their prisoners. At first the soldiers stood firm, but as the mob persisted the soldiers' resolve waned. The prisoners were dragged to an empty lot and beaten to death. Their bodies were burned as the mob cheered, and the soldiers looked on.

Anton was too shocked to react. He could feel the tears streaming down his face, and a cloud of sadness overwhelmed him. "How do you know this?" he finally stammered.

Marta looked up at him, her makeup disfigured from her own crying. "My husband was one of the soldiers."

***

Sam paused the tape so he could catch his breath. He realized that he'd been lost in his own memories for the last several minutes, missing a large part of Anton's testimony. He rewound the tape until he got to a spot he could remember, and pushed the play button.

No sooner did Anton start talking than Sam was again pulled back into the war. He was walking through a compact neighborhood in Linz which, amazingly, had missed the massive destructive impact of heavy Allied bombing. The soldiers of B Company were carefully going door to door, looking for booby-traps and trouble, before the big trucks came through. In one section, six or seven storefronts in succession were marked with stars in yellow paint across the doors. Their windows were shattered and the interior bare or disheveled. A close look often yielded faded red stains on the street just in front of the building.

Sam walked the cobblestone streets in a state of escalated anxiety. In a relatively short time, they entered a square, in the middle of which a chipped, marble obelisk sat in a stone tub. Four streams of water spurted from within the tub onto the base of the sculpture, aligned with the center of the four streets which came together at the square.

The unit came to a stop just in front of the fountain. The perfect symmetry of the spot combined with the crisp, spring air and pleasant gurgling sound of water, was momentarily calming—until…

"Holy Jesus!"

Sam turned left toward the voice, and then back over his shoulder to where the speaker was staring. Three charred husks, of unequal length and girth, hung from a wooden trellis which had been erected on a stage built onto the steps of what was once a large brick building.

Sergeant Yancy yelled, "Cut them down," and the entire Company moved in unison to the gallows.

Reggie Tillingham shimmied up one side of the structure to cut the rope, and Sam and Hoffman were there to carefully lower one the corpses to the ground. As he did so, Sam realized that the bodies were wrapped in an oily, cloth-like substance that had not fully burned.

Hoffman noticed it as well. He rubbed away some soot with his thumb, groaned, "Oh no," and began frenetically scraping away the dirt with his fingernails. "No, no, no."

"What is it?" Sam asked.

Hoffman's face reflected the pain of a hundred generations. "It's a Torah," Hoffman moaned. "Dear God!"

***

"I'm going to bed."

Sam heard Gloria's voice but had no idea where it had come from.

"Sam?"

He looked to the side, and saw her standing in the doorway of his office, holding her shoes in one hand and rubbing the back of her neck with the other. "What are you doing? Is that Anton?"

Sam glanced at the TV, and realized the tape was still running. He turned off the VCR, slowly pushed himself up from the chair using his desk as leverage, and walked over to, and then behind, his wife. He put his hands on her shoulders and slowly, gently began to massage them.

"I got back about an hour ago. You were deeply asleep, so I thought I'd let you stay there for a while."

" That feels good. How is Anton?"

"Not good—really not good. He seems resigned to dying. That's the first time he's been down."

"Is it true? Is he dying?"

Sam sighed deeply. "The cancer has spread. He looks terrible. I don't know..."

Gloria turned to face Sam and put her arms around his shoulders and drew him in. As they held on to each other, Sam was calmed by the familiar warmth and scent of his long-time companion. His eyes tightly shut, Sam floated weightless in Gloria's embrace. He visualized a multi-faceted glass ball, falling in slow motion from the sky. A bright light—the same yellow that covered the walls of Linz—glowed from within the orb. Just before it struck the ground, Gloria relaxed her arms and pulled herself back from Sam's grasp.

"Come to bed," she said, softly stroking his face. "You've had a rough day."

"I will," responded Sam, lightly kissing Gloria on the

forehead. "I just need a few minutes to finish what I was doing. Wait up for me?"

"Sure," she said. "Don't be too long."

Sam watched Gloria climb into bed, turned and went back to his den. He thought about calling Tokyo to check in on the markets, but resisted, concerned that doing so would engage him for more time than he was willing to give. He'd call later, after he'd finished watching Anton's tape.

***

After their father's murder, Anton and Kata threw themselves into the work of rescuing Hungarian Jews from Eichmann's depraved mission. In the second half of November 1944, the Arrow Cross and SS began rounding up Jews from the ghettos in Pest and forcing them, on foot, to the Austrian border, some 200 kilometers. The Swedish embassy aids were positioned along the route to hand out protective passes, food and medicine to the seemingly endless rows of the victims. Anton accompanied Wallenberg to checkpoints further down the road, where they threatened and bribed police and soldiers until those with Swedish passes were finally freed.

The forced marches eventually ended, but the deportation of Jews did not. By mid-December, Jews by the thousands were being herded into box cars and transported by train out of Budapest. This served to further intensify Wallenberg's efforts. In several incidents in which Anton was present, the Swede climbed the train wagons, stood on the tracks, ran along the wagon roofs, and stuck bunches of Schutz-Passes down to the people inside. The Hungarian soldiers were ordered to open fire, but miraculously their shots never struck their target. Anton assumed that the soldiers were either so intimidated, or impressed, by Wallenberg's courage that they deliberately aimed high.

Wallenberg was able to rescue thousands of Hungarian Jews through these tactics, but many more were deported and, presumably, murdered by the Nazis. Just after the beginning of the new year, 1945, Anton was called into Wallenberg's tiny office in the Embassy to listen to a report from a man who served as an administrator for the Arrow Cross party whom Wallenberg had repeatedly bribed. The informant told them that Eichmann himself had ordered the complete destruction of the ghetto in Pest in which some 80,000 Jews had been sequestered. The action, which would involve using tanks and small artillery to shell buildings, massive troop support and the use of flame throwers, would commence within a week's time.

After the informant left, Wallenberg's face was ashen. He summoned into his office several of his most senior staff to discuss their tactical options. The group concluded that the only way to stop the massacre was, somehow, to get to General August Schmidthuber, Commander in Chief for the German troops in Hungary.

Wallenberg was unsuccessful in applying his diplomatic resources, and copious bribes, to arrange a meeting with Schmidthuber. With only a few days left before the planned action, Wallenberg was forced to use his last resort.

Almost since his arrival in Hungary in the summer of 1944, Wallenberg had been working on a rapport, fueled by bribes, with Pa'l Szalay, a high-ranking officer in the police force and an Arrow Cross party member. In the hopes of developing their relationship further, Wallenberg had restrained from asking favors of Szalay until that point, but now felt there was no choice in the matter. In a carefully worded letter, which Anton reviewed for colloquial and grammatical style, Wallenberg pleaded with the Hungarian to intercede with Schmidthuber. He reminded Szalay that the Russians were threatening the German eastern front and the war was near its end. He also noted that there would most certainly be war crimes trials, and that Wallenberg would be in a position to testify as to those who participated in, or helped to stymie, Nazi atrocities.

Anton delivered the letter to Szalay's home that evening, and, as instructed, waited for him to read it and reply. Clearly angered by his first reading of the letter, Szalay turned beet red and flung the paper at Anton's feet. "Here is your reply. Tell Wallenberg to go to hell."

"Are you sure you want me to tell him that?" sputtered Anton, finding the courage to stick to his script. "Oh," said Anton, handing him two sealed envelopes from his jacket pocket, each containing 5,000 U.S. dollars in $100 bills, "One is for you and the other for the General. There's yet another envelope for you at the embassy for afterwards."

A broad smile overtook Szalay's face. "I see. Tell the Ambassador that I will send a note to my good friend the General right away. The course of this war is not lost on him.... Nor is the value of hard currency."

Anton left Szalay's flat with more a sense of optimism than at anytime since before his father's death. He took a seat on a streetcar for the trip across Buda to the Embassy, and was thinking about what he and his sister would do when the war ended when he was jostled by someone who had fallen against his knee and was now on the floor of the car. Before Anton could piece together what had happened, a leather-jacketed Arrow Cross thug came up and hit the man brutally in the ribs, and then in the groin, with a thick, black nightstick.

The man lay there, clutching his stomach and groaning in

agony. While the other passengers moved away, the assailant readied to hit again. Anton instinctively stood up, blocking the attacker's path. The Nazi paused for a moment, then raised his nightstick and swung it at Anton.

Anton deflected the blow with his left arm, and struck the man squarely on the nose with his right fist. Blood gushed from the injury, and Anton hit him twice more before he fell back against the door of the streetcar. The man pulled a whistle from his pocket and began blowing into it furiously, creating a high-pitched sound that lodged right in the center of Anton's head.

At that moment, the streetcar stopped and its doors opened. Anton jumped out and began running, but the whistle kept following him no matter how fast he went. He was tackled from behind before he reached the next block, and stopped his kicking and thrashing only when his head was repeatedly banged into the sidewalk.

A burly policeman, who had been sitting on top of him and was huffing and puffing, finally got off and turned him over. Anton could barely see his face, but could feel him probing his pockets and withdrawing his credentials.

"Jew," Anton heard the soldier say, followed by a sharp kick to his ribs. "You attack a party official, and violate your curfew. You've got a big problem."

Anton was jerked to his feet, and with his little remaining energy, said, "Diplomatic protection--Swedish Embassy."

The soldier held the official-looking booklet in front of Anton's nose, and moved it back a forth in front of his eyes. "You mean this piece of shit? I say it's a forgery, not worth the paper it's printed on." Within seconds, the pass was ripped to shreds and scattered on the pavement.

The last thing Anton remembered before losing

consciousness was the pain of the Arrow Cross brute playing out his revenge with a heavy boot and a sharp stick. When he awoke, he was lying in the corner of an impossibly hot and crowded railcar, on his way to Gunskirchen.

Anton knew he was at Gunskirchen for five months because that's what the calendar said. Living through it felt more like 20 years.

He had lost his father and his sister. His ribs and legs hurt constantly, making sleep impossible. Anton was forced to work in an airless, filthy factory stamping bullet casings for 12-hour shifts with rare glimpses of the light of day.

He watched co-workers scream in agony when their fingers or hands would get caught in the dilapidated machinery, only to be dragged outside for rendering themselves useless and summarily shot.

In the workers barracks, every morning, Anton and one of the few other able-minded inmates would cull from the mass of men those poor souls who had died the night before. Whispering the ancient Jewish prayer affirming man's love for God, the Sh'mah, Anton would drag the corpses into the courtyard where they would be picked up, thrown in the back of a lorry and dumped in a huge ditch behind the camp.

When despair would threaten to overtake him, Anton tried to hold on to the hope that Wallenberg has successfully saved the ghetto. Anton seized onto that dream, telling his interviewer, "It was as if I was holding a piece of shattered glass, a piece of the puzzle from which we might again find God's grace."

He had been hearing the sounds of planes—hundreds of them, it seemed—for several weeks, and noticed that the guards had been growing fewer in number and becoming much more distracted, and arbitrarily violent. Even though the conditions at Gunskirchen were horrendous, and the soldiers cruel, there was a sense that the prisoners were there because there was work to do. But in the last few days, the guards would beat inmates, and shoot them, for almost no reason.

Anton also noticed that the dead were not replaced with new prisoners. In the first few months of his captivity, their ranks grew daily with new deportees from Hungary, the Ukraine and Romania. Recently, however, there was more room in sleeping lofts and fewer crowds in the dining shack.

On the day the Americans arrived, Anton, as usual, was the first to open the barrack doors. A thick fog had descended on the camp, held in place by the surrounding dense forest, blocking the first rays of the early morning sun. He limped outside, pulling with him the lifeless body of Mika, a young man from Szeged who had been brutally raped by the duty sergeant a few nights before. It seemed strangely still. Anton looked around discretely at first, and then more aggressively, straining to find any sign of his captors. Leaving the corpse in front of the barracks, Anton walked into the center of the mud caked courtyard, then to the latrine, then to another barracks, but found no one.

Emboldened, Anton made his way to the east gate, the one the trucks would use when taking the dead out of camp. He was shocked to find the gate wide open, and still no soldiers—not in the watchtowers, or the sentry posts, or anywhere around the camp. It was then that he noticed bodies—hundreds of them—littering the front of the yard.

Anton continued walking out the gates and in the middle of the coarsely paved road leading into the forest. As the sun's rays broke through, the many mounds of dirt piled up several meters from the side of the road became heaps of emaciated bodies. The air reeked of decay, so overwhelming that Anton doubled over with nausea, and fell to the ground.

He staggered to his knees, careful not to look back at the camp. "I must have been delirious," he recounted, "but I was certain I'd turn into a pillar of salt if I turned around. I tried to stand, and immediately felt the strong arms of an American soldier lifting me up. I felt so puny and embarrassed, so shrunken and broken, that I buried my head in his shoulder and began to cry.

"It was the first time I had cried since my father died, and it felt so good to allow myself to feel pain and sorrow again."

Sam looked at Anton on the screen but saw the ravaged figures stumble toward him. He gagged at the stench, as if he were back in the muck of Gunskirchen, 50 years earlier. He reached into his shirt pocket for the ever-present pack of Luckies, and when he looked down to try and understand why there was nothing there, he realized where he was and what he was doing.

The interviewer had just asked Anton to describe his post-war experiences. Sam saw in Anton's face, and detected in his voice, a major emotional letdown. That made sense, he thought. Anything would be anti-climactic, if not banal, after the surge of energy and emotion that must have overtaken Anton when recalling and describing his experiences at the camp.

Nonetheless, Sam tried to listen carefully as Anton detailed the time he spent in a displaced persons camps in Austria, the first six months of which he was frantic, trying to get word about Kata.

Eventually, he made contact with one of his co-workers at the Swedish Embassy, and learned that two days after he was expelled from Budapest, on January 13, 1945, the Russians attacked, repelling the Nazis and liberating the ghetto. Wallenberg immediately went to work, making arrangements with the newly enfranchised Russian military to provide safe passage for his workers. And even though Wallenberg left the embassy under military escort a few days later, and had not returned, the Russians honored the measures that were agreed to and Kata was among the first to leave for Holland.

It took Anton another 12 months to secure his own passage to Amsterdam, where he reunited with his sister under the roof of a maternal relative. Kata married a Dutchman several years later, had two children and taught kindergarten until cancer cut her life short in 1968.

Sam turned the tape player off, realizing it was past midnight. He felt worn out, partly explained by the fact it was the end of an extraordinarily intense day. Walking to the bedroom, Sam tried to convince himself to block out any thoughts other than the matters immediately at hand, like changing his clothes, brushing his teeth and taking his pills, but the tension kept creeping up the back of his spine, into his shoulders and neck , settling painfully into the base of his skull. His arms and back began to itch mercilessly. Sam knew there would be no sleep for him in this state. He'd either have to go back to work, or....

Sitting in a comfortable chair in one corner of the darkened bedroom, Sam summoned one of the few benign memories from his trove of remembrances. It took him back more than 40 years, when, after the War, Sam had finished his undergraduate degree and used the GI Bill to go to law school. He had been married for only a year at graduation, and his job at the downtown law firm hinged on passing the state bar exam.

The pressure was unbearable. Sam had gotten himself into such a state while preparing for the two-day test that he couldn't sleep, and had broken out in huge boils and hives all along his arms and legs. Gloria tried to calm him down, but nothing seemed to work. Finally, in an act of desperation, Gloria told Sam's father about the situation.

Sam was not especially close to his father, who was born in Ireland and didn't subscribe to a "close and cuddly" father-son relationship. But Gloria didn't know where else to turn, and was really worried about her husband's ability to deal with the strain. Sam's father called that night, and in characteristic fashion, and totally devoid of tact, he addressed his son's problem head on:

"Gloria tells me you're having a tough time...can't sleep, irritable, hives. You know, this isn't the first time. You probably don't remember, but before you were supposed to go to Boy Scout camp when you were 10, or 11—I don't remember exactly when. You were a mess. We yelled, and threatened, but you just got worse. So, against my better judgment, your mother—of blessed memory—insisted we let you off the hook and told you that you didn't have to go. Almost immediately, you felt better."

Sam's annoyance was palpable. "Thanks a lot. Are you telling me that I don't have to take the bar exam? And that will make the hives go away? I can't run away from this one. I've got a job at a law firm that goes away if I fail. We've got loans to pay and an apartment to carry. You can't take me off the hook, 'against your better judgment' or not."

Sam's father continued: "I'm not telling you to run away—far from it. Let me finish the story. One day later, after you were told that you didn't have to go to camp, you came to your mother and told her that you *wanted* to go. You had thought about it, there was nothing to be afraid of, and you were ready. So I drove you up to New Hampshire, two days late, and you spent the entire summer without a day's homesickness. We learned a lot about you then, son." The old man's voice was firm, but warm.

Knowing that Sam was listening carefully, remembering the episode from the perspective of the 10- or 11-year-old he then was, his father delivered the one bit of advice that would stick with Sam through over 30 years of battle in one of the world's most intense and difficult professions. "Sam—you're smart and capable but sometimes you think too much. There are times when you just have to suck it up and do something—*anything*—even if you're not sure what. The worst thing is inertia, because nothing good happens from doing nothing. So here's my advice—pour yourself a stiff drink and go make love to your beautiful wife. This thing's a piece of cake."

With his father's words resonating in his head, Sam slid into bed and reached out, gently, to touch his wife. As if she had, indeed, been waiting for him all this time, Gloria turned and shimmied toward him, moving her body so close Sam could feel her breasts and hips through her nightgown. She reached an arm around his shoulder and her kiss was soft and warm.

"I love you," she whispered in between kisses, "so much."

"Me too," answered Sam, never meaning it more than at that moment.

CHAPTER 8

Sam blinked several times, and rubbed his eyes. *Could it really be 7:05?* Had he slept through the alarm? With the comforting sound of Gloria's light snoring behind him, Sam carefully eased out of bed and tiptoed to the bathroom. He had slept well for the first time in a long time, and even though he knew his lateness would mean a nasty drive to work, he smiled thinking about their lovemaking the night before.

In the shower, Sam applied shaving cream to his dripping face and looked in the supposedly fog-free mirror he'd been given as a birthday present a few years back by his son. Rarely did he use the mirror that he didn't think of how odd a gift it was. Jeffrey, the president of a large, prestigious arm of the World Bank, was a sophisticated and well traveled international executive. What did it mean that he would buy his father, for his 65th birthday, a $50 Sharper Image mirror?

Sam's thoughts continued to drift to his only child and the difficult relationship between them, when a synaptic charge jolted him. "Shit," he said aloud. "I never called Tokyo."

He quickly finished his ablutions, wrapped himself in a towel and padded into the den. He turned on his market data screens while dialing the London office. When Jon Lavendar finally answered the call, Sam realized that he had literally been holding his breath.

Lavendar confirmed what the computer screens reflected—it had been a very difficult, and costly, overnight session. The dollar had declined another percent, translating into yet another eight-figure loss for Sam's trading unit.

"What happened?" Sam bawled into the phone.

Lavendar's voice reflected vast tension. "The Japanese Banks were big sellers, probably orders from the exporters. Rumor has it they're also working big stop losses around these levels, and if the market breaks through, we'll go much lower. I've been on the phone for the past 20 minutes with Mike T, and we've cut our position by another 100 million."

"Jesus H. Christ. Why didn't anyone call me?"

There was silence on the other end of the phone.

Sam tapped the receiver on the edge of his desk, now wet from his dripping hair. "Did you hear me?"

Jon cleared his throat and replied, in a whisper, "I thought it would be a good idea to give you a break. Pam told me you were having a very difficult time yesterday."

This time, Sam slammed the phone on the desk, making a large dent in the wood and breaking off a two inch piece of plastic from the phone.

"You thought wrong, goddamn it. I gave explicit instructions about how to handle this and when I need to be called. You don't have discretion to change those plans and sure-as-hell Pam doesn't. Damn it!"

Lavendar cupped his hand over the phone. "I'm on the trading floor, Sam. If you want to continue this, let me go into my office."

Sam plopped into his chair, all the positive feelings from his good night completely spent. " Never mind—what's done is done. I'll check in with Mike from the car, and I'll call you from the office. I've got a stop to make first."

Sam hung up, checked the prices again, and walked into his dressing room. He could see that the lights in the bedroom had been turned on and the bed made. He detected the sweet and inviting smell of brewing coffee from the kitchen.

Sam felt bad that his tirade had most likely woken Gloria, and hoped he hadn't upset her. He dressed quickly and hopped downstairs. Gloria was sitting in her bathrobe at the kitchen counter, cradling her favorite mug and looking at the front page of the paper.

Sam kissed the back of her neck and said, "That was great, last night. I slept like a rock."

Gloria turned and kissed Sam. "So did I. What was the yelling about?"

"Sorry, honey. Hope I didn't wake you. We're just losing more money, that's all. It's simply...ah, it's nothing serious.

'I'm going to put some coffee in a travel cup and get going. I'm planning on visiting Anton on my way in, and I'll call you when I get to the office." He added, almost as an afterthought, "Don't forget to take your blood pressure pills."

Gloria banged her mug on the counter and turned her back to him, her shoulders hunched defensively

"Honey?"

She pushed her chair back and walked away from him. "Damn it, Sam. I can take care of myself."

He watched her climb the stairs, and waited for her to get out of earshot before he hissed "Shit." He left the house lethargically, trying to shake the deep feeling in his bones that this had the potential to be another truly awful day.

Sam called Mike on his mobile phone and got a brief update, and asked that a conference call be arranged among the Firm's key traders and economists, globally, for that morning. He then checked his voicemail.

The first two calls weren't important, and Sam skipped over them summarily. The third, however, was from Stanley. *This won't be pretty.*

"Sam, I'm on my way to Beijing, but I didn't want to wait to express my serious disappointment with the way you are handling the situation. I can't let you blackmail the organization and hold up our business this way. You know I support you, but I've got my limits. You had better work this out before I get back. Otherwise, and I mean this, I'll work it out for you—and probably without you."

Sam clicked the off button on his phone and realized he was trailing the green station wagon much too closely. A hollow feeling in his stomach grew as Sam played out the implications of Stanley's threat. *Maybe it all ends here. Maybe it should.*

Sam shook off the defeatism. He knew that neither Stanley nor anyone else on the Management Committee could really afford to piss him off right now. Sam had enough money to comfortably leave his job for the contractually required three-month garden leave period before setting up somewhere else, and there were plenty of other places around the Street which would be happy to have him, even at his age. Not that Sam would ever want to work anyplace else, but Stanley didn't know that.

In the end, on Wall Street, it all came down to money. Today's certain money always took precedence over tomorrow's maybe money. How many times had Sam railed at the narrow-sightedness of management, over-paying current producers because they had made a lot of money now? How often had Sam, along with a few of his senior colleagues, criticized others for refusing to make the long-range decisions because they conflicted with immediate profitability? And yet, wasn't he doing the exact same thing now—claiming that an exigency excused him from making the appropriate, albeit hard, forward-thinking business decision?

But this is different, thought Sam, almost as if he needed to convince himself. He had to protect Mike T from these predators. What good was all of the power and wealth he'd accumulated over these decades if he couldn't make good on the promise he'd made to his Army buddy on his death bed? Furthermore, Sam knew he owed Mike T a lot. In fact, most of his recent success at GSC was as much a result of Mike's brilliant trading instincts as it was Sam's business building abilities. Mike knew it too. In very un-Wall Street-like behavior, he was happy playing second fiddle to Sam so long as he was protected from the in-your-face antics of those who just didn't understand Mike's need to be left alone to do his work.

Sam logged in to his voicemail again to respond to his boss's message.

"Stanley, this is Sam. I hope your trip is going well. As you know, we've got a bit of a messy currency situation here, which unfortunately coincides with the Management Committee's business planning directives. I've always had trouble thinking and chewing gum at the same time, so please forgive me if I can only deal with one crisis now. I can't risk alienating my team now, when I need all their energies focused on risk mitigation and liquidity. We're all working 20-hour days, and there's a lot of money at stake. I'll continue to work with Todd, but really think this is not the time to talk about letting people go. Word gets out. People lose their focus. Thanks for your consideration, and I'll see you in a few days."

The traffic began to slow considerably as Sam approached the Henry Hudson Bridge to Manhattan. As he inched forward, he began to re-visit the many nooks and crannies of his career, and his relationship with Mike, which directly impacted his ascendancy at the firm, and the material wealth that had followed at a vastly accelerated pace.

Almost two decades earlier, Sam had asked for, and received, a transfer from his cushy job as Assistant General Counsel to a mid-level sales position on a newly formed currency trading business.. He worked his way up through the ranks and, within a few years, rose to run the New York-based effort. Not innately the risk taker, Sam fashioned his business as a sales-oriented one, and that strategy proved successful in increasing the firm's notoriety and allowing GSC to increase its stature and prominence.

During this same period, a similar effort was being undertaken in London, headed by David Morton. Unlike Sam, Morton had a trading background, and not surprisingly, his strategy stressed trading and risk-taking activity while eschewing client relationships.

Their boss was Andrew Smithson, who purposely kept the New York and London operations separate on the "Petrie dish" theory then in vogue on Wall Street. The idea was to allow each location to develop on its own, a function of its unique environment and personnel, without intervention. At just the right time, the boss—Smithson—would select the best attributes from one dish and transplant them to the other, with the hope that independence would be preserved while at the same time providing for the transmission of best practices from one group to the next.

Of course, maintaining a business structure such as this required a master scientist, or benevolent dictator, to determine which attributes to commingle, and to provide order when the needs and interests of one location spilled over to the other. For example, because running two completely separate trading books is inefficient and risky, London and New York would have to cooperate in sharing limits and dealing with customers who desired to trade in both time zones. If independence was stressed, then coordination and cooperation on matters such as these could only occur if a "supreme being" insisted on it.

The problem was, the "supreme being"—Smithson—wanted to become even more supreme, and being responsible for managing the many contentious issues that came up was, as he would complain, "de-leveraging". Thus, to move up the ladder, Smithson finally conceded that a global head of the business had to be appointed.

Anyone capable of dreaming up the Petrie dish approach would not simply choose one person, and anoint him worldwide head of foreign exchange. No, the process would have to be much more market-oriented and much more competitive. Consequently, Sam and Morton were told, publicly, that they would co-run the business globally, and would be required to spend at least four successive months in the other location, two with their colleague in attendance, and two alone, to ensure truly global management. Privately, however, each of them was told that the intent was to choose one leader by the end of a year. And of course, what ensued was an epic battle of will, skill, scheming, plotting and generally carnivorous activity.

Sam could not have won the battle without Mike T. As the grand strategy unfolded, Smithson warned Sam that the New York business was incomplete without a world-class trading effort, and that he should learn from David Morton's business plan and management style. Of course, Morton was comparably warned that his lack of client friendly activity threatened his ability to rise in the organization, but Sam didn't know that (much as David had no idea of the challenge laid out to Sam).

Years later, Sam would muse at the diabolically clever and manipulative game Smithson had played, pitting his lieutenants against each other with a Darwinian twist. But at the time, all Sam felt was the trepidation that set in after his conversation with Smithson, wondering how he would develop the trading side of the business quickly enough to establish his own credibility. He knew he didn't have the skills to do it himself, and reviewed every trader in his group hoping for a savior.

Mike Tillingham jumped right out at him. He had progressed so quickly since Sam brought him on board two years earlier that he was running his own "book," a mini-business where risk was apportioned and gains and losses measured daily. Mike required little supervision and had his father's strong nerves and unflappable self-confidence. More importantly, he had tremendous trading instincts and a mind that handled numbers and mathematical relationships quickly and unerringly.

After several private meetings with Mike, Sam became convinced that he was his only hope in the survival contest Smithson had laid out. Deciding upon Mike would turn out to be the easy part, Sam recalled. Convincing Smithson that Mike should be promoted would be much more difficult.

First, Smithson accused Sam of being lazy by even considering such a junior person for the job. "It's an admission of your own lack of ability, and your management screw-ups by not having an experienced person on the desk already," yelled Smithson when Sam first let him know that he wanted to advance Mike.

Then, Smithson insisted that David Morton interview Mike T, since "Morton's done an excellent job with his traders, and has shown his ability to train, grow and promote them." Sam knew that Morton would be highly critical of Mike if he thought he was any good, not wanting Sam to improve his own standing in Smithson's eyes. Sam winced in remembering the conversation with his boss when he told him this, and how

Smithson had completely blown his top and thrown Sam out of his office. Smithson didn't like hearing that his laboratory experiment had structural flaws.

As it turned out, Morton liked Mike, a lot. Sam was sure that it meant Morton thought Mike was a loser, and it caused him a few sleepless nights, but he had no other option and, in the end, Smithson approved the promotion.

Mike's first month was terrific. He restructured the risk reports, made changes to desk responsibilities, and worked out a course of dealing with the sales team, particularly Betsy, which improved upon much that Sam had originally established. He traveled extensively to the trading offices in London and Tokyo, endearing himself to traders and salespeople alike.

With the addition of Mike, Sam felt well armed in the foreign exchange wars. The markets were supportive, and the trading profits grew to record levels in the New York effort. While London's trading accounts benefited as well, Morton had not hired a sales head to compare with the New York team, and Sam had the growing sense of moving out ahead.

As the unusually hot summer progressed, the trading business in New York was functioning with premium efficiency. The desk had over a billion dollars' worth of nominal positions in a variety of European currencies. The bet was that the central banks of the weaker economies in Europe, such as those in Italy, Spain and Portugal, would either intervene directly in the markets or modify their monetary policies in order to keep their currencies within the European Monetary System bands. The positions were expressed in a variety of ways, including currency forwards and options, leveraged bond trades, and equity index arbitrages.

Sam remembered a quiet moment with Gloria one evening while all this was happening, telling her how delighted

Smithson had seemed with the success of his group, and the sophistication of the effort. He specifically recalled his wife's surprise when Sam told her that Smithson had asked him to make a presentation about the currency business before the combined Management Committee and Board of Directors meeting on the Monday after Labor Day.

At first, Sam was thrilled with the assignment. Smithson didn't ask David Morton to do it, or to share in the presentation. Certainly, the boss wouldn't have asked Sam to represent the business if he were about to name Morton its global head in the next month. He spent the better part of the day feeling satisfied. He walked out to the desk any number of times, put his hand on Mike's shoulder, and complimented him and the trading team on their strategies. He tried to think of an excuse to call Morton, to see if he knew that Smithson had nodded in his direction, but caught himself. There will be plenty of time to gloat, thought Sam.

As he started sketching out the nature of the presentation, though, Sam began getting nervous. The desk had taken on a lot of risk, and the markets were notoriously fickle. *Do I really want to attract firm wide attention to what we are doing, now? What if the market turns against us?* He could just as easily be a goat as a hero.

Should I cut back the risk? That would be prudent if, indeed, the global job was in the bag. But if Smithson hadn't firmly made his decision, and if Sam showed a lack of fortitude now, it might embarrass Smithson in front of his peers and quash Sam's chance of succeeding.

Sam called Mike into his office, and shut the door. Mike had only been running the desk for a short while, but had settled in so seamlessly that Sam felt no discomfort in getting frank with him. "Mike, are you OK with the positions we've got on?"

"Huh? What's going on? Do you know something I don't? We've talked about putting this structure on for a couple of weeks now. Yeah, I like it. So do the guys in London. They've got almost double the position we have, although it's in a more direct form. I figure we've got as much upside as we can get, at a fair risk level, because we've used bonds and equities to take the risk. Unless the central banks decide to devalue, or impose trading restrictions, they have to intervene or change the rate structure. They have to. Sam, I realize this is an important time for you. Are you getting cold feet?"

Sam cleared his throat, and responded without looking Mike in the eye. "Not really. I mean, I agree intellectually with the direction we're taking, and I think you've done a great job in putting it all together. I'm just anxious about the timing. Smithson asked me to make this presentation to the Board and I guess I'm just re-thinking our risk in light of the attention it will bring to me...I mean to our business."

Sam squirmed in his seat, glanced out through his interior window to the trading floor, where he noticed several of the traders looking back at him and Mike. Certainly, they were wondering what the two senior men were talking about.

Mike moved to the edge of his chair, saying, "That's great. You get to do the command performance, not Morton. Sounds like you're in, he's out. So what's the problem? You should be feeling good right now, so why do you look like crap?"

"Two reasons. One: I don't want the attention. I like it better when the Management Committee is only looking at the bottom line. Two: I'm superstitious. I can't afford to screw up. So, what should I do? If we cut the risk, I look like a wimp and Morton gets the job. If I hang in there, and the market moves against us, I'm a jerk and won't get the job." Sam's face had bloomed to a bright, rose-colored red, and he slammed his hand down on the desk. "Goddamn it!"

Mike got up from his chair, stuck his head outside the office door and said something to Sam's assistant. He turned back to his boss, and said, "Relax. It's not a problem. I've asked Pam to get you a Diet Coke and two Advil—that's what you do when you get uptight, right? So just hang in there. The way I see it, we've got to stay in these positions. If the market deteriorates, Morton's screwed too. So, for that matter, is Smithson. We both know that 'shit happens', especially at the worst possible times. It's always a bad time to lose money, but you can't make money without losing it. Don't you think that when you're global head of FX this won't come up all the time? And when you do lose some dough, the bankers are going to accuse you of 'speculation' and treat you like you're dirt. It's just like baseball. Even the best batters strike out, and those that get it right only 30 percent of the time get into the goddamn Hall of Fame. You've got to grow a thick skin, and enjoy the attention."

Pam entered with the drugs, and Sam sighed heavily as he washed down the pills with the soda. He felt ashamed, and uncomfortable. "You're right. I'd be fine if it wasn't for this damned presentation. It just doesn't feel right.--that bastard!"

***

Sitting in his car, stuck in rush hour traffic, many years later, Sam was still able to remember his emotions, recollect his thoughts and recall the distinct images of these scenes with great clarity. It was like he had stored them in his mind, for review at a later date when he would be capable of more objective analysis.

It seemed so clear to him, now. Smithson had asked Sam to make the presentation *not* because he had decided to hand him the prize. No, it was yet another test, another experiment, to determine whether Sam was made of the right stuff to run the business. Would he wilt under the pressure of being microscopically observed by the senior echelons of the firm? Did he have the courage of his convictions, and faith in the people that he hired, to stick with the battle plan?

Mike had picked up on that, intuitively. He also knew that Sam wasn't naturally built in a way for this to be easy. Thinking back, Sam recognized just how important that conversation with Mike had been, and how crucial a role Mike would play in the next few days.

The presentation went extremely well, Sam thought. He had thoroughly researched the history of the business, and put together a focused and analytically sophisticated analysis of the risks and rewards of the Firms' involvement in currency trading. Bob Argent, the Chairman, had sent Sam a congratulatory voicemail that afternoon, and even Smithson poked his head in his office the following day with a "Good job" nod.

Still, the uneasiness persisted. Sam toyed with a variety of strategies that would reduce the risk of a calamitous market move, but discarded each one because the costs would be high, and the effort transparent. Sam felt he couldn't show a lack of *cohones* at this stage of the game.

Two days later, at 4 a.m., Mike woke Sam at home with an urgent phone call. "I just got a call from a guy I trade with at Barings. He told me that there's a buzz on the street, which he's also hearing inside the Bank of England, that the Italians are pressing for devaluation. The forwards are moving out, big time, on it. The guys on our London desk have heard it, too. Of course, those pricks didn't call me—I had to hear it from a competitor."

Sam put Mike on hold while he walked out of the bedroom as Gloria groaned and turned over. He picked up the call in his study, where his slowly focusing eyes reviewed a few computer pages that confirmed Mike's news. "Shit. Shit. I can see the forwards, and it's bad. How are the bonds doing?"

"Nothing in those markets, really. Well, a bit in the bonds, but nothing like the currencies. Either the guys in those markets don't believe the stories, or they're too slow or stupid to figure it out, which is unlikely. I think we got ourselves a real, live bad-assed rumor here, and because there are some big positions on, people are freaking a bit." Mike's voice was remarkably clear and paced for this kind of event, at this time of day, Sam remembered. That alone took the edge off the situation.

"Is Morton lightening up? Are we?" shot back Sam.

"Yes and no," responded Mike. "Yes, those pussies in London have taken off about a quarter of their trades, and have stop losses on another quarter nearby. That I can get off of the computer, but of course no one told anyone in New York that they were doing it. And no, we still have the same sized position we had on last night. There's a change in our risk-of-loss, of course, because volatility has changed and so has our delta equivalent position, but we've taken nothing off. We did have stops that didn't get triggered, and I just yanked them. That's the reason for the call. Sorry to wake you."

"Wait. Are you in office?"

"Yup. I got here about 15 minutes ago."

" I'll be there in about an hour. Don't you think we should reduce our exposure at this point? Isn't devaluation about the worst thing that could happen? And what do you mean you pulled the stops? You can't do that on your own. We've got to have some stops in place with a position this size. It's required procedure." Sam had shifted to a portable phone at this point, and was pulling his clothes together as quietly as he could.

"I know that, and that's why I called. I'm sure these rumors are crap. It makes no sense. The Italians are the last ones, politically, who can demand devaluation. The Antonelli government has pushed monetary union as its number one priority. To insist on devaluation now would be humiliating. It's not going to happen. Trust me. I'm actually thinking we should add to the position."

"Damn it, I knew you were going to say that. Do me a favor. Don't do anything until I get there, unless you feel you have to bail out a bit. But don't buy more, please. Now that you're in the office, I guess we don't need standing stop loss orders, but keep on top of what the London desk is doing. I'll be there in a little bit...I'm leaving now." Sam disconnected the call, brushed his teeth, put on his clothes and rushed out of the bathroom toward the garage. He could hear a faint "Bye, honey" from Gloria as the door closed behind him.

The decisions made in the next two hours were the ones that really forged the steepest upward slope of Sam's career. Like a few other decisions he had made in the past (enlisting in the Army, proposing marriage to Gloria, leaving the law firm for GSC, promoting Mike), Sam couldn't remember why, exactly, he had chosen a particular course. In each case, something more than logic or reason had pushed him over the edge in an uncertain environment. Whatever the force was, as indescribable as it was, Sam was grateful for it, for each time he relied on that instinct, it led him to a successful result.

As the London trading unit, and many others in the market, panicked, Mike did indeed add to the desk's risk by buying out-of-the money Lira call options against the deutschemark. If devaluation occurred, Mike would lose money but only to the extent of the premium paid for the options. If devaluation didn't occur, and the exchange rates moved back to their appropriate spots within the EMS band, the good guys would make a bundle, a much bigger bundle than before the rumors began.

Smithson stopped by the trading desk at around 8:00 that morning, fully briefed on the turmoil in the market and the disparate reactions of his New York and London desks. He asked Mike to quantify the aggregate size of the position, its mark-to-market value, and its risk values, and then walked into Sam's office, where Sam was just finishing a call.

"Well, that's a gutsy move. Did you clear it with the risk police?" asked Smithson, his steely blue eyes fixed straight at Sam.

"I just got off the phone with them. I think I passed the interrogation. Actually, we're only a bit above our risk limits with the new options on, because our portfolio is nicely diversified."

Sam leaned forward on the edge of his chair—the several cups of coffee having their intended effect—and continued with complete confidence: "This strikes me as a classic fake-out. The Italians have got no basis to request a revaluation. I've been on the phones for two straight hours talking to public and private sector folks in Europe and no one thinks this is for real. And the bond and stock markets don't either. I'm comfortable. Aren't you? How come Morton is freaking out? I called him a while ago, but he hasn't returned it yet."

Smithson slowly turned and headed out the door, responding over his shoulder "Well, I suspect he's a bit busy. I guess my portfolio is diversified, too, between you and Morton. Stay on top of this. I've already gotten two calls from the chairman, demanding to know why New York is buying when London is selling. Let me know right away if anything changes. "

Sam thought he detected a smile when Smithson left the office. He wondered what his boss and Mike talked about, and intercom'd Mike to ask him.

"He wanted to know the size of the position, its mark-to-market, you know, the statistical stuff. Then he asked me why I was so convinced the rumors were bullshit." Mike turned to face Sam through the plate glass window separating the trading floor from Sam's office.

"Yeah, so what did you say?"

Mike waved away a junior trader who had yelled a price level to him from an adjoining desk. "I said that you were so completely on top of the situation, and had made such a compelling point, that I couldn't argue with it. I also told him that you thought this was an incredibly attractive time to put more on, when everyone else was freaking out. And we did."

Sam wasn't expecting this kind of a response, and at first thought Mike was kidding him. But a close look at Mike's face confirmed that Mike had just done Sam a real, solid kindness. "Thanks, man. I really appreciate it."

"It's nothing you haven't done for me already." Mike nodded to his boss, lit up a Marlboro, and yelled something to his assistant trader while picking up another phone.

***

"Honk. Honk. Honk."

Getting his eyes to focus, Sam realized he had fallen several car lengths behind as he exited the highway toward Columbia Presbyterian Hospital, and dialed Mike on his cell phone.

"It's Sam. How's it going?"

"Better. I think we're stabilizing. You know we took some risk off overnight."

"Yeah, I spoke to Lavendar. I've should be on the desk in an hour or so. Anything else I should know?"

Mike turned to the trading turret, his back to Sam's office and the disquieting figure that'd been standing there, almost motionless, for the past half-hour. "Not really, other than that Todd creep who's been camped outside your office door all morning. Maybe you should come in the back way?"

Sam smiled at the thought of sneaking in the office, maybe even in disguise, to avoid Todd. "It wouldn't help. He's like a bad dream—sooner or later, it finds you."

CHAPTER 9

Rebecca was getting angrier by the minute. Not only had she skipped her regular swim and work-out session at the gym to suit her father's schedule, but she'd also abandoned her comfort uniform of jeans and t-shirt for more respectable attire. And still, he kept her waiting. She expected some delay—he was a busy man with an unpredictable schedule—but 45 minutes was more than rude, it was an insult. And that's just how Rebecca was taking it.

With a huff, Rebecca bounded from her seat in the opulent waiting room toward the matronly receptionist and asked her, for the third time, to remind Mr. Hart's assistant that she was waiting. And, she added, "Tell Gina that if he can't see me right now, I'm leaving."

The receptionist did as she was asked. "Evangeline will be right out," she reported.

As so she was. Evangeline DeCosta had been Jeffrey Hart's executive assistant since he had joined the Bank over a decade ago. She was a tall, dark and elegant Brazilian woman in her late thirties, and Rebecca wondered whether her relationship with Jeffrey was purely a business one. Nonetheless, her long service exposed her to many of the family's trials and tribulations, and over the years Gina made numerous attempts to calm the troubled waters between father and daughter, with uneven success. Rebecca liked her enough on a personal level, but it was abundantly clear where her loyalties lay.

Gina grabbed Rebecca's hands and offered her both cheeks. "You look wonderful. I love your hair that way. Come, he's almost ready. It's been a crazy day."

Rebecca was led into the private office suite her father occupied as the President of the Inter American Development Bank. Gina left her after a few rounds of social niceties to poke her head into Jeffrey's office and see if the coast was clear. Rebecca used the time to recall how Charley, the first time they met, had characterized the IADB as a "pathologically inept and politically malevolent" organization. While Charley swore at the time he had no idea that Rebecca and Jeffrey were related, she wasn't convinced that he hadn't read her perceptively and fashioned the perfect pickup line.

Gina emerged from Jeffrey's office carrying several bound documents, which she placed on her desk. She looked at her watch and said, apologetically, "He's got a meeting at the World Bank in 20 minutes, which means he has to leave here in 10. I'm sorry about that. Will that be enough time?"

Rebecca felt the heat rising to her face. She glared past Gina and strode into her father's office, ready to let him have it. She could hear the door shut behind her.

"Am I getting you at a bad time?" she asked contemptuously, throwing herself into an upholstered chair across from her father's overflowing desk.

Jeffrey looked over his reading glass at Rebecca with an expression that suggested he didn't know what she was talking about. "You know things get busy during the afternoon."

"Dad, you were the one that suggested we get together today. And that was for almost an hour ago."

Jeffrey leaned forward and got that "don't screw around with me" look she had seen so many times in the past. "Sorry. I just wanted to catch up. What's going on?"

Rebecca looked down at her feet, trying to remember the

reasons why she ignored Charley's advice and agreed to meet with her father. None of them seemed sound just then.

"Nothing's going on. I've taken a leave of absence at Georgetown and I'm going to get a full-time job. That's it."

"Didn't you just start school again?"

He hasn't a clue. "I've been taking courses for almost a year, ever since I got back. I'm having trouble figuring out what a Masters degree in International Affairs is going to do for me. I think it would be better to get some job experience—make some money, you know."

"What kind of job are *you* going to get?" asked Jeffrey in a manner that Rebecca had every right to take as patronizing.

"You know I've been working three afternoons a week at GSC's Washington office. A full-time position has opened up, and I'm going to take it."

Jeffrey shrugged. "C'mon. I thought we agreed that, after the Peace Corps debacle, you'd buckle down, clean up your act and get serious. You swore up and down that you wanted to go back to school, build up your credentials and so on. Now you're saying to want to quit and work for an investment bank? You've got to stick with things for a while, Rebecca. You're an adult now...you can't keep swinging from limb to limb all your life."

She was hoping her father would understand her frustration with school and perhaps even offer to help her find the right job. But, typically, he was finding fault with what she did and making it personal.

"I think the easy way out is to stay in school, father. For me, that's swinging in the air with nowhere to go. Grandpa agrees that a real job would help me feel more grounded, and I'd move on from there. That makes sense to me. I'm ready."

Jeffrey's face reddened. "Oh, so is that what *he* says? I

guess I need to speak to your grandfather about his sticking his nose into places where…The bottom line is that *I* think he's wrong. You've started something—getting your masters—and you should finish it. The additional growing up time will be important, too."

Rebecca, who had been tapping her right foot in an attempt to hold back the tears, exploded. "I should have known this was a mistake. Like always, you've got nothing but criticism. I never should have come."

She grabbed her pocketbook in a huff, swung it over her shoulder and steamed toward the door. Jeffrey stood in his place and said, half-heartedly, "'Becca. Sit down. Can't we have an adult conversation?"

Rebecca pivoted and glared at her father. She raised her right fist and ever so slightly began extending her middle finger at him. As the look of shock overtook her father's face, Rebecca said "Is this *adult* enough for you?" Then she left, almost banging into Gina, who was poised to knock on Jeffrey's door to get him moving for his next appointment.

Two hours later, Rebecca blew past Charley into his studio apartment, dripping wet and steaming mad. She chucked a bulging plastic bag hard against a worn and filthy Strato-Lounger at the foot of the bed. The thud that resulted made less of an impact than the water damage as the bag exploded and the bathing suit it held bounced off the chair onto Charley's pillows.

Charley, all 78 inches of him, stood at the doorway, paralyzed with fear. "Jesus! What did I do?"

Rebecca made no attempt to clean up her mess. She paced the perimeter of the small apartment twice before regaining the composure to speak. "That son of a bitch."

Charley seemed relieved to be out of the line of Rebecca's fire, and moved in, carefully. "Who?"

Rebecca stopped suddenly and glared at Charley. She was stunned that a 45-minute swim at the Y and an intense speed walk to Charley's apartment hadn't burned off at least some of her anger. But her relationship with Jeffrey had a cumulative effect, setting off intense bursts of anger and a mélange of other emotions.

Charley closed the apartment door with a flick of his hip as he placed both hands on top of his head. Rebecca sat on the floor with her legs folded underneath her. It was only after Charley came around behind her, and massaged her neck for several minutes, that she spoke.

"He kept me waiting for almost an hour, like I was a goddamned supplicant, waiting for an audience. And then he criticized me the whole time I was there. *He* busted *my* chops. What a joke."

Charley dug in a little deeper, encouraged by Rebecca's soft moans. "Why'd you go in the first place? You knew he'd still be pissed off about AZTEC."

Rebecca didn't like being confronted with such a simple and accurate example of her naiveté. She leaned forward, away from Charley's hands, and stood up slowly. She thought to herself, in response: *Because he's my father and I need his approval.* But those words didn't make it to the surface—not just because she didn't want Charley to hear them, but because she didn't want to acknowledge how true the statement was.

"I assumed he'd gotten over it. What an arrogant, selfish jerk he is."

Charley snickered and remained on his knees. "If it makes you feel any better, he's still taking a ton of crap about the Bank's policies on third world debt. There's a big article in today's *Post* about Congressional hearings on the Brazilian loans."

"If he can't take the heat…"

Charley got up on one knee. "Huh?"

Rebecca repositioned herself, sitting at the edge of the bed. "When I was a kid and my parents were fighting in front of me—which was always—things would really get nasty. Eventually, my mother would wither under one of his lawyerly barrages and start to cry…a sickening, drunken cry. He'd get right up in her face and quoting Harry Truman, of all people, he'd scream, 'If you can't take the heat, get the hell out the kitchen,' which would really flip her out and send her storming from the room. He'd look at me with this obnoxious, self-satisfied smirk on his face and walk into his study, leaving me alone to think about that phrase. It's almost satisfying to know that he's wilting under the pressure. I wished I had been together enough to use that line against him today."

Charley moved his hands and began caressing her hair. "Re-lax. Take a deep breath. I'm not going to say I told you so…but I did, didn't I?" Rebecca responded by elbowing him in the chest.

"Arrggh. I guess I deserved that. You didn't hit your father, did you?"

Rebecca allowed herself a smile, finally. "No, but I did give him the finger."

"Now, that's telling him!" Anticipating another elbow, Charley arched his back, moving his chest out of harm's way.

Instead, Rebecca reached back and tenderly touched his hands. "My father has this incredible ability to find my weak spots. And he seems to enjoy it. Am I that terrible?"

Charley grabbed Rebecca by the shoulders and turned her toward him. He gently wiped the tears from her eyes with his forefinger and kissed her lips delicately. "It's not you. It's him. From what you've told me, he's got some serious problems with his relationship with his own father and a horribly failed marriage. You're the gem in the family, 'Becca; a beautiful, kind and caring jewel. Don't ever blame yourself for this."

Rebecca threw her arms around Charley's neck and bit his ear playfully. She whispered, "Make love to me."

He didn't need to be asked twice.

***

The sound of the running shower woke Rebecca up. The clock registered 6:44 and she wondered why Charley would be up so early.

Then she remembered. Today was the day he had been planning for several weeks. Rebecca had kept her options open, not really wanting to go and also not wanting to say so to Charley. But after last night, and how supportive he was to her, she couldn't turn away now. She'd have to go to the rally, no matter how inane she thought things like that were.

Rebecca dressed and made coffee. She tried to make small talk at the table but it was clear Charley was preoccupied with the events ahead of him. They held hands walking to the bus station and for most of the 20 minute ride to the Washington Mall.

The weather wouldn't help. From the staging area at 15th Street, just south of Constitution Avenue and on the outskirts of the Mall, Rebecca could see the various camps of protesters moving about nervously as they donned waterproofed jackets, removed umbrellas from backpacks and otherwise made adjustments for the unexpected rain showers. The reporter from CNN had been promised attendance of 5,000 by the protest organizers, who hoped that such a sizeable group would be too large to resist. It was a stretch under the best of circumstances, but now, with the rain, a turnout of half that number would be welcome.

The permit from the District of Columbia police allowed the group to march and assemble between the hours of 10 a.m. and noon, on a route that would take them west on Constitution, then north to the headquarters of the International Monetary Fund on 19th Street and Pennsylvania Avenue. Charley told Rebecca that the protesters had been warned to expect plenty of uniformed and undercover police, given the route's proximity to the White House, and the protesters' reputation for aggressive activity in Europe. He introduced her to Didier Bendit, one of the rally's leaders, while they waited in the drizzle for a critical mass of protesters to arrive.

Didier, a dark, slim and serious-looking man in his late twenties, spoke with a smooth, French accent and looked Rebecca in the eye as he spoke. She would have found him more attractive if not for the ever-present Gauloise which seemed to be attached to his lips. Rebecca had never been able to tolerate cigarette smoke, and she found the cloying smell of French tobacco particularly obnoxious. She didn't try to hide her disdain for Didier's cigarettes, frequently waving away the smoke as they stood together.

Didier told Rebecca that ATAC—"Allied Together against Corruption"—was in the early stages of establishing its base in the United States. He flattered Charley, saying that he and several of his European colleagues had become enthusiastic about working with him, given his intelligence, leadership and dedication to the cause. "I'm also impressed with his choice in women," he said, low enough so that only Rebecca could hear him.

DIVIDED LOYALTIES

Didier made Rebecca uneasy. Maybe it was because he always seemed so calm, so much in control. In contrast to Charley, who was a bundle of energy, moved frenetically and rarely kept still, Didier's motions and words were smooth and seemingly rehearsed.

You never know what someone like that is really thinking, mused Rebecca. *There will always be secrets. Charley shouldn't trust him so much.*

Precisely at 10:30, Didier excused himself and moved to a temporary and rickety stage that had been set up near the entrance to the park. Holding a bullhorn, he called for the small crowd's attention and went through the administrative and logistical details for the demonstration. In a somber tone, he warned the protesters that there would be a lot of policemen—in uniform and undercover—along the way. He concluded with, "Be aware of that when you choose what to say and," as the crowd laughed, "what you *smoke*, in front of people you don't know."

Didier passed the microphone to Charley, who cleared his throat and waited for the crowd to quiet. After a deep breath, he said, "We are here today for one very clear reason. While the U.S., and most of Europe, gets richer and richer, the poorest people of the world get poorer and poorer. Western businesses and governments continue to exploit the under-developed world for their own commercial and political gain. Institutions like the World Bank and Inter-American Development Bank act as fronts for corporate interests in the West, inflicting more pain and suffering on the most helpless of the world's peoples.

"We in ATAC are here to point out these hypocrisies and injustices. We are here to let these governments and phony institutions know that *we* know all about them, the games they play and the lies they tell. We are here, and *we won't ever go away*, until there is a more equitable system put in place to cure poverty, disease and corruption. We are here to make sure the world knows what we know. We are here...and *we won't ever go away!"*

Charley's deep, resonate voice peaked on this last phrase, drawing a huge cheer from the soggy crowd. Rally organizers passed out signs and placards bearing the ATAC emblem adorning anti-globalization slogans while Didier and Charley took their positions in the front of the crowd.

Rebecca felt proud of Charley. She considered that she might be observing a side of him she hadn't seen before--a man who had figured out how to channel his enormous physical and inner strength into a persona people would follow. She walked quickly to catch up with him and Didier as they led the marchers down Constitution Avenue.

Even though the weather kept the numbers down, the protesters were enthusiastic and buoyant striding down one of Washington's main thoroughfares. An ad hoc mixture of cheers and yells had eventually settled down into chant of "we *won't* go away" as they headed toward their destination, a stage set up in front of the IMF headquarters.

Approximately two blocks away, a police barricade stretched across the street. Charley held up his hands to slow the march down, while Didier engaged the police captain in charge of the blockade, arguing that their permit specifically allowed them to proceed to the IMF building.

The policeman took the permit from Didier and walked several yards away, where he called his dispatcher on a two-way radio. A few minutes later, he returned, handing the permit back.

"There's a mistake. This is as far as you can go." About two dozen cops blocked their path, some wearing helmets and holding acrylic shields, and all looking serious.

Charley had now joined Didier, who took a deep drag from his Gauloise and blew the smoke straight overhead. "No, the mistake is yours. The permit is clear; we go to 19th and Pennsylvania. See-- right here," he said, shaking the now soggy document in the policeman's face.

The officer leaned to within an inch of Didier. "Do that again and I'll bust your faggy ass. You're stopping here."

Charley pressed forward, in the direction of the cop, but Didier reached out his hand to restrain him. He turned on his heels and walked to the sidewalk, then up the steps of a brick brownstone on the side of the avenue. Charley and Rebecca followed.

Using the bullhorn, Didier said, "It seems the Washington Police don't want us to go to the IMF, even though our permit allows us to. They probably believe that we will leave. Let me ask you—do you think we should go away now?"

It took a minute or two, but the protesters got the cue and soon the chant of "We won't *ever* go away" began growing like a living organism. The mantra got louder and louder, and when someone got hold of the microphone and added her amplified, screaming voice to the others, the situation took on a concentrated and, in Rebecca's mind, frightening dimension. Charley seemed to sense it too, and he grabbed her hand in an attempt to move to the edge of the street.

The policemen also appeared fidgety, fingering their nightsticks and adjusting their armor. This provoked the crowd even more, which compressed as those in the middle and rear pressed forward.

"Let's go," screamed one voice. "Go through the line."

"Right on," agreed another. "They can't stop us."

"Fuckin' pigs," railed a third.

The throng of protesters moved ahead to within a few feet of the wooden traffic horses set up as barricades. Rebecca grabbed Charley's arm to avoid being swept away, and realized that matters were on the brink of falling apart.

"Craaaccck. Craaaccck."

Rebecca could hear the noise in front of her, near the police—it sounded like glass breaking—but couldn't tell where it came from. There was an odd moment of silence, as if everyone was trying to take in the import of the explosions. Then all hell broke loose.

Tear gas canisters, fired by policemen behind the barricade, signaled a general advance by the armored cops. Rebecca heard the sounds of nightsticks finding human flesh, and cries of pain and surprise, and Charley tried to push her away from the chaos. They had gone only a few steps when she felt Charley's grip on her loosen, and then disappear. She looked back to see him grab at the side of his face, where blood gushed from a vertical gash, before the panicked crowd swept her away.

She was being pushed into the gas, and soon was blinded by it. Rebecca staggered for a few steps, held up the mass of bodies, but then tripped on a curb and fell hard on her side. She tried not to rub her eyes, but the pain was great and her fear of being trampled even greater. After being kicked in the back and legs several times, and not knowing what else to do, Rebecca curled herself into a protective, fetal position against the curb.

Her beating heart almost drowned out the screams and she covered her face and head with her arms. Rebecca's eyes burned almost as much as her throat. Her pants were soaked through, and she was convulsing from the cold.

She cursed Charley for his naïve belief that mass action accomplishes anything, and blamed herself for taking part as a spectator. *Hadn't they learned from Bahia? Nothing happens except good people get hurt.*

She thought about her father, and how angry he was when she was expelled from the Peace Corps. He said her actions were "childish acting out," and "impotent." She hated him at the time for daring to say that to her, but now, curled up like a baby in a filthy gutter, she had to consider that he was right.

Rebecca heard a scuffle nearby and a familiar voice above her. "Get out of the way. Move, goddamn it...'Becca?"

She opened one eye and struggled to see Charley, clearing bodies from his path as he bent down to her. His face was streaked with dirt and blood, and tears were streaming from his swollen eyes. She reached up to put her arms around his neck as he scooped her up from the sidewalk and carried her past a security guard into the lobby of a private office building.

"You OK?" he rasped, putting her down gingerly. "You're shaking like a leaf."

"I'm freezing. Oh...what happened to you?"

Charley reached up to the wound on his face. "I was hit with a gas can—almost knocked me out. I wasn't sure I'd be able to find you."

Rebecca grabbed him and hugged as tightly as she could. She was wet and cold to the bone, but now her trembling was more a function of realizing what might have happened had Charley not come to her rescue.

"You've got to get some dry clothes on. Stay here until things settle down, then you should go back to your place. I'll meet you back there later."

"Where are you going?" asked Rebecca, not wanting to let go.

Charley tried wiping his face with a grimy sleeve. "I've got to get back out and see if I can help. My name's on the permit...there's no getting around that."

"You'll get busted, no way around that either. Shouldn't I call a lawyer?"

It was clear to Rebecca that Charley was laboring as he shrugged his shoulders at the suggestion of another thing he'd have to deal with. "I think Didier said he'd taken care of the legal stuff. I've got to go. Don't go back on the street until it's clear."

Rebecca stretched on tiptoes to give him a kiss. "Please be careful. Please?"

She watched for several minutes until Charley disappeared into the fog of tear gas and bedlam of the mob. Her attention was diverted to a scene playing out right in front of her, where a stocky cop was pushing a pony-tailed young man into the sidewalk with his shield. The man wasn't pushing back, but it was clear that he didn't want to be moved in the direction in which he was headed. That just made the cop push harder, and the man stumbled to the pavement.

A woman of comparable age wearing a yellow rain slicker emerged from the center of the street and reached down to help the man. The cop slashed at her, backhand, with his nightstick, catching her with a glancing blow to the arm. She fell back, more in shock than in pain, and the cop advanced toward her. This gave the young man an opportunity to jump to his feet, and although Rebecca couldn't hear anything, she could see the words form in his mouth: "Leave her alone."

"Wham."

The officer pivoted and brought his weapon squarely down on the man's collarbone.

"Wham."

The second blow smashed his unprotected ribs.

"Whomp."

The third and final stroke was a short one into the solar plexus, and the man crumbled on his side.

To Rebecca's horror, the cop, clearly enraged, turned to find the woman in the slicker. He was about to use the nightstick again against this defenseless target when his legs seemed to give way, causing him to freeze in mid-motion, fall to his knees, and then face first on the ground.

Out of the corner of her eye, Rebecca had seen the reason for the cop's collapse. A slim man in a hooded, brown coat had moved behind the cop and smashed the back of his knees with the side of a discarded police shield. A second hit, to the back of the cop's head, sent him down.

The hooded man called out to make sure the woman was alright before moving to assist the protester so savagely beaten. As he bent over, Rebecca could see most of his face, and recognized him as Didier. With self-assured movements that clearly indicated he'd done this before, Didier first spoke with the man, and commandeered two other marchers to help him up and move him out of the way. He then stood tall, peering around the crowd, presumably looking for other situations where he might be helpful.

Rebecca was stirred by the dramatic scene. She felt bad about her earlier assessment of the organization, the march, and especially Didier. She had allowed her post-Bahia disappointment to make her cynical about the excitement she felt as part of a group of like-minded people, dedicated to an important cause. Remembering the thrill of Mama Baha's workers' crusade, she felt the urge to run to Didier and pledge herself to ATAC's effort.

Three steps out the door, while still on the sidewalk, the street in front of Rebecca began emptying. A District of Columbia paddy wagon, followed immediately by an ambulance, came screeching to stop. About a dozen cops emptied out of the wagon, and before Rebecca could react, she was one of many grabbed, handcuffed and thrown into the back of the vehicle. She sat there for over an hour while more and more protesters were added, providing more than enough time for her re-discovered activist bubble to burst yet again.

***

"I think we may have lucked out here, Sam. I've spoken with the arresting officer, and he recommended that they only hold her overnight anyway. She didn't resist arrest or give them a hard time, so she's good to go."

"Thanks, Duddy. What about the other one, Charley, uh, Robinson, I think? Rebecca made me promise to check up on him too"

Assistant Attorney General Aaron ("Duddy") Feldberg, Sam's moot court partner in law school and a close friend for almost 40 years, let out a short, breathy whistle. "Robertson. Charles Robertson. He's a different kettle of fish."

"What do you know?"

"He didn't need any help from me. He wasn't arrested on site, and voluntarily showed up at the police station to make himself available to the authorities with a high-priced lawyer and a pocket-full of bail money."

Sam got up from behind his desk and slowly paced an arc around his desk defined by the length of the phone cord. "Are we talking about the same guy here? The Charley I know—the one Rebecca has been dating for a while—is a disheveled slob who seems flat broke."

Aaron fingered the two-page fax he'd received a few minute earlier from the FBI. "I can't answer to that, Sam. But the group he seems to be hanging out with, ATAC, is a big player in Europe and been around a long time. They were associated with far left—dare I say Communist—causes in the '70s and '80s and have morphed into an anti-globalization group over the past five years. I think it's fair to say that certain interests in our government are keeping a close eye on them."

"Oh, that's great; just great," Sam whined, watching Mike T heading approach from the trading floor. "Why can't she date a nice, quiet—and rich—Wall Street guy? I've got the perfect one for her right here, standing outside my office."

"That's another imponderable, Sam. You sound busy, and I'm meeting my interns for drinks 15 minutes ago. Don't forget, I'm just a civil servant and get to leave my office after five. Give my love to Gloria."

Sam hung up the phone and motioned Mike into his office. For the next few minutes, Sam pretended he was focused on Mike's battle plans, but really couldn't stop thinking about how he might try, once again, to get his granddaughter and godson interested in each other.

Eventually, Mike stopped talking and stood up to leave the room, snapping Sam out of his preoccupation.

"Where are you going?" Sam asked.

"I need a smoke. And it looks like you need some time," responded Mike. "I'll be back in a few minutes."

"You know, I could use some air. I'll walk out with you."

Sam grabbed his suit coat from behind his door and told Pam he'd be back in 10 minutes. As they passed through the soundproof, glass doors that separated the trading room from elevator lobby, Sam touched Mike gently on the shoulder and said, "By the way, are you around this weekend? Rebecca is going to be in town and she was asking about you."

***

Rebecca got back to her apartment after 6 p.m., and everything hurt. She threw her damp and dirty clothes in a heap on the bathroom floor and donned one of Charley's XXL Georgetown sweatshirts. It had been a really lousy couple of days, and the only thing she cared to think about was a warm bath and a cold brew.

While drawing the water for the former, and screwing off the cap of the latter, Rebecca pushed the blinking red "play" button on her phone message machine. The first call almost made her drop her beer. It was her father—*her father*, not a lackey placing a call on his behalf—calling to apologize for yesterday and hoping they could have lunch or dinner during the week. He signed off by saying, "I love you."

Whoa, thought Rebecca, taking a long, revitalizing sip of Budweiser. *That's got to be a first!*

The second message was from Charley, whom she had seen only for a fleeting moment as she was leaving the police station. He wanted to make sure she knew how sorry he was that she'd gotten mixed up in the day's mess, and was checking to see if she'd gotten home safely. He wasn't sure how long he'd be tied up in post-riot processes, and so she shouldn't wait up for him. If he was running really late, he'd go back to crash in his own apartment so as not to disturb her. He also ended his message with, "Love you, 'Becca."

Damn straight he should be sorry.

The third and last message was from Sam, and she said aloud in a TV announcer's voice, "I hit the trifecta!"

Rebecca grabbed another beer from the refrigerator, pulled the phone over to the tub, and eased herself in. She called her grandfather at the office, the late hour notwithstanding, and wasn't surprised when Pam answered. After a short wait, Sam picked up the phone.

"Are you ok?" he asked. "You had a tough day."

"It's my own fault. I'm a lot better now," Rebecca responded, squeezing the soap bubbles with her toes. "Thanks for getting me out of there."

"You weren't staying long anyway. They may have kept you hanging out for a little while, just to bust your chops, but last time I looked there was still a First Amendment. Want to talk about it?"

Rebecca slipped down so that her chin rested just on the water line. "Not really, sorry."

Sam could hear the exhaustion in her voice. "I understand. Let me make a suggestion. Come stay with us this weekend. I'll send you tickets for the shuttle. Grandma has great seats for Carmen at the Met Saturday night and she said it's your favorite. She really misses you. And, we want to celebrate your new job."

"That's a great offer, Grandpa. I should talk to Charley..."

Sam had hoped Charley wouldn't come up. "Well..."

"Is something wrong?" she asked.

Sam had to think quickly. "No, it's just that Grandma and I haven't seen much of you lately and we were hoping to have you all to ourselves."

Rebecca was disappointed by her grandfather's response, concerned that Sam disapproved of her relationship with Charley. But she wasn't really serious about asking him to join her anyway. After today, she felt she needed some space. "OK. Friday afternoon?"

"Great. Let me know what flight you'll be on and I'll pick you up at the airport."

Rebecca hung up the phone and leaned back against the tub, but couldn't get comfortable. And the water was no longer warm, but her beer was. The relaxation part of her bath was over.

She washed her hair, toweled off and threw on some jeans and a sweater. While drying her hair she felt a deep ache in her stomach, which she reckoned was a combination of hunger and the residual affect of being tear-gassed. She welcomed it when Charley called a few minutes later to ask if she wanted to get something to eat.

Rebecca descended the narrow staircase into the dark, smoky main dining room of the Tombs at Prospect and 36th Street in Georgetown. Spotting Charley's oversized head above the crowd, she pushed her way through the throng at the bar—which featured robed Jesuit professors, white-coated medical types from the nearby hospital, and a handful of inebriated college preppies—and walked to the fireplace in the back.

Charley sat in a crowded booth next to Didier and across from a short-haired, olive-skinned man and an athletic, attractive woman with auburn locks. Because they were engaged in a lively and animated conversation, Rebecca was able to hover in front of them undetected.

Charley tapped his forefinger on the table pensively. "I guess you're right. It could have been a lot worse. I just wasn't expecting the police to come at us swinging. Was there something we should have done?"

Didier flicked the stub of his cigarette into a filthy, blue ashtray and shook his head. "The cops, they were looking for trouble. Nothing short of turning around with our tails between our legs would have averted the attack. That's the unfortunate baggage that comes along with us."

The young woman reached across the table and touched Charley's arm. "It wasn't all bad," she said in a husky voice laced with an accent Rebecca had trouble placing. "Even though

Stein never took the podium, he did stick around long enough to be interviewed by CNN and it made the news. Five seconds on the riot and 30 seconds of a Nobel-prize-winning economist speaking to our message. We should be happy with that."

Didier continued to shake his head. "No. We shouldn't be happy at all. *Tomorrow's* news will talk about the five protesters and two policemen who were taken to the emergency room, and we'll be branded as commie anarchists again. We've got to demand more of ourselves if anything is ever going to change."

Charley seemed disappointed by the criticism. "We had the permits, we had the speakers and the press lined up. The cops screwed us. Not our fault."

"It wasn't the cops. I'm sure the FBI pulled the permit. I'm not second-guessing you, Charley. I'm only sensitive to the impression that we're not competent. When rallies go bad like this, they make us look disorganized and then it's easy to dismiss our arguments. We're just a bunch of losers who bait the police and just cause trouble, yes?"

The woman pulled a cigarette from the blue pack in front of Didier and leaned over to receive a light. With a tone that seemed supportive and patronizing at the same time, she said, "You're exaggerating. This was our first try in the States. It will take time to get as prepared here as we are in Europe. I would say our new friend," she said smiling genially at Charley, "is off to a very good start."

Didier took in a long drag on his cigarette, and exhaled the smoke slowly through his nostrils. "Of course. You put this together in a very short time, with little help. I didn't mean to be critical.

"I'm just getting more and more frustrated that our message seems falling on deaf ears or no ears at all. The situation is getting worse and worse: more children dying, more people falling below the poverty level, more corruption and greed. These things are facts, but they don't resonate. We need something big for Vienna to get people to listen. This just isn't working."

Rebecca didn't understand the reference to Vienna, but she could see that Charley did. The tightening of the skin around his eyes and the observable clenching of his jaw demonstrated the same intense level of concentration as was the case in Bahia. This was Charley in his determined mode, and Rebecca knew it was his happiest state of being.

A waitress nudged Rebecca aside to place her tray of beers on the table, at which point her presence become known.

"Hi, 'Becca," Charley said, almost seeming surprised to see her.

Didier stood up immediately and offered her his place next to Charley. Rebecca and Charley exchanged smiles while Didier moved a chair to the front of the table. "I'm sorry to interrupt," she said a bit sheepishly.

"Not at all," Didier said. "Let me introduce my colleagues Fatima and Karim. Fatima is originally from Lisbon and Assan from Pakistan. Both work in our London agency.

"I'm sorry you had some difficulties today. Is everything alright?'

Rebecca banged her elbow lightly on Charley's bicep. "Aside from a few tread marks on my back, I'm OK. Luckier than some, I'm guessing."

Didier fixed his pale blue eyes right on hers. "I hope it didn't sour you on our organization. From what Charley's told us, you'd be an incredibly valuable member of our team."

Meeting his stare, she responded, "That's tempting, but I'm on sabbatical from my revolutionary agenda for the time being. I think I'll try to earn a living, just to mix it up."

"It's a shame," Fatima said good-humoredly. "A fine woman like you shouldn't be wasting her talents on capitalist tasks when there's a revolution that needs to be led."

Rebecca smiled and opened the menu that had been sitting on the table in front of her. "Maybe next year," she said. "Do you mind if I order? I haven't eaten all day."

***

Rebecca and Charley walked east on Prospect Street while the others headed north. He grabbed her arm and folded it into his own. "I'm really sorry for today. I shouldn't have dragged you there."

"You didn't kidnap me. I admit I was curious, but I'm cured now. I'll pass on the next rally."

"Things really got out of hand."

Rebecca pulled her arm loose. "Stop apologizing. You didn't know what would go on—it wasn't your fault."

"But you got busted for nothing, and almost trampled. I never should have let that happen."

Rebecca stopped walking and turned to face Charley. "Let's make a deal. You stop apologizing, and I'll do my best to stay out of a position where you have to worry about me. You love this stuff, Big Bear, and you're good at it. But it's not for me, not anymore. You do your thing, I'll do mine—and we'll meet at the end of the day to talk about it."

Charley bent over and kissed Rebecca warmly. "Deal."

"My place?" she asked, pulling Charley along.

"I'll walk you there, but I can't stay. I'm meeting up with Didier later at the lawyer's office in Northwest. I don't know how late we'll be."

"Why?"

"I've been told to expect some *visits* from our friends in the intelligence agencies about ATAC, and Didier wants me to get some advice about how to handle it."

Rebecca tightened her grip on Charley's forearm. "That's kind of hairy."

They walked in silence for a few minutes until Rebecca wondered out loud "What do we know about these guys?"

From the instantaneous way in which Charley began his answer, it was obvious to Rebecca that he had been thinking along the same lines. "Not a huge amount. I do know they've been around a long time—since the '60s. Didier told me his father was involved at the beginning, mostly to protest the Vietnam War. They've got a political arm in France—I don't remember the name—and actually have won some seats in the national assembly and locally. He seems serious enough, don't you think?"

"He does look like he knows what he's doing, and seems to genuinely care about people as well as the cause. I guess I'm weird-ed out at the thought that the FBI is taking an interest in you because of them."

"Maybe nothing will happen. They just want me to be prepared. I'll see what they say tonight and what happens tomorrow. Don't worry—we got through Ecuador. At least there's a Bill of Rights here."

Rebecca resolved to change the subject. "I'm thinking of going to visit my grandparents in New York tomorrow. Do you mind?'

"That's good...I mean, that's fine. I'm tied up most of tomorrow anyway, and most of the weekend, because all these ATAC people."

Rebecca slowed their pace a bit. "Those two I met at the Tombs—Fatima and, uh..."

"Assan."

"Right. They're from ATAC. Are there more?"

They were just a few steps from Rebecca's apartment and Charley stopped and turned to face her. "Yeah, a bunch more. I had no idea, but they were all at the rally. They're having a kind of mini-convention this weekend, and Didier invited me to some of the meetings."

Charley looked at his watch. "I got to go. Want me to walk you inside?"

Rebecca shook her head, reached up and kissed Charley tenderly. "Call me tomorrow. By the way, I took the job. I start Monday."

"Cool," said Charley distractedly.

Back in her apartment, Rebecca pulled up the covers and crumbled the pillow to find the perfect position for her weary head. She acknowledged that she was genuinely happy that Charley was getting involved, in a structured way, to accomplish his activist leanings. She had often thought he would be more satisfied working with others who shared his passions, and thought that Didier offered that, and perhaps more, in the form of guidance and mentorship.

Yet, a nagging reservation buzzed at the outskirts of her thinking. Things almost got seriously out of hand today, and people were severely hurt. Why would the FBI take the trouble to actively intervene in a simple protest rally? *Was Charley in over his head?*

Rebecca was so exhausted that sleep trumped her uncertainty. She didn't stir until a combination of persistent telephone rings and sweeping nausea woke her up at almost noon the following day.

"Rebecca?"

"Dad?"

"You sound surprised."

"Sorry. I mean, you never dial your own calls. Usually I get passed from a secretary to Gina before we talk." Rebecca heard the sarcasm in her own voice and wished she could take it back.

Jeffrey's voice stiffened. "If this is a bad time…"

"Not at all. Sorry, I was just…ah… Sorry I didn't call you back yesterday. I got home late and crashed right away."

"That's OK. I called because I was unhappy with how our conversation ended yesterday, and I wanted to apologize. I do think you should stay in school, but I understand your point and it wasn't right for me to dismiss you out of hand."

What's gotten into him? "I…uh….I suppose I appreciate that. Thanks."

"Its no excuse, but I've been traveling all over the place lately and there's no letup in sight. Next week I've got to be in Bogotá on Tuesday and Wednesday, and get from there to Vienna for the IMF meetings by Thursday."

"Sounds like fun."

"Not this trip. I'm expecting every anarchist, malcontent and spoiled brat on the planet to be there, clogging the streets with meaningless protests and making my life generally miserable. I'd pay someone not to go if I could get out of it."

She almost said, "It's not *about* you. It is *about* the poor and under-represented. It's *about Bahians* getting screwed by AZTEC Oil," but bit her tongue. "Oh," was all that came out of her mouth.

Jeffrey asked, "Want to try again? Maybe we could have lunch this weekend?"

"Sorry, but I'm going to New York tonight. Grandma invited me to the opera, and I haven't seen her in such a long time."

There was a long pause before Jeffrey responded, and Rebecca could hear a mixture of disappointment and annoyance in his voice. "Call me when you get back," was all he said before hanging up the phone.

Rebecca sat on the edge of her bed for a few moments, reflecting on her father and grandfather. She knew she existed in the middle of their troubled relationship, and often wondered whether she might be the cause of the tension. In many ways, it was much easier on her when Jeffrey opted out of her life, when she only had one male parent-figure to deal with. Things got unduly complicated when her father decided, for whatever reason, to get re-engaged, and Rebecca had a bad feeling she had just stepped into one of those times.

CHAPTER 10

Sam stood over Anton, stroking his thin, white hair. He was shaken at how much Anton had deteriorated over the past 36 hours. His skin was almost translucent, to the point where the veins and arteries that ran through the exposed parts of his body could be plotted with precision with the naked eye. Salt-and-pepper stubble had been allowed to grow on his face, exaggerating the fact that he had become, for all intents and purposes, merely skin and bones.

Helene entered the room a few minutes after 8 and Sam moved to a chair by the window. He was facing north, to the Bronx. It was a beautiful and clear morning, and the sun reflected reflected off the Hudson River, which had probably never looked so blue. The wooded hills of the Palisades were illuminated as well, and had probably never appeared so verdant. But Sam was overcome by the recurrent gray of Gunskirchen.

Sitting in the mud and muck of the death camp, Sam Hart held the man's dying head in his lap, stroking what malnutrition and disease had left of his hair. While other American soldiers were calling for medics to help prisoners they thought were alive, Sam sat there quietly, trying to stay calm and comforting the poor inmate.

The face of the man whose head he held became Anton's, ashen and emaciated. The yellow star on his chest became the words "Columbia University Medical Center" on a white cotton robe. Sam had exchanged a grimy army uniform for a dark pin-striped suit and silk tie.

Anton slowly opened his eyes, which glowed with a fragment of white light that peered into Sam and provided a surprising balm to his distress. Sam looked around the muddy yard and saw hundreds, possibly thousands of vivid and slender beams rising from the ground—from bodies on the ground—squandered, toward the sky.

"He's asking for you," Helene said. "I told him you were here."

Sam wiped the moisture from his eyes and dragged his chair next to Anton's bed. Helene had propped up her father and brushed his hair while Sam was daydreaming, and he looked much better as a result. Anton's smile was waiting for Sam when he got there.

"You look good," Sam lied.

""Compared to what?" was Anton's raspy response. "A hedgehog?"

"You look *really* good in that case."

Anton chuckled with some difficulty. "It's good to laugh—something I'd do more of if I was home."

"Don't start, Papa. You're not ready to go home yet-- maybe in a few days." Helene rolled her eyes at Sam. "I'll leave you two for a few minutes. I want to try and find the doctor."

"I'm sorry I couldn't come yesterday. Things got complicated at the office and, well…Rebecca got into a bit of trouble and I needed to get involved. Did you get the tape back?"

Anton nodded in the direction of the far end of the room, where a TV and VCR rested on a portable stand. In an increasingly trembling voice, he said, "Helene and I watched it yesterday. It was very hard on her."

"I can only imagine," said Sam, vividly recalling the emotional impact it had on him.

"I gave her your number. I hope you don't mind."

"Who?"

Anton closed his eyes. "Cindy Allenson...the Shoah lady. Please talk to her."

***

Sam collapsed into the driver's seat of his car and stared out the window. The tension between honoring his friend's request and his self-preservation instincts tore at him the entire ride down the west side of Manhattan to Wall Street.

He drove like an automaton. It took him a few moments in the men's room, after washing his face with cold water, to be able to enter the trading floor and face the day.

Pam followed him into his office. "Mark Todd called twice, looking for you. Stanley's office called and asked me to hold open 3 to 4 today. And Mike T said you should read the risk report he put on your desk as soon as you can. And Rebecca called to say she'd be on a 5:30 Shuttle. I think that's it."

The scale of the issues before him was overwhelming. Sam sat in his chair, paralyzed, for several minutes. He shut out the drone of the trading floor, the ringing of his phone, and his secretary's intercom messages. His eyes focused on a single point—the ivory dial of the grandfather's clock in the corner of his office—and let his mind sink completely into a collection of seemingly random images: entering Gunskirchen; Rebecca's hospital room after her accident; the young Cossack in the white tunic with a bullet wound to his heart; the grey and loose skin on Anton's face.

The session was abruptly ended by obnoxious knocking on Sam's door. Mark Todd let himself in and dropped a thick memo on Sam's desk. Without looking at Sam, he reached over and tapped the document with the index finger of his right hand. "I hadn't heard back from you, so I sent this to Stanley as a draft, pending your final approval. It's more or less as we discussed."

Sam thumbed through the first few pages of the document distractedly. He was so exhausted that he was prepared to give up. Accepting Todd's document would get Stanley off his back, buy Sam a year of quality time at GSC in anticipation of a hero's retirement, and give him the space he needed to deal with his other major issues. He knew he couldn't win the fight anyway, so why not give it up now, especially with everything else going on.

He considered telling Todd that he was sure the memo was fine, and to go ahead with it, when he first heard, and then saw, a considerable commotion on the trading floor. Salespeople were standing, some on their chairs, to be heard and seen by the traders who, in turn, were huddled over their computer screens, hands cupped to their headsets. Something had happened, Sam knew—something huge.

Sam bolted out of his chair, scattering the pages of the memo on his desk and headed to the trading floor, ignoring Todd. He made a bee-line to Mike T's station.

Mike held a phone to each ear and was barking prices to a half-dozen salespeople who were on lines to their clients. Sam glanced at a computer screen where the prices of a variety of currencies fluctuated wildly. It only took a few seconds for Sam to determine that, for whatever reason, the dollar had strengthened significantly against all major currencies, especially the yen.

Sam smiled and gave Mike the thumbs up.

The head trader hung up one of the phones and handed another to his assistant. He pulled Sam over to a quieter corner. "Treasury reiterated the Administration's desire for a strong dollar, and the Fed was buying on behalf of the Bank of Japan. The shorts are puking. We're up two percent already, and there's more to go."

Sam did the mental math. "We're back in the black. I wished we hadn't chickened out and kept our whole position intact."

Mike looked somewhat sheepish. "We did. We're up big now."

"What?"

"I added this morning. We're back to two billion."

Sam was staggered. Mike didn't have the authority to do that. At this point, even Sam didn't have the authority to increase the risk to that magnitude.

"It's just a day-trading position, boss. It'll be gone before the day is done. Luckily, we got it right."

"*You* got it right, Mike--balls of steel."

Sam glanced over his shoulder and saw Todd waiting, impatiently, in his office. He picked up a nearby phone and dialed Pam's extension. "Tell Mark that I've got to be out here for a while, and I'll call him when I can to go over the memo. Thanks."

Sam watched amusedly as Pam delivered the "go to hell" message to Mark Todd. Sam was tempted to stick his tongue out in response to the icy glare Todd shot his way when he stormed off the floor, but discretion prevailed.

He realized that this incident with Todd would only serve to make the afternoon call with Stanley much more difficult. Sam shrugged his shoulders, feeling himself again, if just for the moment, and thought, *That's why they pay me the big bucks*, before returning to the suddenly benevolent currency market.

***

Sam recognized that his improved mood was living on borrowed time. At precisely 3:00 p.m., Stanley called. He was in the JAL First Class lounge at Narita airport in Tokyo, en route to Beijing, and Sam could feel the jet lag in his voice.

"I hear you guys had a monster day. A hundred million, is that right?"

"Actually, it'll be closer to one-thirty-five, when the dust settles tonight." Sam was trying to enjoy the calm before the storm.

"I must be missing something, or else our risk reports are messed up. How'd we make so much money?"

Sam smiled at the liberal use of the pronoun. "*We* traded a lot today, Stanley. Actually, it was *Mike* who had us perfectly positioned."

Stanley could be heard taking a deep breath before continuing on. "The *team* did a great job today, Sam. But I have to admit I'm more than a little annoyed about the headcount issue. I still don't have your fingerprints on the staff reduction plan—you're the only one I'm waiting for."

Sam flicked a lever on the side of his desk which released the magnet and allowed his office door to close. "Sorry. Todd was in my office today to go over the draft when the market went crazy. I had to prioritize, and our positions came first."

Sam could always tell when Stanley was getting mad, because his voice took on a high pitched and raspy quality. "Prioritize? You've got a higher priority than complying with a direct order from me? I told you to get your headcount down, and to get me the plan weeks ago. You've done nothing but jerk me around on this. That's over."

Stanley continued. "I hope you read that memo Todd gave you today, because you own it. Lock, stock and barrel. Overall headcount will be down 10 percent. Two senior traders are to be let go by year-end, including Mike T. You're to cut back new hires in sales by at least 20 percent. You had a chance to get your two cents in, but you blew it."

Sam was sputtering. "You can't do that! It's stupid and irresponsible. I won't run this business—that means these people—as percentages, Stanley. We're doing great. Mike T is making miracles out there. And you want me to fire him because we pay him too much money? That's ridiculous!"

"Sam, I want you to listen very closely. Either you will implement this plan, or Mark Todd will. At this point, I really don't care. But it will take place."

Sam fought back, his face swollen with anger. "Don't threaten me. I wonder how the Board will react when I tell them I've been forced to fire the most productive trader in the firm for the past two years. Think long and hard about it before you do something stupid."

Stanley lowered his voice an octave and spoke very slowly now. "I'm not an idiot. I've got the Board behind me on this one. You go against me, you lose. Not even close."

Sam was furious with himself. He had been so distracted by so many different things that he didn't seize the opportunity to shape this situation in his own terms. He knew that unless Stanley was bluffing—a tactic that Stanley employed frequently and masterfully—the odds were against Sam. Losing this fight to Stanley would mean that Sam would lose an enormous amount of power within the Firm and probably have to step aside. Importantly, it would also mean that a number of dedicated, effective and innocent employees would be sacrificed in the process. He suddenly felt too old.

"Are you still there?" Stanley tried to sound presidential. "I really hate doing this, after all we've been through. You helped build this place and you should leave on a high note. Don't fight me. It's simply business—don't make it personal."

"Simply business—I'll try to remember that."

"Good. I'll see you in Vienna in a couple of days."

Sam's first instinct was to tell his boss where he could shove Vienna, but held back. Instead, he extended his arm, released his fingers and let the phone receiver drop to the floor. Sam sensed there was an opportunity here to nail Stanley, to turn his arrogance against him. *Simply business,* Sam thought. *That's it. The Board only really cares about making money. And I'm the only one doing that around here.*

To make this work, Sam knew, he really *would* have to go to Vienna.

Pam entered his office and reminded Sam it was time to go. He would need extra time on a Friday evening to get to the airport, and Rebecca's flight was due in 45 minutes. Sam gathered up the most recent risk reports and a handful of other papers that needed reading from his desk, stopped by to check in with Mike, and then left the building.

Sam looked forward to the drive to LaGuardia Airport and the down time to absorb all the things going on around him. Initially, he thought about how he'd been outflanked by Stanley, and how stupid it was since he'd seen it coming from a long way off.

Sam thought back almost 24 months, when GSC's then-President, Spencer Graham, surprised the Board with his resignation to become the Secretary of State. Within hours, the power struggle began.

All other things being equal, Sam would have had a damned good shot at the job. He ran one of the Firm's most successful businesses and was unquestionably its best known international personality. But Sam was 65 years old at the time, and that changed his profile from contender to king-maker.

DIVIDED LOYALTIES

Stanley Masters was not a leading candidate at first, although it became clear to Sam early on that he would be the least polarizing of those under serious consideration. He thought Stanley was fundamentally stable and honest, and because he was of only ordinary intelligence, controllable.

Stanley wanted Sam's support in the worst way, and offered Sam two major items in return. The first was a substantial broadening of Sam's business franchise to include hybrid securities and principal investments—as a result, Sam would control a much larger and more profitable enterprise within the Firm. The second was that Stanley would guarantee the suspension of the company's mandatory retirement age of 68, allowing Sam to work "until you drop."

Two years later, Sam recognized the Faustian nature of that bargain. Stanley no longer needed Sam's support, and in fact would be a lot more powerful if Sam were no longer around. And while it would be difficult for Stanley to out-and-out fire Sam without a lot of uncomfortable proceedings, he could certainly lead the Board—which had become increasingly *his* Board-- in reinstating the mandatory retirement provisions.

Sam could fight it. He could call in some chits and maybe even turn things against Stanley, to the point where his job security was threatened. If this were 10 years ago, Sam thought, he'd eat Stanley for lunch. *But now...with everything else going on, did it make any sense?*

The more Sam contemplated giving in and giving up, the more he resisted the notion. His work defined such a large part of him that he couldn't imagine not having it there, every day.

Sam scoffed at his contemporaries who retired to Florida and Arizona and focused only on their own, selfish needs. He saw that as a final option, when mental or physical decline limited his abilities to do only one thing at a time. Until then, so long as he could stand tall and think clearly, Sam intended to be fully engaged.

For his decades in the pressure cooker of Wall Street, Sam prided himself on being able to handle multiple, complex tasks simultaneously. He could handle his dying friend and ailing wife alongside a power struggle at the firm, so long as he kept his priorities straight and his head clear. He just needed to stay focused.

Revived from the pep talk he'd been giving himself while driving, Sam pulled into a parking spot in front of the Shuttle terminal and checked his watch. He had made it to the airport early, although once again Sam remembered little of the actual trip. He took his briefcase with him into the arrivals concourse, intending to catch up on his reading while he waited for Rebecca to arrive.

He fished into his attaché and pulled out a stack of memorandums and a brown envelope he had placed there a few days earlier. Sam shuffled the envelope to the top of the stack, thinking seriously about using the time to re-read the disturbing story it contained. Remembering how reading it for the first time had distressed him, Sam rotated it to the bottom of the stack and began to review the first memo in the pile. He welcomed the time to bury himself in the mundane aspects of his business, and got so absorbed in the process that he almost jumped when his granddaughter tugged at his sleeve.

Rebecca didn't seem quite herself. She was uncharacteristically quiet and subdued that evening, her arms wrapped around her torso as they drove north to the Westchester suburbs. Sam felt selfishly deprived. He was looking forward to the effervescent package of energy that his granddaughter almost always brought with her on her visits to New York, hoping to use her vigor to propel his own.

"Are you alright, 'Becca? Did you get the call from GSC today?"

"I'm fine. Sorry, just tired, I guess. Yeah, Kathryn Mantle called. They want me to start on Monday. It should be great. Thanks for all of your help."

Sam could tell that Rebecca was feigning enthusiasm for his benefit. "Something's bothering you. Want to talk?"

Rebecca tightened the grip around herself. "There's nothing to talk about. I'm fine."

Sam let it go for a minute, but couldn't restrain himself. "Everything OK with Charley?"

Rebecca turned and stared at Sam for a long moment. "We're fine. He's just gotten really busy." Then she added sarcastically, "Sorry to disappoint you."

"I don't dislike Charley—quite the contrary." Sam tried to keep his voice soft and calming. "I think he's a nice guy who seems to treat you with respect. But I'd be lying if I said I wasn't concerned about the fact that he attracts a lot of trouble wherever he goes."

"The violence at the protest rally wasn't his fault. The cops started it...they rushed the crowd, smacking people with their nightsticks for no reason. It was obvious *they* wanted trouble."

Stopping at the toll booth, Sam looked over at his granddaughter and could see her face reddening. He recognized that this moment might not have been the optimal one to talk about this, but for some reason he felt that it was important that he not defer points he needed to make. "This faction he's associating with, they're bad news—an extensive history of violence in Europe."

"Are you checking up on them?"

"'Becca, this is serious stuff. ATAC is probably under constant government surveillance, and maybe you are as well."

"Because I was in a protest rally?"

"No, because you're Charley's girlfriend and I know for sure *he's* being watched."

Rebecca brought her heels up to the lip of the car seat and hugged her knees. "That's ridiculous, you know. Charley would never do anything to hurt anybody. In Bahia..."

Sam interrupted. "They know all about Ecuador. Don't forget the Peace Corps is a government-sponsored institution."

"Shit," she said under her breath. "What should we do?"

Sam put his right hand on Rebecca's shoulder. "You don't have to *do* anything, but keep it in mind when you think about where you go or people you meet or, maybe even, what you say on the phone. I know that sounds crazy, but the Feds take ATAC very seriously."

There was little conversation for the rest of the ride. Rebecca tried to call Charley as soon as she got to her room, and left a message when he didn't pick up. She busied herself by unpacking her small suitcase and looking through a few old photo albums, but time was moving excruciatingly slowly and she called Charley about a half-hour later, to the same effect. She needed to unburden herself to him, and was mad when he didn't answer.

Rebecca was grateful for the distraction a few minutes later when Sam called her downstairs for dinner. Gloria was so happy to see her granddaughter that she carried more than her share of the evening's conversation, and eventually the fine wine that Sam poured liberally throughout the meal took hold, and Rebecca relaxed.

Gloria said goodnight around 10 o'clock, and Sam stuck his head into the family room to see if Rebecca—who had been stretched out on the couch, reading through back issues of *The New Yorker*—needed anything before he turned in.

Rebecca lithely swiveled to a sitting position in one move. "I love him, you know," she said, trying to be matter-of-fact.

Sam was caught off guard. "Ah...Umm..."

"He's had a really hard life. He was orphaned when he was four and never adopted. He worked his way through college completely on his own. He had some drug problems—he told me everything—but put himself into rehab and he's been clean for more than five years. The most he'll drink is a beer."

Sam moved toward her, holding out his hands. "You don't have to..."

She brushed away a solitary tear and fixed her eyes on a photograph of her and her father hanging on a nearby wall. "He is so passionate, Grandpa. He cares about people more than anyone I've ever met. The stuff he talks about—fairness and equality and human rights—he says because he really believes in it. I wish I had his certainty and confidence."

Sam sat on the couch, shoulder-to-shoulder with his granddaughter. "I'm sorry I dumped that on you in the car. It wasn't the right place or time. I'm sorry I upset you."

***

Rebecca tried Charley again several times that evening. It was so unlike him not to call her back that she even dialed around to a few friends to see if anyone had seen him. She was getting more and more upset each time she got a negative response.

Rebecca had trouble falling asleep. She worried whether something had happened to Charley—taken in for questioning? She worried that she was, once again, disappointing her grandfather. She wondered whether she was, in fact, being watched. Would she ever feel confident again?

Eventually, she drifted off to sleep and awakened only when Gloria knocked on her door and let herself in. "It's past one. You wanted to shop for some clothes for your new job, didn't you?"

Rebecca rubbed her eyes and looked disbelievingly at the alarm clock next to her bed. "Did anyone call this morning?"

"Yes, but it was for Grandpa. Are you expecting someone?"

"I guess not. Give me a few minutes, Grandma. I'll be right there."

***

There were two calls that morning, both for Sam. The first was Helene. She had taken Anton home the previous evening, for hospice care. Sam's heart sunk when she used that phrase.

"He insisted," she said. "His doctor wanted him to stay and try more chemotherapy, but Papa refused, straight out. At least this way he'll be comfortable. Come by when you have a chance."

The second call came only a few minutes later. It was Cindy Allenson from the Shoah Foundation in Los Angeles, calling at Anton's suggestion. She apologized for bothering him on a Saturday, but she was leaving for Poland that evening, and was hoping Sam might be available to speak with her when she returned through New York two weeks later.

"Mr. Karetske mentioned you were part of the liberation of Gunskirchen, where he was interned, and that you've become close friends. That's a remarkable story which we'd very much like to document, Mr. Hart."

"Ah, I don't know Miss Allen…"

"Allenson. Please call me Cindy."

"I'm not sure I can…I mean…"

"I just want to talk. No notes, no recordings. Let's just talk. If you're uncomfortable after that, of course, that's it. Just give me a chance to explain what we're doing, and how your piece fits into the overall picture."

Cindy's phrasing caused Sam to think about Anton's parable, of reassembling myriad pieces of light into a cosmic whole, and he involuntarily said, "OK..."

"Wonderful. I'll have my office call yours and make the appointment. I really look forward to meeting you."

Sam hung up the phone, grabbed his keys and was almost out the door when he remembered to tell Gloria he was leaving. He arrived in Rye a few minutes later.

Anton was sitting in a chair in the living room, his feet up on an ottoman and a brown blanket draped over his legs. The color was back in his freshly shaven face, and he was wearing a blue NY Yankees baseball cap that covered his bald head. His eyes were half-closed, and his head swayed slightly in time to the Mozart violin concerto playing from the stereo speakers. He smiled when he saw Sam walking his way.

"Much better, don't you think?'

"You do look good....and this time I mean it."

"Ha. I knew you were lying at the hospital. Come, sit. This nice young man, Marcello, brews a wonderful pot of tea."

Sam nodded in the male nurse's direction and said "Yes, thanks, I'll have some tea with lemon." He moved his chair closer to Anton's and said to him, "That woman, Cindy something or other, called today."

"Good. She's very smart."

"I think I agreed to meet with her." Sam rubbed his temples with the thumb and forefinger of his right hand.

Anton raised his eyebrows. "You think?'

"No, I did. But I don't know why. I really don't want to talk about the war, not with anyone."

"It's very important that you talk about it."

Sam leaned forward. "Your story was important. I didn't do anything. I was there...by accident."

Sam thought he saw disappointment in his friend's eyes. "I wasn't there by choice. And what did I do?" Anton grabbed Sam's hand firmly. "*My* story is *your* story. I wouldn't even be here if you—and your army—hadn't turned up. No wife, no daughter, no life. They should hear about survival, and heroism--about the future, and hope. That's *our* story, Sam. You have to complete the picture."

Sam felt a surge of panic at the thought of making these memories public. "You said it all already in your tape. There's nothing worthwhile I could add."

Anton's eyes seemed to bore right through him. "You can't run forever, Sam. Sooner or later, it'll catch up to you. Maybe it already has."

He patted Sam's hand. "This is your chance. Take it. For you, for me, for the men and women who were there. Most importantly, do it for those who follow, so that they can know exactly what happened. Remember the story about Tikkun Olum and the shattered vessel? This is precisely what the allegory means; to make things better and to make sure man's evil side is kept in check, we need to understand exactly what we have done and are capable of doing...good and bad. Each experience—a shard of glass in the story—has a central role in the reparation of humanity."

Sam had all the old arguments arrayed in battle formation, ready to respond. This time, however, he just couldn't find the strength to rally them. It seemed clear to him, finally, after 50 years, that he had been engaged in a battle he could never win. It was finally time to stop being a soldier, and come to grips with the full scope of his own character.

Anton had not taken his eyes off of Sam's face. "Good," he said, relaxing his grip on Sam's hand. "You've made me happy."

***

It was Sunday morning, and still Rebecca hadn't heard from Charley. Her anger at him the night before at least provided some relief. She actually relaxed enough to enjoy her grandmother's company and the opera. Overnight, however, she had been overtaken by severe anxiety, and when once again Charley failed to answer his phones, she insisted that Sam take her to the airport early to catch a morning flight back to Washington.

On the way to LaGuardia, Sam made a light attempt to get Rebecca to talk about why she was so desultory. She deflected the questioning, and was surprised when Sam didn't press the matter. He seemed pre-occupied, himself.

She took a cab from National Airport back to her apartment in Georgetown, and there was no sign that Charley had been there. Rebecca fished out the key to his place from an ashtray filled with small change and took a cab across town. She held her breath as she opened the door, afraid of what she might find there.

Nothing. The small studio apartment was a mess, but it was always a mess. Clothes and a towel were strewn on an unmade bed, but the sheets were cold and the towel dry. Room temperature coffee in a paper cup sat on a cheap wooden table, alongside Thursday's *Washington Post*. There was no physical evidence that Charley, or anyone else, had been there recently.

Rebecca sat on the edge of the bed, unsure what to do. She resisted her initial impulse to call Sam. He had just warned her that Charley was always getting into trouble, and she had defended him. Calling Sam would confirm his assertion. Worse, he'd think she was weak and not able to handle own problems. He'd think poorly of her.

But what else could she do? Should she call the police? File a missing person's report? *This can't really be happening.*

Rebecca took a deep breath and reached out to call her grandfather. As she was punching the numbers on the phone, she saw Charley's answering machine. She hung up, and with only the briefest of second thoughts, pushed the play button lightly, which provoked an androgynous electronic voice to announce "You have no new messages."

How can that be? I've left two messages here myself.

This time, she pushed the play button and held it for a few seconds. The answering machine responded, "You have four old messages…first message, sent Friday at 7:20 pm…"

Rebecca heard her own subdued voice, asking Charley to call her at her grandparents' house, leaving the number. The second was Rebecca again, clearly angry this time, on Saturday afternoon.

The third call came in Saturday evening. A hoarse female voice, barely audible above a wall of background noise, said, "I wasn't sure if you'd left already. If not, call me and we'll get together. Otherwise, I'll see you there on Monday. Ciao."

Huh?

Rebecca played the message back several times, trying to place the vaguely familiar voice and understand the odd references to "if you'd left already" (*going where?*) and "I'll see you there" (*a different "there"?*). The pieces weren't coming together, so Rebecca hoped the last taped call might be helpful.

It was recorded only 45 minutes earlier. "Mr. Robertson, this is Inge Furst from Austrian Airlines in New York. We've located your bag in Vienna. Please claim it at our customer service desk there or, if you want us to return it to New York, please call us. Our numbers are..."

"Vienna?" Rebecca asked aloud. She got up and started to pace around the apartment.

She went to the dresser where she knew Charley kept his important papers and located his checkbook and birth certificate, but no passport. She inspected the apartment more carefully and she realized that his Dopp kit—which he always brought with him when he planned to stay at Rebecca's for any length of time—was missing from the bathroom.

The rush of adrenalin was making lots of things clearer to Rebecca, including the owner of the husky female voice on the recorder. Rebecca had, at the time, put aside any thoughts that Fatima may have been flirting with Charley at the Tombs a few days ago, but now, after this message, that didn't seem so ridiculous.

"Shit-head," she said aloud, slamming the door to Charley's apartment behind her. *He's toast!*

CHAPTER 11

The ride back from LaGuardia Airport was unsettling. Sam used the time to thrash out the complicated set of conflicts that seemed to dominate his life these days. He knew he needed to go to Vienna to protect his career interests at GSC and Mike T's future. Bolstered by Anton's encouragement, he admitted to himself that he also *wanted*, for purely personal reasons, to attend his Army reunion.

Yet, on the other hand, how could he leave the country with Anton so sick? And how sure was he that Gloria was sufficiently stable to leave her unattended for any length of time?

When he arrived home, he found a note from Gloria saying that she'd gone to 10 a.m. mass. He went upstairs to his study and emptied the papers from his briefcase on his desk. Once again, the brown envelope appeared at the top of the pile.

Sam sat down at the desk and noticed that his hands shook a bit as he pulled the contents from the envelope. He leaned into his leather chair and read the story for the second time.

Russian Repatriations and America's Betrayal
By Sergei Pohl.
Translated by Bernice Spivack
When the Second World War ended in 1945, my own personal battle for survival began. I was only a teenager at the time. For almost all of my life to that

point, I had been a nomad. With my parents and my younger sister, Eugeni, we were constantly on the move. First, we fled the Soviet secret police, who were executing a secret order to expel us from our home because we were part of an ethnic group that was, en masse, judged guilty of "treasonous" acts. Then, we went into hiding from the Nazi invaders who captured and enslaved my cousins. Finally, when the fighting was over, we prayed to God for his majesty in letting us survive, together. And just as we thought we would be safe, in the hands of the Allies, fate delivered the cruelest twist. The Americans sent us back to Russia, knowing that we didn't want to go, and knowing that we would be in grave danger there. My father was taken by the NKVD, tortured in Lubyanka, and murdered there in cold blood. My mother, sister and I were convicted of aiding and abetting the "traitorous" conduct of my father, and we were sentenced to 20 years at the Kolyma Gulag. Ironically, I eventually made it to the United States, where I became a citizen in 1980. Somewhat perversely, I count myself a lucky one to have been released in a general amnesty permitted by the Soviets and allowed to immigrate to America. But I cannot write a memoir describing my experiences during the war for this collection and arbitrarily stop the recollection process in 1945 or 1946. For millions of us with a Russian heritage, the War continued and, for many, intensified, until the 1960s when the Gulag system was reformed.

It is hard for me to remember many of the details of my early days, because we moved around so much and always in a panicked state. Both my father and mother came from Volgodonsk, in the Volga River region, where their families had lived for over 150 years. They married there and moved to Kiev, where my sister and I were born, as my father took a professorship position at the Politechnum in mining and metallurgy. My father was a veteran of the Red Army, and lost his left hand in an explosion during the Winter War against Finland in 1940. He returned to us in Kiev, and rejoined the faculty of the university, after recovering from his injuries. We lived a good life, I was told, until the following year when Stalin condemned the entire Soviet population of "Volga Germans" and ordered that they be sent into exile. Even though we lived in Kiev, far from the autonomous region that Lenin had established, we were ordered to leave the city and join the other 400,000 Volga Germans for the 2,000-mile journey to Siberia, our new "home."

My father refused to obey, and moved us quickly and quietly to the Polish border, right into the advancing and traitorous Nazi assault. We were able to avoid detection for a while, mostly because of my father's ingenuity in procuring false identification papers, his fluency in German and the chaos that surrounded us. We lived hand-to-mouth, trading our menial labor for food in the Polish countryside. We lived in barns and sheds and makeshift tents. When my mother would sob after another hasty move, being forced to leave something behind—and most everything we had was precious to us, because we had so little—my father would chide her. "We are together. We are alive. Things could be much worse."

Things got much worse. The ravages of war made it impossible for us to find food or work in Poland. We moved westward, against the tide of the German advance into Russia, first through Czech-Slovakia and then into Austria. Luckily, my father's obvious disability allowed an otherwise able-bodied man to avoid suspicion from the paranoid German population. We were forced to the cities, where my parents could find factory jobs, masquerading as German citizens. My sister and I were hidden most of the day for fear that our poor language abilities would give us away. I remember hiding in attics and cellars of old buildings, scrounging food from trashcans; trying to sleep during the hot summer days on shaded rooftops.

It is amazing to me that we survived those four years behind enemy lines. By the time the war was winding to an end, my parents had connected with a small group of similarly displaced Russians and had moved to Rosenheim, where we convinced a poor German family to rent us two basement rooms in their ancient, and decrepit, stucco house. The town was a shambles, the product of Allied bombing and German looting. I remember the day when the American jeeps rumbled down the road, crossing the bridge over the Inn River into the center of town. A group of about 500 gathered around the Americans, who first pointed their rifles at the people, and then relaxed. My father waded into the crowd, and spoke for a few minutes with one of the town's elders, who was wearing a dirty and wrinkled waistcoat and a black, stovepipe hat. When he came back to us (we were standing across the street, in the shadows of an alley), father was smiling. He said, in Russian, "The war is over," and he kissed Eugeni and tousled my hair with the long fingers of his right hand.

A few days later, we gathered our meager possessions and hopped into the back of an American Army convoy truck, on our way to a "Displaced Persons" facility in Kempten. The camp was situated in an old German army training complex, and was well-stocked with food and medical supplies. When we arrived, we were told we had three days to register in one of several refugee groups, according to our nationality. I remember the heated discussions about how best to comply with this requirement. To register as a displaced Soviet citizen might put us in danger of getting sent back, where we would be exiled to the Arctic or, possibly, executed for leaving in the first place. To register otherwise risked criminal prosecution for falsification. My parents talked about this well into our first night there.

We learned that our concern about going back to the Soviet Union was shared by most of the refugees at the camp. The American military organization had formed official screening panels to review DP documentation and nationality claims. Not surprisingly, a corresponding and sophisticated enterprise had sprung up at Kempten to counterfeit all forms of records, including marriage certificates, baptismal records and other forms of proof that the holders weren't Russian, or had been safely out of the country before the war started. My father decided to declare his Soviet citizenship, and to apply at the same time for asylum. He reasoned that the Allies would understand our plight, and respect our wishes not to be sent back to a hostile country. He also felt that with so many applicants using falsified documentation, the Americans surely would figure things out and not look kindly on those trying to lie their way past the panels.

The Americans didn't mind the lies. They overlooked the obvious forgeries and declared that many refugees were from Poland, Greece and Hungary, even though they were as Russian as the Czar. What the Americans couldn't understand was our direct plea for compassion, understanding and mercy. My father told the whole story to the Americans. He described our flight from the arbitrary and discriminatory edicts of a madman. He detailed the extreme and painful conditions under which he led his family to safety at the hands of the Americans. And he convincingly related his urgent and sincere desire to emigrate to the West; he said that his unique skills would be valuable in his new home.

The panel of three American officers, none of whom were more than 30 years old, listened patiently but rejected my father's position. We were Russian citizens and therefore would be repatriated in a few weeks. There were no exceptions or grants of political asylum. My father was assured that the Soviet government would welcome us back warmly. After all, the country had suffered tremendously during the war, and needed its able-bodied and minded citizens back to rebuild. There was no appealing this decision.

We were placed in the Russian camp for two weeks. The mood in the camp was one of utter despair. Children didn't play. The women huddled together, praying and crying. Young men hunkered in small groups, smoking American cigarettes and conspiring with each other. Old men sat on their bunks, or on benches outside, and stared into the void.

Early in the morning of August 13, 1945, we put our clothes and other possessions into knapsacks and began our walk across the Russian camp to the American trucks that were parked in the schoolyard several hundred meters away. The sun was just breaking through some low clouds on the eastern horizon, reddening the sky. There were 20 or 30 of us trudging toward the yard, and no one said a word. Every few steps, my father would look left and right, as did a few other men in our group, as if they were waiting for something. I also looked, but saw nothing more than a few people milling about.

When we got closer to the trucks, those just 'milling about' formed a crowd of perhaps two hundred. They came at us and formed lines three or four deep on both sides of the street, paralleling our path. They were DPs from the Polish camp, and were chanting, their voices defiant and strong. We stopped walking. I hoped the crowd would absorb us in its midst and take us away. American soldiers piled out from behind the trucks, moving between the Polish crowd and us. One of them said, "Let's go. Move!" as he motioned to my father to keep walking.

At that moment, a loud yell came from the top floor of the six-story school building just ahead of us. A blond man was standing by the window, holding a small boy, perhaps five years old, by the waist. The man kissed the boy, made the sign of the Cross on his forehead and threw him out the window. The body lay motionless on the sidewalk below. The crowd was silent, and remained so when the blond man threw a young girl from the window. Only when the man himself dove clumsily down, head first, to his death, did the crowd react with a collective cry and move in the direction of the soldiers.

The stunned Americans froze in their spots. It seemed as if the crowd would run them over, and we would be free! But within a few seconds, a tall, powerfully built officer emerged in the center of the square and fired off a round of bullets into the air from a submachine gun. The soldiers fixed their rifles on the crowd. Another burst from the machine gun stopped the crowd's advance, and we were whisked into a six-wheel convoy truck before there was any further reaction. Within minutes, we were on the road, heading to the railway station in Kaufbeuren, for the long trip to Moscow.

As we later learned, we were the first, and only, group of repatriates to have left the Kempten camp. The courageous Polish refugees (led, it seems, by a Ukrainian posing as a Pole), continued their insurrection, forcing the Americans to scuttle the plan.

What happened to those lucky people is not clear to

me. But being unlucky cost me my family, and most of my life.

***

Sam rested the document on his desk and raised his eyes to the ceiling. He recalled the first time he'd read it and wished he hadn't. He had been tempted to throw it out, but didn't because Rusty Culliford, an Irish soldier with whom Sam had grown close during the War, had sent it to him at the beginning of the year. Any thought of getting rid of it later ended with word that Rusty had passed away.

So why was he reading it again?

Maybe it was because he learned, from Anton, that he couldn't run from his past.

***

The Gulags in the Kolyma region of the Soviet Union occupy the far northwestern corner of Siberia, on the Pacific Coast. There is no more inhospitable place in the world. There are also fewer parts of the world with greater accumulations of untapped natural resources. It is the combination of these two factors that led Stalin to conclude that forced labor would be the only effective way of exploiting these valuable assets. The millions of displaced Russians involuntarily repatriated after the war, joined the tens of millions of common criminals and political rivals (real and imagined) in working the gold mines, digging the canals, building the railways and harvesting the forests for "the glory of the Motherland." I was imprisoned there for almost 20 years.

After we reached Moscow, my father was taken away

before our internment in a holding camp. I know from the one letter that reached me that he was jailed at the Lubyanka prison, and died a year or so later. We received no explanation of why he was imprisoned, how he died, or where he was buried.

My mother, sister and I were interrogated at great length by a short, fat NKVD officer named Schransky. I can't recall what I said, but it seemed to please him. My mother, on the other hand, said nothing at first. She was threatened with beatings, and isolated from her children for days at a time. Finally, she told them what they wanted to hear, and we were put on a train to Vladivostok. The train car was so crowded that we had to take turns sitting and standing. There was a "waste bucket" in the corner, which was hidden from view by nothing more than a dirty white sheet. There was minimal ventilation, and the stench in the car was so bad that vomiting was commonplace. Thankfully, our three-month journey ended just as the truly frigid weather was beginning, for there was no heat in the train car.

From Vladivostok, we were herded onto a pre-war ocean steamer, for the three-week trip north past Japan, through the Sea of Okhosk, to the port of Magadan. Once again, we were given only minimal food rations, limited fresh water and no privacy.

By the time we arrived at Kolyma, the average daily temperature was negative 10 degrees Fahrenheit. Before winter's end, the temperature would drop to below minus 50 degrees. In those conditions, we would walk five or more miles to the gold mine, where we would dig for eight straight hours with primitive tools and only a 15-minute break for food. We would then walk back to the camp, bathe in cold water, eat our meager rations of fish soup and hard white bread, and go to sleep to prepare for the next day of work. The routine was followed for seven days a week, seven out of eight weeks. On our "rest week," we had one day off.

Many prisoners injured themselves to try and avoid work. Some cut off fingers or toes, others entire limbs. Prisoners regularly committed suicide, or succumbed to the pressures of guards and other prisoners and became stoolies, or sexually prostituted themselves, for extra food rations or better working conditions.

I joined a gang of Volga Germans in the camp. I am humiliated to admit that I allowed myself to degenerate, engaging in acts of extortion, assault and theft in the name of self-protection.

My sister was gang-raped by a group of prisoners who had been allowed into the women's camp by a bribed guard. She killed herself by slitting her wrists in the forest when she realized she became pregnant. My mother never recovered from this. She refused to work, and when her food rations were diminished as punishment, she stopped eating altogether. She died in a solitary confinement cell a month later.

Although the Second World War may have ended in 1945 for America, it extended a great deal longer for the three million displaced persons of Russian origin who were rounded up by American, British, Soviet and other allied forces and sent back forcibly to Stalin's camps and his gallows. The vast majority of these people were as innocent as was our family.

As the world celebrates the fiftieth anniversary of the

end of that war, it is important that all the stories—good and bad, heroic and dishonorable—come to light. Otherwise, all the death and suffering and dislocation will certainly have been for naught.

***

Putting the pages down, Sam thought he could isolate the numbness he'd been carrying since the end of the war to a spot at the base of his neck. Before reading the Repatriation story, the spot was burning hot, sensitive to the touch. Now, as he descended the stairs to the kitchen in search of some Advil and a Diet Coke, he detected some relief.

Sam felt more determined than at any time in the past few weeks. After decades of hiding and lying to himself, he resolved to revisit the place that had so changed his character and re-formed his future. Part of that meant going to Vienna. It also involved talking to the Shoah Foundation.

When Gloria got home a few minutes later, Sam greeted her with a hug and asked her to sit with him in the living room. He explained that he needed to go to Vienna later that week, and why.

"Thank God," she said.

Sam was surprised by her reaction. "You want to get rid of me?"

"Of course not. I'm thanking God for helping you make this decision. It's been a long time coming. I prayed for you today."

"Has it been that bad?" asked Sam

"Not for me. But when you wake screaming from a nightmare or bury yourself in your job, I've known that something is eating you up, inside. You've never wanted to talk about it, and I never felt right about intruding."

"It's been getting worse," Sam admitted, hanging his head. "I used to be able to push it back, but that doesn't work anymore."

"I could tell. Ever since you met Anton...." Gloria stopped in mid-sentence, as if she knew better than to continue her train of thought.

Sam's mind was flooding with images of Anton, the same gaunt and gray as the inmate in Gunskirchen whose head Sam cradled during his last breaths. "He's dying."

Gloria moved over to sit next to her shaky husband. She put her arms around Sam, held him tenderly, and said soothingly, "He's a remarkable man, and he's been a wonderful friend. He'll always be with you."

***

Sam slept poorly Sunday evening. Just when he would finally exhaust his wartime nightmares and be on the verge of sleep, some inner voice would remind him that he couldn't afford the luxury of rest. His wife was still ill and his survival at GSC was tenuous. At 4:30 a.m., he gave up and got out of bed. He was in the office by 6.

With the benefit of a caffeine buzz, Sam started his day on Monday getting his travel plans in order. He called Jon Lavendar in the London office to give him the good news—Sam would indeed be coming to the IMF meetings and the GSC gala on Thursday evening (a/k/a "the prom")—and the bad news—Sam would not be doing any other traveling and would only be available Thursday evening and Friday morning.

Sam cut off Lavendar's consequent whining with a sharp "I'm not in the mood, goddamn it!"

Sam was waiting for Pam the moment she walked in. He asked her to book his flights, instruct the firm's special events department to get him into the Imperial Hotel and provide him with credentials to attend the various delegates' events. He also dropped the Army reunion invitation on her desk and requested that she respond for the Wednesday dinner only and find out who else was coming.

Pam looked up from her desk and said, "Just you?"

At first, Sam had no idea what she was talking about. But he knew Pam well enough to know that there was a reason—usually an excellent one—behind every question she asked. Then he got it.

"Just me. I haven't figured out what to do about her yet."

During his fidgety attempts at sleep, Sam wrestled with the Gloria situation. One solution—asking Rebecca to staywith her for the couple of days he'd be gone --was untenable because his granddaughter would be in the second week of her new job in Washington.

Gloria had seemed much calmer that past two weeks or so, her anger in check. While Sam had to admit she was more subdued than usual, she certainly didn't seem depressed. *Could I leave her alone? It's only for three nights.*

To forestall second-guessing his decision to go to Vienna, Sam wandered out to the trading floor looking for Mike T. He headed to his trading station, and was surprised to find the desk clear of papers and the ashtray empty. "Where is he?" Sam asked of a junior trader.

"He's in London for the next few days, then going to Vienna," was the response.

It had completely slipped Sam's mind, but of course it

made perfect sense. He sat down at that spot, put on a headset and microphone and connected to Mike on the London trading desk.

Mike updated Sam on the market and the desk's positions. As the dollar continued to rally through the afternoon, Mike was able to unload about a quarter of the risk, realizing almost $50 million in cash gains. Sam and he discussed trading strategies for the rest of the day, with the objective of liquidating another 25 percent before the end of the week.

Sam didn't get it right away, but a few minutes into the conversation he sensed that Mike was uncharacteristically low-energy, particularly after such an awesomely successful day. "Are you all right? Jet lag?"

Sam could hear Mike sucking through a cigarette, once again breaking the trading room smoking ban. "I guess."

Clearly, something was wrong. He wanted to keep Mike on the phone long enough to find out, and asked him when he was planning to go to Vienna.

"'Dunno. Not sure I should go."

"What have you heard, Mike? Tell me."

Mike lowered his voice and cupped his hand over the receiver. "Better if I stay here and mind the store, with all this risk. In any event, it's probably a bad idea for me to show up at a shindig for our big clients if I'm being bagged at the end of the year."

Sam was about as angry as he could get. "What are you talking about? Who told you that? You're not going anywhere. Not while I'm around."

Mike was silent on the other end of the phone.

"It's that slimy bastard Todd, right?" Sam hissed.

Sam could hear Mike taking another drag on his cigarette.

"All right, leave it to me. I've got this covered."

Sam hung up and stormed back to his office. Pam flagged him down with two messages: he had missed calls from Mark Todd and his son. Todd wanted to see Sam right away, and Jeffrey was hoping to have lunch with his father in Vienna Thursday.

"Lunch with my son, that's fine. Tell Todd I'm around all day. And please arrange for me to have a private meeting with Stanley before the prom," and then, under his breath, *where I can rip his head off.*

***

The five-mile walk to her apartment took no time, absorbed as Rebecca was in characterizing her anger at Charley. He was, she concluded, nothing more than a selfish, arrogant, lying, cheating son of a bitch. It was comforting to have real clarity.

The waters became muddied, however, only a few minutes later as Rebecca initiated the playback mechanism on her telephone answering machine.

"'Becca, it's me. I just got my messages. Sorry I didn't call sooner, but you told me you were going to New York for the weekend—I just left a message there—and I was sure I'd be back today. As it turns out, I'm going to have to stay…ah… here for a few more days. I'm okay….fine, actually. I'll try and call later. Luv ya."

The sound quality was lousy, but it was clear that Charley's tone was buoyant. On one level, she was relieved to hear he was alright. But still, where the hell was he?

After listening to the message again, carefully, she grabbed some change from her purse, left her apartment and walked to the Georgetown campus. Passing several storefront windows, Rebecca stole a peek at her reflection, and behind, to see if she was being followed. Once she was satisfied that she was alone, she made her way to the student center and occupied a phone booth with an open view of the front doors.

Rebecca dialed her grandparents' New York number, and deposited the requested amount of coinage. Gloria answered, and told Rebecca that Charley had, indeed, called just a short while ago. He left a number where Rebecca could try him, which Gloria read off to her granddaughter. "Funny thing, though. He specifically asked me not to call you, but to wait for you to call me to give you this number."

Rebecca thanked her grandmother and hustled her off the phone. She then dialed the operator, and placed the call to the number Charley had given Gloria using her credit card. After a short delay, and several European style rings, an operator picked up.

"Gruss Gott. Pension Christina."

"Uh, I'm sorry. Do you speak English?'

"Yes."

"Great. Do you have a Mr. Robertson staying there?"

"Mr. Roberts. Charles Roberts. Room 323. Yes?"

Rebecca felt her heart rate increasing. "Could I speak with him please?"

"Moment."

He picked up on the first ring.

"Where are you?" Rebecca demanded.

"I'm...wait. Where are you calling from?"

"I'm on a pay phone at school. I figured that much out."

Rebecca froze for a moment as a thin man in a gray suit walked past the booth and glanced at her. She followed him with her eyes until he disappeared into an elevator across the lobby. "You're a bastard. I've been worried sick. For all I knew, you were lying in a ditch in Rock Creek Park. Where are you?"

"Trying to be careful, that's all. I'm in, ah...Europe."

"You're in Vienna, goddamn it. Why lie to me?"

Charley's response was delayed, and his voice muted, as if he had changed location and was cupping his hand over the receiver. "I'm not lying. I'm just being careful."

"What are you doing in Vienna?"

Rebecca didn't give Charley a chance to answer. "ATAC?'

"Uh-huh," he said

It all came together for Rebecca. "The IMF meetings," she snapped. "It must be an anti-globalization retreat."

"Hardly a retreat. We're working our tails off, setting things up. There's a lot left to do before...before it's over."

Rebecca was getting claustrophobic in the narrow telephone booth. She was also getting mad at being jerked around. She needed some fresh air and clarity from Charley, and barked at him. "What the hell are you up to?"

Charley withheld his response for a few moments, giving Rebecca the impression that he was counting to 10 to moderate his own anger. Finally, he said in an obviously controlled voice, "Nothing to worry about. Didn't you ask that we keep our 'things' separate? This is my 'thing', and I'll tell you all about it when I get back in a few days. I got to go. It's best if you call me—tomorrow?"

***

Sitting outside on a wooden bench, Rebecca tried to sort through her feelings. She told herself she should be irrevocably angry with Charley for his sins of omission and immediately write him out of her life. But that just wasn't how things were settling in. On the contrary, the more she thought about their phone conversation, the more concerned she became about him.

The University Library was just a few steps away. Rebecca ducked inside and headed for the computer room. She emerged, three hours later, knowing a lot more about the organization Charley had allied himself with, and not feeling the least bit good about it.

ATAC had its roots in France in the late '70s as a far-left student group. The organization's constituency spread to Germany, Italy and the Low Countries by 1983, but its anti-American orientation kept it from establishing any meaningful representation in the U.S. or the U.K. When the Soviet Union fell apart, and Communist regimes folded around the world, ATAC found itself a rebel without a cause and with an aging and declining membership base.

Its leaders took up the fair-trade, global justice agenda in the early 1990s and with it a highly confrontational, and in many cases violent, *modus operandi*. Rebecca located newspaper reports of the 1990 street protests in Milan in which government offices were firebombed and two policemen killed. ATAC operatives were arrested and convicted of inciting the riots and causing those deaths. Likewise, ATAC was among several groups blamed for the unsuccessful plot to assassinate the president of the World Bank at the G-6 meetings in London in 1992.

Rebecca found several references to Didier Bendit on the internet, emphasizing his role as a leader of ATAC and in the forefront of the anti-globalization movement. One article, contained in a British political science journal, quoted him justifying the use of "direct action to destroy, not just reform, the instruments of capitalist domination".

"We are at war," he continued, "and we should consider

all the tools of war, conventional or otherwise, to be at our disposal."

Rebecca went back to Charley's apartment and began tearing the place apart. She found it hard to believe that the man she knew and thought she loved would have bought into the message of violence that seemed to be ATAC's hallmark. Rebecca was hoping to find something—anything—that might help her understand.

After a few frustrating minutes, Rebecca picked up a small wastebasket from the floor near the desk where Charley kept his laptop—now missing—and dumped its contents on the bed. Amidst the soda cans, sandwich wrappers and old newspapers was a ball of white crumbled paper. Rebecca unfurled it greedily.

The title at the top said, "Delegates Schedule-Continued." Underneath, the page had a subheading for "Thursday" and one for "Friday. Each day was broken into time periods, with columns for "Events" and "Location." The first entry for Thursday was, at 8:30 a.m., "Breakfast sponsored by DeutscheBank, Hilton Hotel Grand Foyer." Later that morning, at 11:00, was "Dollarization and its Discontents: a paper by Rudi Samuelsson, Monterey Room, Imperial Hotel." Rebecca's eye went down toward the bottom of the page, where some handwriting—she didn't think it was Charley's—appeared in the margin. It said "Hans und Gretel."

What the hell does that mean?

She folded up the paper, put it in her pocket, and went back to the phone booths to ask Charley. Rebecca calculated that it was past 2 in the morning in Vienna, but placed the call anyway. When no one answered in his room, she snarled, "Working your tail off, huh," into the receiver and stormed out of the booth, leaving it dangling.

***

Rebecca slept poorly Sunday evening, and it showed the following day. Most of her co-workers looked at her in a way that suggested they thought she might be sick, hung-over or a mugging victim.

Charley still hadn't answered his phone in the morning, and Rebecca tried to push any thoughts of him aside as she sat as her desk and prepared to start her first day as a full-time employee. All her well-intentioned discipline faded, however, when she saw the memo taped to her computer from Caroline Coleman, her boss. She was being redirected from a lobbying study on futures trading to helping out on GSC events at the IMF meeting in Vienna. One of the senior associates had taken seriously ill over the weekend, and Rebecca was urgently needed to fill in.

Caroline gave her a specific assignment: make contact with the offices of the numerous governmental officials who were attending the big GSC event and make sure that the appropriate credentials were issued. Rebecca was advised that some of the VIPs may request specific details about security arrangements at the event, and it would be her responsibility to get them the information they need, or put them in touch with the Firm's protection department if she couldn't help herself.

Rebecca skimmed through the thick folder her boss had given her. She stopped first at the spreadsheet providing the names of the officials attending the event with whom she was to make contact. As she went through the list, Rebecca saw a number of highly recognizable names, including those of the U.S Treasury Secretary, the President of the World Bank and, she noted with a smile, her father.

She glanced at several documents regarding the logistics of the IMF meetings itself, and after a few minutes of skimming, stopped at a page that seemed eerily familiar, with the heading "Delegates Schedule." Rebecca turned to the continuation page, and remembered where she had seen it before: yesterday, in Charley's apartment.

Looking more carefully at the page now than she had the night before, she realized that the handwritten words were in the margin next to the entry for the "Black Tie Delegates Reception, sponsored by GSC, Schonbrunn Palace." Rebecca tried hard, but unsuccessfully, to derive some meaning from that juxtaposition, and continued to peruse the file.

Rebecca quickly reviewed four or five more documents before coming to a memorandum entitled "Vendors and Contracted Suppliers." The very first entry, for catering, read "Hans und Gretel Lebensmittellieferant" and listed an address and phone number in Vienna.

Hans and Gretel. Caterers.

Rebecca wasn't sure if her headache was from sleep deprivation or a growing sense of foreboding. She called Charley from the office phone, not giving a damn whether her calls were being tapped or not, and again no one answered. When the hotel operator got back on the line, Rebecca asked whether Charley had picked up her earlier messages, and the answer—that he had not—had a deeply unsettling effect.

Caroline walked by Rebecca's desk just after she hung up. She leaned her elbow on the half-wall of the cubicle that defined Rebecca's work space and said, "Are you OK? You're pale as a sheet."

"Oh, yeah," Rebecca said, trying to straighten her posture and force some blood into her head. "I'm fine. I think it's something I ate last night—food poisoning maybe."

"Don't apologize... Here's why I came by. I know it's crazy, but we're desperate. Carrie—the woman whose job you're doing now—her husband called a few minutes ago. Her appendix ruptured Saturday and she's out of work for a while. She was supposed to leave for the IMF event tomorrow night and help with logistics, but obviously that's not going to happen. I've tried two other associates here, but they can't go either for one reason or another. So that leaves you."

"Me? For what?"

Caroline leaned in. "Vienna. You'd work the prom. Leave tomorrow night, and be back on Friday."

Rebecca stared at her boss, working hard to put this new information into context, but the thoughts didn't coalesce.

Caroline clasped her hands together in a prayer. "Between us, if you wanted to stay to the end of the weekend, who's to know? Please say you'll do it—I'm really in a bind."

Rebecca was never one to believe in signs from above, but this coincidence was just too weird to ignore. It was only after she had said, "Sure, why not?" to her boss and accepted her gratitude that Rebecca thought more deeply about the implications of her agreement. Would she tell Charley she was coming, or surprise him, or spy on him, or sneak up on him? Could she really go and *not* tell him about it? What would he think? What would this do to their relationship?

Her head was spinning. She got up from her desk and went to the ladies room, which was luckily empty and paced back and forth. The arguments and counterarguments began swirling through her head.

The only reason for going was to check on Charley, and that was a bad thing. Why should she have to do that? If he wouldn't be open and truthful with her, then the hell with him. She'd go back, quickly, to Caroline and say she couldn't go— make up an important engagement she'd forgotten about.

Moving back and forth among the stalls in the bathroom, Rebecca was fundamentally uncomfortable with that result. She pressed to articulate to herself why: *No, I can't do that. I've already told her I'll go, and reneging now would really piss her off. Anyway, I'd be going to Vienna for work, that's all. I didn't engineer this, it just came along. Maybe I'll see Charley, maybe not. That was a second-order decision that could be made later. Relax...relax...there's no rush.*

Rebecca threw some cold water on her face and breathed deeply through her nose, yoga-style. She stared into the mirror over the sink, willing herself to take control and trust her instincts. When another employee entered the bathroom, Rebecca left and went back to her cubicle.

A red light was flashing on her phone, signifying she had a message waiting. She put in her code, and heard Charley's muffled voice on the recording. "Sorry I missed you again. I'll be at that number in a few minutes, but don't call me from your office."

Rebecca went down to the lobby, bought a bottle of water and found a pay phone against the wall. She caught herself checking out others in the lobby, worrying that her conversation might be overheard.

She let the phone ring five or six times, and an out-of-breath Charley finally answered.

Rebecca surprised herself with her greeting: "Where the hell have you been?"

"Working," he responded remotely.

Charley's tone got her heart racing again. "All night?"

Now Charley's voice sounded indignant. "Well, yeah. There are certain, ah...things that can only be done then. I'm exhausted, so maybe I'm taking it the wrong way, but how come you're busting my chops?"

Charley's observation struck home, and Rebecca tried to calm herself down. "Sorry. All this cloak and dagger stuff is making me nuts. Want to hear something crazy? My boss asked me if I could go to Vienna tomorrow. The company is throwing a big party, and at the last minute they need more people to cover it. They'd even pay for me to stay the weekend, so we could hang out there."

Charley's end of the phone became uncomfortably quiet. "Are you still there?" Rebecca whispered into the receiver.

"It's not a great idea," he said stiffly.

That caught Rebecca off guard. "What's not a great idea? Coming to Vienna, or staying the weekend?"

Charley's response—he'd be to busy to spend any time with her, and the city was so crammed with diplomats, police, media types and protesters that there was no room to breathe—was clearly incomplete. When Rebecca tried to push him into elaborating, he just changed the subject.

She considered probing deeper into exactly what "things" Charley could only do in the middle of the night, and how the Hans and Gretel caterers entered into all of this, but knew it wouldn't get her anywhere.

"Ok, forget it. I've got a ton of stuff to do around here, anyway."

***

Sam was one of the first to board the Austrian Air flight, and took his place in the second row, aisle seat, of the spacious first-class cabin. He exchanged his loafers for slipper socks, put his tie in his briefcase and fingered the sleeping pill in his shirt pocket.

Allowing himself to drift into the memory of his most recent visit with Anton, Sam faced now what he refused to deal with then--that it might be the last time he would see his dear friend alive. He was filling with self-doubt and recriminations about actually going on this trip for purely selfish reasons. What difference did it make whether Sam confronted Stanley and extended his career at the Firm for one or more years? How could that possibly stack up against the chance that Anton would die while he was away?

As if that wasn't bad enough, Sam vividly recalled the disappointment in Gloria's face when he insisted that her sister stay with her while he was away. She didn't argue, but looked terribly hurt. She barely spoke with him after that, not even to say "goodbye" when he left for the airport.

The panic of being trapped in a bad place started creeping up Sam's spine. People were still boarding the airplane, he noticed. It wasn't too late to get off.

Sam reached down for his shoes, and the movement jarred him from that uncomfortable train of thought. He heard Anton's voice in his head urging him to follow the quest to face up to his past. And he remembered his promise to Reggie.

Sam left his shoes in place and folded back in his seat, staring out the porthole of the oversized jet. He couldn't chicken out—not again.

Sam was deep in thought when someone asked, seemingly of him, "Is this seat taken?"

Before he could turn and respond—he intended to comment on the absurdity of the question in the first-class compartment of a long-distance aircraft—Rebecca plopped down beside him.

"Surprise!" she chirped.

He was too stunned to speak.

Rebecca told him the story—leaving out any reference to Charley—of the past two days. She also noted that Pam, when she found out through the assistant's network that Rebecca was going to be on the same flight as her grandfather, arranged for the upgrade to first class and coincident seating.

"I'm here last-minute myself. There are a million things going on that should keep me at home, but..." Sam wondered how honest he was going to be in completing the sentence "I've got a lot of open ends that need tending and a limited amount of time to do it."

Rebecca gave him a quizzical look.

Sam understood that was a cryptic answer, but after almost 50 years of internalization, he recognized he lacked the skills necessary to summarize his complex and emotionally tangled mindset. So, even though he had resolved to dissemble no longer, Sam pulled out a platitude for Rebecca and immediately felt bad about it. "That sounded melodramatic. I just meant that I'm going to retire reasonably soon—30 years at the firm is long enough—and I've got a lot of people to say goodbye to."

She seemed satisfied. "You should write a book about your Wall Street experiences."

Sam touched her hand. "Nah. Who cares about that? It's just a bunch of money-grubbing guys beating each other with clubs. If ever I were to write a book..."

Their conversation was interrupted by flight attendants passing out pillows and safety announcements over the PA system. It wasn't until after takeoff that Rebecca and Sam spoke again.

"Grandpa, what happened to you during the war? Sorry for asking and sorry if it makes you uncomfortable. Ever since I was little, I've wanted to know. You were always reading books about it, but wouldn't talk about it. You showed me pictures, but never told any stories."

Sam softened at his granddaughter's perceptive observation. He thought he had successfully hidden his inner turmoil by avoiding any conversation about his war experiences. Obviously, that was not the case.

Sam took a sip of gin from his glass and stared straight ahead. "At the end of the war my battalion was involved in some heavy fighting. I remember the details of those days like they were etched on my brain. The smells, the sounds, the colors, the horror—sensory overload. I've never known what to do with all that information. So I keep it inside. I guess it shows?"

Rebecca shifted in her seat to be able to look directly at Sam. "That's scary. That's almost exactly what I said to the therapist after the accident. I had stored up every impression of the fighting between my parents and with me. I remembered every aspect of the car crash and couldn't let it go. It was like I was haunted. But they made me talk about it, and told me it would make me feel better. The bad memories haven't gone away, but I guess I've learned to accept that they're part of me."

Sam felt himself on the verge of an unfamiliar place—where his thoughts weren't censored. He could use the long flight to tell the entire story and get the whole thing off his chest. He looked at his beautiful granddaughter and quickly realized that it would not be fair to burden her with his transgressions.

"I was proud of you. It was painful for you to go through remembering, but you did it. The truth is, and I apologize for not telling you everything, that I'm going to Vienna to go through therapy of sorts myself. It's been 50 years. It's about time."

CHAPTER 12

Rebecca desperately needed a nap after the overnight flight, but she was expected at Schonbrunn Palace, the location of the GSC gala, by 10 a.m. for a pre-event briefing and schedule check. She'd just have to tough it out through the day.

She and Sam shared a cab to the Imperial, and they parted when Sam was assigned his suite on the 9th floor and Rebecca her broom closet on the second. She thought about calling Charley, before and after her shower, but pushed it aside and tried to focus on her job. She was escorted into a Mercedes taxi by the hotel doorman, and kept the window open for the entire ride in heavy city traffic to Schloss Schonbrunn.

The air lessened her nausea, but did little to improve her focus. Her thoughts bounced between what she would say to Charley when she saw him and what she might do if she didn't. When the cab finally pulled up in front of the employee gate for the gargantuan, 2,000-room baroque palace on the western edge of the city, Rebecca couldn't shake the persistent tightness at the base of her neck insisting that she find Charley and determine what the hell was going on.

The obvious issue, she recognized, was that her disquietude could very likely be a delusion. She had no concrete evidence that Charley was involved in anything nefarious, or dishonest. Maybe all the secrecy and indirection was simply because he thought he was being watched?

The cab driver interrupted Rebecca's analysis by announcing the fare, which she paid, and left the car. She stood by the entrance of the palace for a moment, still thinking about Charley, and responded automatically when the guard asked if he could help her. She presented her GSC ID, which he compared to a list on his clipboard. He told her, in excellent and accented English, where the other GSC event staffers were meeting and handed her a floor plan of the enormous facility, which he marked with X's to indicate where she currently was and where she would be going.

Rebecca concentrated on following the map. Down an endless corridor, up two flights of stairs, around two corners and down another hallway. Finally, she reached Room 333. The space had been restored to its previous elegance, with gilded chandeliers and pastel tinted frescoes on the fifteen foot ceilings above. Even the conference table seemed a relic of nobler days. Measuring a full 20 feet in length and five feet across, it was supported by curved, ornate legs which met the floor as claws clutching ovoid balls.

Approximately 20 people were taking their seats around the table, and Rebecca recognized several of them from the New York office. The head of event planning at the company, Melanie Holmes, walked over to Rebecca and welcomed her. "You're just in time for the security briefing. We'll talk afterwards."

Rebecca walked down to the end of the table and sat near one of the floor-to-ceiling windows. Looking out, Rebecca could see that the conference room was perched over a large, cobblestone courtyard which was the service entrance for the facility.

Melanie called the meeting to order. She handed out sheets that detailed the precise timing for the next day's event, ranging from when the flowers were to be delivered to when the dessert set up would begin. She made sure that GSC employees knew their responsibilities for each detail, and answered several logistical questions from people around the table.

Melanie introduced a large, crew-cut man in a gray suit, white shirt and solid blue tie. "This is Robert Reynolds, the director of security for the American Embassy in Vienna. He's responsible, as are all of you, for making sure our guests have a safe and secure time. Please listen very carefully to Mr. Reynolds and don't be shy about asking for clarification."

"Thank you, Ms. Holmes. We'll be spending the next several minutes reviewing with you the security apparatus established for the event that will take place here tomorrow evening. I should point out that we have no specific, credible threats of terrorist activity or threats to the safety of our people. With that said, as I'm sure you know, the IMF meetings tend to act as a magnet for many different types of characters and special interest groups, some of whom would like nothing more than to grab a headline or otherwise disrupt an event. There will be many dignitaries here, and they are sure to attract a lot of attention."

Blue folders were handed out by one of Melanie's assistants while Reynolds continued:

"In these folders is a schematic diagram of Schonbrunn Palace. Please note the places where embassy security and local police personnel will be located, indicated by red and green dots, respectively. These people will be wearing tags clearly noting their role. Now, focus on the blue dots. Non-embassy security personnel, who will be undercover, will be located in these locations. Should you need help or see something suspicious, signal one of agents at these locations. Take a few minutes to review these sheets, as you will be returning them to me when this session concludes."

Rebecca tried not to look as uncomfortable as she felt in the three or four minutes of silence that followed. She weighed the known facts against her gnawing qualms, hoping that some clear resolution would emerge. She considered sharing her suspicions with agent Reynolds, but had trouble thinking through the consequences.

Rebecca's eyes wandered away from the handout to the courtyard below. She saw a white van with blue lettering on the back and sides which read "Hans und Gretel Lebensmittellieferant." Now staring intensely, she watched as several people—two women and two men—got out of the vehicle. Rebecca relaxed for a moment when it was clear Charley was not among them, but then almost lost her breath when one of the women walking from the van into the building took off her cap and exposed a mop of ginger colored hair.

Rebecca's heart was pumping as she turned from the window and thought about what to do next. She almost jumped out of her skin, however, when she realized that Melanie's assistant was standing right next to her, holding out her hand.

"Could I have the layout diagram back, please?"

***

The briefing lasted another half-hour, and Rebecca found it hard to keep her eyes from the courtyard and her mind on the logistical information being discussed. When the meeting finally ended, Rebecca used the bathroom recess to run downstairs and find access to the courtyard.

She waited, impatiently, in the shadows for at least 20 minutes for Fatima to appear, and was about to return upstairs when she finally spied her emerging from the far end of the square. Rebecca moved quickly toward her, from behind. Surprised at her own boldness, she grabbed the woman firmly by the elbow and demanded, "I need to talk to Charley."

Fatima turned and pulled her arm away violently. "What? Are you crazy?" She worriedly looked left and right. "Go away!"

One of the other caterers, a tall man whom Rebecca didn't recognize, moved menacingly at Rebecca. Fatima shook her head quickly, sending him away.

Rebecca moved her face right into Fatima's. "I need to talk to Charley. Is he here?"

"I don't know."

"Bullshit," growled Rebecca. "I assume you don't want me to make a scene. But I will. Where is he?"

Fatima clearly didn't know what to do, but just as clearly wanted to get out of there as soon as possible. She glared at Rebecca defiantly and hissed, "He's back at the hotel. He was there a few hours ago. Don't be stupid."

Rebecca had never hit anyone in anger—well, maybe Charley—but the impulse to smack this bitch was almost irresistible. If Fatima had stared her down another half second, Rebecca was sure she'd have done it. But Fatima turned her back, climbed into the catering van and drove away.

Rebecca's impulse was to find a cab and rush over to Charley's hotel. She'd make Charley come clean. *No more bullshit.*

She also considered saying something to that security guy, Reynolds. But as she thought about it, she didn't possess any concrete, actionable facts. She'd look like an idiot, a jealous, emotional jerk, in front of her employer and the Feds.

Rebecca looked at her watch. She was really late. Her absence would be noticed if she didn't get back to the conference room immediately. Still, she wondered, *what the hell was Fatima doing there?*

Dashing up the stairs, Rebecca felt as if she was being torn apart.

Exhaustion compounded her misery as she sat through several hours more of briefings and checklists. They were dismissed at 2 and told to return that evening at 7 p.m. for a final run-through. Rebecca chatted uncomfortably with a group of co-workers for a few minutes, and using jet lag as an excuse, left the Palace and hailed a cab to Charley's hotel.

In the back of the taxi, she tried to organize her thoughts and prepare for a confrontation with Charley. She didn't get very far when the overwhelming need to close her eyes overtook her. The next thing she knew was that the cab had stopped and the driver was waiting to be paid.

Rebecca was caught off-stride immediately when she saw that Charley was waiting for her out front, and he didn't look happy. "What the hell are you doing here? I told you not to come, goddamn it!"

"How did you know I'd be here? Did *she* tell you?" Rebecca knew she needed to regain the advantage.

Charley was reddening. "Stop it. You yell at me for trying to involve you, and then we agreed that you'd stay in New York and let me do my thing here. Now you're stalking me. What do you want?"

"Do you want to talk here, on the street?"

"Ah, shit. No. There's a coffee house down the block. Let's go there."

They walked in silence, entered the *konditorei* and ordered drinks. Rebecca was the first to speak. "You need to tell me exactly what's going on."

Charley responded without looking up from his coffee. "Nothing. We're planning a rally, that's all."

Rebecca knew he was lying. "That's crap. I know something's going on. I saw Fatima today, at the Palace. That's where the GSC party is, tomorrow night. Don't patronize me."

Charley placed his enormous paws flat on the table as if he was restraining himself. He faced Rebecca and said firmly, "You don't *need* to know. And if you were at all smart, you wouldn't *want* to know—it's for your own good."

Rebecca recognized that his statement was tantamount to an admission: he lied to her, her suspicions were accurate, and she needed to do something.

"Charley, you've got to stop whatever it is you're up to. My grandfather is going to be there tomorrow night and I'm going to be there with him. I don't want him embarrassed or put in any danger."

He banged the table angrily with his forearm. "Goddamn it. He wasn't on the list." Charley paused for a second. "Tell him to stay away. Make up something. Keep him out of there."

"I can't do that. It's his event. Change your plans."

Charley pushed himself back in his chair and looked up to the ceiling. "*I* can't do that. It's not up to me. Just keep away from there."

Rebecca was steaming mad. "*You* keep away from there, and your moronic friends, or I'll make one phone call and the whole thing will come down on all of you."

Charley was silent as Rebecca glowered. A patron passed by on her way to the bathroom, and the waitress came over and asked if they wanted anything else. Finally, Charley sighed deeply. "Let me make a few phone calls. It may take a while. I'll call you tomorrow if I have any luck. But if you don't hear from me, stay out of there--just stay away from there. Even if you can't get him to listen—*you* keep away."

"I better hear from you before I leave the hotel tomorrow morning," she said, standing up and throwing her coat over her shoulders.

They left the shop and faced each other in the street. Charley reached out to put his arms around Rebecca, but all she gave him was a cheek.

"I'll call you. I will. Just be careful," he said, and turned to walk back to his hotel. Rebecca couldn't have been more unsettled.

***

Rebecca's hopes were raised, but momentarily, by the blinking message light on her hotel room phone. Neither of the two messages was from Charley, however—one was from Melanie, reminding Rebecca to come back to the Palace that evening. The other was from Sam, suggesting that they get together for a drink before his dinner.

Rebecca knew she would go crazy waiting by the phone in her tiny room, and welcomed the opportunity to escape. She called Sam back, and they agreed to meet at 6:00 at the hotel bar. While showering, Rebecca considered telling Sam the whole story. She longed to share her burden, but Sam didn't like Charley, and she felt the need to deal with this on her own.

She spotted her grandfather at a table just in front of the entrance to the lobby bar, looking relaxed in a black turtleneck shirt and blue sport coat. He was sipping a clear liquid from a short glass filled with ice, and rose immediately upon seeing her.

Sam signaled the waitress over, and ordered a glass of Chablis for Rebecca and a refill of his gin martini, "no fruit." They chatted aimlessly for a bit, but Rebecca could tell that Sam's mind was elsewhere. She wondered if he was sensing the same of her.

DIVIDED LOYALTIES

Sam looked at his watch, and sighed. "I've got to get going in a minute, honey. I'm off to the Grinzing—north of the city, where the vineyards are—meeting some of my old Army mates for a reunion. I haven't seen some of these guys for almost 50 years. I've been thinking about it all day, and I hope I'm not disappointed."

Sam looked at Rebecca curiously. If he had asked, she would have told him everything.

"You handled the demons, Rebecca. Better than I would have. Better than I have, to be more precise." Sam looked at his watch again, picked up the check and signed his name. "I've really got to go. Sorry."

Rebecca was on the verge of asking Sam to stay when he asked, "Can I give you a lift?"

"No, that's OK. I'll just grab a cab."

"I'm busy most of the day tomorrow but I'll see you at the party. Have a good night."

Rebecca watched her grandfather move quickly through the lobby to the front entrance without once looking back. She sat there, weary and feeling very much alone, then left the bar with her wine barely touched.

She checked the front desk, and wasn't surprised to hear that no one had called her or left a message.

Rebecca pushed the revolving door and headed to the cab line at the left end of the driveway. The doorman headed her off with "Miss, taxi?" and motioned her toward a black Mercedes sedan waiting in front of the hotel. He moved quickly to open the back door for her, and said "Danke sehr" as he accepted her tip.

Rebecca slid into the comfortable car and asked to be driven to Schonbrunn Palace. She was thinking ahead to what she would do if Charley didn't call when the passenger door on the other side of the car opened and a man slipped in beside her. He was wearing jeans, sneakers and a leather jacket with a turned-up collar that hid much of his face. He held up the index finger of his gloved right hand to his lips, and with a "Sshhh," raised his left hand from his lap just high enough to display a dull black semi-automatic pistol. Rebecca heard the doors lock with a click as the cab driver turned around, nodded, and moved the car forward before Rebecca could even think about jumping out or calling for help. Within a few seconds, they were on the Ring Road heading west, away from the center of town.

CHAPTER 13

The September evening was cool, and the hearty doses of newly-pressed Austrian wine were fragrant and sweet. The combination powered the conversation among the 17 men arrayed on both sides of two wooden picnic tables under the vines of the restaurant in the Grinzing, a lovely Vienna suburb. For many of the former infantryman in Company B, it was the first time in 50 years that they had seen each other, notwithstanding numerous reunion opportunities along the way. For all of them, it was the first time they had been in Austria since the end of the War.

The talk hadn't reached the reminiscence stage just yet; the ex-GIs caught each other up on what they'd been up to since coming home: sound bites about careers, current and former wives, illnesses and operations, children and grandchildren. The men were, relatively speaking, a healthy bunch—no doubt because only the fittest of the survivors would have been inclined to make the trip in the first place, and they weren't shy about making themselves heard.

Eventually, the conversation came around to, "Hey, what ever happened to Lieutenant Miller," which led to, "Remember when Ritchie Campbell plugged that kraut right between the eyes from 100 yards." As dinner was served, the stories came fast and furious. Some were so funny that the waitress had to come over in response to the laughter and, in grade school English, request that the men "keep it *kviieter, bitte.*"

Two hours after they started, almost 15 bottles of locally grown wine had been imbibed, along with plates of stuffed cabbage, schnitzels, wursts and dumplings. As the table was cleared and dessert menus distributed, there was a brief lull in the conversation. The wine probably had something to do with it. And perhaps it was the poignant reunion after all these years of men who, literally, had daily put their lives on the line for each other. Sam felt something loosening inside, an urge to share feelings that had been bottled up inside for a half-century.

Sam rapped his knuckles on the table to get everyone's attention. "Now that I've got you all shit-faced, I can pose a question I've been dying to ask. Have any of you heard about Operation Keelhaul or Operation Apple? It started up around the time of our furlough in Vienna, remember? Just before we started training for the invasion of Japan."

Sam's suspicions were confirmed by a consensus of shaking heads. Bill Harrington, a sergeant in Sam's division who was now the longest-serving judge on the Supreme Judicial Court of Massachusetts, said, "I never heard of Keelhaul, but Apple sounds familiar. I think they said that was why you and Marty Diamond left—something to do with displaced persons. At first, we thought you guys had found a way to get your candy-asses out of the mission, but the CO told us you were re-assigned because you spoke German. Is that close?"

Sam delayed answering until the waitress took dessert and coffee orders and moved safely out of earshot. He surprised himself with an articulate and succinct summary of the factual account that underpinned the nightmares that haunted him since leaving Europe five decades earlier.

After the Germans surrendered, Company B was sent to Vienna to train for the invasion of Japan. Sam thought he had truly lucked out when he and Marty Diamond were reassigned to a joint British-American unit responsible for rounding up Russian army deserters who had fallen into Allied hands during the war and sending them back home for trial.

As Sam quickly learned, however, the new job was no cakewalk. His unit was charged with collecting not just soldiers, but civilians as well. Women, children, old men, the ill and infirm, were caught in a broad filter and repatriated. Many had left Russia just after the Bolshevik revolution and had settled in Poland and other Balkan states.

The men at the table were listening carefully. Judge Harrington asked whether Sam's unit was operating in a military, or intelligence capacity.

Sam shook his head. "That's exactly what troubled us at the time. We were Army, plain and simple. Nobody could figure out why we were taking these people, other than the deserting soldiers, who had really suffered at the hands of the Nazis and sending them back to Russia. They were unarmed and posed no threat. It made no sense."

Harrington raised his hand and begged for a bathroom break. Several others took the opportunity to avail themselves of the facilities, leaving Sam alone at his end of the table.

Another secret exposed, he thought to himself. *The important secret.* The experiences and recollections of Gunskirchen haunted Sam, for sure. The situation was grim and awful, and the intellectualization of it could and did create profound conclusions. But the truth is, Sam had been little more than a witness to *that* tragedy. He hadn't done anything, really. He'd just passed through.

Operation Apple was different. Sam was an active, "willing" participant in a condemnable and immoral act, probably illegal under international law. Did it matter that he was wearing a U.S. Army uniform, and was simply "following orders"?

Harrington and the others slowly made their way back to the table and the waitresses appeared to serve the coffee and strudel *mit schlag*. When everyone was settled, Steve Connick asked, "Why would we do it? POWs and deserters are one thing. But civilians?"

Sam had asked himself the question many years ago, and had attempted to thoroughly research the answer. Even though much of the relevant information and documentation about it was highly classified at the time, Sam was able to discover a few formal records, which strongly suggested that Stalin desperately wanted all these ethnic Russians under his control. An infamous paranoid, the Soviet despot couldn't stand to have large groups of potentially anti-Communist Russians outside the country, plotting his overthrow.

Roosevelt and Churchill apparently were willing to go along because they were under enormous pressure to get back their POWs who had fallen into Russian hands. The Americans and English were exhausted from the war, and mothers and wives were desperate to have their captured men returned. The President was genuinely worried that Stalin would use American GIs to barter for his own expatriated citizens. "As a result," said Sam, wearily, "American and British soldiers engaged in a series of secret operations to forcibly repatriate Russians back to the Soviet Union. Most of them had absolutely no interest in going back."

"You said 'forcibly'?" asked the judge.

Sam closed his eyes, feeling the weight of all the years bearing down on him.

***

DIVIDED LOYALTIES

When the Bolshevik revolution started in 1917, one of the Communists' biggest targets were the Cossacks, a fiercely independent, religious tribe that had enjoyed a carte blanche under the White Russians and were often employed as the "special forces" for the czar's personal objectives. Not surprisingly, when Lenin took over, many Cossacks fled the country, dispersing primarily to the Bulgarian and Yugoslavian regions. Others left years later to avoid Stalin's purges. When Hitler invaded the Soviet Union in 1941, many of these displaced Cossacks were dragged from their temporary homes, often serving as conscripted soldiers and slave laborers for the Nazi war effort. Some even defected and joined the German army. Most ended up in Poland, Austria and Germany when the war in Europe came to an end on May 7, 1945.

Two weeks later and 24 days after leaving the Gunskirchen labor camp, Sam Hart was training to be part of the Allied invasion force of Japan in an American base outside of Vienna. His battalion had seen significant battlefield action, and everyone in the group was expecting frontline responsibilities for the assault on the enemy's homeland. They were all terrified.

One morning, at mess, Sam was ordered to report to the Liaison Officer's desk in battalion headquarters, where he was informed that he was being reassigned to a special unit, the Liaisons Tactical Squad, to assist in re-locating the huge numbers of displaced persons throughout Europe. He was told that his selection was due to his language proficiencies, and that he was under strict secrecy orders until further notice. Two hours later, Sam was packed and on his way, along with a dozen other GIs from disparate units, to an undisclosed location. He never said goodbye to any of his Company colleagues or friends.

The British camp at Lienz served as Sam's home for the first week. He was told that he had been seconded to the 36th

English Brigade, which included the 8th Battalion, Argyle and Sutherland Highlanders. For the next two days, Sam engaged in light drills with his adoptive unit, a combination of Scottish and Irish troops under the command of Lieutenant Colonel Alec Malcolm. An Irish private, Rusty Culliford, befriended Sam and filled him in on the recent history of this operation. The brigade had been fighting its way through Italy, and as it approached the Austrian frontier, they prepared to do battle with Russian defectors who were reported to have set up a base housing the military activities of the re-formed Cossack nation. To everyone's surprise, what was found was a widely dispersed group of approximately 35,000 people, half of them women and children, who offered no resistance to the British troops. And while some of the men wore uniforms, only a handful were in German Army garb and even they made it clear they had no bone to pick with the British troops. They formally surrendered on May 8th, the day after Germany unconditionally surrendered to Allied troops.

"Thank God," Rusty said to Sam as they were taking a break from a formation exercise on the unusually warm late May afternoon. "Those Cossacks were fierce-lookin'. Black capes, curved swords, long beards and moustaches—it's like something out of the 1800s. And that was just the women!!! Ha, ha, ha."

The 36th Brigade rounded up the various Cossack communities and moved them from the border to a huge camp, in the Drava Valley, in the town of Peggetz outside the city of Lienz. During the two weeks that preceded Sam's arrival, Rusty told him, the English soldiers had worked with the Cossacks to organize the refugee camp by building huts and installing sewer lines. Warm and collegial relationships were established, and many of the Cossacks expressed their interest in joining forces with the West against their common enemy, Stalin. The British distributed rations, but in all other regards, the Cossacks were responsible for their own governance. Officers retained their own side arms and enough rifles for local policing activity.

"They talk about Stalin as if he was the devil himself," Rusty said. "They don't speak much English, and of course none of us speak whatever they speak, but it's clear they hate the bastard. They think we're going after Russia next, and they'll get their land back. Shit, I hope that's wrong. I've had enough of this."

On the morning of May 27, Sam's unit received an order from Brigadier Musson, calling for the total disarmament of all Cossacks by 2 p.m. that day. The tone of the message ran completely contrary to the positive impressions that had been established since the Cossacks had moved into the Peggetz camp. Musson cautioned his troops that their task would require "great patience and tact," and that they needed to be firm and use their weapons if necessary to carry out their orders. Should any of the Cossacks attempt to flee, and fail to obey a first warning, the soldiers were authorized to take whatever action was necessary, including the use of deadly force, to prevent escape. Should an uncontrollable crowd form, the troops were instructed to "kill the apparent leader." These orders were chilling enough, but Musson ended the instructions in a way that affected Sam deeply: in the event a solder used his weapon against these people, it would "be regarded in all respects as an operation of war."

The crisp morning air dulled almost immediately as Sam and Rusty walked back to barracks. "What the hell?" queried Sam.

Rusty was more confused at the turn-around of his superiors and the alarm these orders had generated in the troops. "We've not had an ounce of trouble from these people. We haven't bolted any doors, or gates, and these folks have come and gone as they please. Now, all of a sudden, we've got to lock them away and shoot them if they try to escape? Escape from what?"

All the members of the unit were edgy as they received their specific assignments. Sam and Rusty, along with twelve other soldiers, were sent into two of the officers' barracks where they loaded dozens of revolvers and rifles into wheelbarrows. They expected some resistance. But the Cossack officers were formal and polite, and went out of their way to ensure that the confiscation went smoothly and efficiently.

Over dinner that evening, the mood was somber and nerves were on edge. One formerly affable sergeant was heard to mutter, hardly to himself, "This buggers all. The fucking war is over, and we're walking around with weapons drawn babysitting a bunch of antique solders. Who are these people? What are we supposed to be doing with them?"

The higher-ups were curiously absent. Neither Malcolm, nor Musson had been heard from in days and the junior officers were jittery. But if they knew what was going on, they weren't telling.

The following morning, at 1000 hours, the unit moved from the base to the Peggetz camp, where they provided an armed escort of Cossack officers to a "conference" at Spittal. Sam rode in one of several buses that joined with a number of three-ton military trucks with tarpaulin tops to the assigned meeting point, just outside the Cossack administrative building in Peggetz. Orders that all soldiers were to have "arms at the ready" were repeated. So too was the admonition to quell any demonstrations or objections with directed fire.

DIVIDED LOYALTIES

Approximately 1,500 Cossack officers lined up and filed into the trucks and several buses without incident. Some of the most senior officers were accompanied by their wives, who were allowed to ride in the cab of the trucks with the armed escorts. In addition to the British soldiers on the three-tonners, hundreds of additional, heavily armed soldiers in jeeps, armored vehicles and smaller transports accompanied the convoy. Sam was, again, shocked at the overwhelming display of force and security. *For what? They'd had no trouble with these people.*

The convoy made its way along the Moor River, and a camp appeared over a ridge about a half mile off of the paved road. Slowly, the shape of barracks became clear, as did the barbed wire fences surrounding the camp. The perimeter was dotted with wooden watchtowers, and the images of soldiers manning machine guns in those towers came into view once the convoy turned onto the dirt road. From the front of the bus, where Sam watched over 60 or so officers, he could feel the tension levels rise as the buzz of concerned chatter increased substantially. "What kind of conference was this?" he muttered under his breath.

The convoy drove into the inner yard of the camp, forming a square. Once the gates were locked, a number of British tanks emerged from the woods and surrounded the convoy on all sides. The Cossacks were discharged from their vehicles into the pen where British foot soldiers herded them into groups of 10. The Cossacks were searched and watches, knives, lighters, medals and other regalia were confiscated.

The Cossacks were ordered into the barracks which had been stripped of all furniture other than mattresses. Sam followed the rear of one group into the barracks, and one officer tried to force his way back to the courtyard. He was muttering in English, "We've been tricked. This is no conference. We are going to be killed."

He refused to heed a British soldier's order to stop, and continued to push through the crowd entering the barracks. His mutters became shouts in Russian. Several other officers joined him and the scene became chaotic, with bodies moving in and out. English and Russian shouts and orders were rising to a din of white noise.

The initiator of the incident began to break out of the crowd and make his way through the door. Sam raised his rifle and yelled, "Stop!" The Cossack officer did indeed stop, but only to look Sam in the eye and make it clear that he didn't care if Sam shot him. He continued on. Sam jabbed the butt of the weapon firmly into the officer's knee, sending him sprawling to the ground. One of the rebellious officers came to the aid of his comrade, while others headed for Sam. A burst of machine gun fire stopped them in their tracks and a phalanx of British troops positioned themselves at Sam's side.

"We will shoot," yelled a British corporal. "Get into the barracks, now!"

***

Lying on his cot that night, Sam tossed and turned, struggling to make sense of the day's events. *Why this sudden change of policy?* Sam wondered what these people could have done to deserve this treatment

He had only been asleep a few minutes when the sirens blared and the lights went on. "Everyone up. Everyone up. Now. Now. We are securing the camp. Move, move, move!" Sam couldn't tell who was barking the orders, but it didn't matter. The room was a blur of motion as soldiers threw on their clothes, grabbed their rifles and sprinted out the door toward the gate separating the Army's barracks from those of the Russian prisoners.

Allied troops inside the camp were pulling Cossacks from their barracks and forcing them to lie face down on the muddy ground. Once the officers had been evacuated, Sam's unit was ordered to search the buildings for weapons and contraband. Sam ran for Building F. To the side of the door a body lay on an army blanket. The man's face was purple, his eyes bulged and tongue distended. A thick black line formed a circle around his neck, and his white uniform trousers were stained with human waste. Sam had seen this before, at Gunskirchen: the unmistakable signs of death by hanging.

Sam, Rusty and a pair of other soldiers entered the barracks; two moving to the left, and two to the right. Rusty shoved aside a mattress and discovered another dead Cossack. The casement window above the mattress had been broken, and shards of glass littered the ground. The officer's throat was a bloody mess, as were his hands and wrists. "Oh, Lord..." were the only words Rusty could get out before turning and vomiting onto the floor.

Sam pushed Rusty out of the building. "I'll deal with it."

Another British soldier shouted, "Here's another one... strung up on a hook. What the fuck is going on? "

The sergeant came running in, attracted first by Rusty stumbling out of the building and then by the other soldier's cries. "What the...God. Take that man down from there." He looked at Sam. "You, help me carry this one out."

Sam took a deep breath, located a blanket nearby and assisted the sergeant in moving the bloody body out the door. He could see Allied soldiers scurrying in and out of the other barracks in the compound, carrying blankets loaded with dead and wounded Cossacks.

After a two-hour guard shift, Sam was relieved and allowed to go back to his cot. The Cossacks remained on the ground until dawn while teams of British soldiers cleaned the barracks and removed the glass windowpanes from the buildings. The officers were allowed to move back in, but without their shoes and belts.

Sam was wasted, but would not allow himself to sleep. He walked outside and found a bench by the mess hall. A number of soldiers moved about, also unable to sleep after the evening's activities.

Sam was stunned, and the more he tried to figure it out the more confused and frustrated he became. Finally he asked a British officer, Corporal Wheeler, to explain what was going on.

"Guess they didn't tell you folks at Peggetz. These poor sods are going back to Mother Russia. They're pissin' their pants thinking about what Stalin will do to them after they fought for the Germans against their own country."

"In Peggetz, there are thousands of others: women, children and old people—civilians. Are all of them being sent back, or just the officers?" asked Sam.

Wheeler flicked his cigarette to the ground and shook his head. "Not sure. You're going back there tomorrow, so you'll know better than me in a few hours time."

Sam sat on the bench until daybreak, thinking about what the Corporal had said and fighting off images of Gunskirchen.

The Argyles moved out of Spittal at 0600, thankfully before the process of transporting the Cossack officers to Judenberg began. There, they would be handed over to Soviet authorities. The British troops at the camp were on edge and the Cossacks were desperate. Sam was glad to be on "his bus" and back to Peggetz.

Over the next 24 hours, however, Sam would review that feeling and come to the conclusion that staying in Spittal might have been the easier assignment. By the time he got back to Peggetz, the remaining Cossacks, now leaderless, were panicked. Rumors circulated that the officers were executed and the rest were being sent back to Russia. Petitions were presented to British officers demanding an explanation and insisting on the protections afforded prisoners of war under the Geneva Convention.

The British troops were agitated as well. After the Cossack officers had been removed from the camp, another of Brigadier Musson's orders was transmitted to the troops. The Allied Governments, the men were told, had agreed that all of their own nationals were to be repatriated, meaning that the Cossacks under the Brigade's control were to be returned to Russia. The commanding officer acknowledged that this would be, "on the whole, extremely unpopular" with the Cossacks, and that many of the men would have difficulty carrying out this task because there were so many woman, children and the elderly involved. But they had to remember that these people had supported the Germans in the war. The Russian government had promised to put these people to work on the land and educate them to be "decent Soviet citizens." Musson urged his men on to complete the all-important goal of securing a lasting and just peace, and ended by saying that while he hoped the task could be accomplished without bloodshed, if hostility was required, he "would support them in any reasonable action they might take."

Musson's orders again had a distressing effect on Sam. After weeks of working in close quarters with the Cossacks, he knew that few of the prisoners had done anything to support the Germans. Rather, they were victims of the Nazis themselves, having been conscripted into the German army or used as slave laborers to work the factories and supply chains. Certainly the women and children couldn't be accused of supporting the enemy in any serious way.

Rusty was also visibly upset. After the men were dismissed, he spat violently on the ground toward the officers and growled, loud enough to be heard a good distance away, "What a load of crap. First, he tells us that these people were traitors, and that's why they're being sent to Russia. Then, in the next breath, he says the Russians will treat them well and put them to work. Right! That's just what His Majesty would do with British traitors. That bastard Stalin is going to kill them all, and we're all going to have a hand in it. "

At 1630 hours on May 31, Sam was on guard duty as Lieutenant Malcolm met with the heads of the Peggetz "Camp Committee," comprised of several Cossack priests, two mid-ranking officers who had not attended the "conference" due to illness, and three older men who were considered to be moderate, community leaders. Malcolm advised them that they would all be repatriated to Russia within the next 48 hours.

The Cossacks couldn't understand why the Allies would do this; after all they'd been through with the Bolsheviks, then the Nazis, and now Stalin. They couldn't believe that the British would acquiesce, given the threat that Stalin posed to the West. Did Malcolm understand how many millions of Russians had been killed in Stalin's purges, or had died because of the famines created by collectivization? Did Malcolm know that many of the people in this camp had left the Soviet Union well before the war had started? Did he realize that thousands of Cossacks who had resisted the Nazis' demands were executed, and that most of those in Peggetz were forced to work for the Germans under threat of death?

Sam watched Malcolm carefully, and was amazed when the lieutenant simply shrugged his shoulders, and said there was nothing he could do. How could he ignore these sincere and articulate pleas? How could Malcolm not understand that the entire reason for fighting the war was to protect the rights of individuals from the profane actions of a demagogue? If the war in Europe had been lost, wouldn't all of us be just like these poor people, who've done nothing wrong except try to flee one tyrant, Stalin, only to get enslaved by another, Hitler?

The Cossacks left the meeting in obvious despair. As they walked to their barracks, Sam could see the priests splitting off from the others to confer with the handful of enlisted men who had been waiting outside the meeting hall. The way they squeezed together in tight huddles, looking up frequently to survey their immediate surrounding, suggested strongly to Sam that some conspiracy was underfoot. He considered saying something to Malcolm, but found himself sympathizing with the Cossacks, and turned away.

Two hours later, the Cossacks implemented a general hunger strike. When food was delivered to the barracks, the Cossacks piled it into stacks and guarded it, to make sure no one, even children, broke the fast. Banners made from bed sheets were hung near the discarded provisions, reading, "Cossacks would prefer to die of hunger than be return to SSSR." They hung black flags from the barracks and tents, and many women and old men fastened notes to their clothing, which read, "Kill me. Kill my children. But do not send me back."

The Allied soldiers were put on eight-hour shifts standing guard over the Cossack barracks, adding greatly to the already palpable tension in the camp. Sam was shaving when Marty Diamond rushed in to the latrine, stuck his head under a sink and doused himself with cold water. He emerged several minutes later and stood in front of the mirror, dripping wet, staring at himself.

"What's happening?" Sam asked, offering Marty his towel.

"Un-fucking-believable. I was outside HQ with Amster, on guard, when the priest they call Gregoriev—you know, the one in the red robe with the white beard down to his belt—hands me a box of letters and tells me to deliver them to Malcolm. Then he handed me and Amster each a sheet of paper, and said it was for us. I looked at it after the guy walked away. We took a look at a couple before we brought them inside. One of them was addressed to the U.S. Congress, and started and ended by saying that they'd rather die, to the last person, than go to Stalin's Communist Russia."

He reached into his pants pocket, pulled out a sheet of paper that had been folded into a tight square, and handed it to Sam. It was addressed to Roosevelt, Churchill, the U.S. Congress and the British Parliament. The note stated that the Cossacks had been wandering for over 25 years because of their opposition to Communism, and that sending them back would result in certain death. They pledged their loyalty to the Allied governments and agreed to relocate anywhere but Russia.

Sam read the last line of the petition twice. "If you cannot accommodate us, if you intend to send us to Russia, it would best to shoot all of us yourselves, here in the fields, now." He felt a rush of conviction, certain that these deportations were indiscriminate and utterly wrong. There was no way to justify them.

The petition that had been given to Marty Diamond had also been widely circulated amongst the Brigade's enlisted men, and with a similar impact. Many soldiers refused to hide their dissatisfaction at orders to guard the Cossacks closely to prevent escape, and to break up prayer services in the camp square organized by the Orthodox priests. The private discussions at mess centered on the general disbelief that the Soviet government would go to the trouble of forcing these people back, just to murder them. Some soldiers—Billy Martin, for example—dismissed the Cossacks' resistance as pure whining. "You place your bets, and if you lose, you gotta pay the piper. It's as simple as that."

But many others, including Sam, knew the situation was much more complicated. "It's not quite that simple. A lot of these people left Russia a long time ago, before the war. They left because the Reds stole their land, and outlawed their religion. They had no choice. We're going to be sending back women, and children, and old men. Stalin's already killed millions of his own people because he wanted to, for no other good reason. If it wasn't for the Nazis, we'd probably be fighting the Russians to protect Europe."

Billy turned his hardened, ruddy face toward Sam and glared at the young American. "Ah, listen to you—fuckin' GI with a fancy education. The truth is, nobody cares about these bastards, and nobody should. Say what you want, but they didn't lift a finger to help us. So why should we feed 'em? There are enough folks around who fought the German bastards, who really need our help. I say we spend our money and time on them. Who cares what happens to these Russians?"

Sam held back a retort, realizing he wasn't going to change any minds or make any friends with the next part of his argument.

Billy sighed. "I'm not a monster. I've seen more death and pain than any man should see. I've got a wife and kids in Dublin, and I've been away for over two years. The faster we give these people to the Russians, the sooner I get back to my family."

***

The deportations were to begin from Peggetz on June 1. By 6 a.m. that morning, the Cossack priests walked in procession around the camp, gathering people as they went, to join them in a prayer session in the central square. A huge wooden platform, holding a makeshift altar and an enormous wooden cross, had been built during the night.

On each side of the platform stood a chorus of women and boys, roughly 20 in each group, chanting solemnly as the priests, dressed in their brightly-colored vestments, marched toward the altar holding religious banners. The lead priest, Father Gregoriev, began the Orthodox liturgy by leading the crowd in prayer. Several priests split off from the group and offered communion, and Father Gregoriev continued the formal ceremony.

Sam guessed there were six to eight thousand people in the square, far too many to be comfortably situated. The center of the space was comprised primarily of women and children, and the perimeter was made up of younger men, many of whom were uniformed. These men were standing shoulder to shoulder, with every other man facing in, toward the praying crowds, while his neighbor faced outward, toward the fences of the camp, watching the British soldiers. Sam marveled for a moment at their organization. But interest soon turned to anxiety when he realized that these people would not voluntarily leave, and that violence was now a near certainty.

Lieutenant Malcolm strode to the altar, accompanied by two officers and an interpreter. Father Gregoriev stopped chanting and the crowd hushed while the four men approached. Malcolm spoke loudly and clearly, pausing after every sentence to allow for interpretation. "You will begin loading the vehicles on the far side of the camp in thirty minutes. You are permitted to take only your clothes and a small number of possessions with you. Please finish this service promptly."

Gregoriev renewed the service even before Malcolm had a chance to walk away. The crowd drew in, tightening the square. Cossacks along the edge of the crowd began linking arms. The chanting intensified, as did the monotonic wailing of the priests. A brisk, warm wind gave motion to the flags, banners and colorful costumes of the clergy and the crowd. Energy was being created and stored.

The Argyle Brigade and Sutherland Highlanders formed just outside the square, behind the altar. They were given the order to fix bayonets, and in a collective "clack," a hundred knives were clipped to the ends of rifles in full view of the crowd. "Advance" was the next order, and the troops moved toward the Cossacks, with instructions to move those assembled toward the transport trucks at the southern edge of the camp.

The Cossacks refused to yield, and attempts to pull away individuals from the mass were unsuccessful. The British soldiers hesitated to use their bayonets and rifles on the Cossacks, and a stalemate ensued. The officers kept prodding the soldiers back to the crowds, but the soldiers refused to attack. Sam, who was assigned once again to ride guard on a transport bus, hoped the passive resistance ploy might prove effective.

Malcolm changed tactics. He ordered several trucks moved closer to the square, and sent a large number of Irish riflemen to one corner of the crowd, concentrating their efforts on a discrete area. The focused approach began to work, and the soldiers peeled off several Cossacks from the edge and loaded them, by force, into the nearby vehicles. Rather than dispersing the crowd, however, the group closed ranks, which created a panic. Cossacks clamored over each other to get away from the soldiers, forming a pyramid of bodies under which many became trapped. The throng transformed into quicksand, and the chanting stopped, overtaken by screams of horror and fear.

As the mass of people broke up in one area, it reformed in others. The violence intensified when soldiers became frustrated at their lack of success. Eventually, several truckloads of Cossacks were moved out of the railway station. Sam's bus was ordered to travel into the square, and he took up position at the entrance to the vehicle, making sure that once thrown in, a prisoner remained.

Sam knew that if he was truly to take a stand now would be that time, before he was swept up in events he couldn't control. But everything was motion and chaos. He considered simply walking away, out the gate and then, perhaps, to the CO's office.

Two British soldiers were heading toward him, struggling to hold on to a tall, thin man wearing a white Cossack uniform. His wispy moustache, and full head of dark hair, suggested he was just a teenager. But he was strong and wiry, and was giving the soldiers all they could handle. Finally, one of the soldiers smashed him in the gut with his rifle butt and dragged him to the bus. The soldiers lifted him onto the first step, but got him no further. He turned, kicked one soldier and then the other, wriggling free from their grasp and moved quickly toward Sam.

The Cossack, two feet from Sam, yelled in Russian, "Shoot me. Kill me. I would rather die here as a man."

Sam raised his rifle, and stuttered "Stop...," but didn't have a chance to complete the warning. The young man leapt forward and tackled him. The next thing Sam knew, the man was up on his feet, holding Sam's rifle. He turned the weapon inwards, toward his own chest, and fired.

The impact sent him flying backwards, his white tunic covered with blood. Sam stared at the body, unable to think, unable to move, and remained on the ground as two British soldiers dragged the suicide to the side of the square. The bus that Sam was supposed to have been guarding had become full, and was being waved out of the area to make room for the next one.

Rusty ran over to Sam and helped him to his feet. "Are you hurt?"

"Huh? No. He shot himself."

Rusty held on tightly to his friend, and yelled "Medic," then said to Sam "Take it easy. We'll get you some help.'

"No, I'm all right. He didn't shoot me. He shot himself."

Rusty grabbed Sam's jaw, hard enough that it hurt, and moved it so that the two were looking eye-to-eye. "Listen to me carefully. A prisoner has attacked you. You can get out of here now."

Sam shook his head vigorously. The last thing he wanted now was to be separated from his unit and alone in an infirmary with his thoughts. "Let's go," he said, picking up his rifle and moving to the next waiting bus.

It took hours, well into night, to get all the Cossacks loaded onto the convoys. Even after all the last trucks left the camp, the soldiers experienced no repose. Many wandered around camp, appearing to not know what to do with themselves. Others crowded into the mess hall, which had remained open, drinking coffee or smoking with a dazed look on their faces.

Sam was among them. He was thoroughly exhausted, but because the image of the Cossack teenager with a bloody hole in his chest appeared every time he closed his eyes, he gave up any hope of sleep. His thoughts returned to the German guards who were captured after Company B moved into Gunskirchen. He recalled the way the German officer tried to reason with his captors, claiming that he and his men had been following orders. Sam remembered with precise detail how he had executed the officer without a second thought.

The empty trucks returned to Peggetz a few hours later, having transferred the Cossacks from army vehicles to rail boxcars at Judenberg. Most of the soldiers assigned to that task came straight to the mess tent, disturbed and vocal. Three men, Scots from the Argyle Brigade, sat at Sam's table and swapped stories of the horrible things they had been part of and witnessed.

Sam heard accounts of women and children being thrown, literally *picked up and thrown*, into boxcars which were nailed shut when filled. The cars were minimally outfitted for the 10-hour journey to Moscow.

One of the Scottish soldiers—a short, stocky man with a shiny bald head—was particularly agitated, bouncing his feet up and down as he chain-smoked Lucky Strikes. He banged on his left thigh a few times, as if he was steeling himself to an unpleasant task, and addressed the others at the table without ever looking up. He described how he had been on duty at Judenberg, guarding a cluster of Cossack women who had been off loaded from a bus, waiting for the next train to pull up. A young lady walked up to him and extended her arms, holding out a small baby, swaddled in linen. She tilted her arms downward, and the infant began to roll off her fingertips, down to the rough pavement. The soldier instinctively reached out to catch the baby as it fell.

As he did, the woman pulled a long straight razor from her tunic and slit first her right, then her left, wrists with a longitudinal cut. She moaned something in a language the soldier couldn't understand before collapsing in a heap of cloth and blood. Some of the other Cossacks in the group hovered over the fallen woman, wailing and striking their breasts with their fists. Others ran away, toward the hills behind the train station.

The soldier watched them run, anchored in his spot by the infant in his hands.

Someone yelled "Stop" and fired a warning shot in the air, but the women kept running. Several more shots were fired, and two of the fleeing Cossacks dropped to the ground. The others increased their pace and made it to the cover of the thick woods moments later.

A sergeant scurried over and ordered the men in the guard detail to follow the escapees. No one moved. The sergeant screamed his command again. The bald soldier handed the sergeant the infant, and walked away. The others followed.

The story affected Sam as if it had happened to him. His heart was pumping feverishly, his face was flushed with fury and his hands clenched into fists. He knew he was an accessory to a horrible crime and his only explanation was that he was following orders.

***

In a blink, Sam was back in the present. He looked around the table at the faces of his dinner companions, hoping to find empathy. Instead, these battle-hardened veterans were nervously looking down at the table.

Eventually, someone at the far end asked, "Did you report this to anyone?"

Sam shook his head. "I should have. Not a day has gone by since that I regret my silence."

Connick spoke up. "It was war. Things were crazy. You were a kid. Don't beat yourself up, Hart. That could have been any one of us, and I doubt we'd have dealt with it any differently."

Everyone around the table nodded their agreement—with the exception of Judge Harrington.

CHAPTER 14

The driver left Sam off at the front of the Imperial Hotel, but he was too wound up to go to bed. He walked north on Kartner Strasse, a pedestrian boulevard lined with Vienna's finest stores and restaurants. Many people were out, moving casually from window to window, enjoying the autumn air. The walking was good for his back, which had stiffened severely during the ride from the restaurant in the wine country.

Sam found himself at the entrance to St. Stephan's Cathedral at the end of the street. The main entrance to the chapel was open, and a few tourists were milling about admiring the vestry and the ancient stained glass murals that had miraculously survived the war undamaged. Sam walked slowly down the side of the huge nave to a seating area just in front of the elaborate High Altar and sat in a dark, shadowy spot near the aisle. He closed his eyes and let his mind wander.

Sam was on board the tanker *Revelation*, commandeered from the British merchant fleet to ferry Allied soldiers from Hamburg to Liverpool. During dinner on the very first night of their voyage, at the end of the announcements, an English lieutenant reminded the men who had participated in Operation Apple that their actions were classified and could not be discussed with anyone—including family, friends and even among themselves. Some rumblings were heard when the overbearing officer reminded the men that they were still subject to military protocol and discipline.

The lieutenant left the room, clearly angry, which seemed to give license to the soldiers to vent their aggravation. A respected veteran of the repatriation exercise began banging his fists on the tables, and another intoned, "Liars, Liars," in time to the beat. Within a few minutes, the entire room was filled with rhythmic chanting.

Sam found himself participating with great gusto. He found the scene oddly comforting and cathartic, suggesting perhaps that he wasn't the only one burdened by what had taken place in Peggetz.

When armed MPs entered the mess, the room exploded. A number of tables were turned upside down and a melee ensued. Sam was one of the first to intercept the MPs, and, as a consequence, one of the first to be subdued and thrown in the brig.

His cell was cramped and hot and his bed nothing more than a sliver of wool on a metal base, which did little to comfort the physical injuries he had suffered in the riot. To make matters worse, the entire brig stank of cigarette smoke, a smell that made Sam nauseous ever since Gunskirchen. Nonetheless, Sam was in no hurry to leave.

He lay in his cot for two days. He remembered the events of the past several days with his eyes open, staring straight up at the ceiling as if it was a movie screen. Sam stopped the action at key points, analyzing his actions and questioning whether there was anything he could have done to help the people at Peggetz.

Sam was released from jail on Sunday morning after breakfast. He walked through the labyrinth of the ship to his berth, adjacent to the officer's mess which was used as a chapel for non-denominational services. Sam walked in and joined a small line of men who were sitting quietly, waiting a turn for a private session with the Catholic chaplain.

Sam hadn't made confession since his childhood, and it rarely entered his thoughts since, but today he felt drawn to it. He sat on the plastic chair, hands folded in his lap, trying to prepare himself for the ritual. The memories came swirling into his head—the first man he shot in the heat of battle, the execution of the German sergeant, stacks of corpses at Gunskirchen, the boy in the white tunic, the woman in the red robe—and he couldn't imagine how he could translate his feelings into words. He remained there for several moments, hoping clarity would come, and when it didn't, he got up and left the mess hall.

Sitting in the quiet of St. Stephan's, Sam recalled that utterly helpless sensation as if it was yesterday. His most recent attempt to unburden himself—that night around the dinner table with his GI comrades—just made him feel worse. Sam reverted back to the blocking tactics he'd employed for the past 50 years, but nothing seemed to work. He remained slumped on the bench, feeling much like a broken man, until the cathedral closed at midnight.

Sam walked back to the hotel, exhausted, his emotional turmoil exacerbated by severe jet lag. He picked up his room key at the front desk, as well as a message slip noting that Gloria had called. When he got to his room, he used the bathroom, stripped down to his underwear, and collapsed on the bed. He told himself he just wanted to rest for a moment before calling home, but fell asleep almost immediately.

***

Rebecca was petrified. Moments after the taxi sped away from the Imperial Hotel, she turned to the man sitting next to her and said,. "What do you want?" Without looking at her, he told her to shut up and waggled the revolver in his lap.

Not another word was exchanged for the remainder of the 30-minute ride. The silence amplified Rebecca's paranoia as sinister thoughts flooded her mind.

Robbery? Rape?

The Mercedes pulled to a stop on a quiet side street a few blocks from a major avenue. The driver unlocked the rear doors and hopped out of the car. The man with the gun opened his door, and motioned Rebecca to slide toward him to the sidewalk. She glanced at the opposite door and found it blocked by the driver. No escape.

Rebecca followed the man out of the car. Once he had taken firm hold of her wrist, he put the gun in his jacket pocket and pulled Rebecca up several stairs into the dimly-lit vestibule of an unremarkable row house. He pushed a button for apartment 3D, and moments later they were admitted into the building by a responding buzzer.

All the while, Rebecca tried to assess her options. Should she try to take on her captor—kick him in the shins, or the groin—and make a run for it? What about the driver? If she screamed, would anyone in the other apartments hear her and call the police?

She must have telegraphed her thoughts, because once the door closed behind them, the man pulled out his revolver and said, "Don't be stupid." He put the nose of the gun in Rebecca's back and pushed her up three more flights of stairs.

The door to Apartment 3D was ajar. Rebecca hesitated, putting her hand on the doorjamb. Her captor grunted, "Move," and shoved her hard. She stumbled into the dark room, and tripped on a rug, falling to her knees.

The door was shut behind her and she heard a lock being turned. The man barked, "Get up."

Rebecca refused to budge. *Screw this guy.* What difference did it make if she stood up or stayed down? The more she cared, the more they controlled her.

The man took a menacing step at her, kicked her firmly in the thigh and growled, "Goddamn it. I said 'get up.'"

This time Rebecca did as she was told. She looked over his shoulder toward the door they came in through.

"It's locked from the outside. You're going down that hall," he said, pointing behind her with the revolver that had just reappeared. "Keep quiet and you'll be all right."

Rebecca found her courage and screamed, "Who the hell are you? You can't do this!"

The man grabbed Rebecca by the arm and pulled her down to the end of the hallway. He pushed her through an open doorway, snapped on a light, and closed the door. She could hear a bolt turn and the man's footsteps as he walked away without another word.

Rebecca took in her surroundings. The room was about 15 feet square, and was sparingly furnished with two wooden arm chairs, a beat-up wicker couch and a small coffee table with a glass top. On the opposite wall there was a doorway, which Rebecca could see led to a bathroom.

She was bewildered, still overwhelmed by the intense anxiety of the past hour. Rebecca paced the room, looking for a way out. At first glance, the room appeared to be wholly internal, but as Rebecca studied her environment more carefully, she thought she detected the outline of a plastered-over picture window. Without a second thought, she began digging at the wall with her nails.

***

Sam awoke with a start and in a cold sweat. He looked at the clock in disbelief as it registered 9:18.

He staggered to the bathroom and sluggishly showered and shaved. Standing in front of the mirror, he gave himself a pep talk, directing all his energy to the several business and career-related tasks for the day ahead. He'd have to shake off the emotional baggage and get to work.

Back in his bedroom, Sam reached for the phone to order some breakfast when he noticed his message light was blinking. Sam dialed the operator and was advised that he had two messages. The first was from Gloria, taken the night before. *Damn. How could I have forgotten to call?* He'd conked out last night and forgotten about the message slip he received along with his key. New York was six hours behind, making it around 4 in the morning there. He'd have to wait a few hours.

The second message was odd, and must have been received when he was in the shower. The operator said, "A man called but wouldn't leave his name. He was out of breath, I think—in a hurry. He insisted I call your room several times before he would hang up."

Sam thought about who the mystery caller might be. He dialed the London trading room, asked for Mike T, and was forwarded to his mobile number.

"Where are you?" Sam asked.

"Heathrow. I'm taking your advice and flying to Vienna for the event tonight."

"Great. Did you try to call me a few minutes ago?

"Nope,"

"Hmm. Well, how're we doing?"

Sam could hear Mike draw hard on his cigarette. "We're officially back from the dead. Dollar's higher, and I took some profits overnight. You can take a victory lap if you're in the mood."

"I may need to—I'm having lunch with Stanley in a few hours. See you later."

As Sam considered who else might have called him, a cold chill ran up his spine. *Could it have been Anton?*

That was extremely unlikely, Sam knew. But why did the uneasy feeling linger?

Room service arrived just as Sam finished dressing. His eyes skimmed the *Financial Times* without reading while he drank his coffee and picked at a croissant. He wished he could speak to Anton right then and there, but it was still too early.

Sam brushed the crumbs from his lap, re-combed his hair and readied his briefcase before leaving the room. Jon Lavendar was waiting for him in the lobby to take him to a meeting with the senior officers of the Austrian Central Bank. Sam put himself on automatic, trying to conserve his energy for the much more difficult meeting afterwards with his boss.

***

Sam counted on Stanley's habitual and calculated tardiness to prepare his case. His legal training and negotiating skills taught him to review his client's and adversary's positions intelligently and honestly. He knew that victory had little to do with having the facts on your side. Winning was about exaggerating your own strengths and exploiting the adversary's weaknesses, a kind of psychological warfare.

Sam sipped on a glass of Veltliner and zeroed in on the important issues. Stanley was obscenely rich and extremely influential, but that only encouraged him to seek more. His ambition and arrogance were the very things that left him exposed. Control his ability to increase power and wealth, and you had him by the balls.

Sam, on the other hand, felt himself secure from anything Stanley could throw at him. He had a much more straightforward agenda. He wasn't going anywhere at GSC, had more money than he knew how to spend and maintained no interest in greater power or additional responsibility. All Sam wanted was to make good on his promise to Reggie, and protect Mike T from the venal and arbitrary hazards of Wall Street. If the firm's culture was strengthened in the process, that would be a bonus.

He knew that Stanley wouldn't believe any of that, and would assume Sam cared as much about money and power as he did. And that's why Sam knew he held the winning hand.

He was feeling confident when Stanley arrived. They engaged in some social conversation over aperitifs before dancing around the business issues. Phrases such as "I'm only thinking of the Firm's best interests"; "I respect your position" and "Maybe I'm wrong here" dominated the foreplay before things got more serious and personal.

As the salads were served, Sam and Stanley were at each other's throats as only business partners could be. Thrust met parry, feint neutralized charge. Sam's argument to keep his team intact was refuted by Stanley's point that no part of the company could be treated differently from any other. Stanley's admonition that Sam jeopardized the Firm's culture by refusing to cooperate was countered by Sam's invoking his fiduciary duty to the organization.

Sam could see that his boss was growing increasingly impatient and frustrated. It was his plan to push him to the brink.

"Stanley, I appreciate your points here, but I just can't go along with it. We've got the most profitable part of the Firm and the most successful desk on the Street. Not only would it hamper us tactically, but think of what it says to the market about our commitment to the business. Our competitors would pick off our clients and prospects. We'd lose our best people over this. We'd be screwing our shareholders. I just can't let this happen on my watch."

Stanley's entire head turned cherry red. He clenched his right fist and, ever so slightly, moved his left shoulder forward as if cocking his body to throw a punch. Sam had found the button.

"Your watch," Stanley sputtered, "is over."

"Excuse me?'"

"You're fired. And this conversation is over." Stanley pushed himself away from the table and was about to stand when Sam lifted his hand and showed Stanley his palm.

"I've got a contract and you don't have the authority to terminate it without Board approval. So sit back down and let's work this out."

Stanley extended a long, bony finger a half-inch in front of the bridge of Sam's nose. Still crimson, he rasped, "Fuck you. See you in court."

Sam ordered an espresso as soon as Stanley had cleared the exit. Having just precipitated the crisis, Sam wanted to linger on its ramifications and delight in its consequences. He would refuse to authorize the headcount reductions and fire his traders. Stanley would get the correct legal advice that he couldn't summarily terminate Sam. Getting the Board together to deal with Sam's contracts would take weeks, and would be extremely costly to Stanley in terms of his stature with the Directors. Thus, his only unilateral recourse would be to try to replace Sam as head of the division.

Sam wondered who Stanley would consider, and smiled at the thought. He'd be petrified to risk dismantling his only profit center, Sam knew. *Got'cha.*

Sam went back to his hotel room with a refreshing sense of determination and urgency. It was now 7:30 a.m. in New York, and he called his office. Keeping Pam on the line to place the calls, Sam spoke with three GSC Directors with whom he had fostered strong relationships and two Management Committee colleagues who he knew would jump at any opportunity to knock Stanley down a peg. Sam was careful to speak dispassionately and accurately as he disclosed the events leading up to the confrontation. He knew that the facts would speak for themselves and that any editorializing would seem blatantly self-serving and hurt his cause.

Sam also called his personal attorney. He instructed him to call the general counsel at GSC and warn her that Sam intended to ensure that his employment contract was scrupulously followed and that he was prepared to seek a restraining order to protect his rights. This would really piss the hell out of Stanley.

When he finally came up for air, Sam noticed an envelope that had been shoved under his door. He ripped open the seal, and felt his spirits crash to earth as he read the message from Gloria: "Call me. Urgent."

Jesus!

Sam dialed home and Gloria picked up almost immediately. Sam could tell she was trying hard to control her emotions as she told him that she visited Anton the day before, and that he looked extremely frail. He kept slipping in and out of awareness but he knew who she was and asked for Sam several times. "I think you should come home," she said. "I'm not sure he'll make it through the weekend."

"My God," sighed Sam. It was too late to make any flights to New York that day. He'd be on the first flight tomorrow. "Do you think I can call him?"

Gloria said in a wavering voice, "It's worth a try. I know he'd want to talk to you before..."

"Are you alright?" Sam asked, worried how this unsettling news would impact his wife's own precarious situation.

Gloria's tone took on a caustic edge. "Don't worry. My babysitter is here making sure I don't run away."

She hung up before Sam could come up with something to placate his wife.

Exasperated, he called Anton's number. Helene answered, and told Sam that her father's condition was worsening. The pain was increasing, but Anton refused to take more medications that left him semi-conscious most of the time. Sam asked if he could speak to Anton, and he could hear Helene as she tried to get her father to respond.

Several moments later, Sam could hear a frail, thin voice in his ear. "Hello?"

Sam felt that Anton was barely there. "It's Sam. I'm in Vienna, and will be back in New York tomorrow. I'll come visit you in the afternoon. How are you feeling?"

Anton weakly cleared some phlegm from his throat. "I'd be much better if they'd send me home."

Sam had never heard Anton complain before. "You *are* home, Anton. I'm in Vienna. I'll see you tomorrow."

"Please God. Did you go to your reunion?"

Sam was amazed that Anton would think of him at a time like this, much less remember a conversation they had days ago. "Yes, I did. You counseled me well. I told the whole story, for the first time. I'm still numb. Shouldn't I feel better?"

Anton chuckled softly. "You may need to do more than tell the story once to repair the world. It may take a lifetime."

"Tikkun Olum," said Sam, saying aloud his first two Hebrew words. "I remember."

Anton broke a long silence. "I'll wait for you, please God. Travel safe."

Sam hung up the phone and walked over to the window. Instead of gazing out at the ancient city, Sam looked at his reflection in the glass. The thin hair and sagging skin were still there, of course. But maybe there was a new sparkle in those eyes, which had grown cold since the War.

For those five decades, Sam had classified himself as irredeemable and more or less successfully suppressed his remorse and guilt. Now, thanks to Anton, he was beginning to find the courage to follow a different path.

The phone rang, breaking his trance. Sam picked up the receiver and was told by the hotel clerk that his car had arrived. Realizing how late he was, and with a heavy heart, Sam began to change into his tuxedo. He questioned whether he should even go to the event that evening. After all, he had already set the stage with Stanley for a showdown in New York. He really didn't care one whit about the Firm's clients, at this point. Maybe he should just stay back at the hotel, and call his wife.

As he wrestled with his bow tie, Sam realized he hadn't heard from Rebecca all day. He'd want to tell her he'd be leaving on the first flight out tomorrow.

***

Rebecca lay on her back on the floor and stared at the painted ceiling. Her fingertips were raw and bloody and her wrists ached incessantly. She'd scratched and clawed her way through a half-inch of plasterboard to uncover a window, only to expose a dismal airshaft with no means of egress.

Aggravation turned to anger as she recalled her conversation with Charley at the coffeehouse. He told her he'd take care of things. He seemed genuinely worried about her safety and concerned about Sam. She acted tough, but deep down inside she'd believed and trusted him.

"I'm an idiot!" she said aloud. She had an opportunity to inform the police between the time she left Charley and when she was abducted, but didn't because Charley told her not to worry. Worse, she'd been with her grandfather just before the incident. She could have told him, confidentially, about her concerns. He'd have handled it discreetly. He would have figured out a way to foil whatever these crazies were plotting but in a way that protected Charley.

Rebecca struggled to her feet, humiliated for letting herself be taken in. She paced the room, and in an act of sheer frustration, kicked her heel into one of the interior walls. Instead of the expected "thud," Rebecca heard more of a "ting." She noticed that the wall had caved in at the point of contact.

She kicked that same location with all her might twice more, loosening a watermelon-sized chunk of wall. She got down on her hands and knees and peered into the hole. To her surprise, she saw a hollow space and a sliver of bright light coming through the darkness.

Rebecca put her hand in, gingerly, and felt another wall on the other side of the hole about eight inches away. She groped around the wall until she touched a metallic box, about three inches from the floor and just to the left of the hole. That's where the light had come from.

Looking around the room for inspiration, Rebecca set her sights on one of the old, spindly chairs and dashed over to it. She picked the chair up over her head and smashed it on the floor, loosening one of its legs. Back on her hands and knees, Rebecca shoved the makeshift tool into the hole, against the area where the light had come from. That second wall yielded promptly to her pokes and prods, and the result confirmed

Rebecca's hopes. There was another room behind that wall, and perhaps an escape route.

She was about to continue the demolition when she heard a door slam from the direction of the apartment's entrance. She moved quickly to push the wicker loveseat in front of the hole in the wall, and moved the shattered chair into the bathtub, just before she heard the "click" of the lock.

Fatima strode arrogantly into the room. "Did the princess sleep well?" she hissed through a drag of a newly lit cigarette.

Rebecca advanced and was on her in a flash, driving the palm of her right hand toward the middle of Fatima's face. The blow would have crushed her nose had Didier not intervened with a hard shove that sent her sprawling to the floor.

Before Rebecca could recover, Fatima was on her, stomping on her legs. "Cadela," she screamed, holding the spot on her cheek where Rebecca's punch had landed.

Didier pulled Fatima away, and produced a revolver from his jacket pocket that he pointed at Rebecca. "Charley said you were tough, but I don't think you're stupid."

Rebecca recoiled at the sound of Charley's name, confirming his complicity and her worst fears. "Where is that son of a bitch?"

Didier answered, matter-of-factly: "He's at work with lots to do for tonight."

"Tell him I'll never forgive him for this."

Fatima glared at Rebecca, still rubbing her wound. "What a loss. If it were up to me...."

"That's enough," Didier interrupted. "We brought you some food, but maybe you need to earn it. Behave and maybe you'll get something to eat later."

Fatima gave Rebecca a look of disgust and she and Didier left the room. She heard the door lock and then laughter as they headed down the hallway.

Rebecca waited several minutes before moving the loveseat and exposing her escape hatch. Having company in the apartment would make things much more complicated, she knew. She'd have to work quietly, and assuming she could get out of there, she'd have to find a way around her captors. Forcing herself not to succumb to hopelessness, Rebecca began chipping away at the wall with her wooden stick and the heel of her boot.

Sore, and covered with plaster, Rebecca stopped to survey her work: a rectangular space about two feet square. She looked at her watch: it was almost four. Unless she got out of there soon, she'd lose her chance to prevent Sam from going to Schonbrunn.

Rebecca went head first into the rectangular hole in the wall. The fit was tight and her butt and hips pushed hard against the top and sides of the hole. She pulled herself forward with greater exertion, feeling the rough edges of the sheetrock digging into her back.

Time was working against her, and Rebecca ignored the pain as she pushed herself through to the next room. Her pants were bloodied and shredded in several places, but she was out.

She looked around the new room, not knowing if it was part of Didier's apartment. It was furnished as a living room, with two curtained windows on either side of a fireplace. Rebecca stood up next to the oversized mantelpiece, using it for cover, and carefully pulled a drape aside to expose the window. She looked out onto the street, but there was neither ledge nor fire escape.

She considered opening the window and screaming for help, but stopped when she heard a voice from down a hallway. Rebecca held on tightly to her trusty chair leg and hugged the wall until the voice became clearer. It was Fatima, and it sounded like she was talking on the phone.

"Just got here," said Fatima, making a slurping sound. "I'll feed the bitch and be back in 20 minutes."

Pause.

"If it were up to me, I'd ice her. But Didier will say we have to let her go because of Charley, like we should give a shit about that American asshole."

Fatima said goodbye to whomever she had been talking to, hung up the phone and stepped into the hallway where Rebecca could see her. She walked a few steps to a closed door, unlocked it with a key and disappeared into the room.

Rebecca followed from the shadows.

A few seconds later, Fatima was mumbling hysterically, "She's not here. Shit." She rushed back into the hallway and had gone about two feet when the blow to her stomach stood her up straight. The next whack, to the side of her head, sent her sprawling to the ground and gasping for breath.

Rebecca reached down, picked up the keys and stood over her adversary. "Ice me, huh?' She kicked Fatima hard in the ribs, opened the door and locked it behind her, and ran down the stairs two at a time.

She was in a taxi, on her way to the hotel, moments later.

CHAPTER 15

The approach to Schonbrunn Palace is almost as dramatic as the edifice itself. The initial entranceway to the grounds is framed by eight-foot-high marble columns, topped with black onyx globes on which the imperial symbol—crossed scepters and an eagle, are etched. On either side of these regal columns extend impenetrable arbor vitae for as far as the eye can see. Access to the private park, which surrounds the Palace itself, is gained after presenting credentials to the uniformed guard at the gate. Dense forest turns gradually and subtly into formal gardens and the pavement road converts into cobblestone.

Approximately four kilometers from the gate, the arbor vitae appear again, as do the marble and onyx columns and armed guards. Credentials are again inspected, and as the limousine passes through the gate, the Palace finally comes into view.

It is a magnificent building. The structure is symmetrical, and its height and mass are perfectly dimensioned for the space that it occupies. The façade is a pale yellow limestone, imported from quarries in Hungary, embellished by marble inlay above key doorways and multi-story window settings. The roof is adorned with colorful flags of many countries and the Austrian provinces.

Sam slid out of the limousine, straightened his bow tie and pulled down his jacket. His shirt was too starched, the collar was too tight, and his feet hurt. He was anxious to get out of there and on a plane to see Anton and Gloria.

Sam was directed inside by an attendant dressed in a white waistcoat, black pants, ruffled shirt buttoned to the neck and a red sash moving up from the left hip to the right shoulder. He entered a large room, dominated by two huge chandeliers hanging from the 20-foot ceilings. The Carousel Room, as it has been known since the days of Maria Theresa, served as the reception area for entering guests. Sam noted how empty the huge room felt even though at least a hundred people stood in lines to check their coats and receive table assignments.

The Carousel Room led directly into the Hall of Ceremonies, another enormous room adorned by five monumental paintings of the marriage of a crown prince to a French Bourbon princess in 1760. Sam followed the crowd, where he spotted a cluster of GSC personnel who were involved in the event's organization. When he inquired after Rebecca, he was told that she hadn't been present at the run-through that afternoon, and didn't seem to be in attendance yet that evening.

It was very unlike Rebecca to miss a work deadline, as well as not to check in with him. He went back to the reception area, commandeered the courtesy phone and dialed his hotel, but there was no answer in her room. He called again to speak to the clerk, and was advised that she hadn't been back to the hotel since the day before.

Sam was apprehensive as he walked back into the Hall of Ceremonies. He knew he should have tried to reach Rebecca earlier that day, and felt responsible for losing track of her during his preoccupations. He had an unsettling feeling that there was something ominous about Rebecca's disappearance, and was trying to piece together what little information he had at his disposal when he felt a firm pull at his elbow. Sam turned to be nose to nose with Sir James Evermost, the Chairman of the GSC Board.

"Stanley said you wouldn't be here, something about having tendered your resignation. You will behave yourself tonight, won't you?" The dapper shipping magnate smiled conspiratorially and, looking at Sam's empty hands, barked, "You don't have a drink--waiter!"

Sam took a glass of champagne from a white-coated waiter and tried to shift gears. He clinked glasses with Evermost and said, "It is my party. These are my clients—I've known many of them for over 20 years. Why should I let Stanley off easy?"

"He is rather smug. I've always thought he held himself in higher esteem than the rest of us. I assume this is more than a lover's spat?"

Sam thought for a moment before answering, to emphasize the point. "There's a huge principal at stake here, as well as a huge amount of shareholder value. I know you take your fiduciary responsibilities seriously, Jim, and so do I. Stanley's making this a power issue, and he won't back off unless and until he thinks it will cost him something. I think that works to my advantage."

Evermost raised his glass, acknowledging Sam's point. "Indeed. I won't let on to Stanley about our conversations. Were you able to reach the others?"

"I spoke with Brown and Herzfeld and Brody. Hanratty should be here tonight and Grotta was traveling. That should be enough, don't you think?"

"Don't underestimate Stanley. I'm certain he's made his calls as well."

Sam moved closer to Evermost as the room got more crowded. "Can you tell me what he said?"

The Chairman shook his head. "Suffice to say that nothing that came out his mouth would have surprised you."

Sam turned to follow an amplified banging noise to his left. Several yards away, Stanley was tapping on a microphone, trying to get the attendees' attention so he could begin the introductory ceremonies. As the crowd quieted down, Stanley was joined on the stage by two other men.

Stanley fidgeted with his notes and the microphone for a few awkward moments before speaking. He introduced himself and his co-hosts: William McKinley Langer, the President of the World Bank, and Jeffrey Hart, the President of the Inter-American Development Bank.

He cleared his throat and addressed the crowd. "This is the eleventh time GSC has sponsored this event. I speak for everyone in our organization when I say how proud we are to be able to work with the international community to spur advancement in the lesser developed parts of the world and provide for efficient and effective global flows of capital. Through the efforts of the World Bank and its sister organizations, in partnership with the private sector, a world-wide renaissance of economic and social development have occurred. Over 20 million people once considered living below the poverty line are now...."

"Bullshit! That's a crock of bullshit."

Stanley strained through the lights to see who had interrupted him. Sam looked around as well, and spotted a tall, shaggy-haired man, wearing a starched white chef's tunic, positioned on the side of the stage. He held a megaphone to his mouth and began speaking again.

"You should all be insulted by this banker's false boast that world poverty is being alleviated and that he, or any of these phony organizations, had anything to do with it. The truth is that during a period of time when Western economies were expanding at historically high rates, the standard of living in the poorest countries on Earth has gotten much worse. The World Bank is a fraud. The IMF is a fraud. The Inter-American Development Bank is a fraud. It's all bullshit."

Sam watched as two bulky men, presumably security agents, moved from behind the podium toward the young man. Even after they had pulled the megaphone away from his mouth, he continued his diatribe. The security guards bent his arms behind him in preparation, Sam thought, for handcuffing. In this position, he was able to get a good look at the protester's face, and it only took a few seconds for Sam to recognize him. *Charley.*

Movement on the podium caught Sam's eye. He turned his head quickly, realizing that everyone in the hall, including Stanley and the supranational institution leaders, were looking at the disruptive scene Charley was causing. As such, they were unaware that five other people, also wearing white tunics, were on the stage and moving in the direction of the speakers.

Charley's the distraction, Sam said to himself. A cold chill moved up his spine as he recalled a scene, long ago, where a sniper in a tree served as a diversion to an ambush.

And then a horrible thought entered his mind: *Is Rebecca part of this?*

He moved quickly closer to the stage, trying to get a better view of the co-conspirators. Two were women; one with a swollen face and black eye, and to his great and momentary relief, his granddaughter was not among them. He also noticed that several of them were armed, and he remembered the warning given by his friend, the DA, about ATAC. *My God, they are crazy.*

One of the tunic-ed men grabbed the microphone while others pointed their weapons at Stanley, Jeffrey and Langer. "Let him go," demanded the man at the microphone, Didier, pointing at Charley. The security agents stopped, and looked around for guidance. "I mean it. Let him go now. We don't want to hurt anyone, but we will if we have to. Now!"

The guards unshackled Charley, who ran over to one of the skirted serving tables on the side of the hall. He slipped underneath and emerged a moment later with a portable video camera. He climbed on the podium and began adjusting the controls and the lens, and moments later said, "Ready."

Didier straightened his posture and moved close to the microphone. He looked out over the crowd, much of which was rushing to the exits. "May I have your attention, *please?*" A few people looked back at the stage, but most kept moving away from the speaker. Obviously annoyed, Didier pointed his revolver upwards and fired two rounds into the ceiling, sending plaster chips down into the crowd.

"I said *please*." He fired one more time and did, indeed, get the attention he demanded.

Looking superior and self-satisfied, and mugging for the camera, Didier continued: "We are from ATAC, an international organization dedicated to exposing the self-serving deception which Western governments have perpetrated to the detriment of the lesser developed world. We are taking extreme measures tonight to make sure our message is heard, because these are desperate times. Poverty, disease, exploitation and dehumanization are increasing exponentially throughout much of the world while the so-called developed countries get richer day by day. You dress in your fine clothes and drink champagne while the infant mortality rate in Uganda *sinks* to all-time lows and the average life expectancy in Bangladesh is 35 years. *35 years!*

"The World Bank and IMF are controlled by Western businesses and governments that encourage poor countries to borrow, at predatory rates, supposedly to build infrastructure and invest in the domestic economy. But you know as well as we that the money never gets there. It goes right to the pockets of the patricians and politicians, who do little to improve the local situation. Laborers are paid slave wages, no roads or schools get built, and most of the money ends up in New York or Zurich in private hands."

While Didier was talking, Sam was watching Jeffrey, who was fidgeting and clearly losing patience with Didier's pontifications. Karim hastened toward him and pulled him back.

Sam moved closer to the stage. He wanted to make eye contact with his son, to let him know he was there.

Within a foot of the podium, Sam noticed first one, then several, crew-cut men in tuxedos positioning themselves around the area. He identified them as security personnel from the wires that led from their ears into their jackets. Sam thought they looked as if they were waiting for a signal to storm the stage.

Didier turned and reached out his arm to his captives. "These men, and the institutions they represent, have committed crimes against humanity. They will be tried for their duplicity, and ..."

"Ridiculous," shouted Jeffrey, pushing away Karim's hands and walking defiantly to the edge of the stage. Karim attempted to regain his hold, but was stymied when Jeffrey hammered an elbow into his chest and pushed him at Didier's feet. Jeffrey turned on his heels and strode away, brushing past a cowering Stanley on his way to the stairs.

Sam was halfway up the steps to the stage when Didier sidestepped Karim, squared his shoulders at Jeffrey and raised his revolver. Sam was only a few paces away from Didier, and planned to either draw the Frenchman's fire or knock him to the ground when the crushing pain in his head stopped him as if he had run into an invisible wall. Before he blacked out, Sam saw Didier squeeze the trigger.

***

Sitting on the edge of her seat in the taxi Rebecca questioned herself anxiously. What was she doing going to Schonbrunn?

These people have guns! They kidnapped her! How could she not go immediately to the police?

She was convinced that Charley had nothing to do with her abduction. Involving the police could be disastrous for him, and calling them in could be a huge overreaction. Maybe he didn't know how extreme Didier and the others were. He had pleaded with her to stay away, she recalled, and she got in his face.

She knew her decision to go to the Palace could be the worst of her alternatives. But, damn it, she had to do something!

Rebecca hopped out of the cab at the service entrance and took several deep breaths to calm her nerves and stop shaking. Luckily, the guard recognized her and let her in without her pass. She moved slowly and carefully into the kitchen area, knowing that she would have to get inside the adjoining Hall of Ceremonies without being noticed by the ATAC activists.

Waiters and cooks were scurrying around the kitchen, too busy to give her any notice. Rebecca stuck her head into the Hall and saw Stanley tapping on the microphone with her father standing next to him. She tried to locate Sam in the crowd, but all the men looked the same in their black tuxedos and she was too far away to be able to distinguish features.

Several feet away, Rebecca spotted Sharon Eckerd, another GSC transplant from New York seconded to work on the affair, and formulated her plan. She would ask Sharon to pass a note to Sam, insisting that he grab Jeffrey and meet her in the service entrance courtyard. That way, she could stay out of sight and, with some luck, get them out of harm's way.

Rebecca got her co-worker's attention with a "pssst" and waved her over.

"Where have you been all day?" Sharon looked Rebecca up and down, and said incredulously "What happened to you?"

"It's a long story. You've got to do me a huge favor. Find Sam Hart and give him this note. Please. It's really, really important.'

Sharon looked dubious. "Why don't you give it to him?"

"And that's another long story. Anyway, I can't go out there like this. Please?"

Sharon took the note and stared at it for a few, long seconds. "OK. I'll find him."

Stanley had begun his introduction, and she looked up at the podium just in time to hear someone else say "Bullshit. That's a crock of bullshit."

Rebecca followed the crowd as they collectively turned to the left of the stage. Charley stood there, barking into a megaphone. She remained frozen in her spot, her heart sinking. There could be no denying now that Charley was deeply involved. He betrayed her, and put her family in serious danger. Their relationship was a sham, and she'd been a fool. She had nothing left for him but contempt. Why hadn't she listened to Sam?

When her father pushed Karim away, the adrenaline shot

through Rebecca's system and she began sprinting to the stage. She watched Sam collapse in slow motion on the stairs, and saw Charley leap toward her father, knocking him to the floor. Rebecca screamed when Didier fired his revolver, then again when three explosions on Didier's chest dropped him to the ground.

She reached her grandfather in full stride, before the tuxedoed security detail rushed the stage and disarmed and captured the other ATAC operatives. Rebecca didn't know what to do first. Sam was sprawled on the steps, legs bent awkwardly underneath him. His face was bright red and he seemed to be struggling for breath.

"Help me," she cried, waving her arms over her grandfather. "Help him."

Mike T was next to her within seconds. He gently pulled her away while he felt for Sam's carotid artery and put his head to his chest. He tilted Sam's head back, pinched his nose and blew twice into Sam's mouth, then listened at his heart again.

Moving quickly, Mike pulled open Sam's tuxedo jacket and forcefully pushed down on his chest with the palms of his hand. Rebecca could hear him softly count to 30 before he stopped, and she didn't allow herself a breath until she saw Sam's chest move on its own.

Mike motioned to an emergency medical team that had just entered the hall. "Here. *Schnell*. He may be having a heart attack."

Rebecca withdrew as the EMT workers took over, but never stopped staring at her grandfather. Within a minute, they had Sam on a stretcher and were moving quickly out the side entrance. Mike T touched her arm and said, "I'll go with him." When Rebecca didn't respond, stuck in place at the thought that she might lose Sam, Mike rested his hand comfortingly on her shoulder and asked, "He'll be alright."

Rebecca raised her head, saw Mike's strong, angular face and serious eyes and suddenly felt less afraid. At this critical moment, when Rebecca knew she was desperate for help, Mike seemed a highly competent ally. She'd met him once or twice before, and was aware from talking with her grandfather how close they were, but she'd never really gotten her own sense of the man. Intuitively, she knew where his loyalties lay, and that she could trust him with her precious grandfather.

"Go. I'll meet you there."

Mike turned and ran after Sam and the medical workers, looking back over his shoulder as he exited the hall. After he was out of view, Rebecca became aware of the mass of police and other medical personnel swarming the stage. She could no longer see her father, and began pushing through the crowd to the spot where he had been lying.

Rebecca was almost knocked off the stage by a medic walking backwards, pulling a stretcher. She stepped aside to allow the gurney holding Charley to pass. He was lying on his side, the back of his white tunic covered with bright red blood.

Rebecca could see his face contorted in pain. And even though her initial thought was that Charley had brought this on himself, a sob escaped her.

Charley opened his eyes and met Rebecca's look. His features melted into anguish, and he mouthed "I'm sorry" in her direction. She refused to respond.

Rebecca pivoted and pushed her way back to the area from which the stretcher had come. Where was her father?

She spotted Jeffrey sitting on the edge of the stage, a medical attendant shining a light in his eyes. She stood behind him during the examination and was thrilled to hear him respond lucidly to the questions posed of him. She sat next to him, grabbed his arm and put her head on his shoulder.

"Thank God you're OK. I'm so sorry."

"Sorry? Why....?" Jeffrey glanced furtively left and right, and then at the medic putting away her bag. "Not now, 'Becca. Let's get out of here."

She nodded, understanding her father's warning.

"Where's Sam?" Jeffrey asked.

"They just took him to the hospital. He passed out."

"Let's go," Jeffrey said, grabbing her hand.

A security checkpoint had been set up at the exits to the palace, and a long line had formed as security personnel checked IDs and asked for local addresses and phone numbers before letting anyone out of the building. Jeffrey dragged Rebecca to the front of the line at the main entrance and, flashing his diplomatic credentials, circumvented the queue.

The main courtyard was filled with police and emergency vehicles. While her father spoke to someone who appeared to be an FBI agent about getting a car to take them to the hospital, Rebecca walked a few paces away, watching four people in white tunics climb into the back of a steel grey paddy wagon. As they loaded into the van, each of them seemed to cast an extended look at a long, black plastic bag, zipped shut from end to end, lying on the ground by the side of the wagon.

***

After the first hour or so, once they had gotten the initial report that Sam was not in any immediate danger, Rebecca, Jeffrey and Mike T agreed to take turns in the waiting room while the others got some air or drank coffee in the cafeteria. Jeffrey came back after a series of phone calls to relieve Rebecca, and she stepped outside to stretch her legs.

Her responsibility in all this was clear. She'd had several chances to pre-empt the disaster with warnings to the police, but didn't, because of Charley. She had exercised incredibly bad judgment, acted selfishly and felt utterly worthless.

Rebecca was desperate to unburden herself, but to whom could she talk? She'd endangered her father and grandfather, and been betrayed by her boyfriend. She was completely alone.

Rebecca dejectedly walked around the perimeter of the hospital for a few minutes when she noticed Mike sitting on a stone bench in a small park across the street, smoking a cigarette. She took the spot next to him.

"You were great back there," Rebecca said. "You probably saved his life."

Mike flicked the cigarette away. "He'd have done it for me. Hell, he's saved my butt a hundred times over the years." He glanced over Rebecca's shoulder at the hospital, and said, "I can't tell you how much Sam means to me."

Rebecca was touched by the tenderness in Mike's voice. "Me, too. He brought me up."

Mike smiled. "Same here...hey, there's your father."

They got up and walked over to Jeffrey. He had spoken with the doctor, and they were moving Sam out of the ER into a regular room. He had suffered a minor stroke, not a heart attack, and was resting comfortably.

Rebecca and Jeffrey let Mike go ahead as they returned to the hospital. Rebecca wanted to tell her father everything. "It was my fault," she whispered, successfully willing herself to maintain control. "I could have..."

"What's done is done, 'Becca. Grandpa will be all right. And as far as the police are concerned, all of the perpetrators have been caught or killed."

"Killed? Charley?"

"Not Charley. He took a bullet but he'll make it. Bendit is dead. The others are captured…It's over. We've been cleared to leave the country on my diplomatic credentials, and I'm hoping Grandpa is up to it tomorrow. It's best we get out of here soon."

Rebecca hadn't considered that her actions could have created criminal culpability, and yet, of course, as she thought about it, the risk was real. Thank God her father was there.

That sentiment surprised her. She tried to remember the last time she felt that way, and was forced back into dim memories of her early childhood. Rebecca reached out to take Jeffrey's arm, and was immensely pleased when he pulled her close and kissed her—in a fatherly way—on the side of her head.

***

Sam walked out of the elevator and into the transformed trading floor. Instead of industrial carpeting, the floor was slick with mud and slime. Bodies were piled on the rows of desks that once held computer screens. Traders and salesmen had been replaced by soldiers.

Sam entered his office and saw Anton lying on the floor. His emaciated form was covered by coarse, off-white pajamas with vertical gray stripes. A yellow star was embroidered just above the heart.

Sam knelt down and cradled Anton's head in his lap. He looked down at his own hands and was surprised to see the wrinkled skin and spindly fingers of an old man. Anton's eyes were watery and unfocused and he was breathing unevenly. Sam gently touched his face, and was surprised when Anton spoke.

"Thank you for coming. I needed to see you before I left."

"No, don't go. Please!"

"It's not up to me. I'm ready. I'm done with my work—but you, Sammy. You still have a world to repair."

Sam was hyperventilating. "How do I do that? I just don't know what to do."

"Be honest about yourself, to yourself. Cherish your family. Gather their light."

Sam could feel the full weight of his friend's head on his lap. Anton slowly raised his hand and made a "V" sign with his fingers. He took a final breath and whispered something Sam couldn't hear before closing his eyes.

Sam reached down to hug his friend for the last time but Anton had disappeared. Sam was now sitting among an assortment of multi-colored glass pieces of various shapes and sizes. He picked one up and held it out, toward the ceiling. The glass shard began to glow, and within moments the room was so filled with its brilliance that it was all consuming.

Sam kept his eyes open, and eventually he could distinguish objects from the blur of the bright light. He saw Gloria, standing on his right. A man in a white coat stood over him, pointing a small flashlight into his eyes. He heard beeps and blips and smelled fresh oxygen through a clip attached to his nostrils. He determined that he was no longer dreaming.

"Dear. It's me. Can you hear me?" Gloria asked, looking hopeful and afraid at the same time.

Sam felt no reason to respond. He wanted to get back to the light, so he closed his eyes and forgot Gloria was there.

Sam was sedated heavily during the MediVac flight from Vienna, and drifted in and out of consciousness during the subsequent 48-hour period. When he was awake, he preferred not to communicate with his family or hospital staff. Rather, Sam spent most of his sentient time staring out the window, trying to recall the specifics of the dream that seemed more real than any other.

The following morning, a sunny day, Gloria pulled a chair next to his bed and grabbed his hand. Her face and eyes showed so much stress that Sam overcame his preoccupations and responded to her touch.

"What is it?" he said, dreading her answer

"Sam... I don't want to hurt you, but I can't hold it back anymore."

Sam turned his head away. "When?"

"Three days ago. You were flying back. The funeral was yesterday, but you were...unconscious. I'm so sorry, Sam. I know how much Anton meant to you."

Sam thought back to his last phone conversation with Anton, which merged in his mind with his dream. He took his hand back from Gloria and pushed the bed covers down his body. He tried to sit up and swing his legs off the bed, but his muscles had atrophied and he had no control over his left arm. "Help me get up, please. I need to leave here."

Gloria tried to comfort Sam. "We can go in a few days. The doctors want you to get stronger and do some physical therapy before they discharge you."

"I can't waste any more time. I'm leaving now."

"No, Sam. There's nothing you can do. Not yet."

Sam fell back on his pillow, knowing that Gloria was right. He should use this time to mourn his friend, not run away. He asked her to describe the last time she saw Anton.

Gloria sat back in her chair and closed her eyes while she spoke. She explained that Anton was weak and in pain, but that he greeted her cheerfully and was apologetic. "He was having trouble speaking, and asked me to give you a folder and a letter. I have the letter in my pocketbook. Do you want to see it now?"

Sam shook his head and asked her to read it to him.

"Dear Sam;

I am sorry I did not say goodbye to you in person because there is so much more to say. I love you like we've been best friends all our lives, and feel blessed to have found you. I pray you find the strength to resolve your memories and begin the process of repair. The war is over; what's done is done. You are letting evil triumph over goodness if you allow those shadows to continue to affect you. Recapture the warmth and joy of your life because you have much to be grateful for. Be honest about yourself, to yourself. Cherish your family. Gather the light.

Goodbye, dear friend. May God's radiance shine down upon you and your family for all the days of your lives."

Sam grabbed Gloria's hand and told her that he loved her. The hug she gave him in return was the sweetest he had ever felt, and they remained in each other's arms for what seemed like a very long time.

***

"Grandpa--you're up."

Sam opened his tear-filled eyes to see Rebecca bound in. "My God," he said, the events at Schonbrunn Palace rapidly spilling into his mind. "I was so worried about you."

"It's a long story, which I'll save for when you get home and we've each got a drink in our hands. But I'm OK. Look who's here."

Mike T stepped out from behind Rebecca and greeted him with his familiar glistening smile and a jocular "Hi boss." Before Sam could phrase the question, Mike answered it. The dollar continued to rise on Monday, and Mike was able to close out most of the position at a very substantial gain.

While Sam was recuperating, Mike promised to run the book conservatively.

"As if my being there makes a whit of a difference," Sam quipped, and felt good about having found his sense of humor. He felt better still when he thought he saw an exchange of smiles between Mike and Rebecca, in the manner of people who don't want to hide their mutual interest in each other.

Sam's musings were interrupted by a cold thought. "Where's Jeffrey? Is *he* all right?"

Gloria told Sam that their son had gone straight back to Washington. She was sure, now that Sam was better, that he'd come visit.

Sam heard the disappointment in Gloria's voice, but tried to fight it off by focusing instead on the loving people who surrounded him. *I wish Anton could see this*, Sam thought. *He'd describe them as the "lights of my life."*

CHAPTER 16

Unfortunately, Sam's sense of purpose didn't last long. For several weeks following his discharge from the hospital, Sam went to bed downhearted and woke up depressed. The doctors had repeatedly warned him that clinical depression was a "normal" symptom of a cerebrovascular accident, and that overcoming its effects would take longer than regaining the use of his left arm. It didn't matter how much he read about his condition, talked to his psychiatrist or downed anti-depressants. He couldn't shake the sadness that seemed to be part of every breath.

He was ill-tempered with Gloria. The more she waited on him, the nastier he was. At one point, he backhanded a cup of tea she had brought him off the kitchen table because, he said, "You're smothering me." At another time, he barked at her for driving the car too slowly to his physical therapy appointment, and then yelled at her two hours later for driving too fast down their driveway and into the garage.

One overcast afternoon, Sam sat in the living room with his feet up, exhausted from a strenuous physical therapy session at the hospital. Gloria suggested they visit Helene in New Jersey, and Sam went ballistic. "Oh, that's a great idea—just what I need."

"But dear," Gloria responded sheepishly, "it might do you some good to get out and stop thinking about, uh..."

Sam banged his cane down on the coffee table, destroying a sterling silver frame that held their wedding picture. "You want me to stop thinking about myself? Is that what you were about to say? How dare you," he growled menacingly as his wife fled the room.

Sam hated himself when he abused Gloria this way, and could tell how hard it was for her to maintain her equilibrium in the face of his tantrums. When the shadows would momentarily clear from his own mind, Sam became capable of acknowledging how incredibly selfish he was behaving. After all, he had survived the stroke relatively unimpaired. Gloria, on the other hand, valiantly tried--and mostly succeeded--in keeping her own depression in check while Sam was recuperating.

Just as quickly as the clouds would break and his thoughts became lucid, Sam would again be overcome with waves of melancholy and worthlessness. In his crooked mind, Gloria would revert back to an unwanted witness to his complete breakdown, and he would turn against her.

Sam couldn't find a reason to care about his business, either. Mike called him several times a day at first with updates and questions about various matters, but stopped when Sam told him not to bother him. He treated the many other visitors from the Firm as if they were imposing on him, which is exactly how he felt. They all seemed so trivial, Sam felt, and his decades at GSC were quickly receding into memory.

In his darkest moments, Sam believed the years of stimulating hard work that had provided an outlet for his guilt and remorse ended when he crumbled to the ground in Vienna. His career was over, and Anton was gone. All he was left with was a lame body and infinite time to dwell on his problems.

While he professed his desire to be left alone, Sam was

greatly aggravated that he hadn't seen his son since their return from Vienna. Jeffrey had called a few times, "just checking in," but their conversations were perfunctory and unsatisfying. Sam did little to change that, and the reality that he had no relationship with his son contributed materially to his depressed state of mind.

When he barked at his wife or his friends, or insulted them, or even refused to even acknowledge them, Sam knew what he was doing. He was driving them away, to punish himself.

The only one he couldn't bring himself to mistreat was Rebecca. When she came to see him, she'd sit quietly at his side while he watched television or tried to read. Occasionally, they would engage in a conversation about world events or light social chatter, but she never forced it or pushed him to the edge of his patience. Sam found it easier to relax while he was in her presence because she was cheery and optimistic and seemed to be the only one who had no expectations of him.

Sam also knew that Rebecca had taken it upon herself to help deal with Gloria's "situation". She drove her grandmother to her doctor's appointments, accompanied her to the opera and ballet, and, he assumed, was there to comfort Gloria when Sam turned abusive.

Sam sensed a blossoming relationship between Rebecca and Mike. She wouldn't refer to it directly, but he knew that she was spending at least as much time in Manhattan as she was visiting her grandparents in the suburbs.

It was, therefore, not much of a surprise to Sam when Rebecca told him, three weeks into his convalescence, that she was moving to Manhattan. What he wasn't expecting was the reason she gave for leaving Washington.

"Dad and I are setting up a business in the City."

Rebecca had expected her grandfather's stunned reaction, and kept talking. "He's leaving the Bank—he'll make it official next week. We're organizing an investment fund which will be financed with both government and private money, to invest in local companies in the emerging world for basic infrastructure work."

Sam's mind was racing. Where had he been while all this was going on? Since when would Rebecca make such a big decision without bringing him into the process? Sam instinctively put his head in his hands, sensing another nail being banged in the coffin. His best friend and job were gone. His wife had dementia. Now he'd lost Rebecca.

"Grandpa, what's wrong?"

Sam wanted to tell his granddaughter everything, right then and there—that his life was filled with deceit and shadows, and how it was shattering all around him. He wanted to beg her not leave him for Jeffrey, which in his dejected state of mind would be further confirmation of Sam's abject failure.

Sam would have completely dissembled had he not heard Anton's faint voice, in the back of his head, reminding him of his solemn promise to repair his world.

"Grandpa?"

Sam took a deep breath in an attempt to shake the darkness from his mind. He stared into his granddaughter's glistening eyes, hoping to find additional strength. "I'm sorry. I was just thinking, reminding myself, how lucky I should feel to have my son and granddaughter in New York, and back in my life, again. Now, tell me more about this fund."

***

Sam slept fitfully that night. He awoke foggy and

somewhat disoriented, a condition that was only partially relieved by a hot shower and a large cup of coffee. He growled aloud upon reading Gloria's note explaining that she'd gone to the store, and grumpily grabbed the business section of the *New York Times* from the pile on the table.

Just as he was about to get up to pour another cup of coffee, the phone rang. In reaching for it, Sam glanced at a wall clock and realized it was past 10. He answered the phone, bewildered that he'd slept so late. On the other end of the line was Jim Evermost, the Chairman of the GSC Board. "Sam, I hope I'm not disturbing you. How are you feeling?"

"Right now, I feel fine. What's up?"

Evermost was obviously taken aback by Sam's aggressive tone. "I guess I'll get right to it, then. I was wondering if we might meet in the next few days. For lunch in Manhattan, or...I could come to your house if that's better."

Sam was confused. "Not here. Let's meet in the city. What's this about?"

Evermost paused before answering. "We haven't really spoken since the....uh...*incident*. I have some governance things to talk to you about. How does tomorrow work?"

Governance things? What the hell did that mean?

"Sure," said Sam. "See you then."

Realizing the reason for Evermost's call made Sam feel like a different man. His emotions were emanating from the front of his head, and not the rear, unencumbered by the weight of gloom and doom. His mind was working again.

The following day, Sam met Jim Evermost for lunch at the University Club in Manhattan. The Chairman of the GSC board casually asked Sam his thoughts on a number of current events before moving on to more analytically complicated questions. Sam went along with the interview, knowing full well that his mental acuity was being probed.

Finally, over dessert, Evermost became direct. "Sam, I'm going to ask you straight out. Was there any...damage...from the stroke?"

Sam chuckled and said coyly, "Not as far as I can tell. But what difference does it make?"

The Chairman straightened in his chair and wiped his mouth with a linen napkin that he placed on the table. He looked around and said quietly, "There's a strong movement on the Board to oust Stanley, which I support. I'm prepared to suggest that you be named acting President while a full-blown search for his successor is conducted."

Sam had not seen this coming. *What could Stanley have done to provoke this reaction?*

Evermost apparently read Sam's mind. "His confrontation with you was only the last straw. The Firm's underperformed, Stanley's pissed off just about every Director, and it's clear we need a change at the top. You're a known quantity internally and externally who'd buy us some time."

Sam stammered, "May I think about it?"

Evermost signaled the waiter for the check. "Sure, but I need an answer by the end of the week. That gives you four days—enough time?"

Sam nodded.

Evermost continued, "We'll make sure it's worth your while."

"It won't be the money that pushes me either way," said Sam, insulted by the suggestion that he could be bought.

"Well, if it's not the cash, maybe it's the position. The CEO of GSC carries a lot of clout. Stanley never seemed to channel his position that way, but think back to Bob Argent.

He got a lot done for his business and social agendas while he was at the top. Think about it."

For the next two days, Sam thought about it incessantly. He spoke to several of his current and former colleagues at the Firm, each of whom reinforced Evermost's point that GSC desperately needed him. Only Sam would have the credibility to create a transition process which would avoid a bloody succession fight.

Sam would emerge from these conversations pumped up, ready to re-engage Wall Street. Not too long thereafter, however, reality would set in. He'd focus on the fact that his left arm was still only three-quarters functional, and he tired from even light amounts of physical activity. He worried that his mental abilities had been diminished and wondered how he'd ever be able to perform the complicated intellectual gymnastics required of the CEO of a major financial firm.

Of greater concern to Sam was the urgency he felt to get moving on his self-redemptive acts. He promised Anton—in nightly dream sessions—he'd begin as soon as he felt better from the accident. He'd hear Anton urging him to repair himself by confronting his memories and making peace with what he did, and was forced to do, to survive the War. Sam knew he'd never fully recuperate unless he accomplished those objectives, as demanding and amorphous as they might be.

Three days after his meeting with Evermost, Sam sat at his desk, holding the manila folder and letter Anton had left for him before he passed away. He pondered whether to risk his improving mood by reading Anton's message, and opened the folder for the first time.

Gloria had put these items on Sam's desk when he got home from the hospital. During those dark days, Sam had shoved them to the bottom of the drawer and refused to think about them.

But now, feeling as if he'd begun climbing out of a hole, Sam was drawn to them. He read Anton's letter, written in fountain ink and shaky hand. The simple and direct instructions made much more tangible sense now than when Gloria had read them aloud almost two months ago. "Repair my world," Sam said aloud, almost in a chant. "Collect the light."

Sam turned to the folder. He stroked the front of it gently, visualizing Anton's sparkling, lively eyes. He pulled out a weathered, gray booklet entitled "The Meaning of This War," by Abraham J. Heschel and leafed through it circumspectly. He stopped at a dog-eared page and read, carefully, a passage that had been underlined in pencil:

> A tale is told of a band of inexperienced mountain climbers. Without guides, they struck recklessly into the wilderness. Suddenly a rocky ledge gave way beneath their feet and they were tumbled headlong into a dismal pit. In the darkness of the pit they recovered from their shock, only to find themselves set upon by a swarm of angry snakes. Every crevice became alive with fanged, hissing things. For each snake the desperate men slew, ten more seemed to lash out in its place. Strangely enough, one man seemed to stand aside from the fight. When the indignant voices of his struggling companions reproached him for not fighting, he called back: If we remain here, we shall be dead before the snakes. I am searching for a way of escape from the pit for all of us.

> Tanks and planes cannot redeem humanity. A man

with a gun is like a beast without a gun. The killing of snakes will save us for the moment but not forever. The war will outlast the victory of arms if we fail to conquer the infamy of the soul: the indifference to crime, when committed against others. For evil is indivisible. It is the same in thought and in speech, in private and in social life. The greatest task of our time is to take the souls of men out of the pit. ...

Gloria stood at the entrance of Sam's office for several moments watching him stare out the window into the back yard. Eventually, she softly called his name, and when he didn't respond she walked to his side and touched his arm. "Sam, what it is?" she asked.

"Anton..." Sam said softly, wiping a tear from his cheek. "He was speaking to me."

***

His phone conversation with his son later that afternoon was the longest they'd had in decades. He asked Jeffrey for the details of the new business he would be setting up, trying exceedingly hard to be positive and encouraging. Sam immediately recognized some weaknesses in Jeffrey's plans, but withheld any critical judgments and offered to help in any way he could.

Jeffrey responded: "That would be wonderful, Dad. I've been away too long, from you and mom, and mostly Rebecca. I'm hoping this brings us closer."

"That's my fault. I wasn't much of a father. I know that now. There's an explanation, which I need for you to know, but no excuse. I can't tell you how important it would be to let me make it up to you."

"I'd say you did a lot for me. You brought up Rebecca—which I know wasn't easy—while I hid behind my own self-importance. I'm hoping that when I get to New York, I can take some of the strain off you in helping with Mom."

Sam was silent for while, letting himself enjoy the warmth of the setting sun through the window in his den and delight in rediscovering the pride of parenthood. "I love you, son," he said finally, unable to remember that last time he'd used that phrase.

Jeffrey's voice cracked noticeably. "Me, too."

***

That evening, after dinner, Sam paced from room to room, trying to separate the various issues and the pros and cons of going back to work. He wasn't aware that he was talking to himself until his wandering took him into the living room, where Gloria was trying to read.

"That's it," Gloria said, marking her spot in the book and placing it loudly onto the coffee table. She intercepted Sam heading into the hallway and grabbed him by the elbow. "Come. We have to talk."

She led Sam into the den and gently pushed him down into his favorite chair. She took her usual position on the adjacent couch, and said firmly, "I've known something terrible has been bothering you for as long as we've been together, but I never pried because you always were able to get through it. That doesn't seem to be working now, and I don't think you can go it alone anymore. I want more than anything to help you, but you have to let me in."

His initial instinct was to resist, tell Gloria that she was wrong and that he had everything under control. But the obviousness of her point, and the sincerity of her tone, sunk in. Perhaps he could try to open up, just a little, just this once.

He surprisingly enjoyed the tingling feeling as he began the long confessional to his wife. The memories came out quickly and lucidly. He articulated his wartime experiences in great detail, recalling precise minutiae, such as which way the wind was blowing, who he was standing next to, and what his commanding officer said. He tried to avoid relaying his own impressions or opinions, and report just the facts.

When Sam described to Gloria his attempts to save the Jewish inmate at Gunskirchen, he was aware that it was the first time he'd ever attempted to recall it without any emotional connection. That feeling of detachment was new to Sam, a kind of out-of-body sensation which allowed him to see things in a clearer light.

He stopped to rest after detailing the liberation of the camp, and it was clear that Gloria thought his story had ended. She touched his knee tenderly and said, "I can't imagine how awful that was. I'm so sorry you had to go through that."

Sam shook his head slightly from side to side, and looked at his wife carefully. He could see she was teary, and considered stopping his tale right there. *What was the benefit of telling her more?*

But he heard Anton, pushing him forward. "Don't run away again. It only makes it harder," he was sure his friend was telling him.

Sam took a deep breath, grabbed a tissue from a box on the side table, and handed it to Gloria. "There's more."

For the next half hour, Sam described, in exacting terms and in complete paragraphs, the horrors of his involvement in the Russian repatriation. And when he was done, he was exhausted.

Gloria's jaw dropped, literally, as Sam was speaking. "Oh, my God," she murmured when he had finished. "You poor man."

Sam thought she looked at him differently, pitifully. He was stunned realizing, after 50 years of feeling sorry for himself, that empathy wasn't what he wanted.

"It *was* terrible. We were put into unimaginable situations. I did some things then…and after…which I knew were wrong, but ran away from my responsibilities. Anton tried to show me a better way."

Sam paused, listening to his own words and trying to connect them back to his current dilemma. Then it all became clear.

***

A week later, Sam took the express executive elevator to the thirtieth floor of the GSC building, nervous and uncomfortable in his dark suit and shiny shoes. A soft "ding" announced that he had arrived at the top floor, and Sam took a deep breath before looking up from his feet as the door opened. In the lobby stood a packed throng of suited men and women, applauding and smiling. Sam stood there, taken completely by surprise, until the door started to close. He reached out to keep it open and walked into the lobby, where Jim Evermost stepped forward, grabbed Sam's hand and pumped it energetically. Several other Board members did the same, and within minutes Sam was mobbed by friends and colleagues and well-wishers who were grateful he had come back to save the Firm.

***

Sam put the proposal down on his desk and rested his weak, left wrist on the arm of his chair. "What kind of access can you get to original source materials?" he asked.

Cindy Allenson, the Shoah Foundation investigator who had interviewed Anton, opened a spiral notebook and said, while flipping through a few pages, "Much of the U.S. materials relating to Yalta have just been declassified, so I should be able to get it without too much trouble. Direct military correspondence may take Freedom of Information Act requests, which means lawyers and time and money. The good news is that the issue has been so far down on everyone's radar screen for so long that I wouldn't expect much of a fight."

The next question was a tougher one, Sam knew. "What about the Brits?"

Cindy shifted her position slightly. "That's much more difficult. The topic is still considered a state secret in England, and their version of the FOIA is toothless. While we can and should try to get our hands on government papers, I think we're best putting more effort on anecdotal sources.

"As for survivors, we've caught a break. I located Sergei Pohl through the Columbia University directory. He's the Holstein Professor Emeritus of Electrical Engineering, and still has an office there. He's agreed to talk to me. This could be really huge for us, Mr. Hart. There's a good chance he is still in contact with others to help fill out the story."

Sam shivered at the mention of Pohl's name, bringing back memories of his harrowing account during the repatriations. "I'd want to meet him, at the right time. I'll leave it to you to tell me when."

Cindy nodded and turned the page of her notebook. "So far, no luck finding Rusty's brother, but I've done it all long distance so there is a chance we'll locate him if he's still alive. I'm planning to be in London next week to follow up on him and a bunch of the other names you gave me."

"That's great. Call me if you find anything interesting. Otherwise, let's plan to meet again in a few weeks, when you get back. Do you need money?"

Cindy packed her papers in her briefcase and stood to shake Sam's hand goodbye. "I think we're OK for now. Last time I looked, *Restore the Light Productions* was flush."

Sam followed Cindy out the door and saw his granddaughter sitting outside his office. He enthusiastically waved her in, and hugged her before she sat down on the couch.

Sam took a chair across from her and asked, "Any luck?"

Rebecca tried, unsuccessfully but preciously, to be modest. "A little...50 million!"

"That's a real number. You're making my life too easy, 'Becca. I told you we'd top the fund up to 100, but you might not need GSC's money at the rate you're going."

Rebecca looked a little worried. "You're not getting off the hook so easy. We've still got a long way to go and Dad wants to close by the end of the year."

Sam patted her on the arm reassuringly. "I was just teasing. We're good for it, you know that. It was part of my deal and I aim to make the company stick to it."

"It's a great investment, Grandpa. Your shareholders will be happy you've been so foresighted and socially responsible."

A natural salesperson, Sam thought. *She really seems to have found herself.*

Sam glanced at his watch. "Do you have time to grab some lunch?"

Rebecca shook her head apologetically as she began gathering up her things. "Sorry, no. Mike and I are supposed to meet with the caterers in a few minutes. Do you need to sign a pass or something so he can leave the desk?"

"He's a big boy now, sweetie. He can write his own pass." Sam chuckled as he thought about how the two conditions he insisted on before taking the interim president's job—that the Firm invest in his son's fund and that Mike be made a partner—had worked out so well.

"That may be so, but I still might need help dragging him off of the trading floor. You'd think he'd want a break every now and then." Rebecca kissed Sam on the cheek and rushed out of his office.

Sam walked over to the east-facing floor-to-ceiling windows that adorned his palatial office on the top floor of the GSC Building. The midday sun was suspended in a cloudless sky, lighting the endless strips of canyons and the skyscrapers that formed them.

Sam looked due south. The Statue of Liberty floated majestically in a harbor of glistening glass and seductive aquamarine. The sun's rays were so strong that even the distant horizon had discernible facets and edges.

Sam felt the warmth of the reflecting light on his face, and was pleased. He was making good on his promise to Anton. The wheels were in motion.

For the past week, Sam had reached down, deep inside, to find the determination and strength to resist the throbbing in his chest and the pain radiating down his left arm. He knew that there was just one broken piece left for him to gather to complete his reparation. Sam bowed his head and prayed silently for the opportunity to witness the marriage of his beloved granddaughter and godson before he became one with the light.

RICHARD E. WITTEN

The End

Made in the USA